ACCLAIM FOR
QUEEN OF SHADOWS

"*Queen of Shadows* paints a story that is as enthralling as it is readable. Isabella of France was a child when she wed Edward II of England, but old enough to understand the tragedy of her marriage. Her life as both queen and woman is brilliantly portrayed by Edith Felber in this masterful tale woven from real events and vividly realized characters."

—Mary Jo Putney, author of *The Marriage Spell*

"The medieval world has rarely been evoked as clearly and sensuously as it is in *Queen of Shadows*. The portrait of Isabella, strong, proud, royal to her fingertips, is a triumph. . . . Felber proves herself to be truly a master storyteller."

—Joan Wolf, author of *The Poisoned Serpent*

Queen of Shadows

A Novel of Isabella,
Wife of King Edward II

EDITH FELBER

 New American Library

New American Library
Published by New American Library, a division of
Penguin Group (USA) Inc., 375 Hudson Street,
New York, New York 10014, USA
Penguin Group (Canada), 90 Eglinton Avenue East, Suite 700, Toronto,
Ontario M4P 2Y3, Canada (a division of Pearson Penguin Canada Inc.)
Penguin Books Ltd., 80 Strand, London WC2R 0RL, England
Penguin Ireland, 25 St. Stephen's Green, Dublin 2,
Ireland (a division of Penguin Books Ltd.)
Penguin Group (Australia), 250 Camberwell Road, Camberwell, Victoria 3124,
Australia (a division of Pearson Australia Group Pty. Ltd.)
Penguin Books India Pvt. Ltd., 11 Community Centre, Panchsheel Park,
New Delhi - 110 017, India
Penguin Group (NZ), cnr Airborne and Rosedale Roads, Albany,
Auckland 1310, New Zealand (a division of Pearson New Zealand Ltd.)
Penguin Books (South Africa) (Pty.) Ltd., 24 Sturdee Avenue,
Rosebank, Johannesburg 2196, South Africa

Penguin Books Ltd., Registered Offices:
80 Strand, London WC2R 0RL, England

First published by New American Library,
a division of Penguin Group (USA) Inc.

First Printing, November 2006
10 9 8 7 6 5 4 3 2 1

LIBRARY OF CONGRESS CATALOGING-IN-PUBLICATION DATA:

Felber, Edith.
    Queen of shadows: a novel of Isabella, wife of King Edward II / Edith Felber.
        p. cm.
    ISBN 0-451-21952-X (trade pbk.)
    1. Isabella, Queen, consort of Edward III, King of England, 1292–1358—Fiction. I.
Title.
    PS3562.A9595Q44 2006
    813'.6—dc22   2006013061

Set in Bembo
Designed by Spring Hoteling

Printed in the United States of America

For Dan and Syd, who always knew.

Acknowledgments

With many thanks to my friends and family, for helping me through some dark times, and also for putting up with someone whose head is not always in the same century as her body.

Much gratitude goes to my three children: Michael, Adam and Susie. A special thanks to my daughter-in-law Jeanne Simpson, for all her loving support, and also to Ed Holland, my Brit son-in-law, for patiently putting up with a mother-in-law who constantly pesters him about English history.

Thanks to Renee Ritter, Diane and Gene Arymn and Dee Dee Wolan, for their continuing friendship; and to Barbara Metzger and Joan Wolf, for their general aiding and abetting.

A particular thanks to Claire Zion at New American Library, who asked me about Princess Isabella, enabling me to find Queen Isabella, and then encouraging me to write about her.

Author's Note

It would be hard to find any random six people to agree about what happened on any day last year. It is impossible to find the same number of contemporary sources to agree on what happened more than six hundred years ago. Even the birth dates of some of the historical figures in this book are disputed. Death dates are usually known, but the mode of death and the reason for it can also be cited differently by different sources.

I've tried to be as accurate as possible under the circumstances. Where I have fiddled with history is in the time line of events in this book. Edward Second and his queen, Isabella, were peripatetic rulers; they did a lot of traveling across the length and breadth of England, frequently visiting Scotland and Wales. I did not include most of these travels in the book, because to do so would have made it a ponderous tome.

In addition, please keep in mind that I have, of course, never met any of the real people in this book, so I couldn't know what was going on in their hearts and minds. So I remind you, Gentle Reader: this is a work of fiction, based on the facts available, and on my constant belief that though times may change, the human heart and mind remains the same through the ages.

Part One

Prologue

1284, AUGUST
CAERNARVON CASTLE, WALES

The fish and fowl had been brought in; now the company looked for red meat. So when the troop of men burst into the great dining hall, all present looked up in expectation of seeing something spectacular: a steaming boar's head borne on a platter, flunkies staggering under the weight of a whole side of beef or a beautifully dressed lamb. The King of England entertained lavishly when he was at Caernarvon, now especially, since his second son had just been born here. But there was no new dish being served. Instead the guests saw a single man march in, tracking mud and shedding water on the clean rushes that had been laid on the floor. His soft leather boots were stained, his cape drenched; he was travel-worn, dirty and sopping, but smiling.

When he reached the center of the room, he knelt on one knee and bent his head. "Your Highness," he said, "I've a present for you, from Snowdonia."

All conversation stopped. The fair-haired man at the head of the long table put down his knife. King Edward, Longshanks, was a very tall, battle-scarred man, but handsome withal. He had bright blue eyes and, though of middle years, still had a head full of thick golden hair. A lad of about ten, dressed lavishly in a blue-and-gold tunic, like the king's, sat at his right hand. The boy's fair face was flushed; his blue eyes, a match to his father's, were sparkling.

"Mortimer," King Edward said, acknowledging the new arrival. He raised a hand to show his guest might rise. "It had better be a good present to warrant your bursting in like this in all your dirt and affrighting the poor ladies. And not a few of the men," he added in an aside to his son, with a sly smile to show he might or might not have meant that.

"Oh, I've something to warrant it," Mortimer said, rising in one supple movement. He flung back his cape to show that he carried a leather bag. He drew off the thong that tied it, reached in and, smiling hugely now, pulled out a severed human head. He raised it high, holding it by its long, streaming black hair.

The boy stared. Some of the ladies screamed. One rose and then crumpled to the floor and was quickly picked up and carried away.

"Behold," Mortimer said. "I bring the last of your enemies, a follower of Daffyd, brother to the last Prince of Wales. He's come to join you at your feast, sire." He gazed dispassionately at the head and gave it a little shake. He frowned. "I fear he don't feel like eating much now. I hope you forgive him that."

Some of the ladies tittered; some turned their gazes aside. Most of the men stared greedily at the severed head.

The dead face was blank, but it could be seen that in life the man had been young, dark and passing fair. His eyes were closed as though in pain, and his neck trailed clotted bloody tubes and knobs that looked less human than like the entrails of a chicken.

"Welcome, young man," King Edward said, laughter in his voice as he gazed at the head. "Well done, my lord Mortimer.

Make our new guest comfortable. Send him back to England and hang him high on a pike at the Tower for all to see and so he can finally see the land he dared defy. But for now, if you please, put him away. You did well last year when you brought me the head of Daffyd. And now this. A delightful habit to be sure, and I appreciate it, but some of my guests do not.

"Fie, ladies," he said with a glance at the women at his table. "You've seen worse done on Tower hill and applauded—I've seen it. Nor would you have a tear to spare for this rogue, had you seen him whole. No more than he would have had for you, I'd wager. He was your enemy. But sleep easy. Here we see the last of his kind."

"No, sire," Mortimer said. "Not quite. Some still fight on and stay hidden in the forest, even now, a year after their cause has died. In fact, I've brought you another one such, but unlike this fellow, alive."

The king raised an eyebrow. "Very well. Let us see him. We'll take our entertainment early this evening, and have him here instead of the jugglers and acrobats."

At a gesture from their leader, a pair of armored men at arms walked in, bearing between them a slight, dark-skinned man trussed like a fowl, his legs and his eyes the only things he could move. His face was bruised, he was thin and starved and his clothes filthy and torn, but he raised his head to stare and there was murder in his eyes as he looked at the king. The guests stilled, and looked at their sovereign. Men had been killed for less than gazing at their king that way.

"He says his name is Owain," Mortimer said. "He was in his prince's guard."

"He didn't do his job very well, did he?" the king mused. "Well, what say you?" he asked the company. "Shall we let him bear his prince company in death as he did not in life on yet another pike at the Tower?"

5

The ladies smiled or looked away; not one of them spoke. Nor had their king expected them to. They sat, in their brocaded robes of rainbow hue, their high headdresses draped with multicolor veils, as pretty as a row of flowers, as mute in the presence of their lord as any infidel woman he'd seen in the Crusades. He nodded, pleased.

"My lords?" Edward asked.

The men in attendance weren't as comely as the women. Some were from his court; some of them were his generals, some few Marcher barons. They were all battle-hardened veterans. They had defeated Wales and were in readiness to march to Scotland with their lord to finally settle the uprising there. They scowled or frowned, expecting the question to be a test of their loyalty.

Only one ventured to speak. "Why not kill him?" an old lord grumbled. "Why not spare him? The issue is as dead as their prince. The Welsh have learned their lesson. The rebels have melted away into the forests, save for a few stragglers, like this one. He isn't even of high enough rank to make a spectacle of, not worth the time to draw and quarter him. Hang him or take his head. It makes little difference now."

"Except to him," King Edward mused, watching the captive. "I tell you what, fellow," he said to the rebel. "These are days of celebration. We mark the birth of another son, another arrow in my shaft. I go to Scotland to loose the rest of my quiver there."

His audience, except for the captive, laughed.

"And so I give you your freedom, as a boon, to celebrate that birth. You see?" he asked the boy at his side. "A king must be strong. Granting a boon does not make him weak if he judges his enemy aright. Sometimes, it makes him stronger. This fellow will tell his friends of my charity, and when you are king, the Welsh will trouble you no more."

The captive gasped. "*He* will rule over us?" he cried, straining at his bonds. "But you promised us a prince born on *our* soil. You said we'd have a prince who didn't speak a word of English. You *promised* us that."

"And see how you repay me," Edward said sadly and motioned his growling lords to silence. "I should think you'd had your fill of princes. Had you fewer to begin with, you might have been able to unite and stand against me longer. Or perhaps not. It hardly matters now. But so I did. And my word is strong as my arm. So what shall we do?" he asked his son. "Here is a problem for when you are king. They don't want to be ruled by King Alphonso."

His son, Prince Alphonso, didn't answer. He knew his father well enough to know when he wasn't expected to.

Edward smiled. The smile grew. He motioned a page to his side, whispered in his ear and sent him running. "I have the very answer," he told the company. "We need only wait a moment or two."

The company murmured among themselves. The king was still smiling when an old woman, a nurse by her severe black gown, appeared from behind an arras, carrying a swaddled babe in her arms.

"I don't approve, sire. Indeed, I do not," the woman said. "He's been on this earth only a day and is no toy to show off to the riff and raff and rabble."

"A fine way to speak of us," the king said. "Now be still. Hold up the babe. Here," he said, rising from his chair, and raising a goblet. "I keep my word. Welshman, here is your new prince."

The captive shook his head as though to clear it. "But that's your son."

"So he is. My Edward. He won't be king. My Alphonso here, God willing, will be that, and a right good king he will be too." He touched his son's hair, lightly, tenderly. "He has brain and heart aplenty. He's a marvel at the joust and with his sword, even now. He rides like a centaur and can shoot true with a bow twice his size." The king chuckled and gazed at his son fondly. "They say he is Longshanks' double, and I swear it is true.

"But here is my second son, the infant, Edward Plantagenet," he said, turning his attention back to the man in bonds. "Born here, in this very castle on Welsh soil, one *I* raised on your land. A handsome babe, they tell me. Yet when he speaks, he roars. Because he has no language yet. So certainly, he doesn't speak English. My promise is then fulfilled. A prince for you, one born in Wales who speaks no English." He raised his goblet. "To Edward, your new Prince of Wales!"

When the clamor of laughter and toasts subsided, the king waved the nurse away. "Take him back to his mother, and send my good lady my respects. As for this fellow," he told Mortimer, gesturing to the prisoner, "send him away, with his head. He needs his mouth to spread the word of his new ruler. Then wash and dress, and come back to our feast. Now let's get on with it. We ride out with the dawn."

"And I with you," the prince said.

"Nay," Edward said. "Your mother said you felt unwell this morning. I'll not drag you the length of England until you are entirely better. You go to Windsor, I to Scotland. When you are fit and wholly well, you may join me."

His son sat silently, crestfallen.

"You don't mind the fact that your brother will rule over Wales, do you?" Edward asked his son, as he settled in his chair again. "It will be in name only. You will be king. Come, you will have so much, you don't begrudge your baby brother this little?"

"No, Father," Alphonso said. "I will not mind, if you say I should not."

His father, well pleased, smiled.

"But I want to go with you," the prince said fervently.

"And so you shall, in time," Edward said.

"All of Llewellyn's blood are dead now?" the prince asked.

"All," his father said. "The men in their graves, or with their heads hung high on the Tower."

"And the women?" Prince Alphonso asked.

"Yes, good question. It's clever to be wary," Edward said with approval. "But the women don't matter. Not even those of royal blood. Noble women must be honored, but they are weak and will always submit to their lord. If they are your enemies you need only kill their men, then take them into your house or send them to a nunnery. They must follow the lead of their man, and so are no concern without men."

"But what about Delilah?" the boy asked, frowning.

Edward threw back his head and laughed. "*Delilah?* Wonderful boy. Good! I see you remember your studies. But though words in the Bible are holy, some are only meant as lessons. Her story is there to teach you to mistrust women's wiles. So you must. They are not made as we are and so they're unable to act in a straightforward manner. Some are devious; all are subject to temptation. Remember Eve! But also remember that no female ever toppled a warrior or a king. Such women don't exist. Or if they do," he said, tweaking a silken strand of the boy's long golden tresses, "remember to never let them cut your hair." His expression hardened. "You need not worry about women. I will take you to Scotland to see who to worry about. When I've subdued them, you shall rule over an empire, one England, a land that runs from Ireland to Wales, to Scotland, to the top of the world."

"I do not worry," the boy said proudly, his color running high with excitement.

"Are you well?" the king asked suddenly, putting his hand to his son's hot forehead.

"Never better," the boy protested. "I am well, Father. I am ready."

Edward frowned. It was August, and even now it was chill in the huge cold castle. But not in the great hall tonight. He'd ordered fires because Alphonso was subject to fevers. So the huge hearth was blazing, the firelight intense; torches on the sides of the walls were also ablaze. Surely the brazen light accounted for the glitter in his son's eyes. Either that or it was his excitement and zeal, and that never harmed a lad.

"On to Scotland, then," the king said, rising, and all the guests rose to toast with him.

The feast went on.

The woman who had fainted was carried into an anteroom. Her serving girl chaffed her wrists; a burned feather was waved beneath her nose. She woke, pale and troubled. She didn't return to the festivities. Instead she went to her guest chamber and then to bed. But first, she had a word with her serving girl, who then ran down the backstairs to have a word with a lad in the stables, who then rode out on his mission even though it meant going out into the unhealthy, dangerous mists of the night.

"Sister," the lady's message said, "hide your girls, their cousins too. Send some to me, the others farther. They must go from here now, if not forever. All our men are gone. Be sure the girls know why. Teach them why, and how it was done. Let them know so they may avenge it. Change their names, but bid them remember. Be sure they remember."

One

The bride stepped off the small skiff that had carried her off the mother ship from across the channel. Taking her husband's arm, she went carefully down the little ladder to the sand of the beach, her head high, back straight, with not a false or wavering step to show that she'd just spent four days at sea. Her eyes showed calm and command, her expression was grave but composed, only her hand quivered where it lay on her new husband's sleeve.

He didn't notice. His eyes were searching the shore.

The small well-dressed contingent waiting for the couple had eyes only for the bride. She was something to look at. She wore silk: a sumptuous, expensive, brocaded silk surcoat in a celestial blue that accented the perfection of her wide-open eyes. The undercotte that peeped out when she took a step was a lighter blue. The veil and wimple she wore over her hair concealed it all, except for the tightly braided and wrapped coils of gold at the sides of her head, echoing the gold amulet she wore at her neck. She was slender and supple and, for a wonder, just as lovely as they'd all heard she was.

She had eyes only for her new husband. He stood tall and arrow straight: a well-made, lithe young man in princely raiment, as befit a King of England and Prince of Wales. His surcoat was blue to match hers, and his thick hair was as gold as her own too. His eyes seemed even more of a dulcet blue than hers, his well-carved mouth was unsmiling as his gaze continued to rake the shore. At four and twenty he was every young girl's dream of a husband. But only a fleeting expression of wonder whenever she gazed up at him showed his bride's continuing delight in her good fortune. She had to wed where politics decreed, and arranged marriages were often less than happy matches of age, body and temperament. Her expression showed her immense pride and glee at finally finding herself bound to such a mate.

A group of dignitaries bowed to the couple and began to walk toward them at a slow and dignified pace. Earls and barons and ladies of high degree walked across the chill strand to greet them.

"Your Majesties," one of the gentlemen said, bending his knee. The others in the little group bowed and curtsied. When they looked up, they realized the king wasn't looking at them.

His gaze had sharpened. He looked over their heads, began to smile and, without a word, leaving his new wife standing there on the shore, he started to walk over the pebbled beach and on up the strand. His grin blossomed as he was sure of whom he was seeing, and then he ran toward the man striding toward him: a tall, elegant-looking young fellow dressed in red and yellow, with dark shining hair, sparkling eyes and a matching smile.

The two met and embraced, there on the shore.

"My brother," the king said, when he could, emerging for a moment from that heartfelt embrace. "How I have missed you."

"And I you," the young man answered.

Some onlookers winced. The man was not the king's brother; he had no living brother, though he insisted on calling this young man such. Prince Alphonso had died of a fever shortly after Edward had been born.

The two embraced again. Two handsome, slender young men, standing toe-to-toe and cheek to cheek, of an age and a height: one with hair of gold, the other with hair as dark as night.

The welcoming delegation stood in front of their new princess and looked back and forth from the couple to the deserted bride.

She didn't seem angry, or unhappy. Only puzzled.

"Here," the king cried joyfully, reaching into the purse he wore at his waist. "A gift, for you—I thought of it the moment I saw it. It reminded me of you."

The young man took the heavy golden necklace set with gems, and turned it over in his hands. He looked his question at the prince.

"A wedding gift," King Edward Second, only surviving son of Edward Longshanks, said eagerly, watching his reaction. "I've more like it if that one's not to your taste."

"Oh, but it is. Yours?" he asked with a look at last to the bride, who stood so erect and alone on the shore.

Edward shrugged. "Hers, mine, it's the same now. Given by a prince to a king, and mine to do with as I wish. I wish to please you. Does it?"

"Assuredly . . . for a start."

The king laughed.

His bride did not. Nor did she scowl, or grimace, or protest. She was wellborn and gently bred, the blood of kings and queens ran in her veins. She knew how she must act and why. She could clearly hear what was said, but she herself said nothing. She only stared at her favorite wedding gift as the strange young man slipped it over his head.

"And the other things?" the young man asked with a mocking tilt of one eyebrow.

"Rings, trinkets, boxes, bracelets. Crowns and spoons, golden dishes and silver chests. Estates, honors, riches. There's more, so much more. A fortune in gems and prizes, all mine to share as I please," Edward said. "And you know how I am pleased."

"So I do," the young man said softly. "But won't you introduce me to her?"

The king grinned. "Of course. Come." But before he took a step back to his bride, he impulsively embraced the young man again. "Oh by God, Piers, I'm glad to see you," he said. "I came back as soon as I could, but I wish you could have been there. He is gone. A chill—a gripe in his bowels, something that started small and ended his life as he was on his way to keep waging his endless war with the Scots. There was nothing to save him. But I am saved. I am my own man, at last, though I still must listen to grumblings of his old allies and those he appointed my advisers. But only for a little while longer, until you can take your place by my side. You don't mind? You forgive me?"

"Always."

"Damnation! I shall change things. I won't be stifled again. You should have been there. It would have been fitting. It would have been *right*."

"So it would have been," Piers said, "but I'm here now."

The welcoming party of lords and ladies saw and heard, and scowled or frowned, or shuffled their feet. Someone cleared a throat and they remembered their places and smoothed their expressions as they looked back at their new princess.

At last, they saw sorrow replace surprise on her fine features. But she straightened her spine and took a deep breath.

Her regal bearing and composure impressed them, although they reasoned it might be because she didn't understand the exact nature of the prince's joy at his reunion with his friend. It might be that she thought this was how all men of England behaved. After all, it was her first time in their country. It could also be because such things were known well in her homeland, France. The French, all knew, were up to anything.

Whatever it was, her control was not unexpected in a person of her lineage. Daughter to Philip the Fair, King of France, and sister to three princes, she knew her worth. But it was nevertheless astonishing. Whatever country she came from, however she was raised, she had to know she'd been deserted, and her bridal gifts given away. And she was, after all, only twelve years old.

Two

1321
Thirteen years later
St. Thomas Tower
London, England

"A gift for the queen," the courtier said, entering the bright chamber, sweeping a deep bow and then peeping up at the ladies watching him. He was a peacock, a man of fashion, a fellow who climbed when he could and bowed when he had to. In other words, as his enemies said: a perfect courtier.

He was certainly a rainbow. His cape was scarlet, his hose yellow on one leg and blue on the other, in the latest French style. His tightly fitted tunic was blue velvet with a starry field of yellow worked at the hem and at the ends of his long dagged sleeves. The round hat he swept off as he bowed was red, with a gilded design on its perimeter and a slender liripipe that looked like a red velvet snake at the end. With his hat off, one could see that strands of his hair had been dyed yellow. His shoes had such long, thin points, it looked as though he could sew with them, or so one of the young women present whispered to a friend.

But he was obviously used to being met with giggles as well as sighs and clearly took both as tribute. He preened.

Queen Isabella suppressed a smile and inclined her head. "A present? From whom?"

"From Lady de Percy, who is distant cousin to His Majesty by his mother. My lady met His Majesty at Ludlow last spring. His Majesty admired her retinue and remarked that you had not been so lucky in your ladies at court. He said you had lost three to wedlock and one to God. So my lady begs you accept her gift in the hopes it will suit."

"*It?*" Queen Isabella said, a faint flicker of humor in her voice.

"That is to say, *she*," he said and stepped back, bent double, still bowing. "Here is Gwenith de Percy, Your Majesty," he said, gesturing to the young woman who stood behind him. "She is cousin to my lady de Percy. She is one and twenty and in good health, my lady bids me to tell you. My mistress also desires that I tell you that Gwenith is virtuous, obedient and good-natured. She has no dowry, but my lady will not shame her when she weds. She plays the lute and the harp, and possesses a sweet singing voice. *And* she can read and write."

The queen's eyebrow went up at that. The courtier waited for the surprised murmurs of those present to stop before he went on, with a satisfied smile. "She can sew a fine seam and entertain children with lively but moral tales. She is an orphan, but having no taste for the religious life, prefers to live within a family. If you don't want her," he added, "simply send her back and my lady will send you another more to your taste."

Gwenith de Percy dipped in a curtsy and rose to stand, pale and still, looking at the queen and her ladies, and the children who had stopped playing at the queen's feet in order to stare at her.

She was passing fair. Her white skin was free of scar or blemish, her features even. She was slight and held her head high enough to show spirit, but not so high as to appear arrogant. Her clothing was simple but she'd raised her head a notch higher when the courtier had spoken of her accomplishments, so there was pride as well as modesty there. She wore a light blue underdress with a darker blue one over it. Her hair was tightly coiled and brought forward over her ears in the Ram's horn style, and covered with a headdress. What could be seen of her hair was midnight black. Plain and simple as she looked, still the courtier seemed to have spoken true. Her dark eyes were watchful and intelligent. Her mouth looked made for laughter. But there was a stillness and sadness about her that made the queen look closer.

"My father-in-law, our late and sorely missed Edward, told me about the slave markets he saw while on Crusade," Isabella murmured. "I didn't know we had such here. And yet you offer 'another more to my taste' if I don't care for her. Another what? Fie, sir, to hold a freeborn maid so low."

"I beg your pardon, Majesty," the courtier said, bowing even lower. "It is but what I was told to say. Lady de Percy wasn't sure you'd want her choice of lady for your court."

Isabella nodded, satisfied. This made sense. Many women wouldn't take such a lovely creature into their households for fear of tempting their lords to the limit right under their nose. But Isabella was different. She didn't show envy or jealousy for any woman. Why should she? All said she was the most beautiful woman in England. She took pains with her hair and dress, but not from vanity. She had little vanity, because she needed no reassurance as to her beauty.

On her wedding day, a poet in her homeland, France, had called her the beauty of beauties in the kingdom, if not all Europe. Still, she'd only been twelve years old then, and he, a court poet. Now at five and twenty, and mother of four, the last only recently

18

birthed, she had blossomed and become what he'd claimed those years ago. She was slender, graceful, with flaxen hair and azure eyes, and all admitted she had no peer. And it wasn't as though her husband would notice any sort of female in her company.

"Gwenith," the queen mused. "A Welsh name?"

"Yes, Your Highness," Gwenith answered softly. "I was sent to live with my lady de Percy after my grandmother died. My family lived in the Marches between England and Wales. Many have such names there."

"So at least we needn't fear a Welsh rebel in our midst," Isabella remarked. "How came you here?"

"My lady sent me," Gwenith said nervously, now showing some emotion, her color rising.

"Yes, yes, I know. But how? In a coach, on a wagon, a litter, by horse?"

"Oh," Gwenith said with relief. "On a horse, Your Highness. I had two outriders with me for safety. A coach is not for such as me, and a wagon would be too slow. And my lady doesn't have men to spare to carry a litter on such a long trip at this season."

"It was a long trip indeed," Isabella mused. "And yet you look well rested."

"I don't mind traveling," Gwenith said simply.

"Good," Isabella said. "Too many females do. We travel a great deal. Some of my ladies cannot travel, or if they do, they do not do it well. It is an inconvenience." She looked at the courtier. "Tell your lady I am well pleased and accept her gift with pleasure. We must get her properly dressed though. Simplicity is a virtue, but not at this court. My ladies' numbers are always changing, due to either their happy fate or misfortune," she told Gwenith. "I keep with me none who do not wish it wholeheartedly. I have my ladies who came with me from France, but they are not pleased with all my traveling either."

A murmur of softly voiced protests came from a group of

beautifully dressed middle-aged women standing in a close group nearby.

Isabella waved a hand and they fell still. "At least," she said, "I shall not trouble them with travel. Go now. Bathe and rest. We shall meet again at evening."

Gwenith curtsied again and turned to go.

"A moment," the queen said.

Gwenith turned back.

"They go to their nurses and tutors soon," Isabella said. "While they are here, know them." She gestured to the three bright-haired children surrounding her. "Here is your prince, Edward. He has ten years in his plate. Here is his brother, Prince John, a great lad of six, and their sister, Princess Eleanor, who has four years to her name. The babe, Joanna, is with her nurse. We are much together, and I expect my ladies to be part of my family."

"Prince Edward," Gwenith said, curtsying. "Prince John. Princess Eleanor."

The children bobbed their heads in acknowledgment and turned back to their game.

Gwenith ducked another curtsy and left the hall.

"Clever," a thin, dark woman dressed in black who stood beside Isabella's chair said softly, shaking her head. "That one is too clever. She should be watched."

Isabella laughed. "You see plots in poems. You hear treason in the wind. Hush, sweet Therese. That one *is* clever. Yes, you can see it in her eyes. Good. She may have secrets, and well might have her reasons for being here. We will see. It will add interest. Have I not said I have ennui? If she has a mission, it will not be done with a dagger. I am safe enough. She has fear as much as spirit. She will add spice."

"Take care," Therese hissed, crossing herself. "To wish for excitement is to let the devil hear."

Therese took great liberties. But she was given great license from the family that her own had served for generations. She could have retired with honor, with land and funds of her own, when her princess had married. But she had come to England with her mistress and had seldom left her side since.

"He hears whether I wish or no," Isabella said wearily. "Don't be foolish." She rose. "I will speak to the girl later. Now I wish to be left in peace."

"Little chance of that," Therese muttered, looking up at the sudden activity in the great hall beyond where they were assembled. The hall was in St. Thomas Tower, on the edge of the great Tower compound, close to the rolling Thames. It was where the king and queen lived and held audience, and also where the royal family assembled. Now it was astir. The king was returning from a day's sport.

"Where is my lady?" Edward called as he strode into the chamber. He was clad in crimson and gold, immaculate except for the fact that his hunting boots were stained green from crushed bracken. As he entered the room, he brought with him the fresh scents of fern and forest.

Isabella's breath caught in her chest, as it always did when she first saw him, just as it had done the first day she had. He was no less beautiful today than he'd been then, more than a decade past.

He'd lost the coltish charm he'd had then. He was an altogether grown and beautiful man of thirty-seven years now. When she'd first seen him he had been twenty-four, close to the age she was now, and it had seemed to her then that he was like the princes of *gestes* and fables she had read and adored, tales of great knights and powerful magic, from the dawn of his kingdom. She'd known she was to marry him since she was a child. Seeing him at last had thrilled her because unlike the husbands in most royal and thus arranged unions, his appearance did not disappoint. In fact, he was almost too handsome to be lord of a kingdom.

His father, Edward, had been famous for monstrous height

and strength, a grizzled man made of angles and edges, long-legged and harsh featured, they said. This Edward, his son, was tall, but lithe and graceful and perfect in every proportion. His golden hair gleamed; his eyes were the gentle blue of a summer's sky. His mouth was tender, his nose perfect, and even though he'd acquitted himself well in war, he bore no scars or disfigurement. It was as though Fate itself refused to mar such masculine perfection.

He was now as then, as always when his attention was turned toward her: courteous. He was an intelligent man and, according to his lights, a good one. She could wish now, as she had not known to then, that he could love her.

But as a child she had never doubted anyone's affection. She had been the favorite of her father, King Philip, his only daughter. It was true he loved her more as an instrument to his designs, but love was good for whatever reason you received it. Her brothers cosseted her; she was feted and sung about. She could believe she was a princess in the same story she had first envisioned her future husband in, the stories about his great king, Arthur. She'd been twelve—still a girl, though made a queen by marriage—and had known nothing of romantic love but those stories. She'd loved them as much as love itself. She had learned better.

Now Edward the king turned and smiled at her, and again, she forgave him the unforgivable.

"My lady," he said, and came to her, took her hands in his, and brushed a kiss on them.

"My wretches, my monsters, my devils!" he said and, laughing, bent to greet his children.

Isabella watched the children clamber around him, and smiled, as all around them did. This was true, this was real; he loved them dearly. Not everything she'd done had gone wrong. And now too, there was hope. With all she knew and all that had happened, still, now she allowed hope to dwell in her heart again.

Piers Gaveston, the beautiful youth from Gascony, son of

a bold knight, and a bold lad himself, Edward's beloved friend and constant companion, had been his youthful folly. And singular, since he'd never been replaced in Edward's heart. So Edward vowed, and so now she allowed herself to hope to believe.

At first she'd been hurt by their closeness, their bond of love and loyalty. But after all, what had she known then? Only pain and anger because her new husband loved his friend so dearly that he slighted his wife for him, spent more time with him and certainly had more smiles for him. Pampered since infancy, she'd been wounded at being left out. Worse, she had begun to see the secret signals and knowing smiles they'd always shared: two magnificent youths amused by their world and contemptuous of all others who were not so young and loved and gifted.

Edward had doted on his friend. That was the right of a king. But she had been a princess, and was a queen.

She hadn't been used to being balked. She'd protested. Edward, her royal husband, explained it was not a slight, but a circumstance caused by her youth. That, she'd understood. She'd felt her lack of years as an impediment too, but had realized, as he'd said, that time was on her side. Why shouldn't a young man rather pass time with a fellow knight, a fellow poet, a companion in arms and experience?

And so too she'd realized that the wedding gifts—*her* wedding gifts, which her new husband gave Piers—were given away because of Edward's generosity. How could she be so peevish as to refuse him the joy of sharing with his best friend? His court—the barons and nobles who watched him—were not so easily appeased when he gave Piers their titles and lands. Nor were they happy with the spiteful jests and asides about them, or the insulting names that clever, witty, sardonic Piers invented for them and subjected them to. His tongue was as wicked as the gleam in his eye.

But when she'd finally had enough, and insulted, wept, and raged, and threatened to return to France, both Piers and her husband had soothed her, catered to her, calmed her. They'd included her in their play from then on, as though she were a younger sibling. She'd still been very young, and had liked that well enough.

So too she'd accepted her husband's affection for Piers as natural between two men who had grown up together, however much Therese had muttered and the English barons stared. Had not Piers himself been a gift from Edward's own father? Longshanks had felt his heir to be too cosseted and weak, not like Alphonso, the adored son he'd lost, the boy he'd groomed to be king. So Piers was sent to the young prince when they'd both been twelve, to be his friend, a companion chosen for his wit and strength and cleverness.

So too she'd taken her young husband's refusal to immediately bring her to his bed as kindness. Even now, so she supposed it might have been.

And so when she was fifteen and came at last to her monthly courses, and her glorious husband had at last taken her, so gently, so sweetly, so quickly, she'd believed it was because he'd so respected her. He came to her calm and dispassionate, and even then she'd felt both honored and cheated. But it was ridiculous to think of royal Edward, golden Edward, grimacing and groaning like the peasants she'd seen rutting in the fields.

So she'd believed until the day she chanced to see something she should not have, and had finally realized that her golden Edward could grimace, grunt and moan, and sweat too, if it were Piers with him, on him, in him.

"What? Which of you rascals has gotten your mother so dour?" Edward asked now, seeing the sudden sorrow on Isabella's face.

"None," she said, forcing a smile. "I was but trying to remember a tale I was going to tell you."

The past was long done, and gone, as was clever, wicked Piers, this decade and more. He had destroyed more than her faith in Edward. He had shaken his kingdom's faith in the king's heir as well. It was unthinkable to unseat a king, an act punishable by God as well as man. But with Longshanks gone, Parliament had appointed Edward's grave cousin, Thomas, Earl of Lancaster, who was his senior by only a handful of years, to rule in tandem with him to prevent more folly. But through his four years of leadership, Lancaster had failed to please the barons, and so Hugh Despenser, Earl of Winchester, an older man full of wisdom and political power, and his warrior son, Hugh, were chosen to share the throne with the rightful king instead. Edward accepted this, in part because of his admiration for Hugh the younger. It ate at Isabella's soul.

Nor had this dire judgment changed Edward much. There had been other favorites since, but he was now so circumspect that it was easy for the barons to ignore them and for her to believe they were but his comrades. So they might have been. Isabella couldn't be easy about it, but it didn't matter. He didn't love any of them as he had Piers. She now understood that a man's physical desires weren't always those of his heart. Even if they were, a wise man kept his wife from knowing, and a wise woman looked away.

Now she had a grown man for husband and a life with him, and could believe and would believe that his absolute adoration of Piers had been youthful recklessness, over and forgotten as he claimed it to be. Except by her, and his court, and Therese, who never let her forget, as if she could. Even so, she was Edward's queen and would stay with him, of course. It was her purpose and her penance. The future would mend all.

"I remember now," she said. "We have a new lady in waiting, sent to us by Lady de Percy. She's educated. I have hopes she'll amuse us. Better still, she travels well. But you should see the courtier who brought her," she added, with a real smile, knowing Edward's interest in what was considered style on the Continent, and his disdain for fops. "He is the latest in fashion, and something to behold."

25

"Then behold him I shall. Give me time to bathe and dress, and I will join you later," her Edward, her king, her love in spite of all, said. He took her hand, bowed and brushed his lips over it.

And she, Isabella, Princess of France and Queen of England and Wales, who bowed to no other man, bowed her head to him. She was born a princess and trained to be queen, and would find happiness where she could, even if contentment were never part of it.

Three

1321
LONDON, ENGLAND

Gwenith left the queen's chamber and stopped in the dim hall outside, shivering and breathing deep. She clasped her hands together, bowed her head, closed her eyes and leaned against the wall. The cold stones at her back chilled her and woke her to the moment.

"Well, you've landed on your feet," the courtier who had brought her said with no little envy in his voice. "'A member of the family.' We all should have such families! I think I'll stay a day or two until you're settled, and see if I can lay eyes on our king. I shouldn't mind being a member of his family."

"Nor I," Gwenith breathed, while her heart raced in her breast and leaped up to her throat. Now she was here, at last she'd a chance to become what she'd been born to be.

"Lady?" a young page asked.

Gwenith nodded.

"Follow me," he said.

She followed the lad to the end of the corridor, where a doorway led to a flight of spiraling stairs. She picked up the hem of her skirts.

" 'Ware," the boy said, pausing. "The steps are steep and slippery."

She nodded, head down, one hand trailing along the wall for support. She was too concentrated on the shallow, narrow steps to speak or look up, even if she could have seen to the top of the winding stair.

"Never rush up, if you don't want to come down in a hurry," the boy added, as they climbed.

The steps were hewn of stone, the walls around of thicker stone. The air was chill and damp; it was like walking in ever-tightening circles inside a great beast. Outside, it was a bright day and the sunlight touched the stone, making it white. Here there was only the perpetual gloom of cold, heavy rock. Torches mounted on the walls at every turn gave fitful flares of light, but the stairs were narrow and the footing treacherous. Gwenith clenched her teeth and climbed. It would never do to tumble now.

At last, the lad led her out of the stair and down a hall to another doorway. He stopped to stare in surprise at the man who had quietly followed her.

"I just want to be certain," the courtier explained. "I have to be able to tell my lady I delivered her in good health." But he wasn't looking at Gwenith. His head was up and he was peering up and down the hall.

"Can't come here," the boy said. "Only for the queen and her ladies. Men at arms at the first floor, royalty at the top, which is how it should be. Dungeons belowstairs, and if you don't want to know about that, be off with you or you'll find it's your head that will be off."

The courtier's eyes widened. Then he backed up and fled down the stair.

The page snickered. "No common men allowed, but that's not saying none ever come here. No man ever got topped for looking, but that one wasn't looking for ladies, anyway. Come on."

The room he led her to had a small high window and white-washed walls. There was a woven carpet on the stone floor and three small, demure straw-stuffed cots in a row, like ones Gwenith had seen in the convent. There were three chests for clothing, and her bags of belongings were already set by one of them.

"Come down when you've put away your things," the boy said. "We eat soon."

"Wait! Come down where?" Gwenith asked.

"The way you came up. Someone will point you in the right direction when you get to the great hall," the boy said and left her alone in the room.

Gwenith went to the window and looked down. She gasped and drew back, one hand on her heart. Then she steeled herself and edged back to the window, holding one hand on the wall so she could prevent the terrible feeling that she was being sucked down. She peeped out. She had stood on hilltops and climbed trees, but had never been so high before. She'd lived in houses of thatch and wattle, and in a fine manor house of wood.

But it was nothing like this king's palace. It was terrible and fascinating. This place she was in sat in the sky; it was a stone for-tress, hacked from rock, upon a rock base and high as a mountain. To the right, she could see the last of the sunlight glinting off the Thames, and the ships that sailed there looked like children's toys. To the left, she saw the other towers in the Tower precincts. They were made of red and white and gray stones; she seemed to be at the edge of a stone forest. And directly below, she could see the stick figures of people as they went about their business on the many paths.

She'd been overwhelmed when she came to London. The city was awe-inspiring; some forty thousand people lived within its old

Roman walls. But the Tower was something else altogether. There were twelve towers in all, she'd been told. She'd also heard about the pleasant walks that connected them, the gardens, the men at arms and warders who patrolled there. She'd been told that while some people she would see might be high officials, such as attendants at court, chamberlains, constables or marshals of state, others would be clerks, washerwomen, bakers and servants. There were also crowds of tradesmen from London here each day to peddle their wares. The business of the kingdom made the Tower precincts a small kingdom. "You need never leave it, except in death," the courtier who had brought her had said.

She'd held her breath when she was told that she might see prisoners who were given their liberty every day and then locked up again at night. There was a garrison and a chapel, a jail and dungeons she hoped never to see, a tower for the jewels of state, a dairy and a forge, pens filled with livestock, a falconry, and stables for warhorses and draft animals. Passing by them on her way to meet the queen, she'd wrinkled her nose at an unfamiliar stench, and then stiffened when she heard a roar. That had made her companion roar with laughter. "Lions," he'd said. "Also here at the king's pleasure. But they're never let out for a stroll."

Lions and prisoners, jewels, guards and kings, the Tower was a fortress within a walled city, pent by a moat, accessible by drawbridges, protected by the Thames on one side. No one could get in without leave. No one could get out without permission. It was no wonder that the king lived here instead of Westminster Palace.

Why had Longshanks had to kill her family, deprive them of their land, when he had had all this? Her hatred for him flared again.

And yet, seeing the splendor around her, her heart sank. It was one thing to sit by her grandmother's side in the inconstant light of the dying hearth, with only the dark wild forest outside, safe in the circle of light, listening to the tales of the hideous Longshanks.

There, she could vow revenge for her dead ancestors, for the future that might have been hers, for her grandmother's sake.

"You are granddaughter of a prince," her grandmother had told her, again and again. "Were it not for the cursed Longshanks, one day you might have been a queen. But there were too many Welsh princes," her grandmother had grieved, "and they all at war with each other. Half his work Longshanks had done for him before he left England. Now they are all gone, to the grave or the convent, from whence no new princes or kings can come. All gone save you, child. Your mother was stolen away and given to me. In my turn and in my time, I will give you to one who owes much to your family, your long-dead father. And in turn your duty it is to save your family's honor."

"I will, I promise," she'd always insisted. It had seemed so right, so possible. Was she not granddaughter of a great Llewellyn, heir to misfortune, sworn to restore honor to her royal house?

It was another thing to come here to see this splendor, and realize how small she was, how hopeless her task.

Still, whenever she had said that to her grandmother, the old woman had laughed. "Aye, small you are, yet great deeds you may do. To keep the roof over our heads, watch for mice, I must. Right? Because little mice can do great harm if they are not caught in time. Remember that. So nibble, nibble, little mouse, and you can bring down their whole house."

As a child, she had always laughed at that. She did not now.

"Lady?" a voice asked, and she wheeled around.

Two men carried in a wooden tub, a half barrel with a seat within. They set it in the center of the room. Three maidservants carrying buckets of steaming water began to fill the tub. She was being given a chance to bathe! Gwenith was awed. At home, only the most honored guests were treated like this, and most of them had been men.

When the servants left, Gwenith quickly stripped off her

wimple and her clothes, and stepped into the tub. She'd been given a cake of soap. She sat, luxuriating in the splendor of the hot water and the wonder of the quickly dissolving, smooth, soft-scented soap.

"There you are!" a merry voice said.

Gwenith turned to see a short, buxom, round-faced and pink-cheeked young woman smiling at her. If she weren't so beautifully dressed in crimson, Gwenith would have taken her for a peasant.

"You take the bed by the window," the young woman said. "I sleep by the door because I sometimes have to leave in the night. Sometimes, to the privy—it's at the end of the hall in the wall, by the way, if you haven't gone yet. Sometimes, I just need to stretch my legs before I can sleep.

"Her ladyship des Monde demands the middle bed," the young woman went on, as she came into the room. "She reasons that if anyone attacks they'll get to her last. They'd do that wherever she slept," she added, grinning. "She gives herself airs. I don't. I hope you sleep sound, because I stir in the night. Still, we're lucky here. Most places we stay we share a bed. Where is my head? I'm Agnes of Bray, one of the queen's ladies. I'm not one of her favorites, but at least I don't puke in a coach or piss myself at the thought of traveling in one. My father is a loyal baron. Otherwise, I doubt even my traveling well would make her put up with me.

"I'm not so bad," she added, "at least once you get to know me. It's just that I say what I mean and I have a lot to say. The queen doesn't like that. Or me." She shrugged. "She's French. That might account for it. I'm not sly enough, I suppose. Though they call it being *délicat*. I'm not."

"That's easily seen," another voice said.

Gwenith looked up to see a tall, thin, pale woman standing in the doorway. Her dark green overdress had a richly set pattern of leaves on it, and she wore it over a white undertunic; otherwise Gwenith would have taken her for a novitiate.

"I am Mary des Monde," she told Gwenith with obvious pride. "And you'd do well to ignore anything Agnes says, lest you end up in dire difficulties, as she soon shall."

"So you wish," Agnes said without rancor. "Shall we pull hair or help this fledgling chick?"

Mary shrugged. "That is what I was trying to do."

"Don't fret," Agnes told Gwenith. "It's not hard being in attendance on a queen. In fact it's a pretty thing. You see the world, eat well, dress well and meet many a man of rank and fortune. And those without either who have other things to offer," she added with a wink.

"You have a chance to serve your queen," Mary said sternly.

"And meet men of rank and fortune, as you never would at home," Agnes went on blithely. "There's not much to your duties. We've heard you can read and write, so you've a brain in your head. Just keep a fair tongue in your mouth to match it. We'll tell you what you must know. You ask us what you don't understand. You'll reason out the rest soon enough. Gossip flies here. Don't listen to it or make any, and you'll do well enough.

"First off," Agnes said, "there's only me and Mary, and Joan and Catherine to meet today. Catherine has loose bowels, and Joan suffers from the headache, so you won't see them much. They sleep in a room down the hall. Margaret is gone to a wedding, Ellen is readying for her own. There are two more ladies in attendance, but not at the moment. They went home, and we don't know if they'll ever return. *She* didn't like them, but in truth, the queen hasn't much use for any of us."

"Really, Agnes," Mary said angrily.

"Really," Agnes said, unperturbed. "That's the fact and better she know it right off. We don't even share her room, like the attendants of the old queen used to do. It doesn't hurt my feelings, I don't pretend to anything but what I am. I serve the queen but she doesn't need me." She turned back to Gwenith.

"The other ladies are French, but they're old, and don't do much more than chatter. The truth is that body servants take care of Her Majesty's needs and she has Therese, so she doesn't need any of us, except for show. Therese came with her from France. She's been with the queen since she was a babe. And Therese's mother served Isabella's before her. She is as close as family to Isabella," she explained, "and never leaves her side. She's the one to look out for."

Gwenith stopped washing and looked up. "There is danger here?"

"Oh, God love you," Agnes said. "Of course. More here than there, because who's to hear you if you say something there?" She laughed. Even Mary smiled.

"There are plotters and schemers everywhere," Agnes went on. "We are at war with enemies we know and those we don't. Wales is quiet now, but Scotland still simmers. In truth, the world envies us, and this is the seat of power. So everyone is on guard against treason, and Lord knows there's enough of that spoken these days. But not here, never here. Being close to the throne means being closer to the headman's ax. Still, I hear it was harder when Longshanks was king. And it would be harder still for you, even now, were you a man.

"Men are always suspected of violence," Agnes explained. "Women can be excused many things, although not by the queen, so keep your opinions to yourself. Even I do. I only prattle about things that can't hurt me. Our job is to accompany, assist and obey. Do that and you'll be safe."

"Safety lies in doing your job and keeping still until asked to speak," Mary said, still stern. "And being careful what you say and who you speak to, befriend and, especially, who you pass your time with, day or, most especially, night," she added, shooting a warning look to Agnes.

"Oh, aye," Agnes said cheerfully and winked at Gwenith.

Gwenith continued to bathe. The less she said, she realized, the better for all.

The other two women were as curious as a pair of cats. They didn't actually paw through her possessions, but they looked as though they were itching to. Even the sober Mary came fully into the room to better see them. They eyed Gwenith, her discarded garments and the new gown she'd laid out on a chair. Gwenith was used to bathing in company, and so tried to ignore them and luxuriate in her bath. But they didn't leave.

"Now tell us about yourself," Agnes finally said.

"There isn't that much to tell," Gwenith said. "In fact, I've seen and done more since I left home to come here than I have in the whole of my life. I knew London was populous, but never realized what it would look and feel like. There are thousands of people here! Every street looks like market day at home. And this tower is taller than anywhere I've ever stood in. I looked out the window when I came in and almost swooned."

"You will become accustomed," Mary said.

"Oh, aye," Agnes said cheerfully, "we all do. Have you any brothers? Suitors?"

Gwenith laughed. "No brothers, and too many unsuitable suitors. There are few men of fortune or good birth at home and too many other men looking for advancement. I'm not wealthy and have no dower portion. That's why my lady sent me here. She's a distant relation of mine, so distant I have difficulty tracing our lines. But she owed a favor to my family, and she's all I have left. I have no close kith or kin since my grandmother died. Since I found no one to marry and needed a future it was with Lady de Percy, where every day is the same, or here, or the convent, and I haven't a calling."

Mary nodded. Agnes laughed.

"Well, you'll meet men here, all right," Agnes said. "All kinds come here, from all lands. There are so many men and so many choices that your head will spin. Some are worthy and some are not, but that doesn't mean they must be ignored. Stay with us and you'll learn that you don't have to marry in order to tarry a while with a likely fellow. You can choose one for a matter of days and let him spin your head, and even better parts."

Mary gasped. "Enough! You play a dangerous game. She should not do such things, no more than should you."

Agnes shrugged. "We all can't pass our time in good thoughts, like you, Mary."

"You'll end up alone and disgraced," Mary said angrily.

"Nay," Agnes said. "If I'm unlucky, I'd end up at home, married and probably not to a man of my liking. But who likes a husband chosen for her by others?" Mary opened her mouth to protest, and Agnes added, "We can't all be like our good queen, married to a man she loved, and happy forever after with him because of it."

Mary closed her mouth, and looked away.

Gwenith's bathwater was growing cold, and she finished as quickly as she could. When she rose, Agnes held out toweling for her. "You'll have a maidservant, but I'll play one until you do," she told Gwenith. "Don't thank me! It's not charity. It's because I'm hungry. Let's get thee garbed, and we'll go down."

"Good sense for once," Mary said. "Is this your only wimple?" she asked Gwenith, picking up the garments Gwenith had taken off. "Or have you another?"

"My clothes are travel-stained. Let me open my cases," Gwenith said. "Maybe you can tell me what best to wear now? I want to make a good impression."

"That you will," Agnes said, as she and Mary happily unpacked Gwenith's store of clothes, commented on them, then helped her dress.

Sooner than she'd thought, and much sooner than she liked, it was time to go down and meet the rest of the court. Gwenith wore her best: a violet gown, with a saffron overtunic. Her hair was still damp, so she coiled it high, pinned it, then wrapped and covered it with a wimple. Then she waited until her two helpers pronounced her ready.

She took the long, dark, winding stair down behind the two ladies in waiting, walking carefully lest she tread on the edges of their flowing gowns. The two women had been friendlier than she'd dared hope, and she felt lucky, even though she knew she could never be a true friend to them. She was awkward and guarded because the weight of her task lay heavily on her mind, and for all their kindness, if they knew her mind, they would be her enemies.

She held a hand on the wall again as she descended, her heart beating so rapidly that she feared it would leap into her throat. But not because of the treacherous stairs. She'd come here with her vow forecast in her mind. But after only a few hours at court, the reality of her situation staggered her. What could she do here? She was only one unimportant woman in a crowd of hundreds of lackeys and servants. These people ruled the world. Her goal of reaching court was met, yet now her task was harder. A mouse? It would take armies of men to bring down this kingdom.

And why? All the traitorous thoughts she'd entertained since she'd left home were back with her again. The road had widened, and so had her view of the world. It was bigger than she'd dreamed. Her ambitions suddenly seemed small, furtive, ridiculously futile. The past was done; it was her grandmother's war, her revenge to take, if she could take it from the grave. Edward Longshanks was dead. So were all those he had abused, including her family. She was an orphan and a charity case, lucky to have the clothes she wore, not to mention the skin she was in. Heiress to a conquered land, even Lady de Percy had been nervous to keep her and keep up the pretense that she was her husband's cousin. But she had to, because her own family had a distant linkage to Llewellyn and owed a blood debt. Gwenith was made to understand early on that she was left in peace and still alive only because if she told no one, no one would know.

This wasn't her fight.

She had no fight, no bone to pick except with ghosts, and she could never defeat her own, much less her ancestors' ghosts, the ones that plagued her dreams. Her grandmother had made sure of that. The glorious dead were long gone before she was born but still she saw their mutilated bodies and severed heads as though she'd been there when they'd been tortured and slain. She knew the names of every one of them, all her dead relatives, countrymen and subjects.

This was her *geas*, her unholy quest. She had to travel the road she'd been set on—no matter that she'd only just now realized how formidable the challenge truly was. She'd have to see what fate cast in her path. She had, after all, no choice. Grandmother was gone to live with her ghosts. She had no dowry for marriage. She had but one purpose in this life, to keep her vow to her family. She couldn't do much, but she refused to do nothing.

The stair wound downward, and Gwenith watched her step carefully, every inch of the way.

Four

1321

Gwenith sat at the long trestle table with some hundred others, and could only watch, and marvel. There was conversation and laughter all around her. Although the hall was huge, bigger than any she'd ever sat in before, it was also the most crowded, save for the cathedral at Shrewsbury she'd once attended on an Easter morning. But this assembly was merrier.

Colors swirled before her eyes. Bold, bright flags and pennants hung on the high walls. The walls themselves were painted with stars and flowers, a riot of colors that rivaled even those on the robes of the nobles in attendance. They wore crimson and gold, indigo and green. Their sleeves were slashed to show more contrasting colors. Their hose were striped, their tunics bold. The ladies wore gowns of magnificent fabrics in dazzling shades. There were monks, garbed in white and gray and brown, according to their order, and higher officials of the church in red. By their colors you shall know them, Lady de Percy had advised Gwenith before she had left for London, and so it seemed tonight.

Their queen, Isabella, was beautiful. Tonight she was a pale, slim figure dressed in shades of blue, as demure as a nun, as lovely as a poem. Or so the minstrel had been singing in his praise of her when Gwenith took her place at the table.

But it was the king who dominated the hall, although seated. He wore black and gold, and his slender figure looked regal, even amid the grandeur of the older men, bishops and generals, who sat at his table.

The hall went still as the king rose to his feet to greet his court.

"Today's hunt went well," he declared. "So we feast tonight."

The assembled court laughed at his jest, as if they wouldn't feast even if the hunt went badly.

"My father always said that meat a man kills himself tastes better than dishes provided by anyone else," he added. "So since the good father here has praised the Lord," he said, indicating the black-clad monk who had given the blessing, "I praise the memory of my good father, and urge you to feast!" He raised a golden cup to them.

His bright eyes shone blue in the torchlight; his hair gleamed gold as the cup he held. The center of all eyes in that crowded hall, to Gwenith he looked altogether like a prince from a tale of the olden days, when kings could be known because their God-given power glowed from them.

Gwenith glanced around. She sat closer to the royal pair than most, and though she knew in her heart she despised them, she couldn't help but feel honored. The hall seemed to be roofless, because its ceiling was lost in the early darkness, the high, thin windows black with approaching night. Even the many torches spouting flames up on the walls couldn't illuminate such a height.

But still it was as hot and smoky as any poor peasant's hut might be. The night was cool, so flames in the huge fireplace to the side of the room leaped and raged, fighting over logs that lackeys constantly fed them. The air was filled with the smell of burning apple wood, oak and pine, mingled with the scent of new-mown hay rising from the fresh rushes strewn on the floor underfoot.

Soon the smell of roasted meats and rich sauces wafting through the vast hall made the dogs at the king's feet raise their noses in the air, as did many of the guests. Then there was a murmur of approval as a quartet of lackeys staggered in bearing among them the weight of a platter, upon which rested a roasted boar, gilded like a statue. The court applauded. It wasn't a great holiday and so the treats paraded forth surprised and delighted the company. They cheered as another crew of drudges bore in platters with roasted peacocks, dressed in their own feathers so cleverly they looked like they might leap from the plate and set to scratching the floor.

Though the dishes were presented to the king, they were for show as much as for dining. More mundane food came after. A stream of servers entered the hall and delivered rivers of fish, clutches of fowl, sides of mutton and beef, lamb and ham. There were eel pies and hash in pasties, with so many sauces that soon fresh trenchers were offered for those who needed them. And ale, and wine, an endless supply of rich red wine.

Gwenith had never seen such excess. Or smelled anything so delicious. Though her anxiety had disguised her hunger, she soon pulled the knife from her belt and plied it eagerly. She'd never seen, much less tasted, some of the dishes. Finally she sat back, replete, slightly ashamed that she couldn't finish all she'd taken. She felt better when she saw the eagerness of the servers as they scooped up her trencher when they cleared the table. It made her realize that, as at home, nothing would go to waste, and the lower servants as well as the poor at the gates would also dine well tonight.

Now, the jellies and pastries having been passed around, most of the dining was done, and everyone in the hall seemed to be talking at once.

The king and queen sat at the highest point of table. They didn't pick up choice morsels and feed them to each other, as newly loving couples do. Nor did they exchange smiles or secret glances. But they seemed comfortable and happy. The king didn't do more than joke with the handsome young man at his side, and never exchanged so much as a longing look with him, much less an embrace or caresses. Gwenith was surprised, relieved and disappointed, because it seemed that all the vile rumors she'd heard about his tastes were false. He had no eyes for his wife, but he'd none for any of the men around him either.

So then, Gwenith wondered, had it all been a lie told by his foes? Had the infamous youth the king's enemies claimed was also his lover, the clever, manipulative and greedy Piers Gaveston, been so foully executed for no reason? Piers had been banished by Edward Longshanks for the rumors about his friendship with his son, but returned immediately after Longshanks' death by order of the new king, Edward. It was said he and the king went straight back to their vile habits. But that was said by Piers' enemies, of whom he'd made legion. Edward the king, under duress from the court, and powerful Lord Lancaster and his allies, had been forced to banish Piers again. All said, it was like a joke between the two of them. Appease the barons and then go back to living as they chose again.

But then Piers was abducted and beheaded by his powerful enemies led by the Earl of Lancaster. His murderers sent his head to Edward, who grieved, they said, to this day. But they said many evil things about Longshanks and his ilk in the lands where Gwenith lived. Her people had dreaded and feared Longshanks.

They needed to be contemptuous of young Edward. Because if a man had a weakness, he could be brought down.

Gwenith had hoped the foul rumors true; it was simpler to hate someone who defied God as well as man. She'd never known a man who loved men. She didn't know if she saw one now. She could see no sign of it in the golden young king, no betraying behavior, no trace of lust for any man.

She sighed. What was or was not true? Did it even matter? It wouldn't be the first or last time innocent blood had been shed. Hadn't her own family been murdered for less? Rightful reasons were always plentiful and sensible sounding, after deeds had been done.

Still, it had been easier for her to hate a perverse man. Now she wondered. Had this gallant young king actually kissed and fondled Piers in front of his wife, and his court? It seemed incredible. That would have been more than shocking. It would have been impious.

Had Piers really mocked the barons, tweaking their noses, calling them by cruel and foul nicknames, teasing them by swaggering around court, showing off the riches he'd been given by the king? Had Edward really given Piers Isabella's bridal gifts and jewels in front of his own court the very day he'd brought his bride home? He'd given him estates and riches enough of his own, taken from other lords to gift Piers with. That much was true. Everyone spoke of it still.

But Piers had been a brave warrior, descended from a brave knight, as had been the king, and they'd been together for years as friends and companions in war and peace. Had not Longshanks himself brought Piers to Edward so they could train together? And they'd been just boys then, really, Gwenith thought. Their love might have been pure. It was impossible to know now.

Now, the company relaxed, musicians played as they looked around at one another.

Gwenith noticed a lady seated near the queen, because she was talking with animation. Every time she moved, she showed off the fact that she wore a fascinating steeple cone atop her headdress, from which a gauzy veil flowed.

"The latest thing from Paris, they say," Agnes, sitting at Gwenith's right-hand side, said enviously. "Trust *her* to wear that," she added, watching the lady in the headdress. "She gets to show that she's just been to Paris. Her Highness will love that. Clever to wear it here. She can talk about Isabella's homeland with her. And *then* she can ask for a boon for that drunkard of a husband of hers."

"They say," Mary commented from the other side, "that he games without luck, and without letup, and soon may be without funds at all."

It was marvelous how Mary had relaxed once they'd been seated. Now she gossiped as happily as Agnes did, though Agnes' gaze was usually fixed on the men.

"You must know who we dine with," Mary told her. "Agnes, doubtless, will introduce you to many a knight. But as for the others, who do not dance or dally, you must let me be your guide. Now there to the side, in the saffron tunic, the sour fellow, that's Richard de Bures, the royal comptroller, old as the hills but still in his position. He sits next to the Keeper of the Treasure Tower, no matter his name, you'll seldom see him. And there is Robert le Breton, falconer. Menials seldom sit down to dine with the king, but he is Edward's falconer, after all. Pray God they don't ask the falcons themselves to sup with us!"

She chatted happily, showing Gwenith a dizzying assortment of minor officials who kept the Tower and the household going.

"So," Agnes said, elbowing Gwenith, "what do you think of court?"

"I can't think," Gwenith said honestly. "I am overwhelmed."

"Soon we'll rise to play," Agnes said. "Ring-around-a-rosy,

and other light games. And then if the queen permits, some livelier dances."

"I know no one here to partner me," Gwenith said.

"You've been noticed," Mary said. "You'll have partners for everything."

"Aye," Agnes laughed. "Now some advice from *me*. The tall fellow in blue who's been staring at you? Down the table, yes, him. Don't look away. It doesn't matter if you stare. He's rich, but already contracted by his family to a fine lady. Tell him nay. He'll understand that. But he will ask. His lady has the face of a horse."

Even Mary smiled at that.

"Now the two lads in blue and green, there, to your left," Agnes went on. "They are brothers who find more amusement in besting each other than in pleasing a lady. Tell one yes and the other no, but don't name which you would dance with. That rivalry will give us some entertainment. Who else would you care to know about? That tall, handsome fellow, John Matthewson, has been looking at you for a while too. I'll introduce you if he approaches, but I'd not advise you giving him more than a courteous good evening."

"Very true," Mary said sagely. "He's about to be pledged to Lady Anne, and can mean no good for you."

The two ladies in waiting told Gwenith about everyone in the room. The men they spoke of looked back at them with similar interest.

"Who is the man in the gray who stares at me so rudely?" Gwenith asked, looking at another man she'd seen eyeing her.

"Where?" the other ladies asked in unison, looking eagerly around.

But he'd faded back into the crowd of merrymakers who were leaving the tables and forming a wide circle in the center of the room.

"He's gone," Gwenith said. "He was all in gray."

"All in gray?" Agnes said, wrinkling her nose as though she smelled something foul.

"Yes," Gwenith said.

"Ah. Then trust me. He was a servant, or a monk," Mary said wisely. "An invited guest would dress well. We wouldn't know him. We have naught to do with servants. That may be why he disappeared when you caught him staring."

"So," Gwenith said, "everyone here knows everyone else?"

"Yes," Mary said comfortably. "Or if not, then *of* them. They have but to speak the name of their family, and all is known. This is true whether they come from the north or south. Of course, tonight isn't a festival or a date of any special significance. There are no honored guests from foreign parts. On such occasions, of course, the world comes here, and we cannot know them all."

"I see," Gwenith said. "And so all the people here tonight are related to each other as well?"

"Not all," Mary said. "Most."

The lively music of flutes, tambours and fiddles began to strike up more loudly.

"I go to amuse myself with Harold," Agnes said, rising and smiling at a stocky man in green who was coming toward them. "He shall be my partner. He flies his falcon with the king's," she told Gwenith.

"Take care, Agnes," Mary said quietly. "He flies too high in other ways too. I hear he's almost promised to Lady Beatrice. She's well dowered."

" 'Almost' has never bothered me," Agnes said blithely. "I didn't say I wanted to wed him, did I? I will see you again at last bells, or maybe not," she added, laughing.

Mary looked dour. "You'll get your tail caught in the door one day," she said quietly.

"Mayhap," Agnes said with a shrug. "But it will have wagged a few times by then." She laughed again, and took the arm of a stocky fellow in green, who bowed and then strolled away with her. They didn't go to the center of the room, where the dancers assembled, but walked through the crowd to the back of the hall, and disappeared from sight.

"You take care too," Mary told Gwenith, watching the pair stroll away. "Agnes means well, but she plays a dangerous game with men she likes. And she likes too many. She'll end up disgraced, wed to anyone who can be paid enough to take another man's leavings. Take note of what she does, but don't try it yourself."

Gwenith nodded, looking so sober and distressed that Mary said no more. She rose and left Gwenith to join the dancers.

Gwenith sat quietly and bit back tears of frustration. She was lost. After only a day, she saw how impossible her mission was.

What could she do? Here was the center of the known world. The men and women in this room held all its power and riches. Should she heave a dagger at the king? Push him down a stair? How could she revenge herself on the very sun in the sky?

This Edward ruled a prosperous kingdom; his youthful follies were forgotten. If he was not loved, as his mother had been, or feared, as his father had been, then at least he was not despised. He'd grown into his role. The Despensers surely curbed his excesses. There'd be no more whispers of insurgency from within his land. Her own people were crushed. The Scots might have defeated the king in battle, but now they too were quiet, within their boundaries.

True, the Marcher lords who ruled Wales and bordering England were still tearing one another to pieces, vying for power. But the Marcher lords now only preyed on one another, and they bowed to Edward's rule.

Gwenith despaired again that she couldn't carry out her promise to her grandmother. But she resolved to save her own immortal soul, at least. She'd bide a while here, and then return to her grandmother's grave and pray for her forgiveness. She watched the dancers through a blur of tears she refused to shed, and so saw only the outlines of swirling colors and lights.

"Lady?" a smooth, masculine voice asked.

Gwenith looked up through tear-starred lashes to see a man bowing to her. He had rust hair and bright blue eyes, and a kindly smile. He carried two lighted tapers, one in each hand.

"Dance, my lady?" he asked. "I'm Thomas Dale, friend to Lady des Monde. She said you are new to us. Do you know the candle dance?"

"I do," Gwenith said with gratitude, as she rose and took a taper from him. "And thank you. I should like to dance."

She marked off the paces of the dance, holding her candle so that it would not flicker and go out, and so lost herself for a while in the mindless concentration necessary for the steps and safety of the flame. She laughed at Thomas' outsized expression of woe when a neat turn he made caused his candle to flicker, and go out. She was ready to go back to her seat when another man, this one in scarlet and green, bearing a flaming candle, took her hand and led her back into the dance.

She danced an entire measure, and another with yet another partner, and would have won the game, but an unexpected breeze from the vast door at the end of the hall being opened defeated her, and her light was extinguished at last. It wasn't the only one that died. The sudden draft ended the dance for everyone. Gwenith bowed to her partner and went back to her place at the table, her heart now even heavier because it had lately felt light.

She sat and looked toward the queen.

"Looking won't hurry her," Mary said, as she took her seat again. "We can't leave until she does, and she's disposed to linger tonight. Are you tired? It must have been a long day for you."

"So it was, but I don't mind."

"It is unusual," Mary said, stifling a yawn. "She usually goes to her bed by this time."

Gwenith watched her king and queen. Edward was in an animated discussion with a young man dressed in surpassingly splendid fashion—in fact, far too splendidly even for this rainbow court. The man wore a purple cape, a rose-colored tunic and parti-colored hose. From the many times he bowed and preened, it was obvious he was fawning over his king.

Gwenith's attention sharpened. Was this another favorite? Were the rumors then true? That would make her impossible mission at least imaginable. She held her breath, glanced at the queen and saw her amusement. The young man turned, and Gwenith saw he was the courtier who had accompanied her here. From the king's expression and the look he shot to his wife, Gwenith realized that it was the costume, and not the man, that had entranced him. He looked as amused as Isabella did.

And then she saw the king's head turn. His lucent eyes widened and his color rose as he stared at the man who had blown out the candles when he'd opened the door to enter the hall.

Though the musicians still played, the room seemed to fall still. The man who strode toward the king wore the helm and armor of a knight, and when he approached the king, he went down on one knee, and raised off his helm. His dark brown hair was damp with sweat, but his dark eyes were alert. He was youthful and well made, but not surpassing fair. He had a square, blunt face with heavy brows, and a strong, thick body. Although surely not more than Edward's own age, he looked like a seasoned warrior, with his rugged countenance so tanned by the weather.

The king stared at him with barely suppressed excitement.

Puzzled, Gwenith looked to the queen. She saw the beautiful lady blanch, and stiffen, and for one unguarded moment, something pained and hard crossed her expression. Then her clenched hand relaxed, her face smoothed and she raised her goblet and pretended there was nothing on her mind but the rich red wine in her cup.

"Who is that?" Gwenith whispered to Mary.

"Who? Oh, the man who speaks to Edward now? That is Hugh le Despenser, the Earl of Winchester's son, the royal chamberlain."

Despenser? Gwenith went rigid. The blood left her head. She knew that name. Who did not? It was the stuff of childhood nightmares. This was Despenser? Hugh Despenser, first Earl Winchester, had been a brutal general in the wars against her people. A man of power and ruthless ambition. A ravager and pillager, he would break a treaty if he could, and do it as easily as he would break his enemy's backs. He killed hostages and pocketed their ransoms. He was bitterly hated in Wales, and everywhere feared.

"Gwenith? Are you well?" Mary asked.

"I danced too fast," Gwenith managed to say. "But I thought Despenser was older."

"So his father is. The big, round man in red velvet, who sits to the side of the king. He's bald and red faced, and wears his chain of office round his neck. This man who just entered, he is the son, also Hugh. He's wreathed with honors: knight and king's chamberlain, constable of castles, and keeper of manors and castles."

"I see," Gwenith breathed.

She watched as Hugh Despenser the younger rose at his king's command. As he did, Gwenith saw the king's face light up from within like the candle she had so lately carried in the dance.

She looked at the queen again, and though Isabella's expression was clear, her eyes burned like the blue at the center of a flame as she gazed upon the younger Despenser, and then at Edward's so apparent delight at suddenly seeing him.

And then, so quickly she'd have missed it had she not been looking hard, she saw a brief expression cross the younger Despenser's face. He shot his king a look both coy and promising, so quickly it was only a heartbeat before his expression smoothed to common affability.

Isabella's face didn't change, but now her hand on her goblet showed her knuckles white.

In that moment, Gwenith at last rejoiced. All was not lost. No problem was unsolvable if one could find the key to it. And now she believed she had. All was not perfect. There was a weakness. A chink in the wall, a crack, one just big enough for a mouse. Now all she needed was time, and patience.

Five

1321
<small>That same night</small>
<small>The Tower, London</small>

Edward rose to greet his knight. The great hall went still. He strode to him, clasped both Hugh Despenser's arms and stood with him elbow to elbow, smiling. "Not here, not now," he told him, low, and then turned a glowing face to his queen.

"Sir Hugh brings news," Edward told her with barely controlled excitement. "I must leave the hall. He and I must talk together now."

"I'sooth," Hugh said, bowing to his queen, "I've news of great victories, and equal word of treachery. Not for gentle ears, Highness."

Isabelle fixed him with a cool blue stare. "My father was King of France, a land five times the size of yours, Despenser. My brother is now king. There is nothing I have not heard."

Hugh smiled. "Then know that Gower and Usk have come about, my lady, and now eat from my hand like doves."

"How comes this?" Isabella asked. "Are those lands not the dower and provenance of your wife's sister, Margaret?"

"Aye, Highness. But her husband has fallen into dispute and rebellion. Wales yet chafes under our harness. I took the reins and now there is peace."

"And Margaret? She too is peaceful?" Isabella asked.

All conversation in the great hall had stopped. Gwenith sat up and turned her full attention on the king and queen and the knight who had just come in the hall.

Earl Despenser, the elder, had moved away earlier to converse with a cleric. Now he returned with a quick, yet measured step, his bulk and red velvet tunic making him seem like a great ship with red sails approaching the king.

"Highness," he said to Isabella in his rich plummy voice, bowing, "has my son said aught to make you believe otherwise? Lady, how has he offended you? He patrols your borders, smites your enemies and upholds your law. Where has he failed? Tell me, and I'll have his ears."

There was laughter as his son pretended to shrink back in dismay, because everyone had fallen silent in order to hear the conversation. Edward looked at Hugh the younger with amusement, and pride.

Isabella turned to the elder. "Your son tells me triumphs," she told the earl. "The king says there was also trouble."

"None that can't be remedied," Hugh the younger said quickly. "Hereford defies our king by not coming to court on his summons. There are some who believe he's encouraged in this by Lancaster—well, what can we expect but that of him?" he asked his king with a wry and knowing smile. "He has ever resented our taking over his duties, duties he never performed with grace or care. But now it seems he's supported by Mortimer. This cannot be borne."

"We can deal with them," Edward said. "But not here. My

lady," he said, "Hugh and I needs must leave you and our company here in the hall tonight. You will learn everything we have to say, certainly. But surely you don't wish to join us in private council? Especially," he said with a sly grin at the knight standing beside him, "since Hugh here smells like a hard day's ride on several horses, and must needs bathe. The lady of the manor ofttimes assists a honored guest in his bath. But I wonder, should a queen?"

"Should a king?" Isabella shot back.

The room went still. Edward's cerulean eyes widened. The elder Despenser's ruddy color grew distinctly paler. The younger's expression grew cold. Gwenith held her breath.

Isabella lowered her gaze, doubtless aware she'd spoken too fast and too freely. "Go then," she said with a wave of her hand. "I'll retire as well."

"It would be best," Edward said a little warily. "But where is Therese?" He frowned. "She should be here to show you to your rest."

"She ails," Isabella said, "but promises to be better tomorrow. If she is not, I'll send for another physician, over all her protests. Give you good night, husband." Isabella stood, and looked down the table, obviously thinking deeply. "Gwenith from the Marches," she announced, "give your queen your arm."

Gwenith leaped to her feet and hurried to the queen.

"Play on," Edward said with a wave of his hand to the musicians, before he left the great hall with Hugh the younger.

Isabella walked to the back of the hall, Gwenith at her side.

"Do you need my arm, Highness?" Gwenith asked.

The queen stopped and looked at her, and laughed. "Do I appear decrepit? Am I in my dotage? I have but five and twenty years in my dish."

"You look beautiful, as ever," Gwenith said, bowing her head. "As you asked for my arm, I only thought . . ."

Isabella laughed, and continued walking. "A turn of phrase, only that. I've no need of support. The halls are lined with men at arms. A linkboy goes before me. A queen is never alone. Or," she added more quietly, as though speaking to herself, "seldom so, at any rate. I decided to take this time to get to know you. You stumble? Am I that fearful?"

"I mistook my step, Highness," Gwenith said as they walked out the door and into the cool night.

A linkboy did go before them, holding aloft a torch so that the queen could walk in the light. Gwenith followed the queen to her bower in St. Thomas Tower.

The queen's quarters were large and well furnished, with colorful carpets on the floors, and bright tapestries with symbols of her native country, France, and of her adopted land, England, hanging on the painted walls. She had two rooms, one with chairs and several chests, and in the other, at the center, Gwenith glimpsed a great bed draped with curtains.

Two maidservants rose to attend Isabella. She sat with great weariness in a high-backed chair and let her servants attend her. She closed her eyes as one maidservant took off her wimple, and the other began to unwind the sheer fabric that had bound it to her head.

Gwenith thought she had been forgotten, and wondered if she should leave.

"Tell me of yourself, Gwenith," Isabella quietly said, her eyes still closed.

"What would you know, Highness?" Gwenith asked.

"Well, first," Isabella said, opening her eyes, "where did that trollop Agnes go? Surely not off with Harold du Benett? I saw her leaving with him. That would be folly. He's promised in marriage. She'll get nothing but a bellyful from him. Was she fool enough to go sport with him?"

Gwenith looked down at the floor.

"Ah, you have given your faith already? That is noble. But I am your queen."

"Yes," Gwenith said softly, "she did."

Isabella laughed. "A test, and you passed it. Good! I admire loyalty. But I value respect for your queen even more. What do you think of this place, Gwenith?"

"I hardly know. I have only been here a day, Highness. It is more than I have seen in the whole of my life."

Isabella smiled, and sat back, obviously enjoying the way her servants uncoiled and then carefully brushed out her long pale hair. "So tell me," she said into the air, "what do you like best? And mislike worst? Come, Marcher maiden, amuse me." But she said it with a laugh to take the command from it.

"It's too early to say," Gwenith said. "I like the food."

This earned her a chuckle.

"And the fact that I've my own bed," Gwenith went on. "I think I like the fact that there are so many people here. I don't know. I've never seen so many ladies, knights and nobles, not to mention all those who serve them. Highness?" she asked in a small voice. "What would you wish of me? I've been sent to assist you, but I don't know how. Mary and Agnes said all will become clear to me, but I'd rather know now. If you'd be so good, that is. If you had the time and inclination, if you could but tell . . ."

"Don't stammer, Gwenith. It's a fair question in a good time. You can serve me right now. My Therese, who has been close to me as my elbow since I left France, is ailing. I have my chaplain and my ladies in waiting, and all manner of aid here. But I need someone of my own, someone new, to run my errands, someone quick and educated. You can read and write, they say."

"So I can," Gwenith said.

"Good. More important, you keep faith, but can you keep your own counsel? Or rather, mine?"

"That I can."

"We shall see. I have visitors every day. I send for some, and send others away. I need someone with wit and tact to serve me in this. Now get you to bed. Don't stay up waiting for Agnes. She'll drag in at dawn. That's one of the reasons I don't entrust errands of any importance to her. I can't blame her for making her duties her pleasures, but I can't rely on her for just that reason, either. Mary is a good girl, mayhap too good. She does everything as it should be done, and all of us cannot be so holy, not even your queen." She sighed. "My little Jane was a charming companion, but she's gone to be wed, as has my lady Elizabeth. Joan is ailing with one of her headaches, and she gets them whenever the wind turns. And Anne has a stomach that plagues her. My French ladies have served me well, but they grow old.

"No, it will have to be you, Gwenith of the Marches," Isabella said. "A pretty little creature, with bright eyes and a wise head, they say. Or at least it will be you until my Therese is well again. And who knows? Maybe after as well, if you prove successful. It's no small thing," she said, meeting Gwenith's eyes. "You'll receive royal favor if you do well. Now to your own bed, and I to mine. Come to me before matins. I may have an errand for you then."

The queen closed her eyes, and the conversation. Gwenith ducked her head, and left the queen to her handmaidens.

"Gwenith! Awake!" Mary said excitedly. "There's a message from the queen. She needs you in attendance upon her now!"

Gwenith cracked her eyelids open and stared into the gray gloom of early dawn. Then her eyes widened and she shot upright. "I'll dress and go. But this is before matins, surely."

"So it is. But there's a page in the corridor waiting to bring you to the queen. Hurry!"

Gwenith dashed water from a pitcher she'd used the night before on her face, dressed, hurriedly fastened her wimple, thrust her feet into her slippers and went to the door.

"Go!" Mary said, flapping her hands at her. "You can't linger when she calls."

Gwenith was short of breath by the time she followed the page down the stair and out into the dark, and then to the queen's chamber.

Isabella was pacing her chamber like a bear Gwenith had once seen in a cage at a traveling show, moving back and forth blindly. She looked up when she saw Gwenith and dismissed her maidservants. Once they were alone, she looked at Gwenith gravely.

"I need you to go on an errand," she said. "A young squire goes with you, William. He waits in the hall for my command. But you can't go by litter, or horse. You must walk, and quickly. It is far, but I can't have the attention that a litter or a horse would bring, nor can I send a messenger that will be recognized. William is ever discreet, and you are unknown beyond these walls, and are young and fit, besides. I need a message delivered, with caution. Tell me: can you do this?"

The queen's voice was strained; she was pale and looked agitated.

Gwenith nodded. "Walk, I can. I can even run, my lady."

"No, don't call attention to yourself. In fact, you must keep your veil close around your face, and your head down. Follow William. He'll lead you there. Do not look at anyone but the man you seek. He's a physician. His name is Simon. I have my own physician here at court, but now I need him. You need know no more than that. Tell him no more than that my Therese is sick again, and the leeches here give her no hope. Tell him he must come if he loves me. And tell no one but him that, and then no one ever again. Can you do this for me?" Her gaze was so piercing that it was almost a threat.

Gwenith swallowed, and then nodded. "Highness, I will."

"Then go," Isabella said.

———

The squire who met Gwenith in the hallway was a fresh-faced young fellow dressed in green, with a face meant for laughter, but he looked grave. "I am William. Come with me" was all he said when he saw her.

They left the Tower and walked out into the rising dawn. No one was abroad that they could see, except for some of the warders and men at arms, who nodded a greeting when they saw the squire. Mists coiled around them as they crossed over a drawbridge that spanned the moat. Gwenith held her breath at the stink of it, but as they walked on, a morning breeze brought the freshening smell of the Thames and it overrode all else.

They passed through the gate unchallenged, and hurried on. As she walked behind the squire, Gwenith noted that London was waking: street sellers were setting up their wares; shopkeepers were opening their shutters, servants and apprentices were bustling through the narrow streets. No one gave a second look as she and her companion wended their way along the crowded, crooked roads of London. First they passed along avenues with grand houses of stone and brick, where armed footmen stood at their doors. Then they strode along narrower streets with smaller residences and shops of wood and thatch close as trees in a thicket and, as in a forest, some leaning toward their neighbors.

Her companion's ruddy complexion must have meant he was an outdoorsman, because she realized he walked quickly and without effort. Gwenith soon felt a stitch in her side. But she didn't slow her pace. This errand might be the making of her and she knew it.

They walked on, now on a winding lane that ran beside the river. The few people who loitered there looked drunken, ragged or dangerous. But Gwenith couldn't spare the time to worry, or even look at her surroundings anymore. She could only concentrate on watching the squire's shoes, try to keep step, not trip on the cobbles and concentrate on her breathing. They hurried on. When she began to see small spots at the edges of her vision, and was wondering if she could keep up her pace, they stopped. She looked up to see a house on a dirt path. It was a hovel, on a broken street of similarly wretched-looking huts and low taverns. She looked at the squire she'd followed, sure that he was mistaken. Surely a queen would never send for a physician from this low midden?

"Here," the squire said, and smacked his hand hard on the cracked and crooked door.

A wizened woman opened the door and stared at them.

The squire looked at Gwenith.

"I have a message for Simon, from my lady," she said breathlessly.

"He's still abed," the old woman said, looking at her warily.

Her companion again said nothing; he only looked at Gwenith.

Gwenith paused to gather her wits as well as her breath. She wasn't to tell anyone about this mission, which meant she couldn't tell this female who had sent her. And if she didn't succeed, she might never get such a task again. She might even be told to go home. But she had no home. That was what gave her courage, and wit she didn't know she had.

"My lady could strip him from his bed in a moment, and more, she could strip his lazy skin from him," she said haughtily. "Bring him to me at once."

William shot her a look of admiration. The old woman gasped, backed away from the door, then shut it in her face.

"Well, that's done it," Gwenith muttered, wondering what to do next.

"I think it has," William said. "I think she goes to give him the message."

"And if she does not?" Gwenith asked.

He shrugged. "Who can say? Not I. My duty is to accompany you, say nothing and do no more than keep you safe."

Gwenith was wondering whether to pound on the door again when it swung wide. This time it was an old man in a black robe stood looking at her. His craggy face showed care as well as extreme age. He was tall and lean, and his hair was gray where he wasn't bald. He'd have looked as decrepit as the place where he lived but for his upright bearing and ice blue eyes, which measured her before he spoke.

"I am Simon. Who sends you to me?" he asked Gwenith. "And for what purpose?"

"My lady sends me," she said, and bowed, showing him respect without knowing why. "She says to tell you that her Therese is sick again, and she needs you to come. She says if you love her you will do this."

"And your lady is . . . ?" he asked softly.

Gwenith straightened her back. "If you know who you must see, you know all. If you don't, then I am mistaken. Do you come? Or send me back with a message?"

He smiled. "I go. Tell your lady she did well in choosing you, and that I hope similar discretion greets my coming and going. I will be there shortly." He turned, and then paused. "Your name?" he asked.

"I am Gwenith," she said.

He studied her for a moment. "And more than you seem. That is your right. Now go. It is no more good for me to be seen with you and William than it would be for you to be seen with me." He closed the door.

When Gwenith allowed herself to exhale, William laughed. "You did well, indeed. Simon is a sly one. Now we can go back. This time at a more sedate pace. When we are far from here, you may show your face and see where you're going. I'm William of Haye," he said as they began to walk back, "squire to the king, messenger for the queen and keeper of secrets, including my own. As we all must be these days."

"I did well?" Gwenith asked.

"Extremely."

But the news the queen received was not good at all. She sent for Gwenith again later that morning.

This time Isabella was in a small, bare alcove off the queen's own bower. Isabella looked white-faced and bereft as she stood by the single cot that was there. Therese lay back on her pillows, exhausted and pale. Isabella held her hand, and Simon, the physician, stood by her side.

"I tarry too long," he was saying, but when Gwenith was shown in to the chamber, he fell silent.

"I know, I know, but say again," Isabella said distractedly.

Simon raised a shaggy eyebrow at Gwenith.

"I trust her," Isabella said, "else she would not be here."

"Therese does not," Simon said softly.

Isabella made a hopeless gesture. "I know, but my Therese trusts no one."

Therese gave a rusty chuckle.

"The girl may be more than she says," Isabella said, "but I believe she is clever enough to do as she's told."

Gwenith's face felt hot, and she looked down.

"We are all more than we say," the old man said with a shrug. "I'll say it again, then. Therese has not long to stay with you. What grows in her breast is beyond my potions, salves or ointments. The pain in her chest and her hard breathing tells me that even cutting the canker out will not dispatch it from her body. The medicines she needs now are courage, and prayer."

For the first time, Therese spoke. Her voice was thready. "I knew that. I felt it in my bones. I take leave of the earth with less sorrow than I take leave of you, *m' petite*," she said, clutching Isabella's hand tightly. "But wherever my spirit is bound, I must go home so I can be sure my bones rest in my own country, in Navarre, forever."

"I can give you powders to lessen the pain," Simon told Therese. "But more, I cannot do."

"I know, and I thank you," Therese said.

Simon's eyebrows went up. "A thanks from you, Therese? Is the world coming to an end?"

Therese chuckled again. "An' if it does, we will pass eternity without ever seeing each other again, you and I. Still, I will pray for your soul."

Simon bowed. "And I for yours. I thank you, and wish you Godspeed. You will let her go home?" he asked Isabella. "She will not rest easy else, no matter how much sweet poppy I give her."

"I will," Isabella said brokenly. "You may go."

Simon bowed, and left the room.

Isabella stood silent, holding Therese's hand. Both women had their eyes closed, but tears were streaming only down the face of the queen.

Gwenith thought she'd been forgotten. But Therese opened her eyes, looked straight at her and beckoned her near. Gwenith came forward, hesitantly.

"I must go," Therese said. "And you are the one my *bebe*, my love, my queen has chosen to take my place, and that because she knows no ill of you. Nor do I. I know you are clever, and I know you are closemouthed. But I tell you, though I may be gone from this place, and this world, I will return to curse you if ever you harm her or let harm come to her."

"Therese!" Isabella said.

"So I will," Therese vowed, "though I forfeit my immortal soul by doing it. Do you understand?" she asked Gwenith.

"I do," Gwenith aid.

"Then promise me you will never knowingly harm my angel, my Isabella, your queen," Therese insisted, her eyes blazing as she stared into Gwenith's eyes.

Gwenith's hand rose. She wanted to cross herself, but she stopped in time, lest she admit she was afraid of such an oath of allegiance to the wife of her sworn enemy.

"*Well?*" Therese demanded, and Isabella turned to see why Gwenith didn't answer.

Gwenith blanched. She was already forsworn. She took a breath, thought of obligations and duties, oaths, and then about words and the way they could be twisted. She finally spoke.

"So I do promise," she said.

Therese left London, and her queen, not long after, on a bleak day. She was carried down the stair in the arms of a huge man at arms. Isabella made sure she would have a curtained litter waiting for her, six accompanying men at arms and four female attendants to dance at her every wish, as well as many burly litter bearers to carry them off the ship when they landed in France. It was an impressive party, and a safe one, because they would ride under the flag of the king.

They stopped in the shadow of the Tower, waiting for Isabella's command.

"Too much fuss," Therese protested, as the man at arms carefully eased her down into the padded seat of the curtained litter. She gasped as the two litter bearers, one with the poles on his shoulders at the front, and the other carrying them in back, stood, raising her in the air.

"Softly, softly," Isabella told them. "She must not be jostled. Carry her as you would a precious cargo. Bear her as you would something fine and fragile. Bear her as you would bear me," Isabella commanded.

The bearers nodded, and then looked away, afraid of their queen's disapproval.

Simon was not able to attend Therese in public but he had given her nurse enough packets of poppy, henbane, mandragora and other potions, and instructions as well, to see to her comfort on her passage to France.

"Gwenith," Isabella said, "come with me."

Gwenith went with her as Therese's little procession marched to the wharf and the waiting ship. When they arrived, Isabella leaned into the litter, and spoke softly to Therese for several minutes. Then she retreated, white faced, and stood quietly by the side of the litter. Only at the last, when the men at arms looked to her for her command, did she nod her head, and finally let go of Therese's hand.

Gwenith moved to her side as they walked back to the tower.

"My Therese cannot be replaced," Isabella told Gwenith, "but you may try."

Six

1321
ONE MONTH LATER
LONDON

Gwenith was not a fool. She believed in God and ghosts; she knew both existed as surely as did her immortal soul. But Therese was not dead yet, and still Gwenith felt her disapproving presence in every part of her room. The chamber was bare, except for the bed and a chest, and a chair. But it still smelled of violets, and Gwenith was glad it would not be her chamber. It made her shiver. Instead, she was told she would sleep at the foot of the queen's bed, on a cot of her own. When the queen closed her bed curtains, it was as if she was alone, but Gwenith was closest to her. This was a high honor.

Mary des Monde had gone to France with Therese, along with three of the queen's other ladies and several of the French ladies in waiting. Now Gwenith knew only Agnes, who seemed preoccupied and was suddenly cool to her. Gwenith could understand Agnes might be insulted at being passed over for the honor of the queen's preference.

It was far more than Gwenith had hoped. It was terrifying. She slept at the foot of the Queen of England, wife of her mortal enemy, the despised Edward. But she could not hate Isabella. Isabella hadn't committed atrocities; a woman couldn't answer for what her husband did. And now too, the queen clearly suffered. She was pale and distracted. Her smiles were infrequent and her appetite lagged. Even her time with her children couldn't distract her. Her royal husband had little time for her. He was fully occupied with Hugh Despenser of late. It was not all hunting and games; they conferred for hours together by day and night. Gwenith never saw the king enter his lady's chamber. When he did, day or night, Gwenith was told she would have to leave. But she never had to leave.

Isabella didn't suffer from his absence; it was her lifelong friend and confidante, Therese, she missed. Or so she said this afternoon, after Gwenith was suddenly called into the queen's solar.

"And so you may accompany me where others do not," Isabella said. "Not because I know such good of you, but because I know no ill. And you have honesty in your eyes. Even Therese said so. And what other choice have I?" she whispered, as though to herself. "What you hear must remain in your ears. What you see you must not show in your eyes," she told Gwenith. "If you deceive or betray me, you will never know my confidence again, not this place, nor any other . . . mayhap. I don't mean to frighten you," she added, because Gwenith had gone pale. "Or mayhap I do. I only want to let you know the heavy duty of anyone who has your queen's trust. Can you do this?"

"I will," Gwenith said, with a lighter heart. Because of all the things she'd promised, this was simplest. She saw no reason to tell what she might see or hear. It wasn't Isabella she sought to destroy.

And if there came a day when something she learned had to be divulged, she was, after all, forsworn. Her grandmother had seen to that. She didn't know if prior vows supplanted later ones, and there was no reason to ponder the matter of God's accounting right now.

"You wear bright colors today. That's good," Isabella said, looking at Gwenith's rose overtunic with approval. "I miss my Therese, but not the black she always wore. Now sit quietly, and wait on my orders. I expect visitors."

Gwenith sat on a stool by a high window that overlooked the broad Thames. The solar was where the queen came to relax, and its ceiling was as high as a cathedral's. It had many windows and graceful curved arches with gilded margins to catch any hint of the sun, and the walls were painted with bright designs. The floors were wooden, and shone where they were not graced by fine Eastern carpets. Gwenith didn't want to look like a simpleton, so she stopped staring around the huge room, ducked her head and gave all her attention to the piece of embroidery in her lap.

The queen sat quietly with a book. Books were rare enough, and Gwenith longed to see it. From where she sat, she could only make out the golden borders of the pages, and catch a glimpse, whenever the queen turned a page, of curling bold black letters and illustrations in crimson, blue and gold.

The queen's visitors arrived as the abbey bells announced vespers, and afternoon shadows began to gather. Gwenith peeped up at them from under her lashes. There were three women. Two were richly garbed. One wore a golden circlet over her wimple, the other a golden chain at her neck. The third was heavy, hooded and veiled, and she walked slowly. The ladies had left their other attendants outside the solar. The first two women were about the age of their queen, and passing fair. Their hair was bound, and what showed of it at the margins of their wimples glowed red.

From that, their white skin, small features and wide blue eyes, it was easy to see they were related.

As they crossed the room, the two richly dressed women looked immediately at Gwenith.

Isabella saw it. "My Therese is gone to France," she said. "This is Gwenith, a maid from the Marches. She sees nothing and hears nothing."

Gwenith looked down, and then peeked up to see the two ladies go to Isabella, bow, then clasp her outstretched hands as the third woman settled clumsily into a high-backed chair. She had to be a very old and trusted friend or servant, Gwenith thought, to come in with her lady and sit without spoken permission.

"Elizabeth," Isabella said warmly, "how goes my namesake?"

"Little Isabella is well," the lady Elizabeth answered, smiling. "She thanks you for the doll you sent for her birthday. She's four now. Can you imagine that?"

"I can't," Isabella said. "I'd love to see her. Bring her next time."

Gwenith stiffened. A friend to the queen named Elizabeth with a daughter named for Isabella? Surely this couldn't be Elizabeth de Clare? Gwenith doubted it. Elizabeth de Clare was married to Roger D'Amory, a man rumored to have been the king's favorite after Piers Gaveston, remaining so until Edward turned his affections to the younger Hugh Despenser. Could his wife be friend to Isabella, even so? But rumor was not truth. And if the lady was married to Roger D'Amory, she was one of three de Clare sisters, daughters of a Norman noble, Gilbert de Clare, Earl of Hertford and Gloucester. More important, the de Clare girls were daughters to Gilbert's wife, Joan of Acre, who was in turn daughter of Longshanks and Edward's sister. The sisters were granddaughters to Longshanks and nieces to the new King of England.

That was why Edward had given one of the girls, Eleanor, to Hugh the younger as wife.

Isabella turned to Eleanor a bit less cordially. "I'm happy to see you, as ever."

The queen looked from one woman to the other and saw their matching tension. A faint crease appeared on her forehead as she frowned. "But surely this is strange. You, Eleanor, come to visit with me frequently. And you, Elizabeth, seldom. What brings you here together now?"

"Our sister Margaret," Elizabeth said.

"How goes it with her?" Isabella asked.

"Ask her," Elizabeth said, gesturing to the seated woman.

"Margaret!" Isabella asked incredulously, rising and staring at the veiled woman. " 'Tis you? How comes this? Why so shy with me?"

"Because she is not here," Elizabeth said. "She never came here."

"Ah, I see. But why?" Isabella persisted.

"Because no one must know," the seated woman cried. She cast back her veil and threw off her hooded cape to show a pasty, puffy face streaked with tears.

Gwenith bit back a gasp. This bloated creature was Margaret de Clare? But she'd been Piers Gaveston's wife! Gwenith tried to conceal an involuntary shiver. Margaret had been married to Piers, and then had been given Hugh Audley as husband. Audley was said to have been another favorite of Edward's. All these highborn women had been married off to men who were said to have also been his lovers. Gwenith shuddered. Surely it couldn't be true. These were the daughters of a great Norman noble, whose name was known only too well to Gwenith. He'd helped conquer her people and build Longshanks' castles in Wales, and he had held them until his death.

Isabella went to the seated woman immediately, and took her hands. "How comes this?" she asked. "Tell me all."

"*All?*" Margaret said wildly. "There is not time enough in the world to tell you all. My time is almost on me," she whimpered, putting a hand on her burgeoning belly. She threw her cape open and her swollen abdomen was clear to see. "The babe comes soon. But I had to speak to you, even were I pushing it out as I did. You must help me, Isabella. No one else, not even God Himself, can, I think."

Isabella stepped back and crossed herself.

" 'Tis her woe talking," Elizabeth said quickly. "Leave off the blasphemy, Margaret. You know better. Tell Her Highness why you chanced so much to come here, for in truth," she said, turning to Isabella, "she risks her babe's life as well as her own by doing so."

"And yet you brought her to me," Isabella said.

"And yet so we did," Elizabeth answered. She sighed. "Very well, I'll tell all. Her wits are turned with her fortunes. But still, if I leave aught out, she'll correct me. She recites her woes like a rosary day and night. Hugh the younger Despenser has cast her from her home. Aye," she said, seeing Isabella's eyes widen, " 'tis true. Hugh, her own brother-in-law. He took her castles and lands at Gower and Usk, declared her husband outlaw, and set himself up in his stead."

"But why?" Margaret wailed. "He has so much now, I can't remember all his titles. I wonder that he can. He's Edward's chamberlain, and constable of Odiham, keeper of Dryslywyn, and Cantref Mawr. He has almost all of Glamorgan and is petitioning the king to take Mowbray's home and entitlements as well as the Mortimers'. He's keeper of castles at Hay and Brecknock, and more, so many more, I can't remember all."

And Tonbridge Castle, Gwenith thought, shivering at the thought of the infamous name. Tonbridge Castle, where his father took one of her own blood, Llewellyn Bren, a Welshman, hostage, and murdered him even though he'd taken the ransom for him. After taking the ransom, he'd taken Llewellyn's head. Before that, he'd had Llewellyn hanged, drawn and quartered.

"What does he need with my home?" Margaret moaned. "Or my Audley's life? I live in hiding. My poor husband lives with the beasts in the forest."

"Her husband has raised an army," Elizabeth said sadly, "and is even now fighting, burning down Despenser's castles and lands on the Welsh borders. Even his own old holding. That's why he's been declared outlaw. War begins. . . . What ails the girl?" she asked Isabella.

Gwenith had turned deathly white and held her embroidery in a white-knuckled grasp.

"She's from the Welsh marches," Isabella said, "and ward to a Marcher lord."

"Well, and I'm sorry for it," Elizabeth said. "But that's what's happening. Rest easy, girl. You're safe enough. This is the safest place in the land now."

"Hugh Despenser tortured poor Lady Baret," Margaret went on, weeping. "He had her arms and legs broken, and drove her to madness, they say. Such a gentle soul she was, and a lady of high degree. It didn't stop him. He wanted her lands too, and she fought him, until he caught her. Did I mention Huntington? Hugh the younger has been named keeper of the castle and manor there as well. He holds more land than the king himself."

The room grew deathly still. Elizabeth waved her hand. "No matter. My poor sister's mind is overturned. Don't regard it."

"What does he need with all that land?" Margaret sobbed.

"Indeed, what *does* he need with it?" Isabella asked. "Why not ask your sister Eleanor, who is wed to Hugh Despenser? She sits right next to you. Why me? She surely knows better than I."

Eleanor bowed her head.

Elizabeth answered for her sister. "Come, lady, you know," she said softly. "We've spoken of it often enough. Poor Eleanor knows how to push out his babes, and little else. Hugh uses her as brood-mare. Ten children now, even the castle cat doesn't litter so much.

He doesn't share her bed for anything else, nor her confidence for anything at all. Is that not true?" she asked Eleanor.

Eleanor nodded, looking ashamed.

"So what can I do?" Isabella asked.

"You are Queen of England!" Margaret cried.

"And so what can I do?" Isabella asked again.

They all fell silent, even Margaret, who only whimpered.

"Ah, well, I'll do what I can," Isabella finally said. "But I can't promise anything. If your husband is captured, Margaret, I might be able to do more, at least for him. But if he continues to set his will against the king, there's nothing I can do. Edward would call it treason."

"No! My husband doesn't rebel against English rule. He fights to keep his lands from Hugh," Margaret cried. "Only the Despensers would call this treason."

Isabella's eyes widened and her nostrils flared, but then she shrugged. "I will try, Margaret. More I cannot do. No more than any man does my husband confide his plots and plans and schemes to me. Nor did my father the king share them with my mother, his queen, nor his father with his wife before them. It's the way of the world. We women are prizes traded for our titles and lands. Come, Margaret, you were a child when you were married, as was I, as were we all. I've had one husband, but you, Elizabeth, have had three. Was it any different for you with any of them? You, Eleanor, have only had Hugh, but has he ever given you anything in private—except of course, for your babes?"

They laughed at that, even Margaret smiled through her tears.

"We're put on this earth to obey our lords, both He in heaven, and our king, who rules our lives here below," Isabella said. "Mayhap in heaven we can rule our destinies. Not here. But as I said, I'll keep a close ear, and if I've a chance to spare you and your family, Margaret, I will. I do so vow."

Margaret buried her head in her hands.

"We must go now," Elizabeth said gently. "She can't be found here. I'll send her back with her retinue to meet her husband, and pray for their deliverance. She must not be discovered. Hugh can't have a chance to hold her hostage, as bait in a trap for her husband."

"I mustn't be found with her," Eleanor said nervously, looking at Margaret. "I came out of love for her, but no one can know that I did."

"No one will," Isabella said. "So then go. I'll watch and wait and listen. It is a woman's lot, even a woman who is a queen. You came all this way and risked so much. Don't take such risks again. Send to me and I will keep your messages secret."

Margaret moaned.

"I told you I would try to aid you," Isabella told her angrily.

"I think she groans for something else," Elizabeth said in alarm.

Margaret's hands were splayed over her rounded abdomen.

"Is it the babe?" Isabella asked.

"I don't know," Margaret whimpered. "I don't know. It hurts, but it's two months beforetime. I've had so many. They come quickly now. But it's not time."

"Then wait," Isabella said. "You can't leave now."

Eleanor started to protest.

"What?" Isabella said angrily. "Would you have her drop her babe on the stair?" She wheeled around, paced a few steps, then turned to Gwenith. "Find William, the squire. Tell him to take you back to the physician I sent for before. Bring him back with you. Tell him the urgency and the secrecy, though he knows it well. Now, go!"

Gwenith dropped her embroidery, shot from her chair and ran to the door. She flew down the long stair, and asked the first page she saw for William, the squire. He told another page, and William was sent for. He came at a run. Gwenith told him the queen's command. He didn't ask for details.

"Then we go," he said, "and quickly."

This time, growing shadows were their only companions as they left the Tower. They passed the neat streets of guild houses, but saw few people abroad. All of London seemed to be indoors. Some were at evening prayer, others at their evening meals. Even the broken streets by the riverside were strangely still. No one was fool enough to venture out with darkness falling. Gwenith didn't have to be told to stay close by William. The night was home to too many dangers, human and otherworldly, for her to tarry. She raced to keep pace with him.

She was breathless again when they reached the physician's door. This time she could save her breath because the old woman didn't ask her errand. She looked at Gwenith, nodded and went back into the little hovel. Moments later, Simon emerged. His mouth was greasy, and he still held a chicken leg in his fingers.

"The queen commands," Gwenith panted. "You must go to her."

"Is she ill?" he asked, eyes wide.

"Nay, 'tis . . . a visitor, with a babe that may be coming before-time. She wants you there now."

Simon sighed. "Then I go. Wait. I will go with you. It is dark enough."

He emerged from the house soon after, wearing a hooded black cloak and carrying a bag. "Lead on," he said.

"We set a swift pace," William said doubtfully.

"Then slow it for my years," Simon told him. "I will do any-thing for your queen, but I don't think she wants me to lay down my life right now, before I see her patient. I won't venture out into the streets of London without a youthful armed escort, not at this hour of the night."

William's face flushed. "Nor should you. If she were not so overset, she would have thought of it. We will walk at a good pace, but not run all the way. So come, we must go."

The three of them walked back to the Tower, going at an easy rate Gwenith found she could better endure. William led the way, looking from side to side, his hand on the hilt of the dagger he had on his belt. As they left the forlorn area where Simon lived, Gwenith breathed a bit easier.

"Excuse my ignorance," she said to Simon as they walked on through the growing night, "but I'm only lately come to serve the queen. How is it that you, as her physician, don't live at court as all the rest of her retainers do?"

William turned his head and stared at her.

"Forgive me," she said, looking from William to Simon. "I didn't mean any impertinence."

"Nor have you given any," Simon told her. "Rest easy, William. Better she ask me than any other. I expect you have the complete confidence of your queen, else you wouldn't be here now," he told Gwenith. "So I will tell you. It's simple. I cannot live at the Tower." He laughed. "Indeed, I can't live in London. Or England itself. And that is why you never saw me here."

Gwenith looked down as she walked on. She was disappointed; he'd seemed a wise old fellow. But she supposed she deserved such an answer for her impudence.

"Child," Simon said softly, "I am a Jew."

Gwenith gasped and shrank back. She crossed herself. So far as she knew she'd never been so close to a Jew. Nor did she know much about them but that they hated Christians and were bound for the depths of hell. Would that apply to one who befriended a Jew? But still, Simon's voice was so calm and ironic that she took courage. It might be that he was teasing her.

"But you have no beard," she said. "No yellow badge."

"I did. I don't now," Simon said. "My own grandfather was

pulled from his house by his beard and murdered for the crime of being a Jew. They knew it by his beard and, of course, by the yellow badge he was forced to wear whenever he walked in the streets. Longshanks exiled my people and now his son murders those who came back. I think my grandfather would have preferred exile. I'd prefer to keep breathing too. So I don't announce myself, as required by law."

Simon laughed. "There's a point. If we're not allowed in England, then can it be a crime to leave off the yellow badge? We shouldn't be here at all, so do laws apply to us at all? Does the greater crime surmount and surpass the other? An interesting point. Too bad there are no rabbis left in London to debate it with me. But few Jews remain. We are proscribed, exiled and forbidden."

"Then why are you still here?" Gwenith asked nervously.

"Because someone must be here to wait, and pray, and work for the day when the rest of us come back. We wait for that the way we wait for our Messiah."

Gwyneth's face registered her shock at such heresy.

"That has taken over a thousand years, so far," Simon went on. "I hope it isn't that long until England lets all her children come home again. Mayhap it won't. Moses only wandered the desert for a generation. Can I do less?"

"You *are* a physician?" she asked timidly.

He laughed. "I am, and a good one. Few have my knowledge. I studied in a foreign land with masters of the art of healing. My teacher was a great man, but also an infidel, despised by your people as well as mine. He was killed, but only when he returned to his homeland to aid warriors in their holy crusade. So many on every side were murdered in the name of piety." He sighed. "Now I go to help your queen. Me. A Jew in the hall of an English king. Who could have imagined such a thing? Edward Longshanks stoned Jews to death for *looking* at the king."

"The queen knows?" Gwenith asked.

William turned his head and looked at Simon.

Simon shrugged. "You must ask her that," he said.

"You are said to be a clever people," Gwenith said, seeking to make amends, and to calm herself as well.

"Clever?" Simon asked. "Mayhap. We were not allowed to practice any trade but banking and moneylending, and your people were allowed to practice every trade but those. We were too clever at it. Because when kings need money, they knew who to kill to get it. God save you from such cleverness."

"Simon," William said in a sudden whisper, "put up your hood. We near the Tower."

They walked to the Tower in silence. They reentered by a back passage, and climbed to the solar. "Better I go to her by myself," Simon told them. He went in alone.

Gwenith waited in the dim hallway with William. He looked down at her. "His life hangs on your word," he whispered harshly.

She nodded. "I know. My word is good. It's just that my heart quails. I never met his like before."

"Yes," William said. "He's an excellent physician."

"I meant," she said softly, "he's a Jew."

"I hadn't noticed," William said. "And neither should you."

Seven

1321
THE TOWER, LONDON

William stood silent, obviously lost in his own thoughts. Gwenith waited in the hall outside the queen's solar with him, trying to get over her shock. Her thoughts were tangled. Here was another chink in the wall of the king and queen. But who would be harmed by exploiting it? Not Edward. Only Isabella, Simon, and William and, mayhap, herself. So such knowledge was useless to her. She also had questions about the state of her own immortal soul because she'd consorted with a Jew, however unknowingly. She wouldn't tell anyone what Simon really was, nor ask her queen if she knew his secret. She had too many secrets of her own.

Just as she was wondering how long she would have to continue to stand waiting, Simon left the solar and spoke to them.

"The babe isn't about to be born," he told William. "The lady is only so terrified that even her fingernails pain her. I don't blame her. After ten children, they slip out faster than they went in. I've given her something to ease her care—something I pray won't hurt the babe—because if I do not, her fear will. The queen bids you send for a litter to take the lady from here by the long and quiet way, the way I come and go. I'll accompany you. The men you ask must be those you trust. Now hurry and do so silently. But that, you know."

"I go," William said, turned and ran back down the stair.

"The queen bids you enter," Simon told Gwenith.

She hesitated. "Your secret," she said nervously. "I won't reveal."

"Brave girl," he said. "But I know you won't."

"How?" she asked, suddenly afraid, because Jews were said to have a bond with the devil, and now his keen blue eyes seemed to look into her mind.

"Because you gave your word," he said innocently. Then his smile faded. "Was I foolish to tell you? Mayhap. I think sometimes that I risk all because I'm still here and so many are not. It is possible to feel guilty for living, even if you hadn't any choice in the matter."

Gwenith stood very still. "I know," she finally whispered. "Oh, I do know."

His gaze sharpened. "So you do. I won't ask your reasons. If you ever want to tell me, you may do so knowing that I of all people know the value of secrecy and would never betray you. But I'm being foolish. Forgive an old man. You have a confessor, and doubtless would prefer absolution, not just unburdening your mind. That I cannot do for you, no more than I can for myself. Go in peace, child," he said on a sigh. "Your queen wants you."

Gwenith slipped into the solar, and stood, waiting for Isabella's commands.

The queen was saying good-bye to her visitors. Each woman took her hand, in turn, and exchanged whispered words of farewell. When Simon and William appeared again, with two sturdy men at arms, the ladies waited until their sister was standing between them, supported by them.

"We cannot bring a litter here," William told her, "lest we be remarked upon. But never doubt, lady," he told Margaret. "We have one below and will carry you away in comfort. Until then, lean on your sisters and they will bear your weight between them."

With a last anguished look back, Margaret and her sisters silently left the solar.

Isabella turned to Gwenith, her face set in such hard lines that Gwenith drew back. But the queen's anger wasn't for her.

"Would that I'd been born a man!" Isabella raged, as she paced the room, her skirts flashing around her ankles as she moved. "What use are we females? What purpose is served by giving us feelings, hearts and brains if we are never to use them? Dear God, I don't understand. They say we are cursed by Mother Eve, and so we are. We have no voice in our own destinies; we are little more than prisoners of our bodies, bound by monthly blood and bawling babes, treated like pets or cattle. A woman's land is not hers. Her fortune is not hers, no more than her body is. She's left only with her name, and even that can be stained through no fault of her own. The older I grow, the less I am used to it. It is insupportable!"

Gwenith stirred. "Majesty?" she said in a small voice. "It is not so with all women."

"Aye," Isabella said savagely, wheeling around to face her. "Now you'll tell me what Therese used to, eh? About how nuns are brides of Jesus and holy in his name. And I'll tell you what I told her: then why is the pope a man, and any monk or priest holier than a woman who has taken vows? So it is. Can a woman lead us in prayer, absolve us, confess us, shrive us, bury us, even though we are women too? No, and until they do, even God disdains us."

"I wasn't going to say that," Gwenith said. She was too numbed by her previous shock to react to new heresy.

Isabella stopped and looked at her. "What were you going to say?"

"Not all men ignore their wives' counsel," Gwenith said softly. "Nor do all men discount female wisdom. My father I did not know, no more than I knew a mother, but my grandmother taught me that men need intelligent women. That was why she saw to my education, so I could be a fit wife. And when I went to live with Lady de Percy, I saw that Lord de Percy always discussed his plans and hopes and dreams with my lady. When she spoke, he listened well. He said she'd a hard head and a soft heart, and as he'd a hard head *and* heart, he needed her for balance." Gwenith smiled, remembering. She had lived with the de Percys for seven years, and had never seen violence or undue anger between them.

She looked at her queen. "Even peasants must shoulder their yokes together, man and woman, else they'd starve. So it is with the yoke of the world as well. A marriage is like a teamed pair of litter bearers, or oxen, my lord used to say, to make his lady laugh. But so it is. The load is lighter when it's shared. 'Tis true that a woman is only as powerful as her lord allows her to be. But if she's strong enough, in time even he will come to lean on her. So it was with my lord and lady. I was taught that a wise woman earns confidence and collects power as her due."

"And a foolish husband?" Isabella asked, her eyes glinting.

Gwenith looked down. "I cannot say. Indeed, I've said too much."

"No," Isabella said. "You haven't. We'll speak more of this later. 'Tis time for the evening meal." She stared at Gwenith. "You know, you must never speak a word of any of this to anyone?"

"Why should I?" Gwenith asked honestly. The queen had listened to her, and somehow that more deeply honored her and warmed her heart than anything else that had passed between them.

"Majesty," Hugh the younger said, as he swept Isabella a deep flourish of a bow.

"Despenser," she said woodenly, and turned to her husband.

Edward was gleaming: his smile, his golden velvet tunic, the circlet of gold on his brow. His courtiers and bishops, knights and men at arms, were all smiling. Hugh the elder, Earl of Winchester, was beaming. Gwenith stood silent and wary, behind her lady. They were all in the great hall, Edward, their king, and his favorite by his side.

"We hunted well," Edward said, drawing off his gauntlets. "And not just today. Hugh tells us his campaign in Wales is a success."

Isabella stood very still. "Then he has captured all the rebels?"

"No, Highness," Hugh said. "But soon. They are nothing anyway. Malcontents and fools, the lot of them. Lancaster throws his weight against saplings. They bend before him, and us. We will deal with them. We kill those we find and those who won't tell us how to find them. Soon there will be none left to kill. Then we'll have to go back to hunting boar, a far more difficult game, eh, sire?" he asked Edward, with a wink.

The king laughed, but Isabella didn't. "But men rebel against harsh rule," she said. "Does not killing only feed their fire and grow new enemies?"

"How else to keep them down, and keep the country whole?" Edward asked. "It was my father's dream, and my legacy. He had no patience with such men, nor do I."

The earl nodded. "Such men always appear in times of plenty, just as insects are drawn to ripe crops. Thank God we have such warriors as my Hugh."

"Insects?" Isabella asked, with a cool smile. "How comes this? I heard that the men who rebel do not dispute their king, but only your son, Lord Despenser. At least they protest against his increasing power over them and the loss of their lands and homes to him. They say he swallows up the Marches."

"Would that I could!" Hugh the younger laughed. "Then my king could live in peace forever, as would your children and theirs down the generations. Where did you hear such things, my lady?"

"My new lady," Isabella said, gesturing to Gwenith. "She comes from the region that's in revolt."

The men turned their heads to stare at Gwenith. She ducked a curtsy to them, but her face had turned ashen.

"You mustn't distress your queen with wild tales," Edward told Gwenith, wagging a finger at her. "Your job is to bring her comfort."

Gwenith looked down. "I shall do my best, sire," she murmured.

Hugh walked to Gwenith, looked at her downcast face and tipped it up with one gloved finger. He smiled and ran the finger down her cheek. "New, eh? A pretty maid with big brown eyes . . . she reminds me of a forest fawn," he said, turning to look at Edward. He looked down at Gwenith again. "She's shy as one too. I wonder, sweet mistress, have you speckles on your bottom and your pretty belly as well?"

He laughed. Gwenith stood still, looking at her shoes.

"And with about as much conversation as a forest creature at that," Hugh said. "Don't you require conversation from your ladies, Majesty?"

"As much as silence," Isabella said coldly. "I have several ladies, for the variety."

"Yet when she speaks," Hugh went on, still looking at Gwenith, "she spreads stories of war and terror? Hardly good conversation. Where did you hear such tales, mistress?" he asked Gwenith.

Gwenith shot a look to Isabella and saw her cold, set expression. There was no help there. She had to cover herself and her lady; it was clearly what the queen expected. Gwenith looked back at Hugh. "It was news of my lady de Percy I asked for, sir," she said. "The messenger told me there was rebellion and war everywhere at home. I was distressed, of course. The queen was kind enough to ask why. I never meant to trouble her. Please, sir, if you are lately come from the Marches, do you know ought of the de Percys?"

Hugh studied her upturned face. "Naught," he finally said. "They are neither rebels nor allies. But they live high and well and have much influence in the region. I wonder which way the wind blows with them? Now you mention it, I'll pay them a visit when I return."

Gwenith blanched.

Hugh smiled. "Shy *and* fearful. Why would such a maid serve our vivacious queen?"

"She pleases me," Isabella snapped. "She's my handmaiden, sir, not yours."

Hugh dropped his hand. He smiled at Isabella and bowed. "That is your good luck, Majesty."

"Come, Hugh," Edward said suddenly, looking from Isabella and Hugh to Gwenith, and frowning. "This is nothing. We'll sup and then speak more. I can eat enough, but never hear enough about triumph."

All listening laughed; a few clapped their hands. Hugh smiled down at Gwenith, flicked her cheek with his finger and went to his seat at the high table.

The king and his knight talked all through their meal. Edward was dazzling. He sparkled. He joked. He teased. He made more than one of his courtiers vow there was no need for a minstrel when the king was in high good humor. The Earl of Winchester sat nearby, beaming at Edward, and nodding at everything his son said.

Only Isabella sat silent. She didn't laugh, nor seem to have much appetite.

"Majesty," Hugh said, leaning over the trencher in front of

him to talk with Isabella, who sat at her husband's other side, "you haven't touched your food. Here"——he took a fat bit of venison in his fingers, bending forward and stretching out his arm to offer it to her—"you must try this. It's excellent."

Isabella drew back as though he held a viper before her. It was common courtesy for a man to offer a delicious tidbit from his trencher to a lady, on his knife or with his fingers. But Isabella was more than a lady. She was his queen. There was a sudden silence at the table. Isabella looked to Edward. Edward looked puzzled, and then his fair skin flushed.

"Hugh," he said with an anxious, flickering smile, "my lady is from France, remember? She stands on more ceremony than we English do. She'd never take food from the hand of anyone but her king."

"I see," Hugh said, sitting back again. "But it *is* a very tasty bit. Would you care to try it, Majesty?"

Edward glanced nervously at his queen.

She said nothing.

"Have I offended?" Hugh asked innocently. "But after all, sire, *you* are an Englishman."

Edward smiled, and opened his lips. Hugh popped the bit of meat in his mouth. They gazed at each other as the king chewed his morsel.

Isabella stood up. "I must to bed," she said in clipped tones. "I'm weary, and my head aches."

Edward rose, as did all in the great room. He took her hand. "Rest well, and rest easy," he said.

" 'Well,' perhaps," she said. " 'Easy?' I doubt it."

Edward drew in a breath.

"My head aches so, you see," she added with a twisted smile. Then she left the table, and walked out of the great hall.

Gwenith shot to her feet, abandoned her dinner and went running to Isabella's side before she could mount the stair.

Isabella turned. "No, no," she told her softly. "There's nothing for you to do for me. I need only my body servants now, as well as a little peace. But I thank you, little maid, for past favor. Your silence earlier when I laid rumor at your door doubtless eased the passage of some blameless ladies. I won't forget your grace and quick wit. But for now I will to bed. You may stay and amuse yourself. Only not with Hugh Despenser. I wouldn't care for that at all."

"Majesty!" Gwenith said. "I would never! He's married. He's—"

"A man with much power. He wants more. He wants that more than any need of his body or his soul, because even they are turned to the purpose of gaining him more influence." Isabella looked at Gwenith and smiled. "Not that you aren't charming. You are. But you are also my lady, and that tempts him as much as your pretty face. He'd use any means to gain information, because information is power. His attraction eludes me." She shrugged. "He is not *gentil*, not in face or form or actions. In fact, I find him repellent."

Isabella's expression turned cold. "But I have seen too many succumb to his charm. Don't give him more than good day and good evening, if you want to please me. Or indeed, if you want to save your virginity as well as your immortal soul. Don't be deceived by what seem to be his preferences tonight, in bed or elsewhere. He toys with people of every . . ." She shook her head. "No more. The less said, the less spoken later. You have the face of an innocent. Keep it that way. They say your actions write your past on your face. You look as though you have never sinned, nor dreamed of it. I hope that's so. Now I give you good night, Gwenith of the Marches. Come with me to matins. We both can use prayer."

"But, Majesty," Gwenith protested, "how can I enjoy myself when I know you feel ill? Let me leave with you please." She hesitated and then added, low, "And too, I cannot like the way Hugh Despenser looks at me. If you're not there . . ."

Isabella's smile was thin. "Let him look. You're under my ban-ner. You're my lady. To offend you is to offend me. I am still queen. He's no danger to you . . . at least, not tonight," she said, her mouth twisting as though she tasted something bitter. "But times are changing, and there are portents. Very well, come along now, if you wish."

"If I wish?" Gwenith asked, amused in spite of herself. "But you said I was yours to command."

Isabella looked at her steadily. "Yes, and no. You are duty bound to me, but you're under my protection and that is my duty to you. There can be no serf without a lord, no lord without a king. As God above protects all of us, your king and queen must protect you, and woe to the ruler who neglects or forgets that. Only God has no one to answer to. So if you wish, you may come with me."

"I do," Gwenith said.

And her queen smiled.

Eight

They climbed the stair, and went to Isabella's chamber. Her body servants rushed to help her wash and undress. They combed out her long fair hair, braided it and left her only when she waved a hand at them in dismissal. She climbed into her great bed, and laid her head back against her pillows. But she didn't ask Gwenith to draw her bed curtains.

"I give you good night now, my lady," Gwenith said as she moved toward her cot.

"Nay," Isabella said wearily, raising a hand. "Stay and speak with me. I would sleep, but cannot. If my Therese were here, we would talk. No one else knows me as she does. She was at my side most of my life. But now she's gone and I am truly alone. I think that, as much as anything, is what's causing me pain. Although there is pain enough. You were right, Maid of the Marches, anything is bearable if you can share it. Now no one can help me shoulder my burden." She closed her eyes. They flew open again. "But you can read," she said on a sudden inspiration. "Come, take the book I left there, on the chest. Come to my side, and read to me."

"Gladly!" Gwenith cried, and ran to get the book. She settled herself on a chair near her queen, opened the book with shaking hands and exclaimed.

"Oh, beautiful it is. Such, I've never seen. It's not a book of prayer, nor of hours," she said, turning the pages. "It's stories, not of the Bible, but of lords and ladies. Oh, but it's wondrous!"

"It is tales of King Arthur," Isabella said, smiling now. "I have other such. I own Geoffrey of Monmouth's tales, and those from other lands. This is a favorite."

"I never read any tales of Arthur, not in a book," Gwenith said, caressing the heavy leather covers. "I've heard them sung. Much loved he is in Wales. . . ." She recovered herself, and added quickly, "He is much loved in Wales and bordering lands."

But Isabella scarcely heard her. "He is much loved everywhere. Come then, read to me from any page. I know it all, but love to hear it again."

Gwenith cleared her throat, picked up the great book and began to read. But she'd scarcely started when the door to the queen's chamber burst open. Edward stood there, his eyes wild, his hands on his hips. He strode into the room. Gwenith put down the book, rose and shrank back against the wall. She couldn't leave until her queen asked her to, but it didn't seem as though the king saw her at all. He came to Isabella's bedside. She sat up.

"What is your excuse, madam?" Edward demanded.

He stood with his hands on his hips, glaring at Isabella. "Why defy me in front of my people, my friends, my—"

"Hugh," Isabella said coldly. She raised her head, and stared back at him. "I am queen, and I may say what I will."

"But not to me," Edward shouted, his fair complexion growing red. "I am king, and I will not be denigrated before my court. And leaving my table without my permission? Hugh was not the only one surprised."

"I was not talking to Hugh. Indeed, I see no reason why the

Queen of England must care about what a lord thinks of her, no matter how many titles he has been given or stolen."

"But you must ask me!" Edward said.

"Must I?" she asked, raising one eyebrow.

"Madam, I think it's late in the day for you to be asking me that," he said, both hands at his belt now, roving her chamber with a swagger. "I've given you a crown, four children . . . or perhaps three. Only you can know that."

She became rigid. "Indeed, why stop at three? Why not say two? Or one? Or none?"

His face grew pale. "Why not, indeed?"

"I care not a fig what Hugh Despenser thinks."

"But the barons do," Edward said with a thin smile, because though he loved Hugh Despenser and respected his father, he knew the subject of having any watchdog appointed to keep him in line always nettled Isabella and demeaned him in her eyes. "They chose him and his father to rule this land with me."

"So is he now so much *greater* than his sovereign king that you run to chastise your queen on his request?"

His head went back as if she'd slapped him. "I am still king," he said through gritted teeth. "And one day soon, when things settle down again, I won't have need of him or his father, except as friends. As for now? I don't like the fact that the barons don't trust me. But they soon will. I don't chafe under either of the Despensers' council, because it is only that. They don't rule so much as give me advice, not orders. Hugh doesn't lord it over me, as Lancaster was wont to do, nor does he demean me or treat me like an infant, as Lancaster did, again and again. And Lancaster only four years my senior! The earl is old and full of wisdom. As for the rest? You see things that aren't there. I like Hugh well enough and consider him a friend."

"You like him too much," she countered. "And I do not consider him a friend."

"You? Of course you do not. What friends have you?" he shot back.

"Those he has not killed," she said angrily. "I hear he's been conquering friends by calling them enemies and then taking their land, manors and castles. I know that he stole Margaret de Clare's birthright by naming her husband traitor, and so now her husband seeks revenge. If he was not a traitor before, depend on it, he will be now. And she was one wed to Piers. Fie, sir. I thought you took better care of those who once were"—she paused, and gave him a thin smile—"your favorites."

He ignored her accusation, but turned paler. "Where did you hear this? From Margaret?"

"It matters not," she said, throwing up a hand. "I heard it."

"Not from her sister Eleanor, I'd wager," Edward said with a forced laugh. "She's given Hugh ten babes, and all his own."

"Eleanor has been bred too often. One should not treat a prized mare in such a way," Isabella said dismissively. "She has neither sense nor wit left. Her life and her brain are in her womb."

Edward's glittering smile was chilling. "Well, then," he said, as he stepped closer, "mayhap we'll try to fill your mind and womb as well, and so stop this nonsense."

Isabella sneered. " 'Try' my lord? An apt answer from you. But I don't wish to, and I doubt you're thinking of rapine. No, that's more in Hugh's line. At least, with women."

Edward's eyes flared brilliant blue. "A fine way to speak to your king and your lord. In front of others too. Madam, this is ill done."

"You mean my maid in waiting?" Isabella said with a shrug of one shoulder. "She hears and sees nothing, like Therese used to do."

"I don't mean her," Edward said, glancing at Gwenith, where she stood white-faced and trembling against the wall. He made a motion of brushing a fly away. "I mean, just now, at the table. How dare you question my fidelity with half the court listening? Have you no shame? If not for me, then for yourself?"

"Shame?" Isabella asked, as she sat up. "Oh, but I lost that in Scotland, when you left me behind your enemy's lines and ran away."

"I left so I could fight," Edward said through clenched teeth. "I rode to battle. I didn't know you would be caught." Now his face twisted in a sneer. "But it didn't matter, did it? You did full well for yourself, did you not?" His voice rose. "*You* returned in high good health and fine fettle, which is more than could be said for me. I was in danger, because I couldn't flaunt my pretty ass to ease my way."

"Oh, I have heard you could. Indeed, I have seen it too."

Gwenith stepped farther back, as though trying to shrink into the wall; they were snapping and snarling at each other like two fighting dogs, and she didn't want to be bitten. Her king and queen stood faced off against each other, two radiantly beautiful people, matched in fury now.

Edward clenched his jaw tight, as though holding himself from hitting his queen. But the force of his emotions made him take another step forward. She stood firm, raising her chin. He stopped, and in frustration, stamped his foot. "By God, madam!" he shouted. "What do you want of me?"

"I want to be respected," Isabella shouted back. "I want you to think enough of me to conduct your love affairs in private. I'm not a child or a fool. My father was king, as is my brother. I know the way of the world, *our* world. A man has needs his chosen wife can't fulfill. We two are yoked by politics and expediency. I never thought otherwise."

"Never?" he asked with an arch smile.

She looked aside. "Well, and if I ever thought else," she murmured, "I was but a child when we wed, my head filled with courtly romance and fables. You were a man grown, and already at a man's games."

"Just so! And with a son already, even if out of wedlock, if you remember," he said triumphantly. "So my man's games were fruitful. My Adam would be with me even now, but he is in the field, seeing to my war against treason with my other men at arms. I can't help it if I was given a child to wed. One that never grew to care for me."

"Oh fie!" Isabella cried. "What is this? I grew to womanhood and *that* was when you began to shun me. If not in my bed, because you needed an heir, then in public, because you had Piers."

"Don't mention his name again," Edward said softly. He looked pale and sick now. He raised a shaking hand to his brow. "Please, at least that. Let him at least rest in peace."

"Then give me some peace too," Isabella said, her chest heaving with the effort of holding off tears. "Leave off flaunting your desires. Sate yourself with discretion, with tact and in secrecy. That, I could bear."

Edward threw up his hands. "Is that what this is? But what have I done?"

"You take food from Hugh Despenser's hand like a child, or a lover," she said angrily. "In front of me and all the court. You give him sweet rewards in return: lands and titles and castles until no one can remember them all."

"Oh, this is nonsense," Edward said.

"Piers, I could understand," Isabella went on. "He was a beautiful youth, gallant and amusing too. For good or for ill, he was unforgettable. D'Amory, I did not understand. He seemed common to me. Others, I ignored as passing fashions because it seemed you took them on and put them off with equal ease."

Edward grimaced and raised a hand as though to push her words away. "You are dreaming."

"But now this younger Despenser?" Isabella asked. "Why? He is not even well looking. His features are as crude as he is. His father is powerful, but he is even greedier than his father. I don't care to even think what he does in a bed. It is what he does in the throne room that frightens me. He'd swallow the world if you let him. I fear you might. You have eyes only for him, ears only for him, and he sits at your right hand. Beware, lest one day he *becomes* that right hand, and you find yourself unable to help yourself."

"Well, this is pretty nonsense," Edward said on a weak laugh. "He is my right hand in matters of state, naught else. I need him, no king can rule alone."

"Your father did," she spat.

He grew still. "Aye, madam," he said coldly. "And see how everyone loved him? It makes no matter. Enough. I've had enough of this. I tell you it cannot continue. Surely you must see that?" he asked, almost pleading. "When you defame me, you demean yourself. Can you not stop this nonsense, at least, at the very least, in public, before court?"

Isabella took a breath, opened her lips to speak, then closed her mouth again. She nodded. "So I will," she finally said. "Can you promise not to belittle me so again, in public, before court?"

He looked at her a moment. "I cannot help it when you see things that are not there. Give you good night, madam." He turned on his heel and left her.

Isabella sank down. She clasped her head in her two hands.

"Majesty, may I help you?" Gwenith asked in a soft whisper, as she came near.

"Oh dear God," Isabella said, "what have I done?"

"Naught, Majesty, only what any wife has a right to do," Gwenith said, before thinking.

The queen suddenly looked at her as though remembering she was in the room.

"Forgive me," Gwenith cried, falling to her knees and bowing before the queen. "I didn't mean to speak out of turn." She was truly horrified. It would be disastrous if she were sent away now.

Isabella reached down and patted Gwenith on the shoulder. "Nay, you have not. You spoke out of charity and kindness. Come, let us forget this. You *do* know that all you hear in this chamber is not heard, and all you see is not seen?"

"I know, I know," Gwenith said miserably.

Isabella put her hand beneath Gwenith's chin and raised her head. She stared into Gwenith's dark brown eyes, overbrimming with tears, her own eyes candid and clear and blue as a child's.

"I trust you." She smiled. "But beware. A queen's trust is a fragile thing. Nay, don't shiver or weep. It is also a great thing. Now you must work to deserve that trust. I would sleep. I would not think now. Come, you may read me the story of King Arthur. You do remember that is what you were about to do?"

"I do," Gwenith said and rose and fetched the book.

When she turned again, the queen lay back on her pillows, wan and exhausted.

"Come, Gwenith," she said, gesturing to the chair at the side of the bed. "Sit. Read to me now."

Gwenith opened the book, and began to read.

Isabella sighed, and closed her eyes. The story took them far from this Tower, back in time, to a world of handsome courtly knights with pure hearts who would fulfill their impossible knightly tasks, to the risk of their lives, so they could win their beautiful noble ladies.

Gwenith read on, her voice gaining in confidence as she went further into the tale of the glorious king and his faithful knights.

Isabella heard the words, and sighed. Gwenith's gentle voice and the familiar tale lulled her. She was half asleep now, and half in old beloved wakeful dreams. "I see it in my mind," she murmured. "The way I did the first time I heard it all those years ago. All was in glorious color, as it is on the page and never is in life. All was *gentil, parfait*, as I dreamed it could be, and thought it would be when I wed my own husband."

Gwenith put her finger on words she had last read, and fell still as she listened to her queen.

"But so it was," Isabella whispered in a dreamy voice that grew ever softer. "I remember my first look at Edward, the man grown, the day I married him. I'd been waiting for him at the Château de Vincennes. He was like a virtuous knight come riding, gleaming, banners flying, triumphant at last, returned to his true love. He dismounted with ease, though he was in full and shining armor. He removed his helmet and halberd to show a face fair as the sunshine he stood in.

"His hair was golden," she said, marveling at the memory, "his eyes blue as the sea, and his smile white and winning, like young Arthur's, surely. He took my hands in his, lowered his head and gave me the kiss of peace. And I went into the church with him gladly. He didn't turn away from me. He didn't go to another waiting for him," she said with wonder. "He never left me. That day, there, it ended, so happily. My heart was full to bursting with love for him. . . ." Isabella's voice trailed off, and smiling, she slept, at last.

Gwenith laid down the book. She looked at her sleeping queen. Isabella's face was flushed with rose as she slept. Mother of four, Queen of England, Ireland and Wales, enemy to Scotland and daughter to kings and queens. She herself had said that a person's actions wrote themselves on their face, but none of Isabella's past showed now, as she dreamed. She looked young, defenseless, innocent, beyond mere beauty: ethereal, pure and good. She looked like the princess in the book. Not Gwenith's enemy. Never her foe. But only a sad and lovely woman whose heart might well be pure.

Gwenith went soft footed to her own bed.

She was the one who didn't sleep that night.

Nine

1321
THE NEXT DAY
THE TOWER, LONDON

T he hunting party returned, glittering in the sunlight,
looking like an illustration from the book Isabella had
listened to being read the night before.

Edward, the king, rode head high, at the front of a festive procession of knights, pages preceding him, raising bronzed cornets
and blaring them to signify his arrival. His right hand held his
horse's reins; his left was crooked so that his favorite falcon could
find purchase on it. The falcon's jesses fluttered in the breeze and
the bright ribands on the top of his hood were no more colorful
than those of the rest of the party. Edward's horse was white, and
stepped high and delicately as though it trod in a ring for show. It
was caparisoned in white and gold, as was its rider, and the king's
golden hair stirred in the breeze of his passage. And Edward was
laughing.

Gwenith's eyes narrowed. The king shared the lead step for

step with Hugh Despenser. And Hugh's horse was no less fine, nor was his falcon, nor his garb. Nor his wide and glowing smile.

Isabella, stony-faced, waited for the company to come to a stand in the courtyard. Gwenith was at her side, as were Agnes and two of her other ladies. The courtyard was crowded, the royal falconer and his assistants were there, as were the stable master and his minions, the king's body servants, along with his physician, and several dozen knights, ready to ride to war if they had to. Falconry was a great sport long beloved of kings. But no journey, no matter how trivial, was considered easy or safe in these turbulent days.

The king rode up to his queen, and bowed from the waist. As did Hugh Despenser, at his side.

"My lady, we return," Edward said. His horse blew a great heaving breath as the king handed his falcon to the royal falconer. As did Hugh Despenser. Edward slid down off his horse, in tandem with Hugh, and stood before her, still smiling. As did Hugh.

Isabella nodded. "A bright day and good news of your hunting, my lord," she said, looking only at Edward.

He stripped off his gauntlets and handed them to a servant. "So it was."

Isabella's smile was crooked. "Good," she said. "But now there's a delegation come to see you, my lord. Look to the front courtyard at Westminster, I hear they come with an army."

Edward's eyes widened. He looked at Hugh.

"What's this?" Hugh demanded.

"They come in peace," Isabella said. "But their faces are grave and they say their mission is as well."

"What's this?" Edward echoed. "Who comes to see me on what sad mission?"

"A confederacy of them, indeed, my lord. You know them all," Isabella said. "They are lords of the realm. Earl Hereford is here, Mowbray, the Mortimers, father and son, Lancaster," she went on, noting Edward's color rise, "and more. They come to speak with you, they said."

"I doubt they've come bearing gifts," Hugh said with a sneer. "And though they should be here in chains, they're not. They escape the traitors' tower, but they tiptoe round treason, sire. Mark me well, they're here to protest your rule."

"We've spoken on this already," Edward said angrily. "There's a law against this sort of assembly. I've *asked* them to refrain from unlawful assemblies that disturb the peace of the realm. It seems I must order it. We can't have this. Where is the earl, Hugh's father? What has he to say?"

Isabella tucked in her smile. "No one can find him, my lord."

Edward's eyes went wide.

"I'll deal with them, sire," Hugh said quickly.

Isabella put up a hand. "I think not. They particularly said you are not welcome, Despenser, not you or your father, at least not until they vote in the special parliament they're convening."

"What?" Edward asked, stepping back a pace. "What's this?"

"Villainy!" Hugh said with a snarl. "They're in league with that damned Lancaster. He never forgave us for unseating him as your adviser, sire. You know that. He's been chafing under our authority, waiting for a chance to bring us down." He scowled. "And D'Amory is not here, is he? Of course," he said with a significant glance to Edward. "That doesn't surprise me. Doubtless, he's behind this as well."

Isabella's smile vanished. "*In league*, Sir Hugh? Odd that you should echo them. They claim that the Despensers, father and son, have formed a league to constrain the will of their king. They say you've unlawfully maintained that their duty is to the crown, and not to their king. That's a dangerous definition of allegiance, at least for your king. Or so they say," she said with false meekness, casting her gaze down. Then her eyes flashed again as she stared at Hugh. "They also mentioned that you, Sir Hugh, are guilty of violence and fraud. I was so startled that I couldn't collect my wits, and so can't remember what else they accused you of, but there were many charges, and they are very angry and definitely serious. They wish to speak with their king, and not you. Not now, at least."

"Don't worry," Edward told Hugh, putting a hand on the dagger that Hugh had just drawn. "They want to speak with me, and so they shall. I'll mend all. This is nonsense. I need you. You know that, and so shall they. Wait for me. I'll soon settle this."

Isabella stood, and watched as Edward walked away.

"You'd like that, wouldn't you?" Hugh said at her ear.

She blinked, and then turned to face him. "Like what, Sir Hugh?"

"Oh, don't pretend with me, Highness. I know, too well, that you pray for my ouster."

Isabella looked at him with a bland inquiring expression, but one that nevertheless clearly showed how generations of her family had looked when they gazed at an amusing peasant.

He crowded closer, until he almost trod upon the toes of her shoes. He thrust his face into hers. She didn't retreat. He nodded.

"Aye, well, and too well we both know it," he said in a savage whisper. "Edward told me. But you forget. I *mean* something to my king. He *chose* me. That's a sight more than can be said for you."

Her expression didn't change, but her eyes were cold as the sea. "Though I am queen, I'm but a woman, my lord. And yet even so, I don't get down on my knees to do anything but pray to my God. Now *that* is a sight more than can be said of you."

His eyes widened. His hand rose.

Gwenith, watching, stepped forward. But Isabella stood straight, and looked him in the eye. His hand closed to a fist, and then he lowered it. He took in a deep breath. "This will not be the end of me, my lady," he said softly. "Never think it. Nor will I forget this day." He stepped back, forced himself into a stiff bow and left her.

"Gwenith?" Isabella said in a faint voice. "Let us go back to my chamber. There's no need for me here now."

"We sit and stitch as the fate of the realm and who shall govern it is decided below," Isabella muttered as she paced.

"You do not stitch, Majesty," Agnes said, with a grin, watching her queen prowling her solar. "You only make patterns on the floor."

Isabella waved her hand. "A manner of speaking, but I spoke truth withal. Gwenith, do you sing as well as you read? I'd like distraction. So much is being decided without me that might influence my life. My son, Edward, though only a boy, is there, but *I* cannot be. It's hard to bear."

"I'd sing, Your Majesty," Gwenith said, "but I fear that might be even harder to bear."

The other ladies in waiting laughed. Isabella smiled.

"Shall I send for a minstrel?" Gwenith asked.

"No, again, only a manner of speaking. I don't think you'd even find a minstrel now. I don't doubt even the fool who turned handsprings for us last night is sitting below, watching all that transpires. He is, after all, a male," Isabella said in disgust.

She paced and turned and then, with sudden inspiration, stopped. "I tell you what," she said. "The very thing! Get you below, all of you, and find out what's toward. But cautiously, and cleverly, so you must not say I wish to know. Agnes, you can come close to a knight as his armor. This time don't dally with him—or do, that's your business—but try to speak with one who knows what's going on, and discover what you can." As the other ladies laughed, Isabella went on. "Anne, to the great hall. Matilda, to the chatelaine. Joan, you know Lady de Berkeley. Margery, you know everyone from the south. Ask a few questions, without saying it is

I who asks. Make it seem like idle curiosity. Then later report your findings to me." She turned to the other ladies and body servants. "The rest of you, go too, and bring news back to me."

"And I?" Gwenith said, as the others left the solar to do their queen's bidding. "I know few people here, Majesty."

"And you, stay with me," Isabella said. "You know me. That's enough. Stay, and wait upon me."

Gwenith sat quietly as Isabella paced the solar. The queen only paused when a page came hesitantly to the door.

"See what he wants," Isabella told Gwenith.

The page whispered a few words to Gwenith, and she returned with the message. "He says there's someone to see you. But he comes in secret."

"The times we live in," Isabella murmured. "And how shall I know if he's friend or foe?"

"He says the one who wishes to speak to you comes unarmed and in peace, and that he's a noble knight, Majesty. And it is William who gave the message to send to you."

Isabella's gaze sharpened. "He'd not have gotten this far if he were dangerous. My guards would have seen to that. Today London is filled with visitors, many from the borders. I can't say nay. Show him in then."

A man, his face covered by the hood on his brown cloak, entered. He went to one knee before Isabella. "Majesty," he said, bowing his head, "I come to give you peace of mind. A friend of yours sends the message that her sister does well and rests easy, and that the babe has not yet arrived. She thanks you."

"Rise," Isabella said. "Let me see who brings this glad news."

The man rose, and threw back his hood and cloak. He was dressed richly in shades of brown and red, and was lean and intense, dark haired, dark eyed, with a dark complexion. His very person seemed to vibrate with pent-up energy. But he smiled at Isabella. "Majesty," he said.

"Lancaster," she said. "So you are returned."

"Only for a few days, until this business is done," he said. He cast a look at Gwenith.

"She's at my right hand, as my poor Therese was," Isabella said. "Too young and too recently come to me to know anything of any of this. But she's proved faithful. You may speak."

"Then I shall," he said. "Know this, Your Highness: I don't seek the throne, no matter what Despenser says. But I do seek Hugh Despenser's ouster, as well as that of his father. The barons will not tolerate them any longer."

"The barons?" Isabella asked. "Or you?"

He shrugged. "All of us. The Despensers seek to swallow us up. We will meet in parliament, and I tell you, Highness, we will be rid of them. The earl has already fled, or so I've heard. They say he shipped to the Continent on the first fair tide after he heard we approached. Clever of him. He stole from us, from the people as well as the king, and would still be doing it if we hadn't arrived. He knew what his fate would be. His son, Hugh, is still here. He'll fight being thrust from the trough. What we seek won't be easy, but it will be done. There is still law in England. He's set the borders on fire, and it spreads, as does his ambition. We'll no longer tolerate it. At the least he will be banished."

"Above the king's protests?"

"If need be. We do this not to curtail his power, but to restore it."

"And who shall rule in Hugh's stead?" Isabella asked quietly.

He cast a bright look at her. "Edward, the king, of course. We're loyal Englishmen. There may be another adviser appointed, someday. But for now, we seek only to be rid of the Despensers. They were given great license, but in their overwhelming greed, they took more."

"You gave great power to them," Isabella said.

"Not I," he said with a forced laugh. "But the barons weren't happy with me when I sought to help our young king with his rule. I was an honest man, Majesty, and I tried full well, but it seems I wasn't the man they sought to help our king with his administrative duties. That was partly because of what the Despensers said about me. There were many lies spoken. Be that as it may, the barons then chose the Despensers instead. That was their mistake."

He sighed. "And that mistake was compounded when the Despensers were given ever more by the king. Forgive my plain speaking, but I only say what everyone knows. No one guessed Hugh Despenser would become the king's favorite. He's nothing like Gaveston, nor D'Amory. And Hugh never leaned in that direction, that we knew of, before."

"He'd go in whatever direction he found power," Isabella said. "Neither his heart nor his body has ever been stirred by ought else."

Lancaster nodded. "Had we known, we'd have never selected him."

"*You* did not," Isabella said sharply. "You were ousted. That must still rankle. Tell me whatever you wish, Lancaster, but do not tell me lies."

He bowed. "Then truth, Majesty. I am now one of a band of nobles who see the need for change. We don't want to supplant the king. He's God's anointed, and must continue his rule, lest the kingdom come apart. But we do not have to like his choice of . . . companions. It is not *how* Edward the king loves, Majesty. At least, not so much, save that he flaunts it in our faces continually. It is *whom* he loves that troubles us. The Despensers' greed brings us to the brink of revolution."

Isabella was silent.

"Forgive me," Lancaster said. "I never meant to give you hurt. But you can't pretend this is news to you. What is news was something I did think you should know, and I sought to ease your fears. We're Edward's men, and yours. Nothing of this will change that."

"But if Edward were gone, then you might be king," she said.

He shook his head. "Nay. If Edward, God protect him, were gone, his son would be king. I would not change that."

She looked at him steadily. "Pray God that is so."

"I leave you now, Majesty," he said. "I am needed below."

"Go then, in peace," she said.

He bowed, and left her.

Isabella sat silent. Then she raised her head. "Gwenith, you heard nothing of this."

Gwenith bowed. "Of what, Your Majesty?" she said.

Only two days later, they stood on the wharf, and the king wept. He buried his golden head in the crook of Hugh Despenser's thick neck, and wept, while his wife, the queen, stood and looked on with eyes the color of stone.

They whispered together, the king and his knight. And then, when they embraced, the queen looked away, and out to where the great masted ship lay at anchor, waiting.

"I will be back," Hugh Despenser cried. And Isabella looked up to see him step into the small boat that would carry him to the ship. "Believe that, and believe me!" Hugh shouted, above the sound of the sea and the wheeling gulls.

Edward watched until the boat touched the ship, and his knight climbed to the deck, and when the ship was lost to sight, the king put his face in his hands, and wept.

"Everything," Edward sobbed that night. "Everything I ever loved has been taken from me, every time I dared to love."

"God's breath!" Isabella cried as she looked down at him where he sat, huddled on a chair in his chamber, his head on his arms. "Have done. Don't tempt Satan. You have your sons. You have your kingdom. You have your health and your life and your throne. Give praise and thanks instead. And leave off grieving. This is unseemly, my lord."

He turned. His eyes were pink and swollen, but glittered with anger. "Unseemly, eh? My friend, my confidant, is gone from me through no fault of his own, and I lament it, and that is unseemly? I had to call a parliament and was forced to concede to their demands. First they give him to me, and now they take him away. Of course I grieve. You wouldn't understand. You have no heart, no soul in you."

Gwenith stood quietly by the door, seemingly forgotten. She dared not stir, lest she be told to leave.

"I lost my father after our first son was born," Isabella told Edward coldly. "He never got to see my child. I lost my Therese such a short while ago. She was as close to me as a sister, as kind as a mother, and watched over me all my life. And now she's gone home to die. But you never saw me drop a tear. Not because I have no heart or soul, but because there was no help for it but prayer. Tears cannot change fate. Do you not think I wept enough when I came to England alone, but for her?"

"Her, and a clutch of your other French courtiers, who do naught but eat and gossip about me. And who is here to see me weep but you?" he asked savagely. "And you do not care. I lost Piers, and though I didn't think I could, I lived through it, did I not? But now Hugh? It is not fair. I am king, with no one to confide in and take counsel from now. You loved Therese? You miss her? You found another to replace her soon enough—that whey-faced little creature who skulks about in your shadow. That's why you do not weep. You have never given your heart. You do not *have* enough of a heart to understand."

"Oh, do I not?" she demanded. "How should you know? I was friendless and innocent, and came across the sea to a husband

I hardly knew, only to find he loved another more? And always would." She raised a hand to her head. "Oh, have done, before we tear each other to pieces."

"Have done, indeed," he said, wiping his eyes on the back of his sleeve. "Hugh has promised to return, and I believe him, and I'll watch and wait for that day. But *Lancaster*! That villain! My own cousin! He carried St. Edward's sword at my coronation, and pledged his love, and yet he has ever sought to undermine me. He spoke of unfair taxes and even blamed famines on me, on *me*, to rouse the serfs and inflame the barons. Then he got what he wanted. They gave him power. That was a shame and a hurt I cannot forget. Did they ever wrest power from my father? They did not dare. But once he was gone, Lancaster spread lies and told tales. And what did he do when they gave him power to equal mine? Did he mend matters, increase the harvests and refill the treasury? Nay, the moment he had the chance, he slew the innocent instead.

"He sent me Piers' head in a basket! As though it were a traitor's to be put on a pike on the Tower gate. I still see it in my sleep every night. I wish I could dream of Piers as he was, dream about that handsome laughing face. But all the living memories of him are eclipsed by the one glimpse I had of his poor dead face. My father brought Piers to me, and then hated him and me enough to send him away, but when death took my father, I called Piers back again. I cannot call him back from where Lancaster sent him! That still hurts me.

"What had *Piers* to do with taxes and famines?" he asked Isabella piteously. "He never even spoke of such. He loved a jest, rich food and fine raiment. You remember. A jollier fellow was hard to find. He called Lancaster a sour-faced fiddler. Was that such a crime? True, he enjoyed showing off his wit as much as he did his riches. You know that. But he deserved his prizes. He was a valiant knight and fought well for me. But foremost, he was my friend and boon companion. My cousin Lancaster lured him up north on a false mission, and then took his head, to burden mine. Lancaster! He shall not stand in Hugh's stead!"

"Nor will he," she said. "Calm yourself. He leaves for his home tomorrow. Now you must rule alone. Can you?" she asked urgently. "Because I tell you, if you can, you'll soon be free to make all decisions yourself. You have only to convince the kingdom that you know what you're doing."

He picked up his head. His fair face was blotchy from crying, and his eyes were red, but he looked at her with sudden interest.

"You have only to behave in a manner that renews the barons' trust, and you will have the throne to yourself," she said urgently. "Behave with more circumspection. If you must have affairs, conduct them with tact. Restore estates. Give back castles to their former owners. Quench the fires on our borders. Else, our enemies on every side will see our weakness, and we'll be at war with all, even against our own.

"That is what the barons fear. It is more than their anger at losing their lands, though if you take a man's home he'll always be an enemy. They can stand against Wales and Scotland—Ireland too, if must needs be. But the barons dread war with each other. If that happens, who will profit? It was fear and anger at the Despensers that led them here, and fear at what will befall them with no one to lead them that they have faith in. Soothe them. Pacify them. Show them you can be trusted to do the right thing, and you will never have anyone to rule over you again. I believe in you, Edward. I believe that you can. The question is, do you?"

"I do not know," he said mournfully. "I will try. It is not that which plagues me now. It is the absence of my friend, my adviser, my Hugh. Naught you can say can heal that."

Isabella stood watching him a moment. "I am still here," she said softly. "If I can give you any comfort, I will. You have only to ask me."

He didn't look up again. "I am beyond comfort," he murmured. "But thank you."

She turned away. "Then I'll leave you now," she said.

He waved a hand at her without looking at her, and stared mournfully at the wall.

Gwenith stood waiting for Isabella, and walked behind the queen as Isabella went to her chamber. The queen's body servants rushed to attend to her, but Isabella waved them off. "Not now," she said.

She sank down to sit on a chest by her window. She put a trembling hand to her forehead, and touched her headdress, an elaborate affair of white linen and veiling, studded with pearls, and then she clasped her head in two trembling hands.

"Majesty, let me help you," Gwenith said, and came near. "Shall I call your servants back?"

The queen suddenly looked at her as though finally remembering she was still in the room.

"Forgive me," Gwenith said, backing up a step, and bowing her head. "I didn't mean to speak out of turn."

Isabella raised a hand. "Nay, you have not. You spoke out of charity and kindness." She stared into Gwenith's dark brown eyes, her own eyes candid and clear as a baby's. "I don't need my servants now. I don't want them hovering. I have no face to present to any of my court just now. A queen must always have a calm face, or she spreads rumor and fear. There's enough of that floating about tonight. My ladies brought me a dozen tales of the Despensers' activities since they left us, each tale contradicting the others. They will return. They will not. They lie in wait. They are gone forever. There's nothing to be done tonight, or learned, as yet. We must wait on events. I don't think I'll sup below this night either. My head aches. I'll have something brought up. But you may go."

Gwenith shook her head again. "If I may, I'll stay with you, Majesty."

Isabella frowned. "'Majesty'? What did you call Lady de Percy?"

"Why, 'lady,' of course," Gwenith said.

"Then call me that," Isabella said. "I need not be reminded of my power every moment. Therese took great liberties with me but never overstepped the line. I trust you have similar sense. You stand in her stead, so 'my lady' will do."

"As you will, lady. Shall I call in your servants in now, at least to help you prepare for bed, and get some rest?"

"Nay," Isabella said. "They peck at me. They whisper in corners. Though they try to be helpful, I'd rather not see anyone else just yet."

"May I help you take off your headdress then?" Isabella wore her hair in coils over both ears, wrapped round with the linen from her wimple, which itself was wrapped with veils. "Mayhap that's what makes your head ache."

"More than that weighs on my head," Isabella murmured. But she bowed her neck so Gwenith could remove the filet of gold that was her crown, and then unwind the wrappings of her pearl-encrusted wimple. Isabella sighed and shook her head when her headdress was off, and the careful coils on either side of her head came undone in white gold streamers of hair that fell to her waist.

"I can brush it out for you," Gwenith volunteered. "My grandmother used to enjoy relaxing of an evening, before the hearth, while I brushed her hair for her."

"Yes," Isabella said absently, sitting back, and staring unseeing out the window.

Gwenith took the pearl-handled brush from off a table, and began to stroke it through the queen's hair. Isabella's hair was pale and light, and as Gwenith brushed, it crackled and clung to her hands before falling into place again, still slightly raised, like silk on a cold night.

"My grandmother's hair was white, and thin as spiderwebs," Gwenith said softly. "Yours, lady, is like fine-spun flax."

Isabella smiled.

"She used to love this," Gwenith murmured, remembering, finding the rhythmic stroke of the brush through the queen's fair hair as comforting to her as it obviously was to Isabella.

"You loved her," Isabella said.

"Dearly."

"And she loved you?"

"Yes."

"That is a great gift," Isabella said on a sigh. "You know, little Maid of the Marches, I have ever been valued, but seldom loved."

There was no answer to that, so Gwenith only stood behind her queen, tending to her, until shadows covered them both.

Ten

1322, January
Six months later
St. Thomas Tower, London

The king rose from his throne and ran lightly down the few steps that led to it as the pirate was shown into his hall. The pirate strutted into the room, as the court stopped all activity and stared at him. Laughing, the king threw his arms around the pirate. He embraced him and stepped back, looked at him and laughed again.

"Majesty," his visitor said on a wide smile, "let me bathe and then I am fit to welcome. I smell of brine and bilge."

"How else is a successful pirate to smell?" Edward chortled.

Gwenith stood beside her queen and marveled. Hugh Despenser was returned to London, neither in chains nor disgrace, but rather greeted like a victorious campaigner. His father had fled to the Continent, but not the son. Since his expulsion, the younger Despenser had not strayed far from home and, though homeless, had prospered. He had commanded a ship that prowled the channel and nearby waters, capturing ships of any nations that ventured near, holding their crews for ransom, sending news of the bounteous plunder he'd accumulated, and offering it to Edward. All the seafaring world had feared him. England had spoken of little else. And now the father and son were forgiven, and the pirate was returned with his riches.

"Look at you!" Edward cried. "Browned by the sun till you look like a Turk. And with a beard like old Methuselah. Who would know you?"

"Oh, sire," Earl Despenser said from behind them, "they knew."

"Indeed, they did," Edward said, grinning. "Who did they fear on the open sea more than krakens and whales or sharks? Our Hugh! They called you the greatest sea monster of all. We're a nation of sailors, but there never was one like you. You made the Viking horde seem like gentle monks. You lay in wait in the channel, near our shores. Two loaded merchant ships and their cargo, one after another, snatched up by you."

"And their rich cargo forfeit to the crown," Earl Despenser reminded him.

"Just so," Edward said. "It was one of the reasons we proved successful so soon, Hugh. They didn't want to deal with you on the land, but you showed it would be easier than dealing with you at sea." He stepped away and let out a long sigh. "You're back, where you should be. The madness is done, and so quickly it does my heart good. Back just after Candlemas. Even I didn't expect you so soon."

Isabella sat erect, listening. She bore no expression on her lovely face. Gwenith, behind her, dared show none either, though her heart had felt cold when she'd seen the jubilant return of the younger Despenser.

"But now, sire, your rebellious lords listen to you," Earl Despenser said. "And the brutes who would have taken over your throne are fled like chaff before the wind."

"Aye," Edward said. "If they didn't act out of loyalty, they did so from fear. I saw to that. But all is not well even so. We may have to go to war with Scotland soon again. We hear rumblings. I needed a man of war to marshal my troops, and so I told them. They knew your strength and so they listened. And now I must march against Lancaster. He took the news of your return to heart. He fled, and even now tries to gather troops, against you, against me."

"And that is why the other lords will ride under your banner, sire," Earl Despenser said. "A man may complain about your advisers—'deed, complaining is an Englishman's pastime. But no man wishes to speak pure treason or regicide."

"Except for Lancaster," Edward said, "because he knows how I hate him. I need a strong man at my side now, Hugh. After your recent triumphs, it was clear to everyone that was you."

"*And* after they came to see that their king could rule without being in anyone's harness, sire," Earl Despenser added. "We only advise. The others would manage all."

"Come," Edward told Hugh, a hungry look in his eyes. "We must talk. It's been so long."

Hugh smiled at him. "'Deed, sire, we must. But first, I must also greet my queen."

Edward smiled. "Yes. True. You think of everything, Hugh."

Hugh walked to the throne and bent one knee before Isabella. She stared back at him, pale and cold eyed.

"Highness," he said, "I am returned. And with bounty."

"So I see," she said.

"Nevermore to desert you, Highness," he added, with a slow, curling smile.

She didn't answer.

"Come, Hugh," Edward said, "rise." He clapped an arm around his shoulder. "There's much to tell you, and more you must tell me. We'll go to my chamber so as not to be disturbed."

He wrinkled his nose. "And aye, I'll have them bring a tub, or two, of steaming water there—and three or four brushes," he added, to make all the courtiers laugh.

Isabella did not. And Gwenith didn't so much as smile; she stood frozen, by her queen.

The evening meal that night was a feast. There was music and laughter, fine food and much drink. There were jugglers and musicians, and a fool to cavort for the company, but nothing made the king smile so much as the man sitting next to him, Hugh Despenser.

They were a study in dark and light. Edward's fair hair and face were shadowed by Hugh's dark splendor. Hugh wore crimson, and a jewel in his ear, in the manner of pirates, he explained. He'd cut his beard, but retained the shadow of it. It made his teeth gleam white when he smiled, and he did that often.

Gwenith felt chilled. Hugh the younger sat at the top of the table, and looked around, she thought, with pleasure and proud possession, like a king returned to his rightful place. And Edward the king hung on his every word, and watched his face for every indication of his mood. The queen said nothing, watching it all with a cold blue stare.

Tonight the king's elder son, Edward, sat with his father; at eleven years old, a somber, pale boy. Gwenith was saddened for the boy and his mother, because even she could see that Edward the king couldn't take his eyes from Hugh. They'd passed hours alone in the king's chamber; all knew that. But even now Edward watched him as though not believing his good fortune.

Finally Hugh sat back and stretched luxuriously, signaling he was sated. Then his sly smile and glance to Edward hinted at still other reasons for his looking so replete.

"Tonight we dine in splendor, but soon we must march," he

told Edward. "My father wrote to me about the trouble in the north and on the borders."

Isabella sat up and went very still. There was music and laughter, but Hugh's voice boomed, and he did nothing to lower it. But trouble in the kingdom was something they should have discussed in the long hours they'd just spent together. That Hugh implied they had not was pure boast, as well as a challenge and an insult to her.

Edward's gaze slewed to his queen, even as he spoke to Hugh. "Aye, as I told you before, in my chamber," he said with emphasis.

Hugh chuckled. "Did you, sire? My pleasure at seeing you again must have thrust it from my head."

Edward's face flushed. He was both pleased and nervous. He looked at his queen's still face, and then, as though making his decision, angled himself toward Hugh, so that he couldn't see her.

"We should march before much more time passes. North, first, I think," Hugh said. "To show both Lancaster as well as the Scots our power. In fact, I think we should send men there at once and join them when we can. Will Birmingham stand with us? And what of Mowbray and Hereford?"

"The more that stand with us, the more that will stand with us," Earl Despenser said. "I think that rallying them now is wise. And you, sire?" he added as an afterthought.

"Oh, aye," Edward said, as he gazed at Hugh.

"And you, my prince," Hugh asked the young Edward. "Do you care to march with us? Do battle, and get a taste of what's to come for you?

Before Edward could answer, his mother did.

"No," Isabella said suddenly. "He has time enough to go to war. Would you have him defend his crown before he wears it? I would that he were safe until he grows to manhood."

"Where could he be safer than with me?" Edward asked.

"Or with me?" Hugh asked with a wide smile that challenged the queen to disagree. But there was an undertone to his voice and a look in his eye that made her shudder.

"That you'll do all you can to keep him safe, I do not question," she said quietly. "But fate besets the best of us. And if aught should befall his father, God forfend, then he must be ready to take up the scepter."

"Does he not have a younger brother?" Hugh asked.

Isabella's eyes widened. "As you well know, he does. But John has but six years to his name."

"Ah, I see," Hugh said. "And Prince John, though a handsome boy, is nothing like his father."

Gwenith drew in her breath. Prince John had red hair. She'd heard the rumors about his legitimacy. The facts that the king's proclivities were increasingly famous and that Isabella had been gone from London to Scotland before some of her children's births were enough to fuel a dozen rumors, none of them substantiated. Gwenith was only shocked that Hugh felt secure enough to hint of them here and now. She was also surprised that it was John they questioned, because apart from his red hair, in the rest of his features, there was no doubt he was his father's son. Whatever the prince's lineage, Hugh had overstepped his bounds.

Isabella stood, white faced and tight lipped. "John is too young to take on such responsibility," she said stonily. "I don't even want to talk about such things. And I do not want Prince Edward to march to war yet."

"My father took me when I was his age," Edward said. "We rode to war with the Scots."

"Aye," she said savagely, "and see how well you've—" She reined in her temper. "But things can go awry, my lord," she said instead. "Indeed, though you're a valiant knight, remember how I was trapped with the enemy that time in Scotland? And only returned to you long days later, by the grace of God"—she paused—"and the charity of those Scots that I came to call friend."

It was there in the open now. She acknowledged that she'd heard the rumors. She obviously waited for Hugh to dare say something as openly. She was queen. He was still, after all, with all his titles, only an honored subject.

But he was saved the danger of a reply.

"I'll go if you wish, Father," Prince Edward said soberly.

"Like a good son!" Hugh said. "But there's time enough for that, my prince. Your royal father doesn't intend to fall in battle. Nor will I let him," he added, looking over his head and into Isabella's eyes, and smiling. "Don't fret. We'll have other chances. To ride to war."

Prince Edward did ride out with his father, Hugh Despenser, a few other nobles and an escort party the next day. Isabella said nothing this time, because they went to visit Hugh's ship, the one he'd terrorized the channel with. They went aboard and exclaimed over the pleasures as well as the hardships the sailors must have faced. It was when they returned that they learned they would have to ride out again.

"News, sire," Earl Despenser cried as they walked into the great hall. His expression was feverishly eager and bright, his ruddy face flushed, his eyes gleamed. "Messengers arrived. Lancaster is defeated at Boroughbridge! They think he has taken refuge in Pontefract, his own castle. But now he is surrounded. He dare not leave there. He's trapped."

"Lancaster!" Edward breathed, his eyes wide. "Great news! Wretched man. He'll never be content until I've drawn my last breath and he can seize control in my stead."

"That will never happen while we live," Earl Despenser said.

Edward wasn't listening. "A false friend and a cunning one.

And what of his coconspirators, Hereford and the Mortimers? And what of D'Amory, the most false friend of all?"

"He is dead, sire. Captured and dead before we knew of it."

"And his wife?" Isabella asked. She had quietly followed the earl, but now spoke. She saw the surprise on Edward's face and she added, "Whatever he's done, she is of royal blood, and has ever been a true friend of mine. If she lives, pray find sanctuary for her, my lord, because she had no part in this."

"I so vow," Edward said. "She's but a woman, and not accountable. But the others?" he asked Earl Despenser eagerly. "All who refused to come and make peace with me when I supported Hugh—do they support Lancaster still? Or will they defend me now?"

"Word has gone out to them," Earl Despenser said.

"They'll fall in line," Hugh told Edward. "I promise that. Lancaster was my chiefest enemy too, sire. There are others. But now, my lord, we must to Pontefract to see justice done. We need to set an example not soon forgotten. He must be torn to pieces and flung to the four winds. Hang, draw and quarter him to show your displeasure, else the very word 'treason' will have no bite. The other barons will make peace when they see your vengeance, and see how their former leader will be forced to make peace with God."

"Lancaster, mine at last," Edward murmured. His hands knotted at his sides. "He has done me great hurt, Hugh," he said sadly. But then his face lit up. "Now he awaits my justice. I must go."

"Indeed, you must," Hugh said. "Show that villainy will be dealt with, revolt put down and England ruled by law of her king, not the rabble."

"And I?" Isabella asked. "Am I to pack my cases?"

"Nay, my lady," Hugh said. "Lancaster is caught. The snake will have its head chopped off, but it may still thrash in its death throes. We haven't got all of the rebels. It is not yet safe enough for a female, much less a queen, not even one brave as you."

Her head turned. She looked down her nose even as she looked up at Hugh. "I did not ask you, sir," she said.

Gwenith's eyes widened. This had been an ongoing unspoken war, but now it was coming out into the open.

Hugh looked to Edward, and then to his father, who said nothing, but stood frozen.

"We will discuss this later," Edward told Isabella.

"Why?" Isabella said. "I've made myself plain enough. I wish to go with you. I went to Scotland, did I not, when all was in chaos there? And yet though I was left alone with your enemies while you went to war against them, here I am, returned."

The healthy flush on Edward's cheeks grew hectic.

Isabella's smile was thin. "Aye. So if I could escape harm there, why not travel in my own England?"

"It is cold. There will be ice, mayhap snow," Edward said.

"I have furs. I'll make ready." She turned to walk back to the Tower.

Edward stood still a moment, and then gave a forced laugh. "What has displeased my lady so much, I wonder."

Hugh smiled at him. "The time of the month or the moon, mayhap?"

Isabella's back went rigid, but she kept walking, Gwenith close to her side.

The queen's chamber bustled with Isabella's servants, her ladies in waiting stood by the window speaking together in low voices. Gwenith watched her queen, and sat silent, waiting for her command.

Isabella paced.

"All is in readiness," one of her servants finally said. "Which of your ladies do you wish us to assist now?"

The ladies in waiting stopped talking.

"Oh, I should love to go, but how can I travel?" one of them whined. "I will go if I must, but you know how I suffer from the headache, Majesty."

"And I'm timorous, Your Majesty," another said nervously. "It is a great shame to me, but so it is. I'll go if you wish, of course, but I dread it. I try, but I could never be as brave as you."

"I'll go," Agnes said.

"No," Isabella snapped. "Not you. I want peace in the night, not titters and tiptoeing, whispers, grunts and rocking cots. Don't vex yourself," she added more kindly. "But we've no time for such. Just thinking about how you'd be tempted amid hundreds of fine fighting men makes my head ache."

Even Agnes laughed at that.

"We must travel fast and light," Isabella said. "I'll take Brenna, Anne and Maevis to see to my clothing. Alyce, Elberta and Edwina to see to my other needs. And Gwenith will come as companion."

The others sighed with relief. Gwenith relaxed. She'd been chosen. She didn't want to sit and wait and feed on rumor. She could not have borne not being with Isabella on this journey.

"She's the only one of you that loves to travel, or so she said," Isabella went on. "And she's shy of men. Or so it seems. And brave enough to speak up, so she may not shrink from risk. So how say you, Maid of the Marches? Is your appetite for travel whetted by danger? Or would you rather I pick another?"

"I'll go, and gladly," Gwenith said truthfully.

"Good," the queen said. She resumed pacing as they all stared at her. "Oh, go now," Isabella said irritably, waving a hand at them. "My bags are packed, and I stand in readiness."

The body servants and ladies in waiting fairly flew to the door. Gwenith went to follow.

"Not you, Gwenith," Isabella said. "Stay a moment."

Agnes' eyebrows went up. "I see you rise high, little Gwenith," she whispered, giving Gwenith an elbow in the ribs. "Better you than me, though. Fare thee well," she said before she left with the others.

"Lady," Gwenith said, "what would you of me?"

"Look to my bags. See if aught else is needed," Isabella said. "Therese used to do that for me, and it was marvelous how much she found missing. My servants are good but today they're in a dither. You always keep a cool head."

"Lady," Gwenith said, with a bow of her head, and went to the side of the chamber, where Isabella's open boxes stood ready to go.

Isabella stopped pacing, and watched her. "Gwenith," Isabella said with a faint smile, "*you* don't have to go with me, you know. I spoke for myself, and not for you. You are, after all, not Therese. I knew her since I was a babe. She came here with me, yoked her destiny to mine and only left me when she knew she must leave this earth, and then only because she wanted to rest forever in her own homeland. But your king was not wrong. There may well be danger. I do have friends across the border, in Scotland. But I also have enemies in England now, thanks to the greed of the Despensers. Still, I must to Pontefract. I have friends in England as well and would see none of them hurt."

She paused. "Or if it chance that they must be hurt," she murmured, "then I must see that it's done quickly, without torment and shame and undue pain. There's grace in that for them, as well as for those who must take their lives. But you need not be there."

Gwenith looked into the pale, lovely face of her queen and saw sorrow and pain, and torment there as well, such as she had not seen since she had sat with her grandmother, and saw her reliving the events that had changed their lives forever.

She shook her head. "Nay. I would come with you," she said.

Isabella smiled. "Then, I shall be glad of your company."

"We travel with an army," Gwenith whispered.

"Nay. We travel as befits a king and queen," Isabella corrected her.

The lines of horses, knights, bowmen, archers and men at arms were followed by a train of servants and horses burdened with tents and chests. The horses danced in place in the courtyard, and the men watched for the word to go forward.

"Still, we travel too light because of the haste we must make," Edward said with a frown. "It's unavoidable. When we rode to the north with my father when I was a lad, we took two hundred souls with us. We had many chaplains and surgeons, rather than just one of each, and porters, valets, servants to tend the kitchens as well as our clothing, even those whose sole duty was to transport his bed and robes. There were grooms and huntsmen too. My father was not a man to bask in luxury. It was what he deemed necessary. This time, we must make haste. I won't trust Lancaster until he's dead. We can't take the household a queen requires."

"I can do without," Isabella said.

"But it means there's more danger. Are you sure you wish to come?" he asked her.

"It's late in the day to ask that," she said. "I'm going."

"Your lady has a taste for revenge, sire," Hugh said admiringly. "That's a bad thing in a lover, but a very good thing in a queen."

Edward laughed. Hugh's father, on his stout warhorse, turned in his saddle and smiled.

Isabella's eyes flashed. "Lancaster is of royal blood," she said. "Whatever he's done, that is unarguable. It's not revenge but a sense of what is right and fit for a queen of England to do that drives me."

"Ah," the earl said, puffing out his cheeks as he contemplated what she said. "This much is true. A royal should attend the funeral of another. But his execution, my lady?"

"Even so," Isabella said.

"Well then, less said the sooner we can leave and accomplish that," Edward said. "We must ride. Once more, madam, I ask if you'd rather go in a coach or a litter?" he asked Isabella. "Think of the rain, of the wind. It would be more comfortable for you."

"And much slower," she said. "You'd be days ahead of me. And that is only if all went aright, and things seldom do. Coach wheels get mired in the mud. Litter bearers suffer accidents. If the road is too muddy, we must stop entirely. Nay, I'll ride. When we get to Leeds, I'll go by litter if you like. It makes a better show."

"And a safer one," Hugh commented. "No one would expect their queen to ride among her men at arms, as though she were one of them."

Isabella tilted her head. "An' if I were a man, sir, I would be, and a good one at that."

Hugh threw back his head and laughed. "A lady of spirit! Well said."

"But not said for you," Isabella countered. " 'Tis only truth."

"And what of your servants? You need personal servants and most ladies are not so high spirited as you," Hugh asked, eyeing Gwenith.

"My servants are of my mind," Isabella said. "Some ride in the wagons. Some ride. My lady rides beside me. Riding is another of her accomplishments."

"Then," Edward said, "we ride for Pontefract."

The king raised his hand, and the procession started moving. Those in the royal household who were left behind stood watching to see them leave. They did so in highest style. Edward the king wore red and gold, surrounded by bright banners flying. Hugh Despenser was at his side, the earl riding just behind them, a retinue of mounted knights flanking them. Isabella came next, Gwenith at her side, surrounded by the queen's retinue, with

armored knights beside them. And then came three other noblemen, summoned by the king. Then came armored knights, lines
of men on foot marching in cadence behind them. Seventy-five
souls braved the new morning, clattering over the drawbridge that
spanned the moat, and then went on into London.

Eleven

1322

ON THE ROAD TO PONTEFRACT CASTLE

Gwenith rode a fine, fat, cream-colored mare, with a long, steady gait. Her cushioned saddle made the ride comfortable, and the way the people of London stared and bowed as she passed made her feel important. Once their procession reached the great north gate, however, the pace picked up.

Soon the only ones to stop and gape at them were the serfs in the fields. And then, as they marched on, there was no one to see them but curious crows, wheeling overhead. The king's horse began to canter; the procession picked up the pace and followed. Gwenith was amazed to see how fast the men on foot could march. It was a mild day for the season, but the roads were iron hard from the cold. There was no talking or time for even an encouraging word. She rode beside Isabella and her retinue of mounted knights, marveling at how they rode, steady and upright, even though they were in half armor. As the sun rose high overhead, Gwenith began to feel her strength falter, although her mount kept up the pace.

By the time the sun was moving westward from its zenith, the king raised a gauntleted hand. The procession stopped.

Edward turned in his saddle. "We stop to water the mounts—and ourselves," he cried.

A knight helped Gwenith down. She was unsteady when she was on the earth again, but soon found her feet. She immediately looked to her queen. Isabella stood in the center of her circle of attendants.

"How may I help you, lady?" Gwenith asked her.

"Come with me," Isabella said. "They tell me there's a running brook nearby for us to cool our faces, with a thicket of bushes to shield us while we tend to our other needs. And then we dine, and then we ride. We've many miles to go. Are you sorry you came, Gwenith?"

"Never," Gwenith said. She was a handbreadth away from the seat of all power in England, a stone's throw from the man she'd sworn revenge upon, and closer still to a woman she found herself increasingly attached to. Every other woman Gwenith had known any affection from had wanted something of her. She hadn't known her mother. Her grandmother had loved her well, but had also extracted a terrible vow from her in payment for that love. Lady de Percy was compassionate, but only because she was obliged to be. But Queen Isabella had shown her favor and was kind beyond expectations, and for no reason except that she seemed to be lonely too. The queen was too powerful to be considered a friend, of course. But she was also too human to hate.

Gwenith had no such feelings about Edward. He was beautiful and bright, clever and astonishingly charming, the very picture of a great king. But only that. A kingdom needed more than a picture of greatness. His father, she knew, had not been half so fair of face and had been as cruel as he was strong, and many times more treacherous and cunning. But although he'd exterminated her family and her people, and she hated him no less, she understood that was what a king had to be. She only wished her princes could have been so strong, and had as many men and allies.

Edward the king was not like his father, nor like her slain family. He didn't burn from within or command awe. Increasingly, she perceived weaknesses in Longshanks' son. She disregarded tales of his behavior with the long-dead Piers Gaveston and rumors of his conduct toward other men long gone. But she saw that he was too eager for approval, especially that of the Despensers, and most especially that of Hugh the younger, who now behaved as though he were also a king. Edward, it was said, had called Piers his "brother king." Hugh behaved as if he were already that.

Though they were surrounded by nearly a hundred men, Gwenith and Isabella and her female servants relieved themselves in strictest privacy, with even their guards facing away from them. They washed quickly, because now there was a cool, damp breeze blowing. Then they went back to where they had left their horses. Gwenith was astonished to see that their mounts were gone, and that a bright pavilion, a capacious golden tent, had been set up in the meadow beside the road where they had stopped.

A table had been set up in the tent, and Isabella joined Edward there, Gwenith seated behind her. But Edward the king didn't speak to his queen above a few words of greeting. Instead he sat close to Hugh and spoke with him in whispers.

They dined on cold meat and cheese and cold dishes of cooked autumn fruits. When they were done eating, Edward stood and looked at Isabella. "If you are done, madam, we ride again."

Isabella rose. "I'm ready."

He nodded, and they moved on. They rode on for hours, until the light began to go. This time when they halted, they were at the foot of a dense wood.

Hugh raised his hand. "Here we stay for the night," he called.

Isabella had been riding silently, but now her head jerked up. She nudged her horse forward until she was at Edward's side. "And how say you, my lord?" she asked him.

He looked puzzled.

"Is this where we rest for the night?" she asked.

"Did not Hugh say so?" he asked.

"Aye. But he is not king."

Edward's face flushed. "He is, however, a worthy knight. This looks as good a place as any," he said. "Why should I disagree?"

"Stay a moment, Majesty," Hugh the younger told Edward. "Have you any worries about this place?" he asked Isabella as he kneed his mount closer to her. "I don't. Night is falling. There are no abbeys, no monasteries, no castles nearby. And no sane man would travel through the night, unless there were dire necessity. Though the wood is gloomy, it is also good protection on our flank. What troubles you?"

"Naught," Isabella said. "It was only that I was waiting for the *king* to have the ordering of the day."

"Why, so he has," Hugh said with much mock surprise. "We discussed it not a moment past, did we not, Majesty?"

" 'Deed, we did," Edward said on an embarrassed cough of a laugh. "Madam, you stand upon too much ceremony. I knew how it would be. But you must understand, you are with fighting men in the field now and not puppets at court."

"Thank you for telling me. I have traveled with fighting men before," Isabella said coolly. "I knew what to expect. Then here we stay."

The golden tent was put up again, along with two others, one crimson and one white.

"This one is for you, madam," Edward told Isabella, indicating the crimson tent.

She looked at him.

"The king has his own tent," Hugh explained. "My father and

I have ours. We share it with Earl FitzAlan and two other nobles. This way you won't be troubled by late-night conference, or the coming and going of knights and men at arms. And you will be safe, surrounded by guards," he added.

She nodded and, without another word, entered the tent. Gwenith followed and looked around the interior. It smelled sweet, of freshly cut hay and dried grasses. A wooden bed had been assembled, with a cot at its foot. There were a table and two chairs, and thick rugs had been thrown over the grass that was the flooring. A tapestry hung from poles to partition it, separating Isabella's quarters from her servants. Gwenith guessed that she and the queen's other attendants would sleep rolled in their covers on the floor in the smaller section of the tent.

"It will do," Isabella said. "Take the cot, Gwenith, so you're at my right hand, should I need you in the night. Then summon my servants. I would wash again, though I regret it is too cold to bathe in a tub. You may also wash. And then to sup and then to bed. We ride early tomorrow morning. Are you prepared for that?"

"I am, lady," Gwenith said. "I come from a rough place where women are used to such."

"Rough, at Lady de Percy's?" Isabella asked, arching one brow.

Gwenith's color rose, she wished she could take back her words, but decided to tell as much of the truth as she dared. "Nay. I was thinking of my childhood before I went to Lady de Percy. I was born into a fine house. But when my mother died at my birth and my father having died only months before, my grandmother raised me. I lived not half so well until Lady de Percy discovered us . . . in a rude cottage, where we had to draw our own water and chop our own wood."

"It did you no harm in my eyes," Isabella said. "Don't color up and look down." She laughed. "Would that were the worst I ever knew about you."

"Would that it were," Gwenith murmured under her breath.

They rode hard the next day. It was dry and chill, so the ground was hard, and the horses could move quickly. Knowing the vagaries of the weather, the party pressed on while they could. There was scarcely time or inclination to talk whenever they stopped. Hugh's father, the earl, surprised Gwenith, because though he was old and stout, he was a hard rider, and never complained.

They passed the next night at an abbey. The king and queen, the Despensers and the other noblemen stayed in the guesthouse; the knights and fighting men camped nearby. After matins with the monks, and a hurried breakfast, blessedly warm, they rode on. A steady mizzling rain made it slow going.

They stopped at a convent the next night, and made better time the following day because the sun came out. The king and his queen seemed in better temper with each other, or so Gwenith thought. Hugh Despenser stayed at Edward's side, but was courteous, as his father was to his queen. Edward slept in his own tent or rooms, though each night he visited Isabella to bid her good night and ask her again if she wished to go home.

This night, they pitched tents at the side of a river. When Edward came to bid Isabella good night, her maidservants left the tent. Gwenith went outside as well and stood before the tent instead of joining the others. She needed a quiet moment. Folding her arms around herself against the chill of the night, she stood looking out at the statue figures of the sentries watching over the camp.

A dark shadow hove up out of the night. Gwenith was startled, but forced herself to be calm when she saw who it was.

"A chill night to be wrapped only in your own arms," Hugh Despenser said. "Mayhap you'd like some better comfort, lass?"

Were he a common man at arms, she'd have backed away from him. Were he only an ordinary man, she'd have said something quelling too. As it was, she could only stare at him.

"Your king and queen have need of privacy so they can ease themselves in the night," Hugh said, putting a finger under her chin so she had to look up at him. "We could, as well. Not in my tent because my father is there. But in the king's."

Gwenith was amazed that he would hint that Isabella and Edward were making love. Of all the things they might be doing, she doubted that was one. "The *king's* tent?" was all that she could think to say.

"Aye, that. He has no use of it at present," Hugh said in a thicker voice. "Or mayhap we should go in the forest, you and I. Aye. That would be better. You look like a little fawn anyway. Don't worry. I'd protect you. And please you. Such a pretty petite creature, you are. Shy as a dove, but with promise in that mouth of yours. Don't draw back. There are ways a virtuous maid can be pleasured and give pleasure without losing proof of virtue or her maidenhead. Just ask your friend Agnes. Such promise there is in that in mouth of yours."

Gwenith stepped back, eyes wide. "The queen it is who I wait upon," she said. "I do not have to pleasure the king's men. I give you good night, sir."

"Oh, I could prove otherwise, did I want to," he said, "and make it a very good night for us. 'Deed, I could."

"Hugh!" Edward said as he strode from Isabella's tent. "Good to find you here." He shot a suspicious look to Gwenith.

"Sire, where else should I be but at your beck and call?" Hugh asked.

"My lady insists on going forward," Edward said. "So there are things we must discuss, Hugh."

"Here I am," Hugh said, and walked into the night with his king.

Gwenith took a deep breath, and went back into the tent. The servants came soft-footed, out of the dark, and curled up on their side of the tapestry partition.

Gwenith ducked under the tapestry, to see Isabella sitting on her bed, looking bleak.

Isabella picked up her head when she saw Gwenith. "Such a face you have, Gwenith," she said. "It wasn't made for secrets. What has distressed you?"

"I met Sir Hugh the younger outside," Gwenith said, and would say no more.

She didn't have to. "And he frightened you?" Isabella asked.

Gwenith nodded.

"Pay him no mind. Now, to bed, please. We ride on at dawn."

Gwenith went to her bed and lay down. Isabella blew out her candle.

"Gwenith?" she murmured into the darkness. "A word said outside is heard clear in here. Don't worry. He has no dominion over you. Only I do. Sleep now, in peace."

They were riding two abreast through a path in the wood the next day, a dull day with no rain, but no sun, when their line of passage halted.

Four knights immediately turned their warhorses from the front of the line and cantered back to stand before and behind the queen. Gwenith sat and looked around nervously. Even leafless, the woods were deep and dense. She saw nothing but the trunks of ancient trees and bracken.

And then, in an instant, there was shouting, and Gwenith saw a band of serfs, armed with axes and bludgeons, burst from the forest.

The knights turned, swords out, and formed a circle around the queen and Gwenith. Gwenith could see little of the battle. She could only hear the peasants' rough cries of "Lancaster!" and incoherent shouts and growls, as well as the clashing of the horses' armor as they charged and danced. And then she could only hear cries of pain.

It grew silent. The knights drew back. Their attackers lay dead and dying, their heads hewn, their throats and chests pierced, their blood seeping onto the forest floor.

Gwenith's heart felt as though it would pound out of her chest. She wasn't afraid for herself; she hadn't had the time to be. But though all her life she'd heard about violent death in vivid detail, she'd never seen it. Peasants and serfs were as common as crows in the fields, and no more to her than that. But she'd never seen them die before. The dying groaned in agony, and muttered prayers, just like men of high birth. But not for long. The men at arms roving the forest found them and tended to them, making sure none survived. Gwenith looked away.

"See," Edward asked breathlessly, holding up a bloody sword, and angling his dancing horse up to Isabella. "*That* for your royal Lancaster! He sought to murder us!"

"His vassals did," Isabella said wearily. "It only shows they love him well."

"I see. And you, madam?" Edward asked angrily. "Is *that* why you drag yourself north with me now?"

She eyed him icily. "He is your cousin, grandson to old King Henry and Eleanor of Provence. He is, although God will it never come to pass, in line for your throne if ought befell you. He deserves royal judgment."

"That," Edward promised, "he will get, in full."

"And royal courtesy," she added.

"Sire," Hugh said as he rode up to them, his bloodied sword in his gloved hand, "I think it would be best if you rolled up your banners now."

"What?" Edward cried. "So all may think I fear another attack? I will not. I'm surprised at you for even suggesting it."

"Nay, that wasn't my intention," Hugh said. "I was thinking of the ride ahead. If you show your standard as we go farther north, it could be taken as a formal declaration of war. Let us deal with Lancaster, and be done with it. We need not start a civil war."

"You're right," Edward said. "Yes, clever Hugh speaks again. Very true. So let's get on and be done with it."

Pontefract was a gracious castle, with a walled courtyard and a long keep. The day was ending, and sunset was gilding the upper stories in the great hall when the king's party arrived. The hall was now blazoned with banners: those of Edward II, King of England.

Edward sat at the top of the hall, Isabella on one side, the older Despenser, the earl, on the other, Hugh Despenser standing behind the king. Gwenith and other trusted servants stood silent, behind their noble masters. The Earl of Arundel was there, summoned along with those nobles in the vicinity who had helped trap Lancaster, and other local men of fortune and birth who had been called to this judgment.

"I see now why he thought he could hide from us here," Hugh told Edward, bending forward, low, to have the king's ear. "The place is well fortified. But he didn't have enough men with him. Those that are here will be dealt with after their leader is. Ah, he comes now. Are you going to make him welcome, sire?"

Edward smiled.

The others in the royal party sat dispassionate as men at arms brought Thomas, Earl of Lancaster, into the room, held between two guards. He hadn't fared well in his captivity. His clothing was torn and filthy; his hands were bound. He had bruises on his face and mouth. But he was alert and his regal bearing was apparent. Gwenith, standing behind her queen, felt her heart leap because he looked, in his dark vivacity, very like one of her own people.

"So, cousin," Edward said, as he eyed Lancaster, "how came we here, to this point? You were at my side at my coronation. Why did you try to be there at my funeral?"

"Well said, sire," Earl Despenser said in a loud whisper.

Lancaster looked up, through one swollen eye. He opened his mouth, but before he could speak, the earl again did.

"He is forbidden to speak, sire," he said.

"Then who speaks for him?"

"His deeds, sire," Earl Despenser said piously. "What more is there to say?"

A few of the nobles nodded and murmured approval. A few sat silent, tense and waiting.

Lancaster stared at Edward. "Who is king here?" he cried, before a guard who had been holding him cuffed his head hard.

"Why talk at all? It's not necessary," Hugh exclaimed, balling his hand into a fist and pounding it on the side of his thigh. "There is only one punishment for such betrayal. He should be drawn and quartered, Majesty. Beheaded, and his various parts flung to the four winds or to the dogs. That's the reward for treason." He stared at Lancaster, and wet his lips.

"Then do not vex yourself, Hugh. That is what shall be," Edward said, turning his head to smile at the man behind him.

"No," Isabella said.

They all turned to stare at her.

"It is not a fit fate for an heir to the throne, however ill advised his actions," she said. "It is no fate for your cousin, sire. Death is ending enough to treason. Torture serves no purpose, except to torment. It is not fitting here."

Hugh gave a bark of a laugh. "What? Are we all women then?"

She stared at the younger Despenser. "No. But only three of us here have royal blood, Despenser. And you are not one of them. A king knows that if he so rudely treats one of his own blood, it reflects ill upon him, and," she added more softly, looking at Edward, "it sets a bad example of irreverence. A king must be above the people. Royal blood must be treated with honor, else the rabble begin to think it the same as their own. If you must have his life, let it be done with dignity. In another time, the man could have been king."

"In this time," Lancaster cried, "the Despensers would be king! *Are* kings. Else I would not have acted. . . ."

One of the men holding him hit his head hard. He slumped forward in their clasp.

"No more," Earl Despenser said. "Let sentence be passed."

Isabella stared at her husband. He shrugged his shoulders as though he felt a chill, and looked away.

"Take him outside," Edward said, eyes downcast so he would not have to look at Hugh. "Let it be done quickly, for all to see. I spare him indignity for his blood's sake. Take his head, and be done."

Lancaster looked at the queen, and he slumped. Not from his wounds, but because it seemed he relaxed the tension in his taut form. His arms were held so he could not bow, but he nodded to her.

"We should take him to the Tower," the old earl protested, "and at least have his head off with ceremony there, and then put on a pike at the bridge, with the other traitors."

"We should," his son murmured. "But we dare not take him the length of England with us. At least, not alive. These are treacherous times."

His father frowned, but waved a hand as though to dismiss his objections.

The company filed out of the hall, into the courtyard and then up a hill nearby. A thin sleet had begun to fall. There was already an improvised block, usually used for the slaughter of fowl, set there, in the center of a grassy mound. Lancaster was flung forward, and thrust to his knees. His head was pushed onto the block. When the king, queen and their company were assembled, Edward gave a nod to the man standing behind Lancaster. Lancaster tried to lift his head so he could stare at Edward. He was doing so when the great ax was brought down. There was a gasp. The ax had not bit through Lancaster's neck all the way, and his head was only half off. He made a gargling sound. The executioner raised his ax again, and this time it went sure, and true, severing the neck and burying itself in the wood.

Lancaster's head was severed, it fell, bounced and rolled away. The terrible sounds ceased as his headless body slumped and flailed, and gouts of blood poured forth from his neck. The executioner bent, caught the rolling head and raised it high, by the hair. "So die all traitors!" he shouted. "God save the king!"

Lancaster's still-opened eyes stared unseeing at the assembled party, as blood streamed from his neck. Even as they watched, his healthy dark complexion rapidly drained, fading to a waxen green death pallor.

Edward sucked in a breath, sharply, and crossed himself.

The queen stared at the head, impassive, then finally looked away.

Edward turned to Hugh. "It is done," he said.

"God pray for his soul," the earl said.

"And pray that it *is* done," Isabella said.

"Aye, it is, except for his knights," Hugh Despenser said.

"You will execute knights?" Isabella gasped.

"Dishonorable ones," Hugh said.

"But they are pledged to their liege lord," she protested, "and so were only fulfilling their vows."

"And I am pledged to my king," Hugh said, "and am fulfilling mine."

"See what comes of bringing a woman to war," Edward said, trying to head off a quarrel.

But Isabella had turned, and was walking away.

The journey back to London was a quiet one. Isabella kept to herself. The earl said little, but the king and Hugh Despenser talked for long hours into the night. And Gwenith woke screaming one night.

She opened her eyes to a cool hand on her brow. It was Isabella, kneeling over her cot.

Gwenith went rigid. "Oh, no, it is not meet, Majesty, that you should bend to me!"

"Better I let you shout the tent top down?" Isabella asked with a smile. She pulled back the curtain and spoke to her body servants, who sat up, alert and frightened, as well as to the guards, who had rushed to the entrance to the tent. "A bad dream, nothing more. Leave us."

When they had, she twitched back the curtain. "What was it?" she asked Gwenith curiously.

Impossible to tell the queen that it was her long-dead father's face she'd seen in the bleeding head that had stared at her—or rather, the face she believed he must have had. But possible to tell her half of it.

"I saw dead Lancaster again," Gwenith said softly. "His head, that is."

"Doubtless he does not rest well, either, wherever he is," Isabella said, crossing herself. "But he's in God's care now."

"I wondered . . ." It was only the lateness of the hour, trapped between dream and reality, that made Gwenith speak again. "I wonder, and it torments me, how long could he see us before his spirit fled. What was the last thing he saw? The sound was terrible. Did he hear his own spine cracked? How strange it must be to see the world rolling by, to think and see and hear, yet feel you have no body, to know that nobody sought to save you. . . ."

Isabella stood again. "Strange little creature you are, Gwenith. Still, I asked the same once, long ago. But about a chicken." Her smile faded. "Be easy. Death comes swiftly. The body moves, but without a head it feels nothing. The eyes stare, but see nothing. It is over in a stroke."

"I hope to never see such a thing again," Gwenith said.

"I pray there's never any need to," Isabella said. "Now sleep. We ride tomorrow. By God, how I wish to be home again."

"Home again," Hugh Despenser said with vast satisfaction, as he stood in the great hall at the Tower, and looked around it. He stood with his thick legs apart, hands resting on his belt, an expression of extreme pleasure and pride of ownership on his face . . . even though his king stood at his elbow.

Isabella looking up from the glad greetings of her children, saw it and went still.

Hugh saw her sudden change of expression and smiled. "Sire," he said, "let us not waste a moment. There's work to be done!"

Edward laughed. "Friend and gadfly, that's you, Hugh. Before God, I'm glad you're back home, with me."

"Being king is a lonely task," Hugh said. "I'm here to make it less so for you."

Edward looked up at him with yearning devotion, the same way that his eldest son, Edward, ignored, was gazing at him.

Gwenith looked to her queen. Isabella saw her son, and her husband, and then she looked away.

Part Two

Twelve

1323, March
One year later
The Tower Grounds, London

"This is my favorite time of day," Gwenith said.

"So it seems," young William of Haye, the squire, answered, as they strolled down the path behind the White Tower, toward the gardens. "But why?"

"At this hour, when the sun begins to sink, I can pretend I'm back at my home, walking in the evening after doing my chores for my grandmother."

"You don't like it here then?" he asked in surprise.

"Don't mistake me," she said on a laugh. "I can't think of being anywhere else now. I'm quite spoiled, you know. But sometimes early memories crowd in. The queen says I'm a country girl at heart, and so I am. But as I told her, my heart is with her now."

"And not any lucky man?"

"And not any," she said, still smiling.

"Though you've many a suitor?"

"Ah," she said, turning toward him, "you've placed a wager on it, have you?"

"Why say that?" he asked with great innocence.

"Because you've never asked before."

"Does that rankle?" he asked seriously.

"I don't see why it should," she said. "A fellow is entitled to make some extra coins gambling with the gullible."

"I don't mean that," he said. "I mean, we see each other often, because we both live here, and are of like mind and age. And we talk frequently too. Does it bother you that I've never sought to be more than a friend?"

"Oh," she said, and considered it. "Nay. I assumed you have a lady waiting for you back at your home. Or mayhap a girl you wait for, because you were affianced to her when she was a child. That's common enough. If that's so, then I praise your fidelity. Not many men in this court are faithful, you know. And I'm not such a monster of vanity that I think every man should fall at my feet. I'm happy to have you as a friend and don't look for more."

"Thank you," he said. "I consider you a friend too. But what about de Blaise? He's been moping and whining and calling you a cruel wench for rejecting his suit. He's even written bad verse to your lips. When he gets drunk enough, he reads it to anyone who'll listen."

"Has he?" she laughed. "I'm not cruel, William. But there are many other women far more beautiful than me. Richer ones too, aplenty. He courts me for my lips, 'tis true. But I don't deceive myself. That's because my lips are close to the queen's ear. Being her companion is both an honor and a danger."

"Danger?" he asked.

"There are some men who have neither marriage nor friendship in mind when they speak to me. The only thing that they do lust for is power."

"Ah," he said. "But danger? Oh, I see. Despenser."

She didn't answer at once. "But even power can't touch me, if I stay far enough away, and close enough to my queen," she said softly. "I only have to suffer invitation. Still, even the sweetest invitation can become tedious if you don't want anything to do with it."

"And his is not the sweetest?"

"What do you think?"

"I can imagine," he said softly. "I've heard such invitations myself."

She looked at him curiously.

He studied her in turn. She wore a violet tunic over a cream-colored gown this evening, and her sleeves were tied up with violet ribands. Her hair was dressed high, and covered with a yellow headdress.

"If you're not the most beautiful woman here, surely you're one of the most charming," he said, with a courtly bow. "And wisest," he added. "Are you going to become another Therese?" he asked suddenly.

She stared at him.

He shrugged. "You dance, and jest. You go for walks and have long talks, but you step neatly away from anything further with any man at court. I wondered if you ever intend to wed."

"It's yourself you're asking for?" she asked in surprise.

"Oh, no!" he exclaimed. His fair complexion colored. "I don't mean that as an insult. But I'm not ready to marry. I wondered about you. You've fitted in wonderfully well since you've come here. Have you plans, ambitions for yourself?"

She stopped and studied him. "Aye," she whispered, "I do." She smiled. "But foremost, I have duties, and for now they meet my desires. They are all to do with our queen. I try to make her happier. She hasn't laughed for joy in too long a time."

"Then there is your work set out for you, and good work it is."

"Aye, there it is." She sighed, because she knew she had other, more important work. But even after two years in Isabella's retinue, she still could see no way to accomplish it. No man at court interested Gwenith more than the king did. Neither knight nor baron, nor guest. She would not allow it. And though she knew her object was to somehow see that mischief came to Edward the king, the longer she stayed at court, the more she realized the futility of her mission, and the more she hated his best friend, lover and close adviser, Hugh Despenser, because she had come to love her queen.

Isabella wasn't a warm person. She didn't exchange confidences. She kept her own counsel. But she wasn't cold. The queen loved her children, and seemed, if not in love, then fond enough of her husband. She was regal and demure when she had to be, and wonderfully well informed as well. She was no idle ruler. William was more than a young squire and a messenger. His honest open ways had won the confidence of the queen, and she trusted him to bring her news. Her ladies brought her gossip, and she kept an ear to her kingdom in other ways as well. She managed the household, and kept her court happy, both her old retinue of retainers who had come with her from France, and the new ladies she had chosen. Gwenith both admired her and enjoyed her company.

But Gwenith worried of late, if she were really replacing Therese in all ways, and if she'd grow old here, and die, her mission unfulfilled, as her life would be. The thought made her shiver.

William misunderstood. He glanced at the sky. He stopped walking. "Lady," he said, with a low bow, "it does grow chill. I see by the sun that I must leave you now. I would not, were you not steps from your home. No harm can come to you here. Can you excuse me?"

"You, William? Always. You've come to be the brother I never had. Don't worry. I often walk here in the twilight. I know every step and every flower in the queen's privy garden, so lately I'm exploring. I saw a promising rosebud on a bush near the constable's tower the other day."

He smiled, bowed and left her. She strolled on, alone. There was little to fear here, within the confines of the Tower, even though she walked beyond the queen's quarters. The men she knew at court would never trespass so openly, and Hugh Despenser never strolled in the gardens. Here she was both safe and secure. Men at arms and warders were everywhere. If they noted her at all, they bowed, or nodded to her. She'd learned enough about court to know which people belonged here and which were visitors, tradesmen or even prisoners. She was obviously a lady, so those who didn't belong never disturbed her. Visitors didn't dare, tradesmen wouldn't bother and the prisoners already had enough trouble without approaching a lady.

So she was surprised when a man she didn't know appeared in front of her. "Lady?" he said.

He was neatly dressed in shades of gray; his boots were dark gray, his hat slate; even his tunic was the color of a knight's armor. He was as slender and dark as a Welshman, and his wide-set eyes were also gray. His long, craggy face was serious.

She didn't know him, but she recognized him.

"I've seen you many a time," he said in a deep voice with a trace of a familiar accent. "But never dared to introduce myself. I always saw you laughing with another man, or dancing, or in attendance on your queen."

"Our queen," she corrected him absentmindedly.

His smile was white, and banished all his graveness. "Yes," he said. "I'm Owain de Rhys, baron, knight and, presently, sojourner." He bowed. "Not a great lord, but a lord of the realm, nonetheless. My lands are in Wales, though I'm most often found near Ludlow these days . . . when I'm not here."

"Where in Wales?" she asked, eager to know if he was a relative.

"In the forests, some by the sea, and most no longer mine," he said with a shrug. "Wales belongs to Englishmen now. I've still got my name, my home, what's left of it, and my heartbeat, and for that, I'm grateful."

She studied his face. "I've seen you," she said, remembering. "I saw you the first day I came to court!"

"I had to leave the next, else we'd have met—that I promise you," he said, smiling.

"I thought I saw you again. . . . Do you always wear gray?" she asked. Then she laughed. "Forgive me. It just sprang to my lips."

"No need to forgive. It's an odd conceit. But did I dress in colors of the rainbow, would you have remembered me? Ah. See? In a field of color, it's the gray that's noticed."

"Well, but I thought you a monk."

He laughed. "Far from it."

"What do you do here? It's odd that I haven't met you before."

"Not so. I travel a good deal. Have I interrupted your walk? Pray, may I join you?"

She studied him a moment, then shrugged, curious enough to discover more about him.

"I have a friend here at the Tower," he said. "A dear friend to whom I owe allegiance. He saved my life and, in a way, my home."

She nodded. "A true friend indeed. Do I know him?"

"Doubtful," he said. "He is reclusive these days," he added with a crooked smile. "And you, lady? What brings you to Edward's court?"

"I was sent by Lady de Percy. I'm an orphan and a ward of the de Percys'. This way I can earn my keep. Surely you know I'm in attendance on the queen?"

"That, I do know," he said.

"And that," she said softly, "is why you sought me out."

He considered her. "Aye. I can't lie about that. But now that I have, I forget my reasons."

She laughed aloud. "I see. A minstrel, are you? A jongleur? Because I've seldom heard such an obvious romance. Do you know the tales of good King Arthur too? Those I'd enjoy more, I promise you."

He smiled. "Nay, neither a minstrel nor a teller of mighty tales. What I am is a Welshman, and so of course I can sing, though never for my supper. As for what I said about seeking you out, it sounds foolish, even to me. But it's so. Have you never had a mission, and then discovered that in pursuing duty, you found unexpected delight?"

Her smile faded. "Oh, aye," she said. "That, I have." She turned a serious face to him. "But in the end, it would always be duty that had the first call on me."

"And if duty and desire didn't clash?" he asked. "What if what you had to do, and what you wanted to, didn't conflict? Where would be the harm in that?"

Now she considered him. "I see none. If that's so for you, then you're fortunate. So, Sir Owain, what is your mission?"

"To have you arrange an audience with your queen for my friend. He has a boon to ask of her."

"Oh," she said, her disappointment more profound than she'd expected. "At least, sir, you're an honest man. I like that, though I confess I mislike it too. Now every word you say is suspect."

"And they weren't before?" he asked, raising one eyebrow.

She laughed. "Granted. So who is your friend?"

"Oh, no," he said, "you must give me time, and the chance to win you over. When I think you are tender to me, amenable to my every wish, like warm candle wax in my hands, only then will I tell you his name."

She laughed again. "Then, sir, you will never complete your mission."

He bowed. "Mayhap. But may I try? Will you walk with me now?"

"Walk, I will. Talk too. But become yours to shape? Nay. That, never."

"A challenge," he said. "I do like that. Now tell me. What is it that you like?"

Her eyes crinkled with laughter. "Nay again. It won't be that easy. Tell me about yourself, Sir Owain the Honest. And then, mayhap, do I choose, if I wish, then I may enlighten you." She slanted a look at him, liking the fact that his clothing was clean, his face fresh shaven. He had all his teeth. When he laughed, she saw they were even and white. He was well dressed and shod. All that marked him as a nobleman, of course. But many noblemen she'd met weren't half so fastidious as this fellow in gray.

"Very well," he said as they walked on. "I like horses. I used to breed them. I like good wine and a merry maid. I like good stories, and I like to sing. Well, but I already told you that I'm a Welshman. So you also know that I like to tell or listen to a fine, stirring tale. Now you?"

She shook her head. "It's not that simple, Sir Honest. Tell me the things that matter. Who are your people? Where do you live? Are you already wed? Or promised? And who are your enemies?" She looked away, startled by her boldness, but pleased with how she could speak with him, as though he were already a friend.

"My people are most of them dead, in the wars," he said. "I live, as I said, at Ludlow, when I'm not here. I'm not wed or betrothed, but I was betrothed, and my lady perished. My enemies are those who slew my family and my lady. And you?"

"Oh, a sad tale," she breathed. "But you're a Welshman, so that I could have expected. I could say the same. Save that I was never betrothed."

"Then we can be friends," he said. "Come, enough of this.

Let's talk about trivial things. It's too fine an evening to ruin with sorrows and regrets."

His comment made her realize they were walking into gathering darkness. It was almost time for the torches that guarded the front of every tower and gate to be lit. She looked at the sky. "So it was, but night comes now. I must to my lady."

"Then tomorrow?" he asked. "Here, in the gardens, at eventide? You will meet me again?"

She looked back at him, standing still as an evening shadow in the gathering dusk. "Aye," she said before she could regret it. "I will."

"And your name?" he called after her.

"But you must know that," she said, laughing, and ran lightly back to her queen.

She had never met a man she responded to as she had to Owain Rhys. She'd met many more handsome fellows here at court, though few, she granted, so glib. But then he was a Welshman, a countryman, and his very voice brought back fond memories to her. She could walk with him. . . . Gwenith slowed her steps. He hadn't said he'd see her at dinner, or to sup, or in the chapel for prayer. Only that he'd walk with her. A mystery, one she ought to solve. Her heart and her pace picked up. Now she had a very good excuse to see him again.

They met the next fair evening, and then the next, until Gwenith found their meetings as regular and looked for as the evening star. When it rained, she paced her chamber. When it was fair, she fairly flew to get her cloak and go down to the gardens to meet him.

He had traveled. Owain had seen the Saracens, and the Continent. He'd traveled to see Venice, and the Holy Land. He'd seen cities built on canals, and castles in the sands. Gwenith didn't know if everything Owain told her was truth. But he said it so well she no longer cared. She was very taken with him. The fact that he was a Welshman mattered, of course. It was that, she realized, that put her at ease. His simple garb also pleased her. Too often the knights and nobles wore velvets and silks in shades that put the peacocks, and herself, to shame.

The fact that he never presumed was interesting. He never stared at her lips, or edged closer as they walked, or hinted at other pleasures they might share. That suited her. She didn't have time in her life for dalliance. But he didn't know that. Or did he? He knew so much about everything else.

She admitted she was becoming much too fascinated by her evening companion. And the fact that he never appeared in the long hall or in the chapel, or met her by day, both interested her and made her anxious. Whenever she asked him more, he told her only a scrap of it, and then diverted her with charm and tact.

It had been two weeks since they'd met. They didn't walk every day. The weather wasn't always fair. And sometimes she couldn't be there, and other times, he obviously couldn't. But a fortnight was too long for a mystery. She resolved to clear it up this very afternoon. If she asked and he still refused to answer, she'd pretend to accept that. And then she'd ask William. William knew everything going on in the Tower confines. Doubtless he knew of her meetings with Owain. If she had to, she'd ask him if he knew more. But still, though they were only newly met, she disliked going behind Owain's back.

"Dreaming again?" Isabella asked.

Gwenith blushed, and looked down at the forgotten embroidery in her lap.

"What a man—to put roses in your cheeks," Agnes said. "In your cheeks? Nay, up to your hair!" she added, and the other ladies laughed.

"You've found a man you care for?" the queen asked in surprise.

"Nay. I found one to talk to," Gwenith said, scowling at Agnes.

"And, my lady, that surprises me as much as it does you. But he warned me he's a wayfarer, so I don't expect more than conversation."

"A wayfarer?" Isabella asked, frowning.

"A knight, lady, of high birth. But he's traveled the world, and I think he yearns to again."

Isabella nodded. "My sensible Gwenith, trust you to see it. Travel does that. It takes some men like a sickness. Once they leave their homes they can never rest easy anywhere on earth again."

Gwenith smiled at her. There was the bond that drew her to her queen, beyond her secret purposes.

"Do I know him?" Isabella asked.

Gwenith cast down her gaze, thinking furiously. She didn't want Agnes and the others to know of him. But it was too late now, of course. "He is called Owain Rhys. A Welshman."

"Oh, a Welshman," Agnes said. "Good looks, and fine conversation, doubtless. But he has not as much heft in his purse as he does in his breeches, I'd wager."

"Agnes!" Isabella said with rebuke, but then relented and laughed along with the other ladies.

"Aye, well but you know me, Majesty," Agnes said, unabashed.

"Well I do," Isabella said more seriously. Forgetting Gwenith's blushes, she began to lecture Agnes on chastity, or at least the dangers of promiscuity.

Gwenith didn't listen. She was thinking that Agnes was right. Something had changed. It might be, it could be—it was marginally possible that she might escape her fate. There might be a life for her after all. Because she had accepted that with all she wanted to do here, all she could reasonably do was to try. She'd thought it through, over and again. A single female could not bring down a king. But she had stayed two years, and so at least she could tell her grandmother's spirit that she tried. And failing that . . .

She truly had come to love her queen. She was now Isabella's sensible Gwenith. It honored her, and it terrified her. She didn't want to become another Therese. There had been no man who had threatened to save her from her course. But now?

"Gwenith," Isabella said, ending her lecture, "don't be so silent. I don't rebuke you. You're a reasonable person. I don't know your Welshman. But I trust in your good sense. Meet him and talk with him. If he hasn't been invited to our table, you may ask him. You can always bring a guest to sup or to festivals we have here. But whatever you do, do not follow in Agnes' footsteps."

"I haven't even been asked to," Gwenith said, and then blushed again.

"No?" Agnes said. "Then mayhap he's like William, the squire you sometimes also parade with."

The room fell still. Gwenith looked at her curiously.

"In that he doesn't care for women," Agnes explained blithely. "At least, not in bed. Or up against a wall or—" Her smile froze. Too late she realized what she had said and whom she was speaking in front of. Her hand flew to her lips. The room was deathly silent, as all the women darted glances at their queen.

It was Gwenith who came to her rescue. "I didn't know that," she said truthfully. "I do know he's a good fellow, and a fine friend."

"If your tongue is even half as loose as you are, Agnes," Isabella said sharply, "then you had best beware, for the sake of your soul, and your life."

Agnes kept silent.

And they all tended to their stitchery.

Thirteen

1323
THE NEXT DAY
THE GARDENS AT THE TOWER, LONDON

His eyes were fascinating, Gwenith thought. They changed color with his moods. This evening, Owain's gray eyes sparkled with light.

"You invite me to the feast? I'm honored," he told Gwenith. "I accept, with alacrity. I'd have preferred a tourney, because then I could have carried your colors in the joust."

"If you wished to ask a favor of my queen," Gwenith said, "it would be better to carry her colors."

He smiled down at her. "But I wish to please you."

She cocked her head to the side. "Ah, but which is more important to you?"

He waited only a heartbeat before he answered. "Can you not guess?"

Her eyes widened. So far, their meetings had only been amusing. She was free to let her daydreams go where they would, and they ranged far, but in the safety of her own mind. Now, if he were to suddenly be serious, then she'd have to be too. She didn't know him well enough to venture more than what she already had: light flirtation and growing companionship. She still didn't know who his friend here at the Tower was, or why she only saw him at the end of the day. She'd asked and he'd always answered, but nothing to the point. By the time she realized that, they'd gone on to something else. She'd asked him to the feast for the April Fool's Day, because it was an amusement, and because none but those who had the king or queen's favor were asked or allowed. It was the one thing, the only thing, she was prepared to give him, just yet.

"I'll be there," he said, "on a white horse, of course."

"I doubt he'll get a place at the board," she said with a straight face, and then he laughed with her.

They were strolling the walks at the Tower, watching the light fade slowly. It was a damp, misty evening, with few people lingering outside. Gwenith was very aware of that.

"Actually, a white horse would please Isabella," she commented. "Her favorite book shows King Arthur astride a white horse."

"She's interested in Pendragon?" he asked in surprise.

"Oh, more than that. She loves the tales of Arthur and his court."

"Indeed?" he mused. "My friend, the one I visit, is descended from good Arthur."

Gwenith laughed. "Everyone is, to hear them tell it. No one claims to be descended from river pirates or thieves, though England must have teemed with them. No, everyone must be kin of Arthur. Our king, Edward, claims it too. It is what interested the queen in the match when it was proposed to her. Not that she had anything to say about it, of course. But she told me that she met him when he was a boy, and she was amazed at how he looked like the young Arthur she'd always imagined. He told her it was so. And when, as a man come to France to be wed, all in gold, and so fair, she believed she'd finally found him."

"I've seen my friend's documents. They satisfy me," he said. "But then, I'm his friend."

"And who is he?" she asked. She stopped walking, turned to him and put up a hand. "Nay," she said seriously, "enough. I need you to tell me. I've walked with you and we've shared many a fine jest. But it's not fair that you keep such a secret from me. Not if we are, as you claim, friends."

He took the hand she'd raised in his. She let it lie in his light clasp, and looked up at him, wondering. Carefully, watching her expression every moment, he bent and brought his lips to her hand. She drew in a breath. He smiled, and bent further, gathered her up in his arms and kissed her, lightly, gently, so incredibly sweetly that when he raised his head she still stood, eyes closed, breathing rapidly.

She recovered swiftly. Her eyes flew open. "Yes, lovely," she said more harshly than she had intended, as she stepped back. "But not an answer."

His laughter seemed to take him by surprise. "Good," he said. "Now *that* is sensible Gwenith!"

"You know what the queen calls me?"

He nodded, his expression tender. "Yes, of course."

"Then it's not meet, fair it is not that this secret you keep from me," she said, her accent becoming stronger now that she was on the cusp of anger. She reined in her temper. "You know, if I wished, I could have asked and discovered all about you too. I've not done, because I felt it was underhanded to listen to gossip. But know that no place on this earth or in this kingdom breeds more gossip than the halls in which I live."

His expression sobered. "I know. But by its very nature, gossip is an unreliable handmaiden, mixing truth and falsehood without

understanding either. I knew the name the queen calls you, because it is always included when anyone speaks about you. And it
is warranted. Gwenith, I accept your invitation to the feast, with
pleasure. There, if you wish, I'll tell you all. But first I must ask my
friend's leave to do so. A man's story is as much his as any of his
possessions, and shouldn't be given out lightly. Can you wait to ask
the gossips until then?"

"Have I a choice?"

"Always. But will you?"

"Aye," she sighed, "I will. But it's only a matter of days. Why
don't you tell me now? I know," she said sadly. "It's because the
Fool's Feast celebrates all that is zany and backward and untrue."

"Nay," he said. "It's because I don't want to lose you."

"All festivals are delicious," Agnes said. "But I wouldn't miss this
one for anything."

"It's been a sad winter and a cruel spring," the queen agreed.
" 'Tis time for the Lord of Misrule to mend all with laughter. Pray
we can mend the kingdom so easily."

The ladies swept out of the queen's chambers. They wore pink
and red, yellow and green. Some wore masks, and all wore smiles,
even their queen. She was dressed in white velvet, her hair bound
high, with a headdress sewn with pearls. The only color was a blue
veil, and a great sapphire to match her eyes at her throat.

But when the ladies entered the hall, their brilliant colors
seemed drab in comparison. The hall was draped with boughs
and blossoms, the tables strewn with spring flowers. All present
were dressed in their finest, and they gleamed and glittered in
the torchlight. Everyone was laughing, because the jester was the
Lord of Misrule; he rode his flower-decked donkey backward
and flailed it with lilies as he backed it into one nobleman after
the other.

"Tonight, we have an April Fool. Misrule is our king," Edward said, as he rose to greet his queen. "And so I have the evening to myself . . . and you."

He took her hand and led her to her seat. Gwenith, following her queen, saw Isabella's eyes filled with unexpected tears. Tonight, Edward looked more regal than ever. She gazed at her queen, wondering why she seemed so stricken.

When Edward had seated his queen, Isabella turned her head and saw Gwenith watching her with concern.

Isabella smiled, slightly. "Tonight," Isabella whispered to Gwenith, "he looks like the youth I fell in love with years ago."

Edward the king wore a long white tunic with gold at its dagged sleeves and, round his neck, a heavy chain of gold to match. A slender filet of gold was his crown tonight. His bright hair floated around his fair face when he turned his head, and for a moment, Isabella shivered, remembering the feeling of it on her skin when they had made love. He'd never been impassioned, nor she released. But the very act of love with him—the closeness, the touching and the fact that for that small moment he was helpless but for her—had ever been enough for her.

As he looked at her, his fine blue eyes filled with tenderness and slow, sweet acknowledgment of mutual erotic expectation. She smiled. Then she heard Gwenith's indrawn breath, and finally saw the direction of her husband's gaze and realized he was looking at Hugh Despenser, who also stood behind her.

"You may go to your seat," she told Gwenith stonily.

Gwenith went to her table and sat next to Agnes, but she didn't pay attention to her, or to any female at the long table or in the crowd of merry guests. She was too busy scanning the company, looking for a gap in among the mass of vibrant color, searching for a man in gray.

Agnes noticed, of course. "He must be wondrous, indeed, to get our little Gwenith is such a state," she said with a laugh.

"He's not here," Gwenith said. She stifled her surging disappointment and turned a calm face to Agnes. "So tell me, what goes on here tonight?"

"As much as comes off," Agnes said with a laugh, "if you're lucky. Ah, don't worry. Nothing is expected of anyone, except merriment. We eat and drink, and there are contests to see who can tell the most marvelously ridiculous tale. Some wear masks, and some wear their garments inside out, in the spirit of the Fool. Mostly, we enjoy ourselves. Don't fret," she added in a softer voice. "Mayhap your man found himself unable to come today."

"He's not my man," Gwenith exclaimed. "I'm only surprised because he seemed to want to be here."

"Well," Agnes said with a shrug, "it is the day for all things backward. Mayhap the more he wanted to come, the farther he'll stay away. Ah, don't listen to me. Too much small beer, too much ale. I'd best keep my mouth closed, except for even tastier things. And I do *not* mean the sweets or savories. Fare thee well, Gwenith. I see my man beckoning to me."

"Where?" Gwenith asked.

"*That* you need not know," Agnes said, as she stood and smoothed her tunic over her hips. "Not you, nor his wife, nor his mistress. Give you a good night. We'll meet again in the morning." She left the trestle table.

Gwenith sighed, because now Mary launched into another denunciation of Agnes' conduct. But she did so with such relish that Gwenith began to think that if Agnes reformed, took the veil and repaired to a nunnery, Mary would fall into a decline.

Gwenith stared into the crowd of revelers, watching their swirling colors, hearing their raucous laughter. The queen, beautiful in white, sat watching with a small smile. Her oldest children joined her tonight, Prince Edward, his face ever grave and watchful, and Prince John, also silent and awed by the company. The king, handsome and youthful, looking like the prince in a book of tales, was laughing at every jest, and there were dozens of them and not all from the jester this night. There was peace in the kingdom, at least at the moment, and it was springtime again. This April Fool's celebration was both a pageant and a feast.

The Fool gave the blessing before they ate, and earned himself a kick from the chaplain for it, which made him caper off and leap up on his donkey again.

The food before Gwenith was incredibly good. There was an aviary of birds offered this night: capons and geese, of course, but also gulls and herons, swans and cranes, even tiny roasted songbirds that looked more tragic than delicious to her. There was venison, pork and mutton, as always. But also a sea of eels and salmon, haddock, herring, sturgeon, cod and mussels, oysters and other fish, as well as something strange and thick on the tongue that the server said was whale. She didn't taste it, but then she hardly ate at all. Her trencher held a bit of many things, all in good rich sauces, and all untouched by her.

She had no appetite. The beggars would eat well tonight, at least those who got her trencher when the meal was over would. She scarcely emptied her cup and wouldn't have known it except that, when the pages came round to refill it, they offered her different brews before they passed her by. How foolish she was become, to think a man who owed her nothing, met her in secret and kept his own secrets would keep his word. She told herself she was well shut of him. But she felt as though she'd lost something important, even if it had only been hope.

"I've been waving to you for this eternity," a soft voice said at her ear. "Fie, fickle lady, to not even have looked for me."

She turned her head and stared into bright gray eyes. But tonight he was dressed in brilliant shades. His tunic was red as blood, his hose, bicolored, one leg yellow and the other brown. His brown hair was covered with a soft, flat yellow cap crowned by twining green peacock feathers.

"You like my disguise?" Owain asked. "A peacock among peacocks becomes invisible, though, I confess, I hurt my own eyes."

He was smiling. She couldn't help but smile back at him.

"But why must you be in disguise?" she asked.

"Because it's the Feast of the Fool," he answered. "And I didn't feel quite fool enough. Are you done eating?"

She nodded, too excited and delighted by his presence to speak at all.

"Then come, let's play. We'll dance and jest. And then," he said more softly, "we will talk. That, I promise."

They did dance, and they jested, and they roared, along with everyone else, when the donkey pitched the backward fool off his back and into a group of food servers. The Fool emerged, dripping gravy, the servers ran away and the court couldn't stop laughing.

There was a great deal of drinking too, but Gwenith still touched little, and she never saw Owain raise a cup to his lips. She thought things really must move backward this day, because as time went on and the feast grew more riotous, her worries and fears began to emerge and grow again.

"You're frowning," Owain said. "So time to talk, I think."

"Oh, aye," she said.

He drew her out of the hall and into the corridor, and then out a door into the cool, damp night. They paused at last, under the inconstant illumination of a flaming torch that flumed and sputtered on the wall of the White Tower.

"The night air isn't healthy," he said. "Nor is it safe, even here. But we'll only venture out in it for a little while, because this is the only quiet place tonight—at least, the only place close by. I'll tell you all now. First, please, come, give me the kiss of peace."

She stared up at him. "Because you think I won't after you speak with me?"

His smile was tilted. "Sensible Gwenith, aye."

Her heart was heavy as she raised her face to his. But the touch of his mouth was as gentle and sweet as she remembered, and the warm, solid warmth of him as he held her close made her forget her fears. He raised a hand to the side of her face, and moved closer still, his mouth seeking, his tongue speaking of things she didn't know but longed to learn. She was entranced.

And then he stepped away.

She'd never known such a kiss. It wasn't just the thrill of it or the warmth she felt in her nether parts; she felt as though she'd found a home again. The feel of him, the taste of him, his very touch banished the loneliness that had become such a part of her that she felt strange, and liberated, without it. She looked at him with hope and gladness.

But he looked at her without lust or joy.

"Gwenith," he said, "I come here every day to visit my liege lord. He's a prisoner in the Red Tower. But he saved my life, and I owe him my loyalty and my good right arm. It isn't only a vow forsworn. I confess I've hopes that one day he'll restore all to me: my castle, poor though it may be in comparison to the wonders of London; my lands, all of them; and my soul's peace again. Because I also swore myself to the defense and succor of my people, and that must always be foremost with me. My people lost everything," he said softly, "as did I. My liege lord spared my life, and refused to have my home burned to the ground. I work to restore myself, and my people, and by that, I mean to restore him to power, and freedom."

"Have you petitioned the king?" she asked.

His smile was bitter. "There's no chance of mercy from that quarter, I promise you."

"Oh," she said with a sigh that drained all hope from her heart. "I see. It's Isabella you would have an audience with."

"Nay. Not me. My liege lord. Did he but have a chance to speak to her, I know all would be righted."

She fell still, remembering Lancaster, and how little chance enemies of the king had to speak, to anyone.

"Who is he?" she asked, although she knew it didn't matter anymore. At least, not to her.

"Mortimer," he said. "Roger Mortimer."

She gasped, drew back and crossed herself. "Mortimer? The beast?" she hissed. "He who would have killed every living man and woman and child in Wales? He who bore brave Llewellyn's head to Longshanks? Curs't Mortimer, whose very name is poison to every Welshman?"

"Nay, hush, not so," he whispered, looking to see if anyone was out in the night who might hear. "Am I not a Welshman? Have I not said that he was my savior? It was his uncle, Mortimer of Chirk, who took brave Llewellyn's head. Mortimer was blameless in that. His own father was killed in the wars. Longshanks placed him under the guardianship of Piers Gaveston, and then he was knighted. And now the king declares him a traitor? I vow he has no more love for the enemies of Wales than we do. Aye, I said 'we.' Because you are a Welshwoman, Gwenith, tell me what you will of living with the de Percys. I see it in your eyes, hear it in your voice and know it in my heart. Mortimer rules Ludlow now. He has sympathy for us. But he hates . . ." He closed his eyes and shook his head. "Rather say that he has no sympathy for errant kings with greedy advisers. He's seen enough of that.

"It was his support of Hereford and Lancaster, his riding to their cause, that brought him to the Tower. But he was a brave general for His Majesty in Ireland, and in Wales, respected by his men, and even by his enemies. He has done no harm but only acted out of love of country. There are men in England now who plunder her, but not Mortimer. Nor would he. That, I vow."

She put a hand to her head. "I've been a very great fool." She laughed. "Indeed, this is a good and fit night for you to tell me this, is it not? But I vow you'd have done better asking Lady Agnes, or another of Isabella's maidens. Not me. I'm unused to the ways of court, indeed, in the ways of life, I suppose."

"Nay," he said. "Or mayhap, aye. True that I sought you out because of your ties to Isabella. But she has many ladies, and I only sought you."

"Because I'm the least informed," she said, nodding. "The newest come to her, the weakest link. I see."

"Nay, because you called to me. There are others who would have been easier to recruit to my cause, those who think less and want to feel more, or who are ruled by flattery and dumb to lies."

"But none closer to the queen, nonetheless," she said bitterly.

"What I did then and how I feel now are very different things, Gwenith."

"Aye, and of course you would say that."

He paced a small way from her and came back. His expression was stark. "There's no way I can prove it. But so, I swear it is. I would do so on a Bible, on my vows as a knight. I can see you don't believe me, nor do I blame you; too many knights have sullied their vows out of greed and ambition. Still, whatever my vows are, or are not, I need your help. If you will not out of love for me, and I can't blame you for that, then think of your love for Wales. Mortimer *will* restore it, so much as he can.

"I do not say he will do it out of love, but from necessity. He needs friends on his borders. No man wants to spend his life fighting, forced to leave war for his heirs. He's only a Marcher lord, but he can give back those lands that lie on his boundaries, and will, to those he owes, and those he trusts. One thing I know, he will restore me and what is mine, and that is my life's goal. Meet him, see him, speak with him, and you will see for yourself. The man is devoted to England, and no enemy to good men of Wales. Nor is he Isabella's enemy. He is not, and never was. All he wants is a chance to speak with her. A chance to plead his innocence. He's marked for death."

"Because he's the king's enemy," Gwenith said flatly.

Owain said nothing. He did not deny it.

She fell still, hearing the echo of her words, thinking about what she'd said.

Owain stayed silent, watching her as she stood, eyes downcast for a moment. And then, slowly, she looked back at him. Thoughts of love, which had both comforted and overwhelmed her, had vanished. Her head was as clear as her heart was cold. It was a relief as much as it was a crushing disappointment. But she had no time for it now. She remembered her goal, her purpose in life. She considered him. "He thinks Isabella will free him?"

"He doesn't know. It's something we must try."

"And if she can't or won't?"

"Then he will attempt other means of escape from his unjust sentence."

"But no man can escape the Tower," she said.

"No man has," Owain said, "as yet."

Fourteen

1323, April
All Fools' Night
The Tower, London

"I will not have it!" Isabella whispered fiercely. "Do what you must in private but I will not have you making mock of me in front of everyone."

Edward the king ran a hand over his bloodshot eyes. He'd been drinking heavily this night. "That's nonsense," he muttered. "I wasn't even thinking of you." They stood in a darkened niche off the great hall. Gwenith stood nervously in the shadows, because she'd followed her queen when Isabella suddenly rose to go and hurried out of the hall, fearing she was ill, never suspecting Isabella was going in order to berate her husband, the king.

"And why did you call me here?" he complained. "I thought there was some great difficulty. Instead, I find you here waiting to attack me. Fie, madam, this is no way to behave."

"And fondling Despenser is?" she exclaimed.

"Fondling?" he laughed. "A gentle touch in passing is now

fondling? Now I think it's you who had too much wine to-night."

"A gentle touch on his *ass*?" she asked. "He stands beside you, in front of all the court, and you reach out and fondle his but-tocks?"

"It's a festival, in celebration of Fools," he said. "I meant noth-ing by it. It was a rude jest—that's all. No one but you thought ought of it."

"Have you learned nothing?" she cried. "They took Piers' life because of your blatancy. Next time, it may be yours."

He straightened and a cold, sane light sprang into his eyes. "Is that a threat? Because it's a hollow one. I am king. I touch whom-ever I choose, whenever and wherever I want. And be damned to you for mentioning Piers in such a way. My enemies killed him. I have killed them. Let them all be, for God's sake, madam."

"And Despenser grinning back at you, your hand still on him. In front of his father, and the court, preening like a village slut who has just been picked from the midden to be tupped by her lord," Isabella went on, tears in her eyes now. "His father is naught but a pander. But I will not be so belittled. I am queen!"

He waved a hand at her. "Oh, aye," he said wearily. "Queen. Princess and queen. And your father was king, and so is your brother, and so all your brothers are or will be. Aye and aye, can't you learn a new tune? I've heard it before. And so what? *My* father was king. *My* ancestors were kings. What of it? It's of no moment. Speak of village sluts? You rail at me like the lowliest one might do, if she dared. Have done. Men stray. They have their diversions. So do women. They are no better. By God, madam," he said with a snarl, "you of all people know that."

She put her hand to her forehead. "Then stray. Go where you will with whom you choose. Lie with a pig for all I care. But not in front of me, and your children, and your court."

"I will do what I will, when I want," he said. "Accept that, and let me be. Your jealousy does you more harm than my play ever will."

"Play?" she said incredulously. "Were it only that, I might. But to remind everyone of why you favor him to the point of slighting others? You deck him with prizes stolen from your loyal lords. You recall him from his exile in spite of the wishes of the barons."

"In spite of the wishes of my *enemies*," he said with sudden dignity.

"The Scots are your enemies, the Welsh, the men of Flanders, and mayhap many more. Pay attention to them in public, not to your lover. Can you not remember what happened before?" she asked. "It may well be that the court doesn't care who you lie with. You have good reason to know they do care how you reward your lovers. I only ask that you do not repeat history. Lie with Hugh Despenser—do whatever you will with him—but do it with discretion."

"Discretion? Ah, there it is. You *French*," Edward said coldly. "That's all you care about: discretion, tact, good manners, even when you knife a man in his back. I am an Englishman, and I'm King of the English, and I do as I damned please. Right, Hugh?" he asked and turned so Isabella could finally see who stood in the shadows behind him.

Hugh Despenser shrugged and spread his hands in front of him. "Sire, it is not my place."

"See?" Edward said, facing Isabella again. "*There* is tact. *That* is discretion. What more do you want? Well, whatever it is, I haven't got it. I give you good night, madam. I need laughter, not anger. There's a great feast going on without me in my great hall, and there's not a sorrier sight in the kingdom than a feast without a master, eh, Hugh?"

"Nay, sire," Hugh said, smiling. "Go then. I'll join you. But first, I've a word for your gracious queen."

"Best make it tactful," Edward said with a measure of spite, "and discreet." He hiccoughed, then laughed, made a great show of swatting Hugh on the rear and left, laughing.

Isabella watched him stagger down the hall.

"Majesty?" Hugh said softly.

She turned to him.

He smiled. "Your lord drank too much this night," he said. "That's all."

"And so I am to forget all I saw?" she asked coldly.

"Oh, nay!" he laughed. "Remember what you will. And this too: I mean him no harm. I do him no harm. Nor would I ever do any to you. I know, I know," he said, throwing up a hand as if she had threatened to hit him. "You've heard terrible things about me. My dear wife has your ear, has she not? I've asked her not to burden you, but she's weak and delights in whining. I don't doubt she's lamented on your shoulder. She's a good woman. She's given me a quiver full of heirs. But her sisters nag at her and make her feel guilty for whatever peace she has found in our union. And our marriage, like yours, was nothing to do with how we felt about each other when we met. We are all of us pawns on a great game board, and we go through the major moves in our lives without knowledge or even consent. But our pleasures? We take them where we may, do we not?"

She stood rigid, not answering him. As she looked at him, she wondered again what it was that Edward found appealing in the man. His face was dark and blunt, as was his body. He was sturdily built, but one day would no doubt have the same great belly that his father carried before him like a prize. She distrusted and disliked him, knowing him as her enemy, and not just because he had Edward's love—she'd long since ceded that would never really be hers—but because he did have Edward's trust and approval, which in the long term, mattered more. And she had no doubt that Hugh wanted to be in their lives for a very long time. Still, knowing Edward's past infatuations, she marveled how this rough man had

managed to capture much less keep Edward's ever-wayward affections.

"He is what he is," Hugh said softly. "And those who love him
accept that."

"And you love him?" she said bitterly. "And would, I suppose,
even if he were not king? Strange that is, when no one can remember you loving a man before. You prey upon his weakness."

His laughter seemed genuine. "Nay, lady, I foster his strengths.
I make him happy and ease his mind. He is no less a man for
where he finds surcease. Never think it. No man is, so long as he
finds a willing partner."

"Oh, aye"—she sneered—"that I believe. He has found a very
willing one, although it is odd that his partner was never so inclined before. He takes from his king what he would not from any
other man, but that only because he *is* the king."

"Wrong," he said, with a smile. "He takes from me, lady, in
all ways. And that only because he knows I know what's best for
him."

She closed her eyes in pain, remembering what she had seen
once of her husband's lovemaking with another man, and opened
them again. They blazed with anger. "Do not brag to me about
your play," she whispered. "Nor think that you ever have the superior role, whatever position you hold. He is still king. That will
not change, unless you speak of treason."

"Nor do I want to change it. You doubt my feelings for my
king?"

"No," she said. "I know what you feel for him. If it is lust, it
is lust for more than flesh. You want the rewards that come with
his affection."

His smile grew. "Ah, there it is," he said, nodding. "You don't
understand. I am a man of many parts. I do like women. Very
much indeed." His gaze went over her with thorough insolence.
"But there's also great pleasure to be gotten from a man, pleasure

of a different sort, though no less keen. It's like loving a part of your own self. Aye, you were right. I never did desire men before, but now? I do. At least, one of them. Yet I still desire beautiful women. And why? I tell you, Majesty, I know more of the flesh than you do. I know that there are more ways to pleasure than you can guess."

He moved so close to her she could smell the ale he had drunk and the sauces he had eaten on his every exhalation.

"Ours is such a short and brutish life," he said in a low purr. "Why not take pleasure when and where we can find it?"

"Because a man is more than a pleasure seeker," she said. "And I tell you, Hugh Despenser, what you do with my husband is not love, but only what any castle whore does up against a wall, for her livelihood. Only she is more honest about it, and more deserving. Because you have enough riches, and only seek more."

His smile faded. "Another thing I know is that an empty bed gives a woman a hard heart," he said. "I can understand that. My Eleanor is as tender as a dove. I've given her ten children. But what are you to do? We're far from Scotland here."

She was shocked that he'd throw old gossip at her, his queen. But she recovered quickly. "Eleanor must bless her king," she said through her teeth. "At least now she has some rest, and some solace. She can know her trials were never her fault. A man who *loves* as you do can never return love to any woman . . . or man."

"Eleanor," he said, taking a step closer, "values me and obeys me. She does my bidding with alacrity. And with joy. She never has to suffer the pangs of loneliness, because she too knows the love of her king."

Isabella's eyes widened. He stood too close, but she refused to back down. He could not mean what he had just said.

He nodded. "Aye, just what you think," he whispered. "Our king likes good company at all times, even when he's at all kinds of sport. So do I. It's delicious, the best of both worlds. I see you understand what I mean. You blanch? But why? A man on the side is no better or holier than one on either side of you. At least not in the eyes of the church. But you know that. You're not so holy, Majesty, nor so untouchable, are you?"

She gaped at him.

"My father is the fellow for tact," he said. "Me, I'm a plain-spoken man. It is what it is. You heard aright. Edward enjoys my company, in all things." He waited a moment, and then added, "You might think on the joys of accommodating us both, as my dear Eleanor has learned to do. You can ask her if you wish. She'll tell you straight enough, after she makes her usual moans and protests. . . ." He grinned. "Aye, she'll tell you that those moans and protests turn to cries of pleasure soon enough."

They were now almost nose to nose. Isabella's voice was soft, and shaking, but also cold and deadly. "Touch me, but once, Hugh Despenser, and you will be dead, your privy parts on a pike with my banner and arms on it."

"Oh, don't worry. I never would without permission," he said, laughing. "But I remind you that Edward is your master, madam. As for tonight, I'm sorry. I regret I have a feast to get back to, and already have made my plans and promises for this evening."

He bowed and, smiling, turned and walked away.

Isabella stood, one hand on the wall to hold her up, until Gwenith at last stepped from the shadows, and stood beside her.

"You heard?" Isabella asked.

"Aye, Highness," Gwenith said in a shaken whisper. "I was here. I'll always be beside you, to see if you need help."

"I do," Isabella said. "But you cannot provide it."

"Have done!" Edward cried, clapping both hands to his ears and holding his head.

"Have done?" Isabella asked in a furious whisper. "The man as much as said you shared his wife with him! Eleanor? Poor, dragged-out Eleanor? She's bred so many times her breasts must be dugs by now, her body like a slug. Her mind has certainly gone soft. Is it so?"

They were in her chamber. At least he'd come alone to visit her when she'd sent word that she must see him immediately. He sat huddled in a chair by the window. The clean morning light showed his complexion to be sallow. His eyes were still red, and they were puffy. She didn't doubt that his head hurt. What time his revels had ended, she didn't know. She'd gone to her chamber after Hugh had spoken to her, and she'd sat up, thinking furiously, until the dawn.

Gwenith sat quietly in the corner, unnoticed. The queen hadn't asked her to leave. At times like this, Gwenith began to realize she was really becoming like Therese—so expected that she was unseen, so powerless she wasn't regarded. The idea appealed as much as it repelled her. She could learn much this way. But she could still do nothing.

"I tell you the man suggested I share you with him," Isabella told Edward fiercely. "Or that you share me, it scarcely matters." She shook her head. "His *queen*? How *dare* he?"

"Oh, Hugh," Edward said weakly. "He'd dare anything."

"I am your queen," she said. "How could you allow him to say such a thing and still remain so calm about it?" She blinked. "Edward. There were vile rumors about Piers and the two of us, but they were without grounds. We both know that. At least so far as I was concerned."

"You were a child, a babe," Edward said. "He loved you like a brother, nothing more."

"So I know. But this Hugh Despenser," she went on relentlessly. "Did you tell him to ask such a thing of me? Did you know of this? Do you countenance this?"

He waved his hands as though fending off a cloud of gnats. "No, no, I never said—" He stopped and looked up at her. "Hugh

176

has diverse tastes. He has long admired you." He looked away from the growing fury in her eyes. "I merely congratulated him on his good taste. That's all there is to that. You are Queen, as you never tire of reminding me. You don't have to do a thing you don't want to do."

"And what do you want?" she asked.

The room was still.

"I want to be left alone," he finally said, piteously. "I want you to be happy, to have you stop attacking me. But as I love Hugh like a brother, I wish him to be happy too. He's not such a bad fellow, only unlike anyone you've ever met."

She drew herself up. "Does he touch but the hem of my skirt and I will call my men at arms and have him slain on the spot. Does he try but once more to gain my bed, by word or deed, and I will leave this place and go back home to my brother, the king, and I will return with such an army as England has never seen, and I will scatter all before me, and have Hugh Despenser's heart on a spear and his head on a pike. Know this, Edward. Do not forget it. Tell your lover as much, or by God, I will. You know that if I do, then he'll say something vile, and I will get angry, and all we have built will be sundered."

"Peace! Peace!" he cried. "What is this nonsense? Armies? Destruction? You are a woman, and my queen. Have you run mad?"

"Nay, I've come to my senses," she said.

"Enough," he said, flapping a hand at her. "Enough of this madness. Hugh will not trouble you again. This will never be spoken of again. It was but a fancy, a jest gone too far. Forget it, and for God's sake, let me be."

"Never!" she said. "Promise me that."

"I do. I shall. It's over. My head is splitting. Have you said all?"

She nodded.

He rose. "Then I'm leaving. Let me be."

Isabella gave another curt nod and, holding her trembling hands together tightly, watched as he left the room.

"Gwenith," Isabella finally said, without looking into the corner of her chamber, "you heard all, but then, you saw all last night. But not a thing you saw or heard must ever leave your mouth, unless it is spoken to me. It that understood?"

"Highness, it always has been," Gwenith said softly. "I only wish I could do more for you."

"You were here," Isabella said, "as my Therese would have been. That comforts me. Nothing else can be done."

He looked every inch a king. Lean and well proportioned, from his neatly barbered dark gold hair to the small, well-shaped beard on his strong jaw, and his intelligent dark blue eyes, he looked, Gwenith supposed, the way the man he claimed as ancestor must have done. Except King Arthur was long dead or might never have existed, but Roger Mortimer, Baron Wigmore, definitely lived, at least for the moment, imprisoned at the Tower.

Gwenith had thought for days about meeting this man, until she felt impelled at last to try to do something to wake herself from her inertia, to risk herself at last. She'd stayed awake the night before, dreading this visit. At least this time, she didn't have to wait for the evening to come. It was only late afternoon. The prisoners were herded back to their rooms at twilight. She'd endured many a jest because of her request to be free this afternoon, and much teasing besides. But Isabella was preoccupied and had listened with half an ear. She'd absently waved a hand to still her ladies, and granted Gwenith the time to herself. Gwenith knew it was a good day to have it; she wouldn't be missed very much, because everyone at court was recovering from the Feast of Fools. But she felt like the greatest fool of all.

Because although Roger Mortimer was a commanding figure, even an elegant one, he was only yet breathing because his date with the executioner hadn't been set. There was no way this man could help himself, much less Gwenith's long-lost cause. He was marked for death. And with sinking spirits, she realized she was a fool for worrying, for imagining herself daring, for even thinking a visit from her could mean anything.

He didn't act like a doomed man. He was calm and dignified. He exuded confidence and power, though his jailers watched to be sure he didn't stray from the paths he was allowed. He bowed to Gwenith when they met, and then strolled the small circle on the paths he was permitted with her and Owain.

"No sense inventing tales at this point," he told Gwenith. "You know very well why I need to speak with your queen. There is no one else I can appeal to. I am not England's enemy, nor good Isabella's, not by any sense of the word. I served my country well all my life. I was lord lieutenant of Ireland for Edward, and drove the Bruce and his cohorts out of power in his name. I've kept order in my part of the Marches for him for years. But I did not support the Despensers, and for that, my head is forfeit. I only wish to plead my case."

"I've asked about you, as though at random, ever since Owain Rhys mentioned you," Gwenith said carefully. "Edward the king's greatest complaint against you is that you refused to answer his summons last year when he was tallying the loyalty of his barons. That was when Hereford and Lancaster were plotting against him, and that is what put you in the enemy camp."

Mortimer looked at her with approval. "You've wit. I don't know that Owain might not have done better to seek the aid of a pretty fool. I jest," he said, when she frowned. "A fool is a man's worst ally. So let me tell you the truth: I refused the invitation to London because I questioned the rule of the Despensers, not my king. He has ever had my loyalty."

Gwenith fell still. She didn't believe that, but it wasn't her place to say so. And his disloyalty to the king was not, after all, contrary to her own purpose. She kept looking at the baron, trying to assess with her eyes the likelihood of this man ever helping her cause. He was strong and determined, well spoken and obviously accustomed to battle. On his forehead, he had a scar that ended in his eyebrow, and another across his cheek. They only added to the sense of force in the man. He was, even if a step from the execution block, a man to be reckoned with. If he ever were set free he could rally an army. He could . . .

But she doubted he ever would be free. Such a man was too dangerous an enemy. Still, though she didn't know how she could achieve it, she didn't see how Isabella speaking to him now could hurt her or her cause.

"The queen coming to visit you would excite gossip," she said. "Edward might even forbid it."

He nodded. "Just so. I may have visitors, and I have done. And a lady would never show her face when visiting me either in my rooms or anywhere here in the Tower."

"I am visiting you," Gwenith said.

He nodded. "But you are with Owain, and all already know Owain is my man. Still, if you are afraid this visit will harm your position, leave now, and I will understand."

"I've considered it," she said. "I won't stay long. And when I leave you, I'll go to see Sir de Brough, an old friend of the de Percys, who is also in the Tower. I do not know what his fate is to be, but all know he was ever a friend to my lord de Percy."

"You think things through," Mortimer said with appreciation "Now can you not think of a way for me to speak to your queen?"

"You ask a lot," Gwenith said. "How can she be sure you won't attempt to harm her? How can I be sure of it?"

"Because I give my word," he said, then laughed. "A dead man's word is good for nothing, I understand. But she may come with guards, if it please her. I will not harm her. What purpose would it serve? If I wanted to die sooner, I'd take my own life."

Gwenith was still, thinking about it.

"I pledge my life that she will come to no harm," Owain said.

"Life is cheap here," Gwenith answered. "Let me think on. I cannot say aye or nay until I do."

"If aught goes awry," Owain persisted, "your name will never be mentioned."

She looked up at him gravely. "If aught went awry? I serve Isabella, and would now, I think, even if I did not have to. I'd never put her in harm's way. If aught went awry, I would myself arm against you, and not rest until you were repaid for your treachery."

"So small a lady and so fierce a one," Mortimer said with a laugh.

It was the one wrong thing for him to say, because it made Gwenith reconsider him.

"I would not want to be her enemy," Owain said quickly. "Size never accounts for spirit, or bravery, or power, not in the long run, else we'd be ruled by giants, my lord."

"Too true. Forgive me, my lady," the baron said. "I never meant to offend."

She smiled, but was not reassured. Still, though it saddened her, it did not make her question his honesty. Most men didn't credit females with sense; fewer still feared their anger. Why should they? However clever a woman was, she thought sadly, she seldom had any power, and that was what ruled the world, in whatever shape or size it took.

She took a deep breath. "I said I will think on, and I will. I'll let Owain know my decision. I wish you luck, my lord, and hope for your ultimate deliverance."

Mortimer's eyes narrowed. "Deftly put, but not too comforting, since my deliverance now depends on you."

Fifteen

1323, May
The Tower, London

Isabella couldn't sleep. It was the height of the night, and the Tower was silent. She had never felt so alone. Her children, her one solace, were in their beds, sleeping. Her brothers were far away across the channel; her closest friends were gone in one way or another. Eleanor was Hugh's wife, and his willing cuckold, or so he said. Isabella hadn't been able to bring herself to speak with her since the night Hugh had made his vile proposal. Elizabeth de Clare, her dearest friend, like her, a pawn of politics and fate, was pent up in Barking Abbey with her two children.

Isabella could not even seek out those pledged to her, her retinue, the two dozen or more who had come with her from France all those years ago: her chaplains, her doctor, her old family friends of high degree. It had been good to talk with them, but increasingly, as her shame grew, it became harder to do, because of the pity in their eyes. Those that had come with her from France were loyal, but she had learned that nationality did not bring any commonality of spirits. She was ashamed of how she was treated in front of them, and they were shamed for her.

She adored her children, especially her son Edward. To look into his eyes was to remember a time when she had believed she was loved. But he was only a boy, and so she fought her love for him because she knew too many boys who had never grown to be men, through war or sudden disease. Childhood was not an easy passage. She had lost one great love in her life, a secret from everyone but her Creator. She refused to allow herself that depth of emotion again, lest she lose another.

Isabella had a kingdom, but no equal here: no confidante, no loving nurse. Of all the hundreds in the Tower precincts, whom could she call friend? She could have woken her servants to divert her. But it was midway through the night and that would cause gossip she didn't want to deal with. She trusted only Gwenith, but didn't want to disturb even her. Her bed curtains weren't completely closed, and she could see the girl was sleeping peacefully on her cot at the foot of her queen's bed.

But Isabella's body prickled and itched, and her thoughts went round and round in a circle. She couldn't sleep for thinking of things she should have said, worrying about things that might happen and grieving for the way her life was unfolding. She was so distracted she couldn't wait for morning. She had to leave her bed. She sat up.

A dark shape immediately rose at the foot of her bed. Gwenith sat up too.

"You weren't sleeping?" Isabella asked, secretly delighted to find a companion in the darkest hours of the night.

"Nay, lady, I could not." Gwenith had sensed her wakeful mistress and seen in it the chance she'd been hoping for. Gwenith had stayed awake until she felt it the right time to make her move.

"What? Is something troubling you?"

"Many things," Gwenith said. "Pardon me. Did I keep you from your slumbers?"

"Your thoughts may have been racing, but I didn't hear them," Isabella said, chuckling. "But well met. I cannot sleep either. What troubles you?" she asked, eager to have any respite from her own tumultuous thoughts.

"Nothing I should bother you with, lady," Gwenith said softly.

"I just asked you to," Isabella answered.

"Aye, lady, but what troubles me is a thing I was asked to ask you about and . . ."

Isabella laughed. "I hope your sheets are not as tangled as your thoughts. Come, tell me. Whatever it is, I wish to hear it."

She heard Gwenith take in a long, shuddering breath. "Lady," Gwenith said, "I'm grateful for the dark, because I could not say these things to you in the light." But it was as if she could see the sudden impatient gesture Isabella made, because she went on. "You know," she said, "that I have been walking out of an evening with a man, a knight, a Welshman."

"Ah, me," Isabella sighed, disappointed. She felt a sudden stab of sorrow. She missed her faithful Therese keenly at that moment: Therese, who would never have dallied with any man, but who devoted her life to her queen. "You didn't take my advice. You followed in Agnes' footsteps, did you? Folly. Though I do not say it is moral or right, Agnes is clever and experienced. She sins, but prudently—that is to say, she knows enough to practice restraint, or has her lovers do so. Poor girl, you don't know what I'm talking about, do you? The villain. I'm afraid the only answer for you is to wed him, or that being impossible, return to Lady de Percy, have the child and then come back to me.

"I'll not let you be entirely ruined," she said, before Gwenith could answer. "I will find a match for you, as soon as may be." And another companion for myself, she added silently.

"Oh, no, lady!" Gwenith gasped. "I have not dallied. Nor has he asked me to. He is a noble knight."

"He is a man," Isabella said. "So mayhap he is promised to another? Or has another in his eye?"

"Nay, not that I know of," Gwenith said. "We have not come to that." Isabella's silence was enough of an answer for Gwenith to add quickly, "Nor is he uninterested or"—she hesitated and, as if on sudden inspiration, added—"or like . . . William, in his preferences."

Isabella laughed in spite of herself. "You mustn't listen to Agnes in anything! She thinks any man who doesn't want to bed her is a man who doesn't want to bed any woman. I have no idea what William prefers. Is that why you took up with your Welshman? Did you fancy William and think him uninterested?"

"Nay, lady. William is a friend, nothing more. Owain is . . . something more."

"So where is the impediment? What keeps you awake in the night?"

"He asked a boon of me, and I hesitate to ask it of you."

"You may wed," Isabella said, "and with my blessing. I do not keep you prisoner here."

"Nor do I want to leave you. But what he asked concerns you. If I do not ask you, I'll disappoint him, grievously. Yet if I ask you, I may do the same, to you."

Isabella leaned forward, as though by doing so she could make out Gwenith's expression in the dark. "Then ask me. Ask my pardon first, and then ask. The worst I can do is say nay. At least then you will have pleased him, and left me in peace."

"He has a friend, his liege lord, who is a prisoner in the Tower," Gwenith said in a rush. "That is how we came to meet. Owain visits him daily, and despairs for this man. More, he grieves for him, because he says he's innocent and yet attracted the king's ire and faces death unless someone speaks up for clemency. I, then, lady, am that someone. I have met the man, and he is exceeding fair, and noble. I cannot believe such a vital man will soon have his head on a pike on London Bridge. I remember Lancaster. 'Deed, I cannot forget him. I do not say he was misused, but I mislike thinking of such a fate for this man. If you would but meet with him once, you would then take the burden off me, and Owain, and mayhap the man himself."

Isabella sighed. "Your Owain plays you like a lute, Gwenith. Whether or no he has taken your body, he seeks your soul."

"Mayhap," Gwenith said meekly. "But he seeks his friend's life. And I'm not sure I would not do the same were I he."

"Or I," Isabella agreed. "So who is this friend?"

"I hesitate to tell you, because in truth, when I first heard his name, before I met him, I wanted nothing to do with him."

"I have said I will hear you out," Isabella snapped. "Tell me, and have done. What is the man's name?"

"Mortimer," Gwenith said. "Roger Mortimer, Baron Wigmore."

Isabella gasped. "He who fought against Edward the king?"

"Nay! He who loves England, and so fought against the Despensers' rule. So he says, and I believe him. Oh, lady, he is a gentle knight, all grace and charm, but that is not what convinced me. Despises the Despensers, father and son, he does. That is what will cost him his life, if no one intercedes. But who will in this court? All fear the Despensers. So they sought me out, because if there is to be any grace in this, it falls to you."

"What can I do?" Isabella asked in a whisper, as though she were asking herself.

"You? You are Queen of England," Gwenith said. "You can do anything."

"Would that I could," Isabella breathed. "It is Edward who has the power over life and death. My dearest Elizabeth, sister to Hugh Despenser's own wife, is imprisoned now, with her children. Her husband, D'Amory, once Edward's favorite, was slain when he was captured, because he was part of the barons' revolt. But she is blameless. If I cannot help her, how can I help anyone?"

"But she's not in the Tower," Gwenith said. "She's in an abbey where she will at least be gently used. Mortimer's life is in peril. Men are killed in the heat of battle, but when there is peace, there is reason. Surely, a gentle word from you could win him some time to prove he is innocent of treason. Owain said it is the Despensers who wish Mortimer dead."

The queen seemed to shake herself out of reverie. "And your Owain does this all out of love?"

"Nay," Gwenith said softly. "He seeks his home again, his lands, which Mortimer won. The Despensers would take it for their own, along with all of Mortimer's properties, wealth and goods. War is about love and loyalty, Owain says. Not politics. Politics is all to do with wealth and power."

" 'Owain says' and 'Owain says'? He hasn't touched your body, you say, but he's made you his creature. Gwenith, take care."

"I do. I have. But if my plea makes you see Mortimer, and see for yourself what and who he is, then where is the harm in that?"

"There might be harm for Edward, the king."

"Forgive me, lady, but I heard nothing of that. But yes, there might be harm for Hugh Despenser, both the younger and the elder, for they are the ones Mortimer dared defy."

The room was still.

"And how can a queen visit a condemned man without condemning him more?" Isabella asked slowly. "That is to say, *if* it is only the Despensers who want his head."

"A queen can wear a hood, lady," Gwenith said. "Many ladies who visit the prison Tower do so. She would not have to visit his rooms either. She could stop and speak with him in the gardens, at twilight, as I did with his man, Owain."

"Aye," Isabella said. "But whatever she does, if she cannot persuade her husband, the king, there is no help for him. No one has ever escaped this place."

"Not yet," Gwenith said.

"You know you speak treason?" Isabella asked, amazed.

"Nay, Majesty, only truth."

"Let me think on," Isabella said. "Sleep now."

Gwenith obediently lay down. Her heart was pounding and her pulse racing. She'd done it. She had waited so long she'd begun to wonder if she was becoming only a shadow. She'd considered just giving up her cause and slinking away from London forever. But Owain had given her heart, and Mortimer, hope.

If the queen met Mortimer, if she heard his plea, if Mortimer were pardoned, if he could then raise an army and then march against the Despensers . . . perhaps she could have her revenge on the king after all, because whoever fought against the Despensers would be Edward's enemy. However it turned out, it would be her only chance to shake the throne. Her lonely mission would be resolved, her hopeless vow fulfilled, her debt to her grandmother and her people paid.

And sweet Isabella would also be free of the pain Gwenith saw daily in her eyes. Gwenith closed her own eyes, whispered a prayer, and on the first surge of real hope she'd felt in a long while, followed it out to the farthest shores of sweet possibilities, and finally, at peace, she slept.

But her queen sat up, weighing, judging, and deciding, throughout the rest of that long night.

"Highness," Mortimer whispered two afternoons later, as he bowed, "you honor me."

He was dressed in shades of blue, and his grave blue eyes met her gaze clearly. The setting sun illuminated him, casting gold on his hair and beard, outlining his face like the profiles found on ancient Roman coins of the sort still found in the earth here in London. He looked regal, and unconcerned by his present situation. He smiled. "You are as I remembered you, Your Majesty. We met, once, a long while ago, when you were first come to our shores."

"Forgive me, but I do not recall."

"Nay, how should you?" he asked. "You were a child. A beautiful child, but nonetheless, still a girl. I seldom saw you after, because I was in Ireland upholding the king's law, and then on the borders defending my home. We are ill met now, in this place, where I cannot offer you hospitality. But even so, I am glad to see you. Thank you, good Gwenith," he said, bowing to Gwenith. "And you, of course, Owain, my good friend in this dark time."

"I have not said I will help you," Isabella said.

"The fact that you come to hear me out is enough for me to give thanks. You are grown now, my queen, and there is no one in the land who speaks ill of you. Indeed, you have both the affection and the sympathy of your people."

At the word "sympathy," she drew herself up. "You presume, Mortimer. A foolish thing for a man in your position to do, unless, of course, you are content with your fate? A man who seeks to keep his head should speak flattery, and little else."

"A man, in any position, Highness, should speak truth. You say you expected flattery, but how foolish I would be if I spoke it now. You are known for more than your beauty. I respect your intelligence, my lady, else I might merely fawn, and flatter."

"Ah, there's superior flattery!" she said.

They laughed. The warders who were always stationed on the paths smiled. Their captives paid them well for privacy when they entertained visitors. The two ladies were wearing hooded cloaks, as so many of the nobility did if they had to come here, and extra coins always ensured their privacy on the paths the prisoners walked and, in some cases, in the rooms they lived in, as well. The wellborn lived well in the Tower until the very hour that they died here. Nobility was spared the common killing ground. Their executioner's block was not far from the gardens where both the living and the soon to be dead walked.

"Shall we stroll?" Mortimer suggested.

"I'd like that," Isabella said.

They began to walk, Gwenith and Owain falling into step behind them. Isabella and Mortimer spoke in low, murmurous tones. Owain looked down at Gwenith.

"You're very quiet this evening," he said.

"I was not the one invited here to speak," she said in return, keeping her gaze cast down.

"Ah, that is it," he said. "You believe that if Isabella had not come to see Mortimer, I would not see you again."

She looked up at him. He was dressed in gray again, and looked stern and strong. He also looked like a man she could lean on, learn from and devote herself to, although she now knew that he didn't need her devotion, only her help for his own purposes. But she had her own purposes as well. He still took her breath away, but now, not her heart.

"It makes no matter," she said. "You have your goals. I have mine. I don't blame you. I just feel a little foolish. We're moved around this life like chess pieces, as I was once told. But I'm unaccustomed to the games at court."

"You really think I would not have asked to see you more if the queen had refused?"

She nodded. "But what of it?

"You're wrong. Whatever the outcome of my request, I was well and truly caught. It was too late for me."

"Nay," she said. "It is only *now* too late for you to claim otherwise."

He stopped in his tracks. "So you will not see me again?"

"Did I say that?

He resumed walking at her side. "Gwenith," he said, "you have learned the games at court so well you could teach them to others. But what am I to do? You're right in that I cannot claim it would have made no difference, if only because you would never believe that. But so I do say, and I pray that as time goes on you will learn

I never say what I don't mean. I'm not a model of honesty when it concerns my life or my life's ambition. But I don't stoop to lying to a friend."

"Never?" she asked. "Fie, sir, there's a lie! Because if your life or the life of one you loved was concerned, I would think less of you did you *not* lie."

He chuckled. "Wretch, you've caught me, and now you are pleased to skewer and roast me?"

"Nay," she said, "I've only learned to play a new game."

"I pray you, don't play such games with me," he said seriously. "I can't defend myself. I can but hope the day will come when you believe me."

"Your day will come, and so, I pray, will mine," she said.

They strolled on in silence after that, behind Mortimer, who spoke in whispers to the silent hooded lady, who was his queen.

Prince Edward was pale and subdued. He was a prince without airs, always a quiet boy, a serious one who listened, not only to his nurses and his mama, but to the chatter around him. He was still Isabella's secret, quiet joy, because he showed that which came out of an act of sorrow and rage and sympathy could yet be a balm to her soul. But she never showed this to anyone, not even to Edward, her son. Gwenith knew of her favoritism, though, as did anyone who watched the boy and his mother when they were together, or who saw Isabella's eyes when he entered or left a room.

Today Isabella sat with Edward and her other children, and her ladies, but her eyes never left off following him—until his father came into the solar.

The other children ran to him. Edward walked slowly, with a dignity to match his eleven years.

"Well, how goes it?" Edward cried, catching up little Eleanor and tossing her in the air, before he caught her again in his arms. He took care not to throw her too high. He held her secure. For all his sins, Gwenith thought, he was genuinely attached to his children—except perhaps for his namesake, for reasons she didn't care to explore.

"Papa!" Eleanor cried. "The kitchen cat has had kittens, and Mama says I may have one."

"If she takes care of it," young John put in.

Edward the king grinned and sat on the floor so he could play with Eleanor. He let her tumble over him, mussing his fair hair, putting her chubby hands on the filet of gold that was his crown, reaching for it as though it were just another sparkling toy. When he was like this, Gwenith wondered how she could ever doubt him or her queen's place in life with him. Too soon, he rose, shaking off John's and Eleanor's pleas to remain.

"I shall not leave, but you must," he said. "I've a thing to discuss with your mother."

They complained, but they understood, and let their nurses lead them away. The queen's ladies and young Edward remained.

Edward the king raised an eyebrow. His son's fair complexion colored but he spoke up readily.

"I am nearing my twelfth year," Edward the prince said. "Almost a man. Mama said I should take more interest in affairs of state. But I told her I could scarcely take more interest, because I already care very much. May I stay?"

"Well and good," Edward said brusquely. "Stay if you wish. Madam," he said to Isabella, "you sent to me?"

"I did," Isabella said. "I would not have, but I haven't seen you of late. And I can scarcely speak to you privately when we sup. I've been petitioned. That is to say," she said, looking down for a moment, "I've been petitioned to beg clemency for a prisoner in the Tower."

"A prisoner destined for the block?" he asked, amazed.

"Aye. And worse, mayhap." She looked at him steadily. "He was sent to the Tower because he spoke against the Despensers, and is sentenced to die for it. I have heard the request, and considered it, and pass it on to you now, as I promised."

"Who is he?" Edward asked.

"Mortimer," she said, "Roger Mortimer, Baron—" She got no further.

"Have you run mad?" Edward yelped.

Gwenith winced. The queen remained calm.

"Mortimer, my enemy?" the king shouted. "Mortimer, who defied me and went with Lancaster and that lot? He spoke against the Despensers? He spoke foul treason! He surrendered to us at Shrewsbury, and it was all I could do not to take his head then. But Hugh was right. He must be made an example of. And we may make more of him than that."

"He never rode with Lancaster," she said.

"Aye, an' if he didn't, it was only his cowardice that prevented him. He supported Hereford. I will hear no more. Hugh and I have enough foes. You ask me to pardon one of the worst?" Edward paced a step, turned and shouted, "Who asked you to do this? Who petitioned you, for by God, they'll share a cell with Mortimer, or, if of lesser rank, better still, we'll drag them to the block in the streets of London and be done with them at Tyburn, where the common rabble meet their ends. Who is it? Madam, I demand to know!"

Isabella lowered her gaze. "Softly, softly, my lord. It was someone blameless, I can promise you."

"Who?" he cried.

"It was an innocent."

"One of his children? He has a clutch of them—ten, I am told. Or his wife?"

"Nay, it was not her," she said, with a glance to Gwenith, who lowered her gaze and stared at the floor. "It was a maid who has no part in this, save that she was fostered by a family on the Welsh border. And Mortimer, as you know, is—was—a great Marcher lord. A friend of hers came to London to petition you on his behalf, but discovering how she was situated, begged her to ask me to do it instead. And so I have done. She has a tender heart and is a valued servitor of mine. That is all."

"All?" Edward muttered, running a hand through his hair. "It is enough and too much. Tell your innocent: no and no and no." He glowered straight at Gwenith, and then deliberately turned from her. "And if she asks again, tell her to go. And at that, tell her she's fortunate I don't insist on her name and send her to hell instead of back to the Marches."

"Very well," Isabella said softly. "But there is more. What I overhear from others disturbs me and robs me of my sleep at night. You are well loved. But there is such a gathering storm of hatred for the Despensers, both father and son, that I fear for you, and me, and the children." She glanced to her son Edward, who stood listening intently, his gaze on her and then the king.

Edward scowled. "Do not try to deceive me. It isn't what you hear that disturbs you, but what you see each day and night." He walked toward her and stopped. He stood, feet apart and hands on hips. "Madam, know this: I *will* have Hugh Despenser at my side. I will have his father as my adviser. I love them well. Any who seek to hurt them hurts me. And I shall hurt them, in turn."

"Even your queen?" she asked. She stood too and looked him in the eye. "Know this, Edward my king: I hate them well. And I cannot pretend otherwise any longer."

"You are merely jealous," Edward said. He looked at Edward the prince and laughed. "Good. I'm glad you're here to learn this, my son. A woman is a goodly creature, full of comforts and sweet sighs. But she is not a reasoning creature, as men are. Emotion rules females. Jealousy is in their very bones. As is spite and deception. From Mother Eve to now, they have deceived us and they will drag you down if you let them. 'Ware, Edward. Let this be a lesson. Give your hand where and when we tell you, and your body to get your heirs. But never give any woman your heart, or your mind.

"Madam," he said to Isabella, "I want no more of this. Mortimer will die. The only questions are how and when. We keep him at our pleasure in hopes he can raise a goodly ransom for his life. But there is no price high enough to excuse treason."

"We?" she asked. "You, my lord? Or Hugh and his father?"

Edward's laughter was genuine. "We: Hugh and I and his father. We are England. It is time you came to terms with that. You are here to give me children, and you have done. Hugh is here to give me advice and counsel, and understanding such as you could never provide."

He turned and left. Isabella sank to her chair again. Gwenith let out her breath.

"Mother?" Edward said. "Don't weep. It is just this Mortimer he hates, not you."

"He hates anyone who doesn't share his love for the Despensers," she said bleakly. "And I do not, and I will not, and I cannot."

Sixteen

1323, July
The Tower, London

"To lie with a man is no easy thing. Oh, I'll warrant it feels like the easiest thing in the world. Just lie back in his arms and open to him. Easy and sweet and fine. But the devil is in it that it stays easy for them, whatever happens after. The 'after' can be sheerest hell for us. 'Tis not fair. But so it is. I am caught," Agnes said simply, as she folded her garments and laid them on her bed. "And the devil's to pay for it, not the fellow who got me that way. He's a knight, and full of honors, and has spoken for another lady in front of God and man. He weds in a month, all holy seeming in God's eyes. I am left in disgrace with his get.

"Now that is unfair, is it not?" she complained. "A man takes his pleasure, leaves with a grin, and forgets it, belike, most of the time. Why should we pay for a moment's bliss with months of discomfort, risk our lives in so doing and ruin our names? Do you think God hates females?"

"He surely doesn't love the babes gotten that way," Mary said. "Male or female, they are cursed."

"Thank you," Agnes said, too sweetly. "Trust you, holy Mary, to tell me that. Were I going to keep the babe, I'd hate you for it. But I'm not. He, or she, will go to some family far from my home, and go without my name. I will go into wedlock with whomever my father can bribe enough to take me now. Be warned, Gwenith. I don't have to warn Mary. I doubt she'll even bed her husband. But when you smile at your handsome lord, remember the high price we pay for a moment's ecstasy."

"We warned you," Mary said.

"Oh, aye, you, and the queen, and the church. I enjoyed myself full well even so for a long time too, though, didn't I? The thing is to have them pull out at the right moment or, rather, just before it," Agnes added conversationally.

Gwenith blushed to her ears. Mary gasped. Agnes laughed.

"Well, so it is," she said. "Remember, it only means a second's pause, a moment's care, for him. He spouts without, as they say, and he is still satisfied, and no damage done to you. Or you can use your hands or lips to drain him instead, if he complains overmuch. But I forgot my own advice with him. He was so . . . Never mind. I am caught. That's that. Not all the midwife's herbs can dislodge it. I must leave and grow the babe, have it and dispose of it. I can never return here."

"God go with you." Mary folded her hands in front of her and left the room.

"God's blood, but she should have been a nun and spared us the sermons," Agnes said. "Cold comfort she is. And you, Gwenith the sensible, do you curse me too?"

"Nay," Gwenith said. "I am sorry to see you go, and sad to see you unhappy. For all you said and did, you did bring merriment with you always."

"Aye, and I did have a good time always. Life's too short for sorrow. I only hope the man my father finds for me is either to my liking, or too old to care what I do for my liking." Agnes laughed. But then she grew serious. "That's fine for me. It's how I'm made. You are a more tender maid. Take care with this gallant knight you spend all your time with. Do not end up like me, because you won't be able to bear it as I do—in every sense," she said, laughing again.

"I wish you well, Gwenith," Agnes said. "You have always been gentle with me, even though I know you disapproved of me as much as good Mary did. So I tell you to take care. It has been months. Spring turned to summer. Every fair evening you walk out and meet your knight, and come back, glowing brighter than the setting sun. The days that it rains, you are sad, because you can't walk with him. What shall you do when winter comes? You're not a flower to be so ruled by the weather, or a child to be so dependent. You must make your own happiness."

"I will," Gwenith said. "I do. And I wish that for you too."

He caught her up in his arms, and kissed her, and as ever, everything she knew no longer mattered, and everything she feared was gone. But the second he drew back to look at her, it all came rushing back.

"What?" Owain said, looking at her expression.

"This is not right," Gwenith said. She remembered all the things she had sworn to tell him when they met next. If she didn't tell him now, as she hadn't the week before, and the week before that, the force of it would grow larger and larger and stop up her throat until she was sure she wouldn't be able to breathe.

He was like the goodly knights in the stories she had heard, like the heroes in Isabella's beautiful book. Handsome and true, brave and on a crusade for his leader. He was a *parfait* knight, too honorable to do more than walk with her and talk with her, share her thoughts and make her laugh, and then kiss her, and leave her to hope and dream of their next meeting. She'd been thrilled with that. Time had passed. However she felt about him, she now knew there had to be more. She wasn't the heroine in a tale. She was flesh and blood and that was what called to him now. He didn't seem to hear, or know, or care.

"We meet, we walk, we talk, and then we embrace," she said. "Then we return to our separate rooms, and wait for the next fair day. I don't even know where your lodgings are. We never speak about that, or the future, save that which has to do with Mortimer and the queen. I was your conduit to her. If that is why you sought me out, then there is no more need for it. Isabella visits with Mortimer as often as I do with you. Since they met, there is not a day that I meet with you that she does not meet with him. So your mission is accomplished. You don't need me for that anymore, and as it's clear you don't need me for aught else, there should be an end to it."

"And what do you need?" Owain asked.

All that Gwenith wanted to tell him was in her eyes. But she would not say it.

"Not for nothing are you called sensible," he said, on a sigh, touching her cheek gently with the back of his hand. "I want much more, Gwenith, so much more that I am amazed at my forbearance. I yearn to ask you to visit me in my rooms. I ache to ask you to stay with me in the shadows, and know the physical truth of my love. But I will not dishonor you. And," he added, before she could speak, "I cannot ask you to marry me."

She stood very still, her eyes large and her gaze locked on his face.

"Whatever happens with Mortimer will reflect on me," he said, "in many ways. If he is executed, I won't have a home anymore, nor a liege lord. When he is gone, the Despensers will take his home, and mine, and all his worldly goods, and mine. My riches are not kingly, but sufficient. My estate is not huge, but it is a goodly portion of land with a good number of serfs to work on it, and it has a mill and a defensible castle. It sits by a wide river, and is on high ground. Be sure, the Despensers would want it. And take it.

"So then what should I do? Ask you to take to the road with me? Shall we sing and dance for our suppers, or act out the Easter plays for our coins? How should I support our sons and dower our daughters? Nay, I'll be a landless, homeless knight. I'll offer my sword for hire, but that is an uncertain thing, and who knows if I will be able to return from battle, or only send you my sword to keep for our son?

"Gwenith, I have nothing to offer you now but my body and soul. If you take my body, you will be disgraced, because with all my caution and care, there's no telling what may happen in the act of love. As for my soul? You have it, and have had it for a long time now."

She bit her lip. It took all her courage to speak what she had promised herself she would. But it wasn't courage. She understood that now. It was despair, because she longed for him. His kisses promised more, and she was ready to know what that was.

"But Lady Agnes told me . . ." she said. "She suggested, her-self she was speaking of, not knowing about us, of course." Her Welsh accents became stronger in her distress, but the thing had to be said the way a morsel swallowed the wrong way had to be coughed up. "She knows ways, she told me. There are ways, she said, that a woman can love a man without risk or harm."

He shook his head. Then he laughed, but his laughter was brittle. "Jesus love Lady Agnes, and at that, he may be the only man in England who has not! Aye, there are ways to play, pleasing ways indeed. But you are not a toy, Gwenith, nor your love a thing ever given and then taken back. Do you think you could lie with me, even only to play at such sweet games, and then, if need be, forget me? I don't give myself airs! You could and should find a far richer, wiser man. But I think I know you well. Would or could you once you had given yourself in intimacy with me? Some women can, and do. I don't think that is you. If I am wrong"——he shrugged—— "I will be glad to oblige. Better me than someone else."

She stood, looking down, her courage gone, only shame and sorrow left. He took her in his arms. She buried her face against his chest.

"Ah, me," he sighed, "what's to do?" He drew back and tried to look down into her eyes. "One thing I can tell you, Gwenith, my own, when this is done, one way or the other, if I do survive it, then it's clear that it will be me, and you, for so long as we are given. For I'll never want another."

"I mislike this," Isabella said.

"Aye, so you've said often enough. You wouldn't like it were we going a-hunting little birds, or for a ride into the countryside to count the flowers," Edward said. He laughed loudly, signaling those behind him they could laugh too.

But Gwenith and those of the queen's court did not smile, because she frowned.

The king sat his horse at the head of a small army. There were knights on horseback, a pack of bowmen, archers and more of simple foot soldiers. Edward was dressed magnificently in full armor. Hugh, at his side, looked no less grand. Edward the prince sat a horse a pace behind them, near to Hugh's father, the earl. The boy looked sober and solemn, as always. Isabella bit back tears.

"This is no simple jaunt. There is danger," she said again.

"Aye, that's why we go," Edward said. "As for the boy? It's time he left his mother's tit and went with men. We will teach him a man's games," he said. "There are none finer." He laughed at the look in Isabella's eyes. "I mean of war, of course. Do I not, Hugh?"

"Aye, sire!" Hugh cried, laughing so hard he startled his war-horse and set it to prancing in place.

"There is trouble on the Marches," Edward told Isabella. "Revolt. We ride for the sake of the kingdom. I remind you, it will be his one day. *If* we save it for him now, and he is man enough to help me."

"We will watch over him," Hugh said, "as we watch over his sire."

Isabella raised her head and spoke only to the king. "Then go in peace. But come back the same."

"What?" Edward asked, slyly, sliding a glance to Hugh. "This time you don't beg to come too?"

"It pleases you to be cruel today, I see," Isabella said. "Say what you will then. Only bring my son back to me."

"Your son, indeed," Edward said with a cold smile. "And mine, I hope—that is to say, I hope you mean to say."

He was playing for Hugh's approving laughter and he got it. Isabella sucked in a breath but was still. There was only so much humiliation she would bear in front of her people.

"Then we go," Edward said. "Edward, say good-bye to your worried mama. She does not believe you are almost a man grown."

The young prince angled his horse forward. He looked down at his mother, his eyes grave. "I shall be careful," he told her.

She reached up on her tiptoes. He bent his head down. "Be careful of Hugh Despenser," she said into his ear, "and his father, by night and by day." She stepped back. "Godspeed you home safe again," she added, rejoining her ladies to watch the troop of men and horses march away.

When they were out of sight, Isabella dismissed all her ladies, but Gwenith, and went back into her bower. Her agitation was apparent. She paced a while, lost in thought. She was so distressed Gwenith dared not speak to her.

The king was gone but the kingdom moved on. The Tower was a fortified palace. There were hundreds here at the queen's command, from the keepers and stewards, chamberlains and constables, clerks and minor officials whose duties included everything from wolf catching to baking, banking and overseeing the buttery. There were dozens of squires and pages as well.

"Who shall I trust?" Isabella finally muttered. "Alas, if only my poor Therese were here. But she would have only given counsel. And I fear she would certainly never condone what I'm about to do. Can I trust you?" she asked Gwenith.

Gwenith bent her head. "If not now," she whispered, "then never, my lady. I am yours."

Isabella thought a moment more, and then nodded. "You have not yet betrayed me."

"I never would," Gwenith said and realized she meant it.

So did Isabella. "Then bring me William, the squire. And let no one else know your errand. Then return with him, to me."

Gwenith ran to do her bidding. By asking here, and sending there, she finally found William. "Come with me," she told him breathlessly. "And tell no one."

As soon as they arrived at the queen's chamber, she spoke. "There is a thing that you must do for me, William. A thing no one may know of, now or ever."

He rose from his knee and put his hand on his heart. "As ever and always, Majesty. Only tell me."

"Summon the constable of the Tower to me. Bring him by secret ways, and swear him to silence. And now.

"Stay," she told Gwenith as William ran from the room. "Be still and listen, and keep whatever you hear close as your own heartbeat."

The constable was so surprised and honored by his summons that he bowed almost double when he greeted his queen, a difficult thing for such a portly fellow to do. His was an important office and he was a wealthy man, but known to be ever greedy for more. Every boat that sailed to the city had to moor at Tower wharf, and he took his tribute from them in the form of wine, livestock, cockles, herring or perfumes, whatever cargo they carried. He had fine lodgings, and his own garden and those to tend it for him. He ate well and slept on feathers, because he also collected rents from the wealthier prisoners in the Tower. He was also said to take bribes for special favors for them. The wealthier they were, the more his purse swelled. But now he was swollen with importance because his queen had summoned him to her in secret.

"What I say to you now must be kept to yourself," she said without preamble. "A few people I trust, but no more. So what I say cannot be shared with your wife or your lover, your king or your God. If I heard you did otherwise, and I would, you will lose more than your position here."

He turned pale. But he bowed again.

"Mark me well," she said. "I mean what I say. Is that understood?"

"Aye, Majesty."

"If you cannot do this, you may leave now."

He blinked and squirmed, and finally nodded. "Aye, Majesty. I can do that."

"Do you so vow?"

"I do," he said, looking anxious, and considerably smaller than when he'd arrived.

"I have a friend," she said. "This friend has a friend, at present a prisoner in your keeping in apartments in the Devyll's Tower. She needs to visit with him in private, and for however long she wishes. She cannot have that privacy during the hours she walks in the gardens with him. She must be let into his rooms and left in peace until she is ready to go. You will be well rewarded for your pains, but ill served if you fail."

"At once, of course, I will do this," he said eagerly, since it was a thing he had done many times before, for considerable fees.

"No one must know," she insisted, "or even I wouldn't be able to help her. If you do *not* do this aright, if word gets out, if aught is known, it will be her downfall . . . and yours. Again, can you do this?"

"Yes, I will. I can. Only tell me when," he said, babbling in his eagerness to assure her, "and who? I mean, where she is to go."

She nodded. "She will be cloaked and hooded. The squire that brought you here will bring her to you after compline, this night. Do not fail me or her."

She told him the name and he nodded. He bobbed his head, and bowed, and left her when she dismissed him.

Isabella turned to Gwenith. "Again, I burden you. The least I can do is to ask if you're willing."

"Your will is mine," Gwenith said, and meant it entirely.

Isabella resumed pacing.

She entered his rooms, at last, and looked around her. There were two rooms, each with a small window. Both were well furnished and comfortable. She could see a goodly sized bed in the second room. Not until she heard the door shut behind her, and the bolt being drawn on the outside, did she meet his eyes.

He stood before her, and he smiled. He opened his arms. She fell into his embrace, and met his lips, holding him close, so as to forget where she was and who she was. The feel of him against her: warm and sturdy, strong, filled with evident desire for her, and yet gentle, withal, made her fears disappear. Then she reveled in his kisses as she had never done before. It wasn't only the excitement of being with him at last. It was the knowledge of the gravity of what she did that made her heart race and the breast that covered it tingle and pucker at the tip as he cupped it in his hand.

"Wait," he said against her ear and drew away, taking her by the hand into the other room.

She followed, her eyes on his.

He looked at her and laughed. "You haven't ever taken off your cloak. We won't be disturbed. This is our time together, at last. We are well out of sight, even far from the window. And it is dusk. But I can still see you in the last of the light. So come, come to me as you are, your only covering your skin, and mine."

She swallowed hard. She hadn't expected that.

"Are you afraid?" he asked.

"Nay, not of you. But nudity between lovers is a rare thing. Privacy comes at a high price, because nakedness makes us vulnerable. It requires time, and confidence, and the desire to bare oneself before the other."

"We have all of that this night," he said. "Do we not?"

She nodded. "Aye," she said, breathlessly.

His smile showed he exulted. He drew off her cloak, and let it fall in a puddle around her feet. He assisted her in taking off her tunic and her undertunic, her hose and her shoes, as though he were a lady's maid. He carefully drew off her heavy headdress, and put it aside. Then, at last, when she stood before him as God had made her, he stared at her and sighed.

She hesitated then, wondering if her body was to his taste.

"Mine, at last," he breathed, and pulled her back into his arms.

"I must greet you as you do me," he eventually whispered in her ear, when his lips had left hers. "Have I your leave?"

She nodded, and whispered, "Aye, I'd like that."

She watched as he drew off his tunic and smallclothes, hose and braies and shoes, and then in spite of her apprehension, smiled when she finally saw his naked, clean, muscular frame.

He led her to his bed. She sat, and he took her in his arms again, and she could feel his heart racing as fast as her own was. His skin was heated, his desire apparent; she took it as further tribute, and smiled. He laid her down, and then lingered over her body, saluting it with kisses. But she was too anxious. She wanted him too much and too urgently for that. She pulled him down to her, and opened herself to him, locking him to her with her legs clasped behind his back, at once frightened and ecstatic, and relieved and damned, as he entered her at last.

Once before she'd given herself in haste and rage and furious sorrow. She could not regret that because of what had come of it, though it weighed on her soul and she knew one day she would answer for such a sin. This wasn't like that. Often before, she'd given herself in love and sorrow, because she knew her lover's desire for haste and regretted his need for it each time, and every time she thought of it. This certainly wasn't that.

He moved in her, and stopped and smiled down at her, and moved again, perfectly in control, deep inside her, slowly, deliciously, making a feast of her for himself, and for her.

Isabella closed her eyes and gave herself to Roger Mortimer with anger and with regret, and glorious sorrow. She gave herself as payment owed to one who didn't want her, never wanted her, and to herself as recompense for her grief.

Seventeen

1324, August
London

"What news of the Earl of Wigmore?" Isabella asked her husband.

"What?" Edward said, looking up from his trencher. "Wigmore? Oh, aye, you mean Mortimer. He is due to leave us soon," he said, and turned his head to grin at Hugh.

Hugh Despenser sat at his side every time they dined these days and nights. Isabella kept her seat on his other side—at least, she did on those evenings that she joined them. She came to the great hall for her evening meal less and less, preferring to eat with the children, she said, or with her ladies. Edward and Hugh both knew it as an insult. Neither cared, which was the greater insult.

"He leaves?" she asked, keeping her voice level and calm with effort.

"Aye, the only question," Hugh said, winking at his king, "is whether he is to go in two pieces or four."

"Nay!" Edward said, laughing. "Such a bad mathematician

you are, my Hugh. It's two, or *five*. If he is quartered, you have four pieces, but the head is always taken too. Thus, five."

"And if he is to be castrated, it is six, or seven, or even eight, depending on how that package is divided and delivered," Hugh said.

Edward wagged a finger, and laughed.

"He is to be executed?" Isabella asked, her hand tightening in her lap.

"He was to be executed months past, but he keeps saying he's raising more ransom, and that had a lovely sound to it, did it not, Majesty?" Hugh said. "Still, a year has come and is almost gone, and so too should he be. We don't want to keep him waiting, you know."

The king laughed, as did Hugh's father, a bishop and a few nervous courtiers. But most went still. Death was not a favorite subject here. To be close to a king meant also to be near his executioner, and few forgot it.

"When?" Isabella asked.

"Why do you ask?" Edward replied.

But she had expected this. "One of my ladies has been walking out of an evening with one of his neighbors who visits him here in the Tower," she said calmly. "A Welsh knight. When the earl goes, I fear her lover will too. Not to the ax, perhaps, for he has done no treason, and seeks out Mortimer for charity's sake. But I fear he will be gone as surely, nonetheless. He has made no promises to her."

"By God, madam," Edward said, "now I remember. You asked about him before on her behalf. The one you called an innocent. There is a lie and a jest! Which one is she?"

"Gwenith, stand forth," Isabella said.

Gwenith, wide eyed and trembling, stepped forward.

"This one?" Hugh laughed, strolling over to her. "Again? The one who looks so meek and mild and acts like a nun? Her mouth promises heaven," he said, running a finger across her lips. "But her lips always speak denial, at least to most men. What did this one offer you?" he asked Gwenith. "Something no other man could? That, I doubt."

Edward looked from Hugh to Gwenith and scowled. "Your ladies have the morals of kitchen cats," he told Isabella furiously. "The big, rosy-cheeked one who was always goggling at me left with a bundle under her apron, got from who knows—I doubt she does. She bedded every man who ever smiled at her. And now another maid falling from grace? What are you feeding them?"

"Tales of romance, sire," Hugh said, putting a hand on his chest and screwing his face up in a comical exaggerated kiss. "I've passed the bower and heard the stories sung and told there. Old stories about gallant knights, fair maidens and true lovers parted— that sort of thing. Your lady is French, you know. They think they invented romance. And they make a story and a song out of it for their minstrels to sing every time a lass gets tupped, which, in France, is every minute."

Edward laughed.

"I remind you that 'the king's lady' is your queen," Isabella said coldly, rising to her feet. "And I am no more French now than I am English. Rather I am both, and proud of it. I should not expect you to appreciate romance," she told Hugh. "But I do wonder why you hide in the hall outside my bower to listen to what we say. Mayhap you are lured by the stories? If so, come in and listen. We will give you a piece of embroidery to keep your hands busy while the stories are read. If not, I suggest you stay away. I do not like the idea of a knave creeping about my door. In the future, in fact, I will tell my men at arms to be sure no one is about."

"I am no knave, lady," Hugh said.

The room went silent. Knives were put down, cups raised to lips that parted to gasp, not drink. Edward the king went very still. The prince, at his mother's side, was silent and watchful, as always.

"You are, if you spy on your queen and tell the tale to amuse the court," Isabella said. "But mayhap I had better to call you a minstrel? That would explain your desire to entertain the court."

Edward the king slowly rose to his feet. This night, he was resplendent in red and gold. But his face was pale. He looked from his queen to his knight, and seemed incapable of speech.

"Hugh," a firm voice said, "beg your queen's pardon. Your Majesty, I apologize for my errant son," the Earl of Winchester said loudly. "He spoke without thinking, and I am sure he never meant to bring offense."

"My lady," Hugh said, bending his head in a mockery of a bow, "I am ever obedient to my father."

Isabella stood very still. She looked at her husband, and not Hugh Despenser. But the king was looking at Hugh. She turned away and left the hall.

"Forgive me, Gwenith," the queen said, as they climbed the stair. "I used you as a pawn."

"Nay, lady," Gwenith said. "A queen need not apologize to her servant. I knew the danger. It was as we agreed."

"As for your Owain, I can do nothing," Isabella said. "But Hugh Despenser I can yet control. I will keep him from you—that, I promise,"

"If aught is to be done," Isabella said later that night, "it must be done soon. My idle inquiry stirred up a hornet's nest. If Hugh Despenser but thinks I have a care for what happens to you, for any reason, even for the comfort of my lady in waiting, he will cause your execution to happen sooner. I left off, bit my tongue and held my peace tonight, though it went against the grain and still vexes me sore. I did it because I knew if I did not, he would cause mischief at once, for me, and for you, and for poor Gwenith.

At the moment he is only annoyed with me. But when he thinks about it, he will remember what we were speaking of, and your life will be forfeit. What shall we do?"

Mortimer stirred. He lay still, on his back, exhausted from their lovemaking, his arm still around her, his legs still tangled with hers. His chest rose and fell in a long sigh. "Then we do what we must," he said. "It is time. You will have no part in it. My men and my friends will risk their necks. They are eager and ready. You've done enough."

She sat up and turned, scowling down into his face. "But it was you who asked me to inquire!"

"Softly, softly, aye, I did," he said, sitting up and folding her in his arms. "That's not what I meant. You requested clemency. When that failed, you paved a road for me. You have risked yourself for me. Now I need endanger you no more." He dropped a kiss on her forehead, tenderly as a father might. "Yet there are a few things that mayhap you could do. . . ."

"Tell me," she said, her cheek against his heart, her hand splayed on his chest to feel the beating in it.

"The constable has been obediently blind to you for these months past. No one knows who visits me, but for him, and your Gwenith, and Owain de Rhys. Since the constable is so obliging, can you bind him further? As you said, the night I leave, it would be easier if I did not have to do murder. We will if we must, but the less blood spilled, the less outcry after. Your king is not so beloved that there will be uproar for my head, if I can accomplish this cleverly. All the world loves a rogue. If I can but get to the moat unseen, I can slip in, swim to the other side and meet my men on a ship waiting on the Thames, one that will bear me away to France, as we agreed."

She nodded. "It is done. I have only to tell the constable when. He is eager to keep his position and his head. Money and threats are the keys to him. I assured him no one would die. Some of his guards will get wine with a potion to send them to sleep. You will be the only villain, and accounted the cleverest man to ever bide in the Tower. Do you not wish this?"

"You know what I wish," he said in a low growl. "But your physician, do you trust him so far as to include him?"

"Nay. Good Theobold is a fair man, but a prosy one, too moral at the wrong times, and he is as often in cups as not. I have another physician I trust with my life, because I hold his life in my hand. As for the other warders, some will not be there, and some will have to be put to sleep, less gently. But they will live to breathe the tale, as we planned, all as we agreed." She paused, and added in a softer voice, "But if it is so simple, why has no one done it before?"

"Because no one has had the aid of a queen." He stroked her naked back. "A lady who can strike the right men blind at a word, and the wrong ones deaf at her command. We are ready. All is in train. Tell your Gwenith to bid farewell to Owain."

She shivered. "It *is* a good plan," she murmured, as if to herself. "I have gotten the constable's promises. Half of his men will be elsewhere, not near this cursed Tower. I've secured from a physician a potion that will give the guards who will be here a certain night's sleep and no more than a headache in the morning. Your men can slip in to aid you, or distract searchers if aught goes awry. All is in readiness for the first dark night, whether that be caused by rain or fog or a sliver moon. But no one," she whispered, "has ever escaped the Tower."

"Yet," he said and kissed her.

He kissed her. He framed her head between his hands and kissed her. And then he let her go.

"Nay," Gwenith said and laid her hand on his chest. "My queen will not need me tonight. Tomorrow night, Mortimer may need you." She raised her head and looked into Owain's eyes. She summoned all her courage, grown out of fear, and added, "To-night, let me stay with you, wherever that may be."

His hand shook as he raised it to stroke her back. "Nay, for all that I would, I could not. A fine thing, to take you for the first time if it is to be a last time! And if we prove successful? Then you've a reminder of me for your life long, and one that will ruin you. Nay. If you love me, let me go, and bid me well, but do not ask of me what I most want to do with you. I try to be a gentle knight, an honorable one. Don't tempt me to stray."

"Mayhap," she said, "there is such a thing as too much honor? Mortimer is an honorable man. He loves his . . . lady. But he does not deny her."

"She is a queen. She has a husband. If Mortimer does not return, and she has a babe, no one will know whose it is but herself. Mortimer is a different sort of knight than I am. He is a married man, with a full quiver of children, and yet for all he has done, I still hold him to be a good man. He was fixed in marriage as a boy, and has no more love for it than his present lady does for her own vows. I will not speak more treason, because that does not matter to us. As for me, I made a holy pledge, and I hold to it. If aught should happen to me, give me your prayers and save a place for me in your memory, but live and laugh, and love again."

She balled her hand into a fist, and lightly struck his shoulder. "I would that you were not so honorable! I am frightened tonight, and I'll be terrified tomorrow. The king and Hugh Despenser already think I'm a slut and a slattern. The queen promises to protect me, but that is not enough for me, not anymore. When shall we meet again? Neither of us know. Pray give me something of you to keep."

"My kiss," he said, and kissed her brow. "My heart, but I cannot tear it out to give to you. My ring, but I dare not endanger you, if it be found on your person or in your effects. There will be a hue and cry raised such as London has never known, whether we succeed or not. No one will escape notice. That is why I'll go with Mortimer. You can claim that you never knew a thing about this. Blame me. Call me a villain. Weep like a waterfall. Insist you were betrayed. Edward does not credit females with much sense anyway, nor does Despenser. It might gall you, but that will save you. As will Isabella, if the waters get too deep. Ah, sensible Gwenith," he said, tipping back her head with his hand so he could look at her, "listen to me. Do not grieve. I may live to become such a cantankerous old man that you will rue the day you met me."

She closed her eyes. A tear fell from her eye.

"Listen," he breathed in her ear. "Leave off lamenting for me. I'm not so goodly a knight. I am no holy man. I sought you out. I courted you so that my liege lord might gain your queen's ear. I aid him because I need him to regain power so I can regain my home. Nothing I have done is noble, save for refusing to despoil you. Leave me that one thing to light my way to heaven, should I fail in this. Because if you ask again, I will say aye, though in my soul, I know it would be wrong, mayhap the worst wrong that I have done or will do."

She drew away. "Then go with God. And I shall never forget you."

"Nor will I let you," he said and smiled.

And she was for that one moment content.

The next night was dank and still. There was a thick fog; no moon was seen. Indeed, it was hard for anyone to see to the end of his arm. The few warders who patrolled the paths shivered; the torches flickering in their places high along the Tower walls couldn't banish the darkness. The glare from their bright flames was suffocated, absorbed into the dampness of the night.

And so no one saw the two cloaked figures slip into the prisoners' Tower. They walked cat-footed past the sleeping warders. Inside the entrance to the Tower, they stopped. A portly man in black, white faced in the night, was waiting for them. He wore a clutch of keys at his belt.

"Go, go, go quickly," the constable whispered nervously. "Go, get him and be gone. You know where his apartments are. Hurry. All are gone from their posts, or sleeping, or as good as. But sleep won't last forever and those gone may return. Here is the key."

One of the men nodded. The other was already halfway up the stair. He fitted the key into the door and drew back the bolt. Mortimer was waiting just behind the door. His smile was a slash of white in the dark.

"Good, good," Mortimer whispered. "Now my sword."

His liberator reached under his cloak and drew out a sword. He dropped to one knee and presented it to him.

"Aye, good," Mortimer said. But he didn't sheathe the weapon. He nodded, and ran quickly down the stair.

He stopped when he saw the terrified constable waiting for him at the foot of the stair.

"Go in peace, my lord," the constable said in a rushed whisper. "But go!"

"Aye," Mortimer said. "But first, you will." He raised his sword in two hands and slashed, so that the blow neatly severed the constable's head. He crossed himself. "Thank you," he said, stooping to rip the rest of the keys from the convulsing body. They were already slick with blood, as were his hands. "Here," he said, tossing the keys to the men behind him. "Let everyone here out. Quickly. Then join us."

One of the men took the keys. The other stood frozen.

"You promised no bloodshed unless necessary," he said.

"It was for our safety," Mortimer said. "Forget it. He has. Now let out the other prisoners. The more running from here, the more they have to run after. And I'm the only one with helpers, and a plan."

The man stood silent.

"I had to do it," Mortimer added quickly. "Now there is no mouth to tell who helped us. A man bought with gold can be bought by fear or pain too. This way, our lady is safe. Now do you wish to stay for the funeral service? Or will you come with me?"

The man moved. "Follow," he said, and ran from the Tower into the dark night.

No one noticed them, but the beasts in the menagerie heard their passage, sensed their agitation and smelled blood. They began to roar and bicker. The men ran on, down the garden paths to the moat.

They stripped off their cloaks and stood a moment, looking into the water.

"Aye, no one in his right mind would swim in it," Owain told Mortimer. "Which is why it is the best route. It will stink. It's thick and brackish at best. It might make you vomit, but it won't kill you. I have done it. I wouldn't send you this way else. I'll follow you. We'll meet on the other side."

He waited until Mortimer slid into the water, then slipped into the moat himself, his entry as silent and seamless as a sea tern seeking fish. Then, following Mortimer to be sure he fared well, he swam quickly and quietly out to the other side of the moat. Where the Thames met the Tower, there was clean water, and a boat was waiting to meet them.

Isabella was woken just before dawn.

"Prisoners have escaped the Tower, Majesty," the page told her.

She exchanged a quick look with Gwenith and, waking her other servants, dressed in haste.

Isabella and Gwenith heard the rising noise as they took the

217

stairs down to the great hall. It rang with angry voices. The huge hall was filling, as men from all branches of Edward's government and the church arrived and clustered before their king. Most of them looked hastily dressed and confused. Menial servants and maids, washerwomen and cook's helpers stood behind them, craning to hear whatever was said. Isabella's ladies came after her, hushed and clearly frightened.

At the head of the hall, Hugh Despenser was raging. His father was grave. Edward the king sat in his throne chair and looked by turns anxious and angry. Edward the prince, at his side, was silent, watching and listening to one speaker after the other. Three monks stood, hooded and silent, nearby. Isabella quietly took her seat near Edward, took her son's hand and listened to the speakers fume and threaten and plot.

"Escaped from the Tower!" Hugh the younger shouted as he paced in front of them. "Where are my men at arms, my warders, my guards?"

Then Isabella spoke, low and emotionlessly. "You mean Edward the king's men at arms, warders and guards."

"Oh, aye," Hugh snarled. "What's the difference? We fear for our kingdom. Bad enough to have the Bruce and the Scots on the march to our north, the Welsh rioting to our west, the Irish plotting always, and the French and the Flemish lurking, waiting their chance to strike as well."

"The French?" Isabella asked with deadly calm.

"Do not tell me you haven't heard that their new king, your brother, is bringing up the matter of ownership of Gascony again," Hugh barked.

"I will tell you nothing when you speak to me as though I were a criminal in the dock. I am your queen," she said angrily.

He raised a hand as though to brush her away. "It's a good thing the villains put paid to the constable, although I would have chosen a slower death for him. His keys stolen, and thrown to the prisoners! Eight prisoners escaped! Seven captured again. But Mortimer got away."

"The constable is dead?" Isabella asked.

"Aye, his head taken off on the spot, as well as the keys at his belt."

She took a deep breath.

"And Mortimer got clean away," Hugh said in frustration. "We've sent men looking for him on the road to the west, should he have gone to his home. But only a fool would do that, and he is no fool. We have companies riding in other directions as well. I think he took to the sea. The wharf is close by. We will discover how he fled, in time. But if he swam the moat, he could have crossed to the river."

"He could have bribed the guards at any gate," the earl put in.

His son shook his head. "We'll find *that* out, soon enough. Those that guarded are themselves guarded now in the dungeons. They will speak, and truth, if it takes every last drop of their blood to get it. But I think we'll find out he went to sea. I have good reason to know that is where a man can best hide and enlist other villains to his cause too."

"But you were a great success at warfare on the sea, Hugh," Edward said in a small voice, as though he needed to be reassured. "Do you think you should sail after him?"

"Majesty," a master of the royal fleet said, as he bowed, "we have dispatched ships. They sail even as we speak. But if he escaped in the night, on the tide, he could be in France by now."

"Mortimer," Edward said, thinking. His clear blue gaze found his queen. His eyes opened wider. "*You*, madam, are the one who asked after him only the other week! You asked because you said you were worried about your lady in waiting. I remember. She was walking out with a knight in Mortimer's service, or some such."

"Aye, I remember your meek little lady in waiting," Hugh

snarled. "Where is she, the one who was seeing the traitor's friend?"

Isabella sat silent. Her ladies clustered together, white faced. Gwenith caught Isabella's eye, and at her slight nod, Gwenith rose.

"I am here," Gwenith said.

"You!" Hugh said with a sneer. "All holy and prosy until your queen's back is turned, are you?"

"I knew of it," Isabella said. "I saw no harm in it. He was a knight."

"More results of your stories and romances, madam," Hugh said. "Not all knights are honorable. Not all ladies in waiting are honest."

"She is," Isabella said clearly. "And you shall not take her from me to torture lies out of her. She walked with the man. She did no more. I would swear to that."

"Would you?" Hugh said. "No matter. What's his name?"

"Owain," Gwenith whispered. "Sir Owain de Rhys, baron and knight."

"A *Welshman*," Hugh all but spat. "Where is he?"

"I don't know," Gwenith whispered, in all honesty.

"Don't know, or won't say?" Hugh yelled, rounding on her.

"Don't know, my lord," Gwenith said, her voice trembling.

"You coupled with him and you don't know?" Edward asked angrily.

"I did not. We never did," she stammered. "We were friends, but never more. I don't know, Majesty."

"Think, Edward," Isabella said in a weary voice. "If he had half a wit in his head, would he have confided any plot to a girl—and one, I'm sorry to say, that he most thoroughly deceived?"

"Aye," Hugh growled. "Only a fool would tell a woman more than 'lift your skirts again.' Mortimer is hardly that, nor would his man be. Is this knight being searched for?" Hugh asked the captain of the guard.

"Now he is, sir," the captain said, bowed and strode from the room.

"What do we do now?" Edward asked Hugh, as he watched the other man resume pacing.

"We wait," Hugh said. "We watch. And we get a new constable of the Tower, one clever enough to keep his head."

Eighteen

1325, FEBRUARY
SIX MONTHS LATER
KING EDWARD'S CHAMBERS,
THE TOWER, LONDON

"Your brother has turned on you. He does not love you, madam," Edward said, "else he would not threaten war against us."

Isabella sat up straight. "He loves me well, my lord. But he loves his country more, which is what a born leader of a nation must do. The love of his heart is never so pressing as his love for his people. It cannot be. *That* is noble, and honorable, and kingly."

Edward scowled.

"Nor is he your only enemy now," she added. "My father was not, in his time, else he would not have given you my hand in marriage. My brother was not. But the pope has heard of what you have done, and he is mightily displeased. Before God, when will you see it?"

He raised a hand. "I see it. I know it, and I do what I must. *That* is what a king must do!"

Her smile was twisted. "Ordering the arrest and imprisonment of all Frenchmen in England, confiscating their lands and property, is what a king must do? Nay, rather it is what Hugh Despenser must do. Even my own retinue, my chaplains, all who came here with me reduced to beggary and sent to live in monasteries or convents?"

"And your brother does not confiscate *my* deeded lands in France?" Edward countered.

"But he does not try to break you!" She choked, and added in a broken voice, "My *children* taken from me and sent to live with Eleanor Despenser, Hugh's wife? For fostering, you said. With that milch cow? Fostered with her and her husband, a man who loves his king too well? What sort of upbringing is that for a boy who will himself be king one day? Nay, my lord, this goes beyond anything. I cannot bear it any longer."

Gwenith shivered. She stood by the door, wishing she could hold her queen's hand and comfort her, as she had done in the months since the children had been sent away.

" 'Deed, you haven't had to," Edward said, leaving off his pacing of his chamber, and glowering at her. "You're scarcely ever near me. This past year you were gone from me as surely as your children are from you. I do not trust this, madam. I ride to war on the Marches, in Scotland, from Leeds to Kent, everywhere in the kingdom where there is need. You go on pilgrimage, and when you are here and I am, you avoid me. You are everywhere but with your husband."

"And that is a shame because he loves me and needs me so much?" she asked, holding her head high. "Despenser has your love, and now it pleases him to belittle me, shame me and destroy me because I am your queen. But I'm also Queen of England. This is folly, Edward. It is not only cruel to me. It may open doors best left locked for you. If the queen can be so belittled, why not the king? How can you allow it?"

"You refused to take the oath of loyalty," Edward said, turning away.

"An oath 'to live and die with the Despensers?' " she asked. "Never! I did not come here to marry the Despensers. I wedded the king. Again, how can you permit this? The country is endangered. Lancaster's men still plot against you. There is revolt spoken and fomenting in all quarters. Not because of me. I don't know how the people feel about me. I've traveled the land this year, and I do know that the people hate the Despensers for their greed and arrogance, even as I do. That means you may have to go to war with all quarters of the nation. And if my brother, the king, is so angry with England, then how can you fight on every front at once? My people came to these shores across the channel and conquered once before."

"Your father was a reasonable man," Hugh Despenser said, as he walked into the king's chamber. "Your brothers are not. Philip the Tall refused me sanctuary when I was in exile, but he did not turn away Lancaster's men who had survived our wrath. No, he welcomed them."

Isabella was speechless a moment, her gaze going straight to Edward. Not so much because of what Hugh said, but because no one should be able to walk into the king's sleeping quarters without first asking permission. This meant that their intimacy had reached a level she could scarcely comprehend. Edward's fair complexion gave the lie to his seeming lack of interest in Hugh's breech of conduct. His face became pink, and he looked down.

"But now my brother Philip is gone," she said. "God rest his soul. And I have always found my brother Charles to be reasonable. I could always speak with him."

"Aye, so why not go to him as an emissary of peace?" Hugh said. "God knows, we will not. We'll go to him with an army, nothing less."

She kept still, with effort. She avoided sharing a glance with Gwenith. So simple in the end, then? He had casually suggested what she had been begging Edward for these last months, since he had shamed her, taken her children and as much as accused her of treason. She wondered why. What new scheme did the Despensers have in mind? Did they think she'd leave England, never to return? Then the earl would have the running of the land, and Hugh would have Edward, entirely, and his sons, and his kingdom one day. There was nothing she could do to stop it, unless she could leave England.

"Go to my brother? I would, if I might," she said fervently. "You know that."

Hugh smiled.

So that *was* it, she thought. It was Despenser's idea. Did he think she could negotiate peace? Or did he think when she left she would never again return? Either thing would please him. But then her spirits fell. It would be very like him to offer something he could then refuse, just to see her pain.

"You think you could calm your brother?" Hugh asked.

"I do not know, but I do know that he loves me," Isabella said.

Hugh looked at Edward, and nodded.

"Then," Edward said, waving a hand at her, "go."

But first Isabella had to speak with those few she knew who loved her in this suddenly alien land. She held an audience in her chambers.

"I cannot go with you, Majesty," Simon the physician said. "I am too old. I will send my nephew, by your leave. I have taught him everything. And he is braver than I."

"Braver?" Isabella said, raising an eyebrow. "But there is danger here for you."

"A danger I know, my lady, as I know the pocks in the road

to avoid when I walk. France has no love for my people either. They have burned down sections of the cities where Jews lived, with them still inside their homes. No, I would rather continue to avoid the dangers I know than try new ones. My nephew can more easily adapt. He does, and can, and will pass as an Englishman in your service."

"I will miss you," she said with sincerity.

"You will return," he said.

"William," Isabella asked, turning to her squire, "do you come with me, or leave me too?"

"I am your man, Highness," he said, hand to his heart. "And," he added, smiling, "since I may be known as such, I'm far better off being with you."

"And you, Gwenith?" Isabella asked.

"Lady," Gwenith said sadly, "how can I not go with you? My life is already in danger. Hugh Despenser made a promise to me with his eyes. I can't face him alone. Only with you may I find refuge now, wherever that may be."

But that was only half a truth, Gwenith thought later that night. She couldn't sleep and lay in her cot at the foot of Isabella's bed, her eyes wide, staring into the dark. Her soul was deeply troubled.

"What ails you?" Isabella asked.

"How did you know I wasn't sleeping?" Gwenith asked in astonishment.

"Your breathing. You don't snore, but you are not exactly silent when you sleep either," Isabella said, with a hint of laughter. Then her voice grew serious. "Come, tell me. You have grown thin of late. You refuse your dinners and go without. Is it fear of Hugh Despenser? I have told you he will not trouble you. We will be beyond his reach. Do you fear going to France, or do you fear leaving England more? My homeland is beautiful. You'll be treated well. I cannot say what your Owain will do. But I know what I can do for you, and that is provide for your comfort. Still, in truth, if you do not want to leave your home, I will understand, and you may go home."

"My home is where you are," Gwenith said. She sat up and, locking her arms around her knees, buried her head on her arms. "Majesty," she said in a muffled voice, "I cannot sleep because I have a confession to make. I cannot eat because it stops my throat from swallowing. I've told no one, not even Owain. He could not help me in this, and there is no priest that can absolve me. Only you can. I have a heavy burden in my heart. I must tell you, even though I know it may be that you will never wish to see me again, or may even order me put to torture, or death. Yet if I do not tell you, I will surely suffer even more."

But then she didn't know how to go on. She only knew that she could not go forward until she had unburdened herself. She had seen Isabella's growing sorrow all these months and had found, to her amazement, that she shared it.

"Go on," Isabella said softly.

"I came to you to do mischief," Gwenith said in a rush. "But you were kind and just with me, and treated me better than anyone ever had. My grandmother loved me, but she ruled me with tales of terror and never let me forget the past so I could become her instrument of revenge," she said, feeling her way, only understanding what she meant after she said it.

"But, Gwenith," Isabella said, interrupting, "I used you too."

"Aye, but not through fear. And not by threat. You asked me to help you, and I did. When my grandmother died, Lady de Percy took me in, only because it was a blood debt to my family. She fed and clothed me, but I don't believe she so much as noticed me. She surely did not need me. But you! You changed me without my knowing. I admitted you into my heart and it was like a bright light that banished all the darkness from my soul. I do not think I could have come to care for Owain had I not . . ." She suddenly smiled, realizing what she said was true. "You banished my brooding and beckoned me to partake of life. I cannot live with the darkness anymore. I must tear the rest of it from my soul, at whatever cost.

"Lady, I was not born in the Marches, but in Wales, and of royal descent, from Llewellyn. But Edward Longshanks destroyed my family, leaving me only a heritage of sorrow. My cousin, Princess Gwenllian, was taken prisoner and banished. My mother was taken into hiding. My grandmother raised me and taught me to hate England, especially Edward and his get. I promised her I would seek vengeance. I came here to do that, and I did. But the one I harmed was you. That I cannot bear."

"How did you do that?" Isabella asked, astonished.

"I arranged for you to meet Mortimer. That is what set this all in motion," Gwenith said miserably. "I knew you would like him. Who would not? He is regal in style and manner, and clearly a victim of the Despensers too. And I knew your gentle heart."

Isabella laughed. "Nay, ease your mind, and lighten your own heart. Mortimer did not cause Edward to turn against me. In fact, Mortimer lightened my life."

"But my vow to do harm to Longshanks' family—"

"That, you may well yet achieve. And that alone disturbs me. Get up, Gwenith."

Gwenith rose from her cot and, shivering, watched as her queen pushed apart her bed curtains and stepped out of her bed as well.

They wore no clothes to sleep. Isabella was a slender, indistinct white figure in the darkness, like a statue of the holy virgin, Gwenith thought, and trembled.

"I care not for foolish vows made by a child," Isabella said. "But I do care for my son, who will be king, and my other children as well. They are as innocent in this as you were when you gave your grandmother your word, so it cannot bind you. Now you are grown to woman, and an oath is a holy thing. Give me your vow, on your life and your immortal soul, that you will never do them harm, that you will protect them as you would me. That or leave me now."

Gwenith dropped to her knees, took Isabella's hand and laid her forehead against it. "I do so vow! I do so swear on my life, on my immortal soul."

"Rise," Isabella said. "Now do you wish to come with me? Do not forget, when it came to it, I was the one who betrayed you to Edward, again and again."

"And then saved me, again and again," Gwenith said.

"Mayhap only to expose you to more danger. You must have been sadly manipulated, and treated with too little grace before you came to me, because you are too grateful for too little, Gwenith. That saddens me. I will not order you to anything now. Should you rather stay here?"

"Lady, my heart is yours," Gwenith said passionately. "My mind is yours. I have come to love you. Wherever you must go, I will follow."

"Then good," Isabella said. "I go to sleep now. Remember your pledge to obey me, and rest easy." She turned and climbed back into bed.

Gwenith lay down on her cot again. The lump in her throat, which had prevented her from eating all these past days, was gone; the weight on her chest had vanished too. Her grandmother was at rest, for Gwenith had fulfilled her vow, however it turned out. She had done her best to confound the son of Edward Longshanks; she'd helped free Edward's enemy and aided his queen in leaving him. She could not be expected to do more. Her family was gone. She was not sure where Owain was. But she rejoiced. She was not alone anymore. She was promised to her queen.

It was not until June that same year of 1325 that they stood on the deck of the ship and watched the shoreline of France coming closer. It was a clear day, with a busy breeze, and Gwenith's hair threatened to escape its bounds as her spirit longed to do the same, to get to France the faster. She stood, hands on the rail, beside her queen, and waited as patiently as the queen did, though her heart was also threatening to burst from its bonds.

"There is a party waiting on the shore," Isabella whispered, as though to herself.

They were as easy to see as a rainbow after a storm. A band of brightly garbed knights, a clutch of beautifully dressed women, a company of gaily festooned horses and two gilded coaches waited on the golden strand. Gwenith's eyes skimmed them all, searching for the one she had hoped to find.

The anchor was thrown down, a longboat lowered, two sailing men carefully handed her down to the boat, to wait for her queen's descent. Then, once the queen was beside her again, as the oarsmen bent their backs, Gwenith turned again and watched the shore.

The queen disembarked first. Gwenith came after and stood statue still, looking for the one face she yearned to see. Her thoughts were like a litany, recited as she tried not to weep. He owed her nothing. He had given her nothing. He might have moved on in his thoughts as well as his person in the year and a half since they had last met.

"Gwenith," Owain said, and she turned to find him striding toward her.

She was in his arms in a moment, laughing too hard to cry, crying too much to laugh, as he whirled her round and round in his embrace.

"My lady in waiting has found her love," Isabella told the French courtiers as they rose from their curtsies. She smiled and then lost her smile, entirely.

Gwenith turned to her with a glad smile, lost her own and looked to see the cause.

Isabella looked past them all to see the man who had slipped down from the saddle of his great white warhorse and now was coming toward her. He was dressed in silver mail. He was strong and well formed, his hair gold in the sunlight, as was his beard. His dark blue eyes were only on her. If she had once longed for the young Arthur, now she beheld him grown and in the richness of his wisdom and years. And this time, he came to her and bent his knee to her. Then Roger Mortimer rose and took her in his arms, kissed her lips, held her, kissed her again and nearly broke her heart with joy because he had no eyes for anyone else but her on that shore, or in the world.

Part Three

Nineteen

1326, July
A year later
Château de Vincennes, France

The queen was admiring herself and so was Gwenith as they both gazed in the tall polished silver looking glass in Isabella's bright chamber. It was one of the few times they had been alone; Isabella had asked her retinue of servants to leave them. Privacy was not as valued in the court of France as it was in England.

"I never tire of this palace, this chamber," Isabella said, lifting her arms and turning around to see her reflection from every angle. "I never tire of being back in France. England is a land of pastels, soft rain and shades of green, blue and gray—the colors of the mists that rise every dawn and come back with the twilight. Here, the light is golden, bright. Here it is as I remembered: gracious, elegant, luminous. The very sky is clearer and the sun more constant. Do you not agree?"

"It is lovely," Gwenith said carefully. "But lovelier to you mayhap, because it is your home. I have come to love the mist."

Isabella laughed. "It's more than that, little March maiden. The people there may speak French as I do, but that is all the two lands have in common."

"I can't deny that the people here in the court seem to live more luxuriously," Gwenith said. "The nobility always dress lavishly. They always seem to be laughing or flirting or telling amusing tales. They wear the latest fashions or they create them, and they dress their hair and even their feet with the same concern as they do their faces. They love fine wines, not just ales, as we do at home. They dine with as much deliberation as they dress. And they eat everything because they sauce it so well. The luxury of it all amazes me."

"It is said there is no better-looking court in all the world, save mayhap for the Italian," Isabella said with pride. "Here at my brother Charles' court, it is not just the food and the wine that must be exquisite. Here a bad smell is as unforgivable as a bad meal. We anoint ourselves with flowery oils and perfumes, and amuse ourselves with stories and ballads of high heroes and deserving knights, just as in the books you love so much."

Gwenith nodded, but didn't dare speak what she thought. It was not quite like the stories of Arthur and his court. She found that the nobles here had great affairs of the heart and the body, and didn't value one above the other, at least, in their songs and stories or the gossip they tattled about constantly. Wherever they loved, or however often, they spoke about it constantly. Hugh Despenser had been right about one thing. The French thought they invented romance, and Gwenith believed they had.

France was the hub of the world. Isabella's brother was surely the most influential man in Europe. The pope himself now lived in Avignon. Isabella was happy here in her brother's illustrious court. It showed in her face and her eyes. Everyone lauded her looks, and that too was lovely for her. She confessed to Gwenith that it was as though she felt the shame and burden of the past years had slipped away, and knew again how life had been when she was young. She laughed more often, and even dressed with more care. Today being a special occasion, she wore an ivory tunic over a yellow undertunic, and her hair was bound and plaited with daisies. The flowers looked so perfect it didn't matter that they weren't real, especially because they were made of gold, ivory and pearl.

In all, Gwenith could see that her queen was happy. Mortimer was with her, and no lady ever had a more tender, affectionate swain. Her old friends were at her side. The people of France gave her due respect and treated her like a princess.

But she was still a queen without a kingdom. That, and few other things, weighed heavy on her heart. She didn't have to confide that to Gwenith. It was obvious from those odd moments, as now, when Isabella's lovely face went suddenly still, and she seemed to look inward. Her beloved Therese was now utterly gone, her remains in a small churchyard in Navarre. Isabella's favorite son, Edward, was in another land, as were her other children. And her throne was there as well.

And today her Gwenith was to pledge her allegiance to another, while keeping to her original vow, or so she swore. Because it was to be her wedding day.

"I can wait no longer," she told her queen. "Nor is it couth or kind to keep Owain waiting."

"Or safe," Isabella had agreed with a smile. "I see his eyes when they are upon you. His forbearance is astonishing. How does he do it when he sees you and desires you every day? Or has he?"

Gwenith ducked her head. "No. We haven't, though we are sore tempted. He says his goal is to make me happy, and that I'm too serious at heart and pure of mind to be happy meeting him behind hedgerows or in dark corners, no matter how pleased our congress would make me."

"A formidable man," Isabella mused. "Yes. I give permission.

More, I give a dowry. I only ask that you continue to serve me as I need you."

Gwenith's eyes opened wide. "But what else? I am yours, lady. As I am, so is Owain. We will be one in your service and defense, but two in our strength in that service."

"I'd thought no less," Isabella said, though she was secretly vastly relieved, even more so than she'd thought to be.

"You must leave us, my dear sister," King Charles of France said.

Isabella wheeled around in surprise to see her brother had come into her chamber. "Leave us?" she asked him, her white brow creasing in confusion. "You want me to leave here?"

"So much as we have delighted in your company, dear Isabella, it is now time for you and your party to depart," he said calmly.

"You jest, Charles?" she asked her brother. "Surely you do. You told me I was welcome here. You understood my reasons for coming to you. You were furious at our people being made outcasts in England, and outraged that a princess of France was treated as I had been, not to mention a true queen in her own right."

Gwenith eyed the king from beneath her lashes. To look directly at any nobleman from this court was to invite attentions she didn't want to deal with. Even though Gwenith was protected by her queen, just as she had been in England, still the king was used to female approval and fancied many women.

Charles was a handsome man, tall and fair of hair and skin as Isabella herself was. He wasn't as handsome as his late father, it was said, or his brothers, all kings, had been. But few men were. Their father had been as well known for his masculine beauty as he had been for his skills as king. Even so, Philip the Fair's son was passing fair to look upon. He hadn't been Isabella's favorite brother when she was young. But he had been generous and kind to her and her entourage since she had arrived here a year past: giving fetes and feasts, and staging tourneys in her honor. Gwenith too believed he was jesting now.

But his face was grave. Isabella frowned. "You mean it, then? But where am I to go? And why?"

Charles shrugged. Today he wore rich purple robes, trimmed with gold. It pleased him to dress elaborately every day. "The pope is displeased," he said. "Gossip is flying. Your living with Mortimer, dear sister, is adulterous and a mortal sin. He disapproves."

Isabella laughed. "And he approves of the fact that my husband beds a man? A strange liturgy he sings, is it not?"

Charles shrugged again. "He disapproves of Edward, also, of course. But my court also gossips. Mortimer is not your husband. And too, must he be so openly affectionate with you? He flaunts your affair."

"A simple caress? A light kiss on the brow? This concerns you? And the fact that he is not my husband? That disturbs you? *You*, Charles?" She laughed, with a sidewise glance at Gwenith.

Gwenith hid her smile. The king's affairs were numerous and well known.

Charles didn't laugh. "It is different for a male, and very different for a king. But that is not the point. Let us leave it. Why do you linger? Your husband, whether you choose to cuckold him or not, sent you here to negotiate peace. He has flooded us with letters to that effect. Yet you have not even attempted that."

Now she shrugged. "Mayhap that is not what I want."

"Ah," he said, "now we come to it. What is it that you want?"

"The same thing you do," she said simply, "if for different reasons. I do not consider myself an adulteress, because I do not consider myself married. Neither does my husband. Edward is in no way my husband anymore, if indeed he ever was. He has had many lovers. I, of course, overlooked that, even though all his lovers were men. It is no secret. The only shock in it now is that he flaunts them. At least they were content with his largesse and did not seek mine. His present lover seeks to oust me, humiliate me and discredit me in the eyes of the court. Despenser wants to be king *with* Edward, and who knows what after that?

"They have taken my property, my lands, my friends and my children. They seek to punish me for merely living. I feared the day would come that they would try to remedy that, as they have already achieved all the rest. They insult not only me, but you, brother, and your entire nation, making the pact between us invalid."

"I know," Charles said. "And so I took back that which was ours. I seized all of his possessions in France. But I regret that there is one I must give up. You must leave, sister."

"Ah," Isabella said, "so you send me to my death?"

"Don't be foolish," he snapped.

"Why else do you think I linger here?" she demanded. "I feared that would be their next move, so I came to you under the flag of trying to win peace for Edward and concessions to him. That is not what I want, nor, I think, what you do . . . under the present conditions."

"Go on," Charles said.

"I want the throne back," she said. "For me, and for Edward, my son."

"And your lover, Roger Mortimer, does he want the same?"

"Of course," she said.

He shook his head. "Think carefully before you answer, my dear sister. Your Mortimer sought to overthrow his rightful king. He has already shown his hand. It may be just as much a mistake to trust such a revolutionary as it would be to trust a dog that has already bitten once. Do you believe Mortimer sought you out only because of your so very blue eyes? You are very beautiful, true. But the world is filled with beautiful women. Or could it be because you were the queen, no matter what you look like? Such a man might love the glimpse he has gotten of absolute power. He might come to love it too much. And then where would you be?"

She stiffened. "*You* would know about such things as desire for the crown, Charles, not he. He fought against the Despensers, not Edward."

"But Edward and the Despensers are one now," Charles said relentlessly. "And well Mortimer knows it. He wants all their heads. He cannot take one without the others. Have a care that your Mortimer does not seek more than you can give him. A man who kills his king overthrows the rule of God and man. Beware of such a man."

"Should I then beware of you?" she asked.

Gwenith looked at the marble floor she stood on. There were stories about the king's older brother, Philip the Tall's, brief reign, because of his seeming good health, and then his sudden illness and death, followed by that of his newborn son.

As Charles grew still, Isabella nodded. "For our family does not have the most savory reputation, either. I heard nonsense about what happened after the death of our poor brother, Philip, God rest him. Or was it? Rumors flew faster than storm clouds rush across the channel. When he died, he left a thriving infant son. Yet somehow the infant died soon after. And so our dear brother, Louis, God rest his soul, who said he knew nothing about it, became king."

Charles stiffened. "Infants die suddenly—some at a change in the wind, some for no reason we can see. Kings cannot proclaim immortality. It is God's will."

"And too," she mused, "I was heartsick at hearing of how you dissolved your marriage to poor Blanche. Divorce—ah, pardon, annulment. The pope did not seem to mind that, did he? Not even when you wed your lovely Marie within the same year."

"There were reasons," Charles said icily.

"Oh, no doubt. I only say that a man sees what he wishes to

241

see. Let us be done with this sorry squabble. My aims are not that different from yours. Nor are Mortimer's. We seek Edward the king's ouster. He is no longer a fit ruler. He is too easily influenced by his lovers. Despenser uses him like a castle whore. And that in itself tells a tale, since Hugh Despenser never desired any other man before. Was none so appealing? Or is it that no other man was king?"

"Just as I said," Charles said smugly. "Some men love where ambition leads them. I hear your Mortimer has a wife and children— not only children, but ten of them. A prodigious amount, is it not? And so, does he desert them and love you because of your beautiful eyes or because you helped him escape death or because you can win him England?"

She cast her gaze down.

Gwenith clamped her lips tightly together. This had always bothered her, but it never seemed to dismay Isabella. Mortimer seldom spoke of his wife, and the queen did not seem to regard it; like all nobility, he had married according to the wish of his father, and at a tender age. Nor did Isabella ever mention his clutch of children. Children after all were often inevitable and having many of them to ensure a succession was vital, since so many failed to reach adulthood. Still, Mortimer neither spoke dislike nor love for his family; he never spoke of them at all, only of his love for Isabella.

"Hugh Despenser has the same number of children," Isabella said, raising her head. "That does not stop him from buggering another man. Or is such a union considered more holy now?"

"What is that to us?" her brother asked. "It is your behavior we are responsible for."

"I am responsible for myself," Isabella said. "I left England in fear of my life and my sanity. The Despensers rape England. Her king revels in it. I want Edward to turn his crown to its rightful ruler now, and that is Edward, my son. I cannot leave France until he is allowed to come join me," she said defiantly. "He is fourteen now, a man. I want him safe, and that means with me. For that, I need your cooperation. Gossip flows from this place. What we say aloud today, they will hear in England by tomorrow's dawn. The more we seem in concert, the more we may be able to make Edward and the Despensers believe that any peace treaty we agree upon here must be signed by a representative of the crown.

"Edward coming to you to make peace will never happen. It would rankle him," Isabella went on. "He sent me to you because you are my brother, and because he thought you might oblige me with a peace treaty. But he wouldn't be surprised if you did not. After all, he also sent me because it was a good way to be rid of me, because he doesn't value me. He doesn't think much of women, and Hugh Despenser thinks even less of them. They would certainly understand if you said you could not value any treaty *I* might sign. Tell them you want Edward, or his son, to come here to make peace. Since Edward would never come to you except in triumph, and that, surely, you would not like, let us wait for my son."

"And then you will go home to England?"

"With an army behind me," Isabella said. "No other way."

"You are mad," Charles said, turning away quickly, the silk of his rich robes whispering.

"Nay," she said, "I am only determined. Think of it, brother. Edward has fewer allies every day. The greedier the Despensers are, the more they take, the more the frightened lords, barons and landless knights will align themselves with me."

He waved his hand, without turning around. "I see," he said sarcastically. "You will do what no man has done."

"That is true," she said. "Because I am a woman, and a queen, and my son is a prince of England who will one day be king. Why not hasten that day?"

"And you expect us to march on England with you?" Charles scoffed, at last turning to stare at her. "Now? You are mad. It is not time."

"Nay. That would be war between nations, an entirely different thing. Then the people will fight to defend their king, any king. You may stay here. What I expect is for you to help me get the funds to march on England. The people of England will welcome me. They suffer now. Wait. Hear me out! They will not see a Frenchwoman at the head of the conquering army. They will see their queen, and their prince, and an earl of the realm. And so they will see it as a liberating army."

Charles was silent in thought for a moment. "And you want me to fund such an army?"

She looked at him and smiled.

He raised his hand to stop her from saying anything. "This is a thing we must think about."

"For a certainty," she said. "But later. Today is a special day. Now we have a wedding to attend. On that head, be gracious, please, and generous to the bride and groom, brother. He is a steadfast, worthy knight, and she is an innocent girl and a true heart."

"You still love the old ballads and romances, do you?" Charles asked.

"But of course," she said. "To my joy and regret."

Gwenith walked on roses. She picked up the hem of her gown and, looking down, went up the stone stairs to the cathedral with great care.

"Is aught the matter?" Owain, at her side, whispered to her.

"They are so beautiful," she said. "It seems a pity to crush them under my feet."

"They are tribute," he told her. "They were born to the purpose."

She smiled up at him then, able to look him full in the face because they had got to the door of the cathedral. The priests waited for them there to perform their longed-for wedding.

Isabella and Mortimer came after Owain and Gwenith, and then stood behind them, waiting for the priest to finish saying the words. William came next, at the side of Simon the physician's nephew. A retinue of English knights and pages followed, as did Isabella's other ladies. Then came the court of the King of France, murmuring to one another, all in silks and velvets as colorful as the stained glass in the great cathedral's magnificent high windows.

The priest, done with the vows, nodded. "You are wed in the eyes of God and man," he said. Then he turned and led them into the chapel for the service to follow their vows.

Gwenith knelt at the altar and stood, and moved her lips in the prayers, but it all seemed fantastical to her. Here, across the sea, she had been joined in marriage to a man she loved. Neither of them knew what lay ahead for them. But neither wanted to go on without the other any longer.

"We cannot return," Owain had told her, weeks earlier, as they strolled in the elaborate gardens at the palatial chateau. "Both our homes, Wales and England, are closed to us now. I could not offer you more than my heart and my hand when we were in England. But when you chose to follow Isabella here, you gave up everything for her."

"For her," she said and bowed her head, "and you."

"Oh, my poor Gwenith," he said, taking her into his embrace, "whatever happened to my sensible Gwenith?"

"She grew even wiser," Gwenith said, her head resting against his heart. "She realized that life without love is no life at all. And where once her only mission was to bring destruction, now she wants to heal all those she loves."

"And so you would give up your vow to your grandmother?" he asked, craning his neck to see her face.

"It was supplanted by another," she said. "The first was made in ignorance, this one, in love. I am pledged to Isabella now."

"Would you take another vow?" he asked. "To me? I am still Mortimer's man. My lands are now truly lost to me, at least for now. They can only be regained through blood and struggle, and anarchy. But I still have, by the grace of God, my good right hand, and my skills at fighting. Let me use them, and my heart and soul, in your service now. I cannot harm you by loving you now," he said more softly. "So can you, will you marry me, at last, my love?"

After she kissed him and after she wept, and yet still after she had kissed him again, she had said yes. And then she had grown fearful, because there was one last thing to do. Isabella had to give her permission.

"I would not leave you, even so," Gwenith had finally blurted, after she'd made her request to Isabella. "Owain is pledged to Mortimer, as I am to you. We would stay on with you, if you desired, if you give us leave."

"But of course," Isabella had said, laughing. "Better marry than continue to languish, wanting him. Better still, not to sin, for that would weigh far too greatly on you, my sensible, but oh so good Gwenith."

And now here they stood, outcast and exiled, treasonous to their king, Edward, loyal to Isabella, Queen of England and her chosen knight, Mortimer, being wed in the eyes of God and under the protection of the King of France. A strange fate for a girl from Wales, brought up in shadows in a peasant's hut, fed tales of blood and revenge. A better fate—Gwenith thought with gratitude to the suffering God on the hugh cathedral wall whose painted eyes let in sunshine as they seemed to look down on her so far below Him—than she had ever guessed or even deserved. How long she would have it she did not know. Sooner or later the piper had to be paid. But for now she stood beside her new husband and thanked God for him, and continued to ask for mercy for herself, and him, and her queen.

The court of King Charles IV of France loved a festival. There was no better excuse for one than a wedding. All the guests had to do was what they did best: laugh and sing, eat and dance, gossip and tell tales. The food was so plentiful, so lavishly prepared, that Gwenith thought the feasts she had been agog at in London at the court of Edward were like those for peasants by comparison. The cooks did more than cook dead beasts and birds, coat them with gilt or feathers and send them forth. As she had told Isabella, she never stopped being amazed at how these cooks prepared meat, fowl and fish so lovingly, and no less elaborately, but in pies and stews and dishes made with flavored sauces and strange herbs, and exotic fruits and spices from the south.

The music was constant. The dancers and jugglers, minstrels and jongleurs performed in the center of the great hall all day and into the night. The very air was perfumed, every guest wore his or her finest and Gwenith had never seen finer.

The King of France gave a toast to the couple. The Queen of England did too. And Gwenith knew that never again in her life would she have a day so wrapped in splendor. Nor a night, she discovered later, so longed for and fulfilled.

The couple had been given their own room in the château for their wedding night, a mark of high privilege. Most others of their status from the English court slept on cots together in the halls or on the floors, or in the stables, or beside their masters' and mistresses' beds.

"This is a high honor indeed," Owain said, as he glanced around the small, spare room. "But there is no table, and no tub has been brought. There lacks a chair, and a glass for you to see yourself in. Were we home, you would have that and more."

"I have you," she said. "I need no more."

He laughed. "Spoken like a bride! Give you a week, and I make no doubt you will change your tune."

All laughter fled. "Were you married before," she asked, her eyes searching his, "that you say such a thing?"

He put his hands on her shoulders and looked at her. "I told you I was promised, but never wed, and so I was not. Gwenith, we two live midst lies. We've had to trade in deceit, you and I. But between us, let there never be a lie."

And so she told the truth when she told him she found him handsome beyond belief when he had disrobed. And he told her the same when he said her body was perfect, after he had helped her remove her garments. He told no lie when he murmured that her hair was like silk when he unbound it. She only spoke truth when she gasped she was ready after he bore her down to their bed, and kissed her and tasted her until she writhed.

She told no lie when she said she was ready and would die did he not serve her. He could not say anything as he came into her at last, because he was trying so hard not to go too fast, because she was small, and it was obviously her first time.

They didn't speak as he began to move in her, nor could. And if he took more pleasure than she did because she didn't as yet know how to, and he could not help her discomfort, she didn't tell him, because she would not lie. Nor would he, nor did he, when he had come to his moment, and lay beside her again. He only said, "Thank you, my love. This will only get better for us. But now you are mine, and I am yours, and as our minds are attuned, so now we have the time to perfect our love, in all ways."

"Do we?" she asked softly. "Who can say?"

"We have tonight," he said, rolling to one elbow and looking down at her. "And for us, each night we do have, we will make our eternity."

Isabella raised her head. Mortimer was still gasping his relief, though his hand kept stroking her hair.

"You like this very well," she said, inching up and resting her chin on her arms on his hard abdomen, and looking up at him. "Do you like it because it feels so good?" she asked. "Or because it is the Queen of England doing it to you?"

He sat up and rolled her over on her back. He smiled, then kissed her. He brought his mouth to her neck, and then his mouth and his tongue to her breasts, and then as she moved beneath him, to her stomach, and then, he parted her, and kissed and tongued her as no man ever had done, but for him. He only paused once before he brought her to ecstasy.

"Do you like this because of how it feels," he asked her, as she lay there, dumb with pleasure, shaking with the need for him to finish what he had begun, "or because the man who will soon free you in all ways is doing it for you?"

She could not gather her wits to answer, and so he completed it for her before she could tell him, which was as well because she no longer knew.

Twenty

———

1326, AUGUST
CHÂTEAU DE VINCENNES, FRANCE

Now she could see a glimpse of the man he would be. Isabella's son was not tall, and likely never would be. Nor was he as beautiful as his mother, or any of her handsome family. But he had grown, he had filled out and his face had lost its boyish cast, becoming strong, rather than pretty. His eyes had changed the most, Gwenith thought. They were watchful, as always, but now they were also wary, no longer a lucent baby's blue, but instead the blue of flint rock, and they showed the strength in the mind behind them.

But he was here. He was in France. He was with his mother at long last. Isabella smiled and allowed herself a moment to luxuriate in the love of him before she pulled herself back to the arduous work ahead of them. The queen and Gwenith watched Edward roam her chamber, impressed, they could see, by the tapestries and furs, silks and fine furnishings that adorned it.

"Your uncle, the king, has made us comfortable here," Isabella said.

"I see," Edward said. "And where does Mortimer stay?"

She looked down and then, refusing to be chastised by her son, looked him full in the face. "With me," she said.

His expression didn't change. "So it is true," he said.

"There are rumors?" she asked.

He nodded.

"Then why did Edward allow you to come here?"

"He does not care about you and Mortimer," Edward said, with a shrug of one shoulder. "He wants a treaty with Charles. He desires his possessions in France returned to us. And he does not want war. At this time," he added.

"Do *you* care about me and Mortimer?" she asked. Before he could answer, she added, "Please do not. I am a woman grown, your mother, and still Queen of England. Edward the king and Hugh Despenser beggared me in body and spirit, as well as claiming my rightful possessions. Had I stayed, I doubt I would have lived. My poor Gwenith will testify to that. I would have died at their hands, or my own." She crossed herself to dispel the sinful thought, and went on. "Mortimer saved me and promised to save us."

"Did you not save him?" Edward asked.

"That," she said, "I will not ever say. It no longer matters. But you know that if you return to England as things are, even if there were a treaty, your life would not be safe? The Despensers aim too high. We need a strong arm to support us, as you are yet too young to defend yourself or your country."

"I know," he said coolly.

She wondered at the control he had of his emotions, even at such a young age.

"And so, the treaty my father wants is not to be?" he asked.

"No," she said. "My brother Charles will not give up what he considers his rightful possessions, nor would he even if they were not. But that is not why I summoned you. You will be king one day. If we wait on it, until your time comes, there may be nothing left for you to rule. And there well may be a usurper on the throne who will not relinquish it. Hugh Despenser and his father want to gobble up England. We cannot let that happen. *I* will not allow it."

"How will you prevent it?"

"We will have funds from my brother. I intend to raise an army and return to England to make sure it is not stolen from us." She waited for him to smile. He did not.

He cocked his head to the side. "Your brother also may want England."

She smiled. "You are very wise to wonder." She lowered her voice, though only Gwenith was in the room with them, and her son was used to her having a constant servant as companion. "But Charles does not want war as yet. He does not want the pope's condemnation, either. If I am a scandal because of Mortimer, just consider how happy they will be with me as a warrior queen! Not to fret. I do not. We are to go to Flanders. There we will stay with my cousin, who is wed to good William, Count of Hainaut and Holland. And there we will raise a mighty army. And then, and only then, we will return to England and reclaim our throne."

"And Mortimer?" he asked.

"You regard him too much. That is your father speaking, not you. Mortimer is also a victim of the Despensers. He wants his titles and lands back. Everyone in my court does," she added wryly, "even my sweet Gwenith, for she wed a knight whose lands Mortimer had, and now Despenser owns. She is willing to spy, and lie, and fight for them."

Gwenith folded her hands and nodded.

Isabella smiled. "Do not think she is of no moment. She is only one small woman, but she can be multiplied by hundreds more like herself. Too many in England have been robbed. They want recompense. We'll give it to them. We will have the hearts and hands of many others too, whose holdings, honors and lands are in jeopardy. We will to war, if we must. Mayhap it will be a short one. God grant it is a bloodless one. But only God knows how it will be.

"Are you agreed to join me in this?" she asked him, her eyes searching his. "If you are not, though I love you more than you can know, I'll send you back to England, to Edward and his friends, and will trouble you no more. But I will weep for you."

"Do not weep, Mother. No more than you do I want my legacy stolen. I came here with friends, baron's sons, noblemen, even Edmund, Earl of Kent. They all want their kingdom back. So do I."

She smiled and reached out to touch his cheek. "So you will have it. And don't worry about terrible rumors getting back to England. Soon they will hear only the truth, and it will be terrible enough for those who fear hearing it. As Mortimer says, our cause will be like a mighty mill wheel set loose, which, once turned, will keep on spinning, faster and faster, until it rolls over all opposition in its path."

"Here are the mill wheels you spoke of, Mother," Edward the prince commented, as they rode along a path by the North Sea.

"Nay," she said, as she looked at one of the giant mills in the distance. "They are windmills. They use them to tame the wind and drive back the sea. This land was once at the mercy of the sea. Now they've civilized it and built dykes and canals. They have water. The water does not have them. They've been clever. I can only hope they still are."

Edward fell still. The company moved on, their banners fluttering in the breeze. Travel abroad was said to be dangerous, but Isabella the queen's party feared no one. It was made up of her chosen knights and ladies, Edward's friends and their knights, some of Mortimer's men and a company of King Charles' knights, one hundred fifty souls, in all. And they rode under the banner of the King of France.

Gwenith stayed at her queen's side. Owain followed, with the knights and men in Edward's train. They camped in the fields, or stopped at monasteries or convents, and were never insulted or attacked as they left France and rode through Belgium. It was not a long journey. But it was an interesting one. The landscape became flatter. Windmills churned by the sea as they rode farther north along the coast. There were no incidents.

The land they reached, by the North Sea, was a comfortable one. They saw plump, contented serfs working in the fields, fat cattle, fat geese and fields filled with grain.

Still Mortimer grumbled. "He is merely a count. I still don't understand why your brother the king sent you to him," he complained as they spied a castle in the distance.

"There are no kings in Holland," Isabella said again, patiently. "William, Count of Hainaut and Holland, is as powerful and rich as any king. Indeed, I've heard he has more riches than a king. He's said to be amiable. His people call him William the Good. He is also said to be mad, but in a charming way. He is ambitious, which is good for us. Charles thought he could help me more than any other ruler in Europe, and that he'd be more inclined to spend money and effort on our cause. We then must believe he can."

The land was flat, but as they approached the count's castle, they could see that his city was beautiful, with gracious dwellings along canals that shimmered through the streets, the tall trees at their sides bending to their reflections in the water.

Isabella's party had been seen, and were expected, and so they were admitted through the castle gates at once, and shown into their host's great hall. The count rose from his chair and came to greet them.

Count William was a happy man. It showed in his face, round and smooth, and beaming. "Welcome, Highnesses," he said, bowing to Isabella and Edward and their party.

His wife, Isabella's cousin, Joanna of Valois, was at his side. Isabella couldn't remember having met her, but she had the signature beauty of her family. She was a tall, graceful and slender woman.

But then, anyone would look slender next to the count. He was wide, solid, not so much fat as well padded. He was not handsome, nor was he ugly. He was a comfortable-looking man who resembled a merchant more than a nobleman. He had a round head and most of his yellow hair, and sandy eyelashes, his red cheeks the only thing on his face that gave it contrast and distinction. His palace was rich. His clothing was simple, but the materials opulent, his chuckles were frequent. His light blue eyes even twinkled.

Isabella bowed her head to him. Gwenith, seeing the perpetually smiling count, did not trust him at all.

Mortimer made him a flourishing bow.

"Come," the count said, "we have room for all of you. You, your ladies and trusted advisers, your companions, your body servants too. Your knights and men at arms will have to stay with mine, but that is no hardship—they can tell you! You honor me with your presence. Please take time to rest. Refresh yourselves. We can talk at dinner. We shall have a feast to celebrate your safe arrival! We always enjoy a feast, and what better excuse? We entertain the Queen of England, and her son, the prince. In truth," he said with a chuckle, "we started preparing when we got the first message from your brother Charles the king. Please make yourselves comfortable."

Isabella inclined her head. "Thank you. We shall."

She and Mortimer followed the count's servants to her quarters. But before Isabella rested there, she made sure that Gwenith and Owain, and her most trusted knights, had rooms nearby to her own.

He was a count, but lived like a king. The food, both delicacies and hardier fare, was served in never-ending waves. There was fine ale and strong wine. Though Count William had no jester or minstrels, it was as well. They wouldn't have been heard, because the company was so loud and the laughter so frequent.

The count ruled over the proceedings. When he smiled, everyone laughed. When he ate, he made sure everyone else had full stomachs too. His wife sat at his side, lovely, distant, silent. As for his children, the boys were stolid, the girls, pale versions of their mother, with, unfortunately, their father's scant eyelashes and brows to make them indistinguishable. If they were not gowned so well, they would have been well nigh invisible. But then, their father was so loud and colorful, it was hard to notice anyone else.

"So," the count said, when he looked down the table at his royal guests, "the food and drink were to your liking?"

Isabella noticed that he never addressed a remark to Mortimer, but only to her or Edward. She didn't take it as insult, though Mortimer seemed displeased. But he was only her rumored consort, so though it irritated him, it only made sense to Isabella.

"All was delicious," Isabella said.

"Thank you. Now," the count said, as he dipped his hands in a bowl of water and rubbed them together, "we talk, Your Highness. Or would you rather wait until tomorrow, when you are rested?"

"I would rather wait for privacy," Isabella said.

"Oh, that, yes, of course," he said. "Not here. We will go to my chambers, now if you like."

She inclined her head.

The count rose. "Then please accompany me, Your Majesty, if you please, you and your son, Edward the prince."

"Me," she said coldly, "my son, Edward the prince, and my companion, Roger Mortimer."

He shrugged. "As you will."

She was glad that the room was too noisy for Mortimer to have heard this. He was insulted enough by their host's ignoring him all through the feast, and it might be that they all would have to work together one day.

The count bowed and, with a flourish, indicated that they should come with him.

Isabella got to her feet, as did Mortimer and Edward. Gwenith followed. But before Isabella left, she signaled to her trusted squire, William, who stood a few paces behind her, as did all the more highly placed servitors.

"We negotiate now," she told him softly. "Watch, and tell those of our party where we go. Tell them to be prepared. When we are done, if things do not go well, we all must leave this place. They will not dare do us harm. But if they cannot do us good, we cannot stay."

They sat in the count's chambers, except for Gwenith, who stood behind her queen.

The count lifted an eyebrow, when he saw Gwenith take her place.

"Gwenith de Rhys is my trusted companion," Isabella explained.

The count shrugged and looked away, as though he realized Gwenith was of no account.

Gwenith didn't mind. She no longer felt like Isabella's cast shadow, because she knew Owain waited for her. She looked around with wonder. She'd seldom seen such comfort, even in a palace. The chairs were covered. The tables had richly embroidered cloths. The tapestries on the wall were magnificent. The room even had its own hearth, which was almost unheard of, even in France.

The count made sure they all had some of his fine red wine, then waved his servants away.

"So," he said jovially, but without preamble, facing his guests, with his back to the fire roaring in the great hearth behind him. "You are here because you want to attack England, kill the king and take the reins."

"Nay," Isabella said coldly. "We wish to return to England, displace the Despensers and have the king abdicate the throne in favor of his son."

The count spread his hands in a gesture of surrender. "If I misspoke, forgive me, Majesty. I am a simple man. But I also was given to understand that your husband, the king, has discovered your aims and demands that you return to England, to him."

"And my brother, the king," Isabella said, "has told him nay. He said that as I came of my own free will, I may return freely, if I wish. But that as I am his sister, and if I prefer to remain with him, he refuses to expel me."

"So why have you left him?" the count asked, and then seeing her darkening expression, quickly added, "Forgive me. I am of a playful nature. I know why. Now, as I understand it, your brother has given you ample funds to achieve your purposes. He does this for his own purposes as well, I don't doubt, as he is not a foolish man. But he doesn't want a war and all its possible results laid on his doorstep. So he sends you to me. Now you must assemble an army. I can help you do that. The Continent swarms with landless knights, wayward ones, those who look to regain their fortunes, those who wish to make them, as well as those mercenaries who will sell their swords to anyone who asks and pays. I can find them for you. You will need generals with tongues like lashes, and swords at the ready, as well. I will find them for you. It will be a motley army, but a conquering one. All this I can help you with, and shall be pleased to do so.

"Still," he asked slyly, "once they are assembled under your banner, how will you get them to England? I can assist there too. But it is no simple thing, and money alone cannot buy my cooperation, because this goes beyond mere war. It is the toppling of kings. There is danger in it, and I am a prudent man."

"What do you want in return?" Isabella asked calmly.

"Oh. Well. That," the count said and paced a few steps, then turned to face her again. "I have money in plenty. God has blessed us with His bounty. The land is rich. We sell and trade. Our fields prosper and our seas give us more bounty. Our nobles *and* our serfs grow fat. God has also blessed me with a bounty of children. I have sons, and five daughters, one lovelier than the other. Although how that can be, I do not know, for if one is truly lovelier than the other, who then is the loveliest?" He chuckled.

No one else in the room smiled.

"No matter," the count went on. "My daughter Margaret is already wed to Louis, Duke of Bavaria. Last year, it was, and such a wedding as few have ever seen. The bridegroom is destined for great things. But the bride's sister, almost the same age, and no less good and beautiful, is not wed yet. This pains her, and her mother, and me. We want her to have a husband who also is destined for greatness. Can you blame her, or your cousin, my wife, or me?"

"How old is she?" Isabella asked.

"She is rising thirteen, a maid, with a good mind and of an obedient nature," he replied promptly.

So she could be any one of the washed-out-looking girls at the feast tonight, Isabella thought. No matter. A king did not wed for love, nor a queen, if she was wise. And the count was a wealthy man with ambition and power, connected to the great houses of Europe. Charles must have known about this, Isabella thought, and sighed. She glanced at Edward, sitting silent at her side. His face was impassive. Mortimer stood next to him, looking aggrieved at being ignored, but he was wise enough to hold his tongue. It was not his duty to negotiate. They had discussed it and agreed.

"I see," Isabella said. "Nor will I pretend to misunderstand. So what do you offer in exchange for my son's hand?"

"Sailing ships," the count said with a smile. "Round ships. Great-bellied carracks. Ships that can carry an army, and their weapons, and heavy cannon, should they be stopped at sea or in the channel."

"How many?" Isabella asked.

"Three," he said.

"Three?" she asked incredulously. "You hold us cheap, sir! Three ships for the hand of a king?"

"For the hand of one who *migh*t be king, one day," he corrected her.

She drew herself up. "Who *will* be king, no matter what else happens. This, I promise."

"Four, then," he said. "Four great men-of-war."

She laughed in his face.

"I will have to buy, beg and borrow. What man has so many ships?" he asked.

She said nothing.

"Six," he finally said.

Her smile was withering.

"Seven then, but that is all I can muster," the count said. "And that will involve building new ones as well."

She glanced at Edward. He nodded.

"Eight," she said.

"Eight?" the count asked, his mild blue eyes widening.

She nodded. "Eight."

"Done," he said.

Twenty-one

Their army was a motley one. But a mighty one. They sailed in the ships that Isabella had been promised. Eight mighty round-bottomed carracks, outfitted for war. Their massive hulls and towering fore- and aftcastles dwarfed not only the traders and other vessels at the docks, but the wharves from which they left.

Each ship was filled with knights, their full armor, their weapons, their pages and servants. If the armored knights were toppled onto the deck they would never survive; if they were cast into the sea, they would sink like stones. Below, the knights' warhorses were secured. The poorer knights made their own group. The lower decks were filled with archers and common foot soldiers, who carried lances and maces, swords and clubs and blessed holy charms to save them from death on land or in the sea. The men aboard the ships shouted to one another until the wind and the sea took their ships farther apart. Too far to talk, but close enough to see, the ships sailed in a string, their big-bellied sails filled, catching the wind.

Each carrack had a castle fore and one aft, each able to hold at least eight fighting men. The miniature castles were like their namesakes, but each a man's waist high, so that the rocking of sudden waves could not pitch the men in them over to the deck or the sea below. The castles were painted and shaped with turrets to look like those on a real castle, and afford the same protection to the men behind them. In the center, high above the sea and the ship itself, where the lookout on another ship might be, there was yet another castle for fighting men to shoot arrows and throw lances from. And every vessel flew the golden lions of England on its pennants.

There was a moderate breeze and it was a fair tide, and the sails on each ship snapped and belched with every gust, but held the wind and sent the huge ships flying, instead of wallowing like the great sea beasts they were.

Gwenith rested her back against her husband, Owain, where they stood on the forecastle on their ship, and felt the sea breeze on her face. They were leaving at last, returning at last, and at last she was frightened, but she never wanted him to know it. It wasn't just her fear of what would happen in England. Now that she had let love in, she had something to lose. Now her own life was as important as her previous mission had been. And that life included Owain and the queen.

Things had moved so fast for her, sometimes she felt as though she was spinning out of control. But Owain was her anchor, and Isabella her lodestone. Still, there were times in the night when Owain lay sleeping beside her, when she would marvel at the change in her life and wonder how it would change her. She loved a man who bore a hated name, and loved a woman who was wife to the man she had vowed to bring down. So, nightly, silently, she said a prayer to her grandmother, asking forgiveness. And each morning she prayed to thank God for Owain, and then asked Him to protect the two people she loved so dearly.

"Again," Owain now said in her ear, "I would wish that you had stayed here with comfortable Count William, and waited for me to come get you when this dangerous work was done."

"Again," she said with a long sigh, "I tell you that I will go where my queen goes, because I pledged myself to her."

"And me?" he asked.

She quickly turned around, her eyes searching his. "But you knew this. You said you understood it, as I understand your allegiance to Mortimer. You said—" A sudden sea swell made her lose her balance, and she felt Owain's arms go around her again, holding her steady.

"So I do, and so I did," he said. "But that does not mean that I cannot still wish to have you somewhere safe now. When this is done, I vow you will be done with danger, so long as I am granted to live." He glanced to the other side of the forecastle, where the queen stood with Mortimer and her son. "Isabella knows that you will go with me when this is over," he asked in a lower voice, "does she not?"

"She does, and she is not the one who insisted I stay with her now. It is what I must do." Gwenith angled a glance at him and, in the new way she had learned in her life with a lover, added flirtatiously, "And that way too, I can keep my eye on you."

"Afraid I might succumb to one of the lusty men on board?" he asked, smiling back at her.

"Of course," she said comfortably.

"As to that, I want you never out of my sight unless you are with Isabella," he said seriously. "There are men here who are skilled at war, but that does not mean they know how to live in peace. This army of ours has noble and worthy knights, but also the human refuse of a dozen lands, men who spill blood for money, and men who would do it, and gladly, for nothing. There are malcontents and madmen in our company, and never forget it."

"And madwomen," she said, nodding. "As I am, for you."

He laughed, causing Isabella to turn and look at the couple.

"Now there is a brave woman," Gwenith heard her say. "My Gwenith would walk with me into fire. Her Owain would too."

"He will be rewarded when this is done," Mortimer said. "I have sworn to it."

"How rewarded?" Isabella asked him.

"His lands returned to him, his castle, his acres, his serfs, all restored to him, with extra land as well."

"And a heavy purse of gold from me," Isabella said. "There is no adequate way to reward loyalty. But gold will do, for a beginning."

Mortimer laughed. "And as for me?" he asked. "What reward do you have in mind for me?"

Isabella's laughter faded. She glanced at Edward, who stood at a turret near them and looked out over the sea with concentration. She was not deceived. She knew he was listening close.

"For you," she said, "a new title, honors, your lands returned, and gold."

"And . . . ?" Mortimer asked playfully.

"And my gratitude," she said, "as well as my son's. Is that not right, Edward?"

Edward turned. "Aye, madam, that is right."

Isabella blinked. In that moment, he sounded so like the man he was named for that she felt herself grow chill.

"I wonder," she said softly, "if we shall get the chance to reward anyone. If this venture will be a success."

"It will be," Mortimer said. "We will not fail."

"Even if we don't fail, even if we succeed, I wonder how I shall be received," Isabella said. "Nothing we do is a secret. The world grows smaller every day. One may as well try to keep a secret from the wind. Edward the king has written me scores of letters, each more furious, since he heard of our relationship. His spies are everywhere. And so I am declared outlaw by him, forbidden to set foot in England, as is my son. Who would have thought it would have come to this? There's no turning back now. You know the rumors that he had paid some in my brother's court to kill me. I scoffed, but I did not entirely disbelieve it.

"One thing I am sure of," she said. "They know what we plan. Such an army, and such a fleet as we have, cannot be a secret. They may await us with an army. They may be planning our defeat as we set sail. And I have heard what they are saying about me in England now. They call me the She Wolf of Paris. Oh my dear, blessed Jesus, how can they turn on me like that?"

"They also call you worse," her son remarked dispassionately. "But that is because of what my father, the king, says. I heard he wears a dagger now too, in his hose, at all times. He tells all that it is to kill you with if he ever sets eyes on you again, and if it cannot, he will use his teeth."

Isabella stared at her son.

Edward's grave eyes turned from the sea to her. "But it will never happen. You will not be harmed. I will not allow it."

"We will not allow it," Mortimer said.

Edward shrugged and looked out to sea again.

Isabella stirred. She reached out a hand to touch Edward's shoulder, and then drew her hand back. Theirs was not that kind of familiarity. But she wished she could tell her son about how she understood too well, how she too knew all the qualities of loneliness. She knew he saw Mortimer as an enemy, and she could not blame him. How else should a boy feel about the man his mother was committing open adultery with? She wondered how a boy would feel about going to war against his father. She didn't even know how her son felt about Edward the king, and suddenly did not wish to know. There was only so much pain she would endure.

But she wished she could explain to him about the fear she had felt, so alone in a suddenly strange land, with a man sworn to protect her who was in love with a man determined to destroy her. She wished she could tell him about the vaulting joy she'd felt when she'd realized someone wanted her just for who she was, and would, were she a servant, or a queen. But she still did not know if this was true.

"We will win," she said instead. "We will prevail. And England will be yours, Edward. I—*we*—will allow no one to steal it from you."

There was an army massed on the shore and the hills above it. Those on the approaching ships could see it plain. The sun glinted off armored breasts, the shining armor on their warhorses, and the helms and shields of the bowmen ranked on the rocks that ringed the beach.

"We can land here, and fight," Mortimer said, as he paced the forecastle. "Or we can turn and land on a different shore. But that will be seen as weakness. They are horsed, and in position. I don't know how well we can commit ourselves as we leap from the ship, but we can try. Surely the Norman William the Conqueror, who defeated another king to claim England, faced such odds, and he won the day. And too, we can hove close to the shore and let our arrows fly, and then rush the beach and attack on foot and horse. They have horses, but we have height, from our ships."

"Aye," Owain said. "But first, and before all, my lord, we must find a safe place for our queen, and her ladies."

"There is no safe place in a war," Mortimer said. "But aye, we can try. They must go below and wait until we can let them out in triumph. I think the young prince should be with them, to protect them, of course," he added when he saw the strange look Edward

266

gave him. "The knights he has brought with him can surely help him do that."

"Apart from the fact that they will fight, as will I," Edward said, "and fight anyone who seeks to deny them, as will I, I think there is another choice. Look closer, Mother, and tell me what you see."

Isabella studied the shore. Her smile grew as she did. "My clever boy," she said. "Aye. Some of the banners are Lancaster's. Some are Leicester's, and there are other noble houses. In fact, none I see are my enemies. And those pennants that are not theirs are white, to show they come in peace."

"I would see," Mortimer said. He squinted, shaded his eyes and peered at the shore. "So it seems," he eventually said. "But even so, Lancaster leads them. His banner is foremost. Can we be certain that the house of Lancaster really means peace with us? You killed their leader."

"Not I," Isabella said. "Their quarrel was with Edward, not me or mine. Thomas, the last earl, died at Edward's command, not mine. I tried to make his death easier. And I believe we can trust Henry, his brother. If not, there's no one in England we can. Not money nor titles nor land would tempt him. Their family is ancient, royal and honored. Henry is now earl, but the house is wealthy beyond a mere earldom. That's why Edward and the Despensers tried to beggar them."

"True," Mortimer said. "But I have heard of them since. The king gave back the lands he had stolen from his brother to Henry, the new earl, because he claimed innocence in the matter of the revolt. Rich men need to grow richer. Royal blood can be contaminated too. Where do you think his allegiance really lies?"

"With the one who spared his brother indignity, and would have spared him altogether, if she could," Isabella said. "And I see no reason why any man, earl or serf, would forgive his brother's murder."

Mortimer nodded. "As I cannot forgive the murder of my uncle, Roger of Chirk, after I escaped the Tower. They couldn't lay hands on me, so they punished him in my stead. I know you did not lament his passing, but I do. Even did I not, blood must avenge blood. And so then, we must chance it. And you, my queen, must go below decks until we discover how right you are."

"Nay," Isabella said, drawing herself up. "I am Queen of England, and a Princess of France. They call me a she wolf and I think I will begin to earn this new name. Do you think Edward the king would be gentle with me should I lose this chance? If I am to lead England, and hold it for my son, I must begin now. If I am to lose England, better I lose my life quickly, in battle, than torturously, with humiliation ending only on the block. I will go ashore now. My son and I will lead our armies, as we will meet our fate, head high. That is what a queen must do. That is certainly what a future king must do, however young he is."

Edward smiled at his mother.

"And, Owain de Rhys," Isabella said to the knight standing beside Gwenith, "ask your wife what she would do. Ask her what she wants to do. Let her tell you. I will not order her or any of my men or ladies to do aught that will endanger them."

"I will not leave you, lady," Gwenith said immediately.

"I know that," Isabella said. "But it may be a trap. It could be a cheat. I cannot promise you that it isn't," she told them.

"We do what we can, and what we must," Owain said.

Isabella took a deep breath. "Good. Then make your peace with God, my son, my friends. We must try our luck. There is only one thing I must do before I disembark."

They all stood silent, watching her.

"I am wearing simple garments, for traveling." Isabella said, fingering the skirt of her plain blue gown. "That will never do. I must change my clothes and come to England as her queen."

When Isabella signaled she was ready, and robed as befitted a queen, the ships began to move. They pulled as close to the shore as they safely could, and let down longboats, which were immediately filled and swiftly dispatched to the shore. Knights in armor led their horses off the ships, mounted and rode through the surf to the beach. The towers on all eight men-of-war were filled with archers, poised, waiting for a signal, as were the bowmen lined at the railings.

The army on the coast was still, watching, knights sitting their horses in silence, helms down, lances held erect, only their banners moving, teased by the wind. The lines of armed men ringing the spot did not stir either, except for their pennants, which fluttered in the sea breezes.

The figure of a slender woman, dressed in gold to vie with the noon sun, was the first thing they saw. She could hardly be avoided. She wore an elaborate headdress, trailing a flowing veil that fluttered like a banner. She detached herself from the first group to land, and waved the others back. When she stepped forward by herself on the sand, a horseman in a ring of waiting knights moved as well, kneeing his great white horse. He wore no helm. His hair was jet, his complexion dark, and his face unsmiling. And he held a great sword in his right hand. He saw her, stopped, slid down from his mount and approached her on foot.

She stopped, but did not falter.

He bent to one knee before her, and laid down his sword at her feet.

"Your Majesty," Henry, Earl of Lancaster said, "welcome home."

That night, they dined in a tent, on fish and bread, but Isabella vowed she had never tasted anything better. Nobles from many houses were there, and it became a feast, with laughter and merriment.

Gwenith couldn't bring herself to smile. Whenever she gazed

at Lancaster, she saw his dead brother's face; they were as alike as twins, and she wondered if that was a bad omen. Still, what he had to say gave her heart.

"I doubt you will get a chance to blood your sword, my prince," he told Edward. "The king's supporters have fled. In fact you may find they slow our passage if only by their haste to leave London. Your father," he said seriously, "made more enemies than even we guessed. From the commonest man to the lords of castles, there has been a swelling of resentment and anger, which now bursts like an angry boil. He took from the rich, but he plagued the poor as well."

"Not he," Isabella said gently. "The Despensers."

They all turned to look at her.

She raised her head high. "I do not champion him. Indeed, I do not forgive him. But I believe I knew him. He is not evil, or cruel. He is but too easily swayed by those he loves. 'Deed, I almost believe," she said, looking at Lancaster, "that had your brother not slain Piers Gaveston, none of this would have happened. Piers was a creditable knight, for all his excesses. He never wanted to rule England, only to enjoy life and flaunt his riches and successes. The Despensers took advantage of Edward's weaknesses as Piers never would have done."

"A king should not have such weaknesses," Lancaster said.

"Then it would be best to have no human man as king," Isabella said. "But as we must, we can only pray that he puts his kingdom before himself, whatever his human failings."

Edward nodded. And Isabella fell still.

"We march to London with first light," Lancaster said, as he rose to his feet. "Sleep well, my prince, my queen. Tomorrow will be fair. I pray it will be safe for you as well."

Twenty-two

1326, September
The road to London, England

Isabella's army grew as they marched toward London. The weather was with them; they had a spate of fine, clear, early autumn days and nights. Nobles, landowners, men of means and their serfs joined them as they went on. The company grew merrier as well. There were only two incidents, when they were attacked by stragglers from Edward the king's army. The attacks were subdued as quickly as they came, and so the queen never saw any of the gore. More often, she saw the backs of retreating horsemen and foot soldiers.

"They might not want us, but they are smart enough to know that to fight against us now is suicide," Mortimer said with satisfaction, "and that it is a crime against God."

Young Edward laughed, as did those men who had heard Mortimer. But Isabella could not, not now that she could see the walls of London looming in the distance.

"I will ride in first," she said.

Mortimer did not misunderstand her. "No," he said, "you will not."

She straightened in the saddle and stared at him. "You cannot gainsay your queen," she said stiffly.

"I don't. I only ask her not to be foolhardy. The first blow is always struck by the most stupid, the most expendable. If there is to be any resistance, you must give us a chance to counter it, swiftly. If you please, Your Majesty," he added with a mockery of a bow. "And too, I do not think you want to endanger your son. He would defend you. A wise man never puts his king immediately in the first row, even when he plays chess, at least not until he has paved the way with his rooks."

Her smile bloomed. "Aye, and I suppose you consider yourself a rook?" she asked.

"I am a knight, of course," he said. "I ride wherever I so choose."

"And I?" Edward asked.

Mortimer shrugged. "You must do as you wish, Prince. And be what you will. But were I playing on a board, I would position you to protect my queen."

Isabella looked at Mortimer. In that moment, she was as proud of him as she had never been before. He was the quintessential *parfait* knight. Smiling, exultant even as he rode to war. Riding a fine horse, in his shining armor every inch the returning conqueror. Easy living on the Continent had added bulk to his muscular frame, yet that made him look even more like great Arthur, the king he claimed descent from. Her son, at his side, for all his bravado was clearly still only a boy. She was glad Mortimer was there to protect him. And glad, again, that she had begun this mad adventure with Mortimer, though she knew she might be cursed and damned for it. She was wed to another. He was too, but God's laws did not seem as important right now as life on this earth.

"Will you stay with me, Edward?" she asked. Because though

she willingly risked her life, she knew it would not matter if she lived, if by any way or means she caused her son to lose his.

"Aye," he said quietly. He stayed with her when Mortimer signaled to her to drop behind him. And he rode with her as Mortimer, Lancaster, Leicester and their allies and armies rode into the city.

There was no resistance at the north wall. Nor any challenge. The streets were eerily empty as the company clattered through into London.

"It looks like a place that a plague has visited," Lancaster said, his voice too loud as they rode down the echoing streets.

Isabella crossed herself.

"Nay," Mortimer said. "There are no corpses, at least, not yet. It looks like a place that knows we are come home, at last."

They rode on, noting the shuttered doors and windows, the guild houses closed. Even the barrows that usually thronged the street with goods, their mongers crying their wares, were mysteriously vanished. They rode to the Tower, and finally paused, by the drawbridge over the moat. The bridge was down.

Nevertheless, they waited for the guard to challenge.

No one spoke. All they heard were rooks cawing, and a gull's scream as it wheeled in the sky overhead.

All was quiet on the wall facing them.

"Are there archers?" Lancaster asked, bemused.

"Nay," one of his knights answered. "We would see them. I sent men round to the side. It is the same there."

Murmurous whispers of what he said ran down the lines of the army poised at the bridge.

"We have won, without drawing a sword," Edward marveled.

Isabella let out a long sigh of relief and sat back on her horse, offering a silent prayer of thanks.

But instead of being pleased, Mortimer was enraged. "Ride on!" he shouted, pointing forward with his lance, rising in his stirrups so they all could hear and see. "The villains are fled, and we must find to where!"

"Gone!" Mortimer said angrily, as he paced the great hall in St. Francis Tower. "Gone with all the riches they could carry, gone in as many different directions as the wind, or so I am told. Despensers and their comrades and the king. Gone!"

"Doubtless the Despensers went to ground," Leicester said. "But where? They have castles all over England."

"Aye, they have Bristol Castle, on the isle of Lundy," Edmund, Earl of Kent, agreed. "An island. That is where I would go."

"And they have a fine manor at Gloucester," another noble said.

"Bah!" Lancaster exclaimed, clearly impatient to be gone. "They swallowed all England, and were hungry for more. They could be anywhere, the only thing slowing them, the weight of the gold and treasure they took. We must act swiftly."

"Their most defensible castles are at Caerphilly, and Neath," Owain said. "I know the land there. Had I enemies in pursuit, that is where I would go."

"I would go there too," Lancaster said.

"Mayhap they are there," Mortimer said. "Mayhap they are nearer still, or farther yet. I will stay and wait on more news. Someone must know where they have gone. There are few secrets from servants. If gold doesn't loosen their tongues, the rack doubtless will."

Isabella listened to their words and thought of the dungeons in the Tower, and those who would be taken there. Innocent or not, they would be taken to their limits. She looked around the vast hall and saw ghosts pacing.

"I would go west, to Wales, with Lancaster," she said. "To Hereford, to wait. If they are near there, we will find them, and if they are not, there we will wait upon word."

"Very well," Mortimer said absently.

Gwenith raised an eyebrow and looked at Owain. Their queen must ask permission? her glance said. He looked back at her, with sorrow.

Isabella stirred, as though she would speak, but then fell still.

"But who is to protect my mother?" Edward asked.

"She does not go alone," Mortimer said. "Do you insult good Lancaster? He will have worthy knights with him, an army of them."

Edward stood lost in thought a moment. "I think," he finally said, "that we cannot leave the command of that army to anyone but myself. I want to find the Despensers, father and the son, but I want to see to my mother's safety even more."

Mortimer frowned. "Then, well and good. She will wait here, while we go on the hunt," he said. He turned to the other nobles. "Send swift messengers every day to tell us of your progress. We will do the same. They shall not escape."

But they had to wait. There were no feasts, no celebrations at the Tower that autumn to celebrate the hunt at the closing of the year. Hunting had begun, but it was for human prey. Isabella and Mortimer's men spread out across the land, searching. The Prince of England took his knights and supporters and sought his father and the Despensers. It was as if London, and England itself, held its breath as the King of England and his supporters went to earth, and remained out of sight.

As October commenced, the coming winter announcing itself with cold winds, chill rain and blood. Though the hunt wasn't fruitful, throughout the land slaughter began, the killing of all farm animals that could not be fed over the winter. Pigs and cows, ewes and rams—the farmyards ran with blood that month. There would be sausages and blood puddings, hams and roasts hung high for feasting at Christmastide.

Then one bright late October morning, a messenger was announced in the throne room.

"News, Highness," a messenger cried, falling to one knee before his queen. "The king is said to be at Chepstow. But he has sent the Despensers to secure the town and castle at Bristol."

She rose from the throne. She had got in the habit of sitting and waiting for news there. "Then there I shall go," she said.

"Lady," Gwenith said anxiously, "nay. There will be danger. The prince and Mortimer are far from here. They cannot defend you."

"But they left me an army," Isabella said. "I will not sit and wait when there is work to be done. I will send word to them. I will call my son to my side. You do not have to accompany me, Gwenith, no more than you ever have had to."

"If you go," Gwenith said, "then there I will travel too."

Isabella smiled. "Then don't fret. I am no fool. I will not endanger you. Even without Mortimer or the prince, we will go by circuitous means. We go to Gloucester, where we have welcome, and thence to Berkeley. Now that the Despensers are not there, though they once claimed the castle for themselves, I can give it back to the rightful owner, Thomas, Lord Berkeley. And so there we will raise more supporters. Then, and only then, will we go to Bristol. And there we will end this matter of the Despensers."

There was such calm conviction in Isabella's voice that Gwenith grew calm as well. She bowed her head in praise and agreement.

"Don't despair," Isabella added. "Just think. You will be near your beloved Wales again."

"It is no longer my home," Gwenith said.

"While your heart is still there, it will always be your home," Isabella said, "wherever you may bide."

Then she summoned her knights, and her favorites, sent out messengers to her lover and to her son and prepared to set out on her roundabout road to Bristol.

———

"We have caught the earl, the elder Despenser," a road-weary messenger told his queen at Bristol Castle. "Lancaster sent me to you. I am to tell you, Hugh Despenser, Earl of Winchester, is yours."

"And the others?" she asked.

Prince Edward, who had joined her as she reached Bristol, leaned forward to hear.

"The younger Despenser and . . . the king," the messenger went on, rushing over his words. "They tried to get to Lundy, we think." His excitement made him so bold he spoke to her as he would any lad he knew. "But failing that, they fell back and ran to Caerphilly and Neath. That is where they are."

"Then there we will be too," she said.

But first she had to see to the disposal of Hugh the elder, Earl of Winchester. He was tried the day after his capture. Isabella and her troops rode to the castle where he was being held, her son at her side, as was her lady, Gwenith.

Like Thomas Lancaster, whose death he had presided over, the earl was not allowed to speak in his own defense. It did not appear that he wanted to. Always robust, always genial, he was suddenly a broken old man who stood bowed and silent. He was charged with many things: treason, theft and the death of Thomas, Earl of Lancaster.

After the sentence was passed by the nobles Isabella and Lord Berkeley had hastily assembled, he was immediately taken out and brought to the block.

Gwenith, at her queen's side, shivered. This was a thing she had seen before. She didn't want to be there, but she didn't want to desert her queen. She, who had vowed bloody vengeance on the kings of England, now trembled. She hadn't known what bloody death was then. She did now and, again, wondered that she had ever vowed to bring death to any other being, much less thought she could be the death of kings. She looked at Owain, standing with the other knights, and kept her eyes on him so she would not have to see the earl's fate. Watching Owain's stern, grave face, she wondered if it was love that had made her so weak, even as it had made her so protective of life.

But her queen stood immobile, watching without blinking, with no expression on her smooth, beautiful face. Prince Edward stood quiet and impassive, as he often was.

Two men at arms walked the old earl to the block. He wore his full armor. When they stopped him from going farther, for the first time, he looked up and seemed to see his captors. His eyes fixed on Isabella, and there was a plea in them.

She nodded. "As he dealt Thomas, Earl of Lancaster, so shall he be dealt with," she said. "Behead him and send his head to London, to sit upon a spike at the Tower as warning to all who would do treason."

The earl looked at her with gratitude.

She stayed and stood quietly when the old man's head was taken. She did not flinch at the blood, or the sounds of his death. When she was sure he was dead, his body at last stilled, she turned and left, after ordering that that body be split into four parts, and shown round the kingdom.

And then she rode out to capture the King of England.

She met with little resistance on her way. No one along the route had given the king sanctuary. He was, all said, on the run toward Wales. Two weeks later he was found, along with Hugh the younger, betrayed by the Welsh they had tried to hide with. Some said they would have given him up to whoever came seeking him. The king was the son of Longshanks. Hugh Despenser, they had heard of. Whether it was that or the mighty army that came to collect the escapees, the queen was cheered as she rode into the courtyard at Caerphilly Castle accompanied by their prince, and her lover, Roger Mortimer, who had joined them on the road.

Isabella sat her horse and saw Hugh the younger being led

out in chains. He was not looking anywhere but at his feet as he walked, seemingly deep in thought.

Isabella stayed only long enough to see Lancaster's men escorting Edward the king from the castle he had taken refuge in. He was pale and confused, shaking, blinking at the light, looking like some spineless sea creature that had just been wrenched out of its shell. He did not see her. She did not wait for him to do so. Instead, she turned and rode away. She did not stop to speak with him. Nor did her son.

But they made sure to come to the trial of Hugh the younger, and then they came to see the ending of him.

The prisoner was brought from his cell into the open air that cold day at the end of November, out of the castle at Hereford and into the courtyard. "He tried to cheat you, Majesties," the jailer at Hereford Castle said with a cozening smile. "He has not eaten since he was brought to me, hoping to starve himself and escape the executioner."

"We cannot have that," Isabella said to her son. "He has been tried and convicted of treason, murder, coercion and other vile crimes. He must pay."

"He prays all the day, and begs forgiveness," the jailer added.

"That is God's concern, not mine," she said and crossed herself.

She watched as Hugh Despenser the younger was stripped of his armor, then stripped naked. She could see how gaunt he'd become. He did not seem to feel the cold. His dark, brutal face was dull. He stepped along with his jailers to the foot of a ladder propped against a gallows. A fire had been built at the foot of it and it leaped and crackled as the guards fed it straw and wood.

Hugh did not turn his head to see who had come to watch his execution. He seemed both diminished and yet still dangerous in his unearthly calm. His guards prodded him upward on the ladder. Once at the top, at last Hugh turned, looked down at his tormentors and spoke.

"I repent my sins," he said. "Blessed Jesus, forgive me."

And then they slipped the noose round his neck and drew him up into the air. He was hanged. As he choked his last, they cut him down. And then as he gasped great gulps of air, he was drawn up on the ladder again and bound down to it. The executioner came close to him with a huge knife. Hugh Despenser's testicles were cut off and held up high, before his eyes. Then they were thrown on the fire that burned beneath him. But he had closed his eyes by then.

He did not groan or shriek. The onlookers marveled at that. The executioner brandished his knife and then neatly gutted him, slicing from his chest to his groin, then holding up his pulsing bowels to show to the crowd as they fell out. Then Hugh Despenser made sounds, but they were not speech. At last, they dragged the twitching body to the block, and beheaded it.

Gwenith was too busy being sick to see it. But Isabella stood, unflinching and granite faced, her blue eyes cold as the deep sea, and watched until her enemy was cut into quarters. She didn't like what she saw but she was Queen of England and her son stood beside her, and so she had to be strong. She steeled herself against womanly weakness, knowing that Hugh Despenser would have done the same to her, her son or anyone in his path, had he had the chance.

In time, instead of flinching, she marveled to see how her chiefest foe could so easily be reduced to less than than a suckling pig. She watched as the body that had so entranced her husband, to his ruin, was reduced to carrion. She rejoiced, in some corner of her soul, at how the man who had harmed so many and who would have shared her bed simply to show his power, was taken down to rubbish. She grieved, on another level, for all the things that had led to this. She clung to these remote, distracting thoughts, because she refused to allow any others.

"He has surpassed himself," she commented at last, turning from the butchery. "He was cut into eighths."

Mortimer looked at her curiously.

"A jest he once made," she said. "No matter. Now we are done."

"Aye, but for the king," Mortimer said.

"We are done with bloodshed," she said fiercely. "Royal blood shall not be spilled. Cannot be spilled! And there is no reason for it now. He has agreed to renounce the throne and appoint Edward, my son, as king. That is enough punishment for him. I have one more journey before I return to London. I will go to Kenilworth, where he is bound, and see him sign the document ceding all to my son, and then take my farewell of him. Because howsoever old he grows, I shall not see him again."

"I shall come with you," Mortimer said.

"Nay," Isabella said, "not you, or my son. This is a thing I must do alone. I will be back in time to celebrate Yuletide with you."

Twenty-three

1326, December
Kenilworth Castle, London

Isabella took her most trusted knights and pages, her ladies and body servants and an army, and went to see her husband, the king, in his prison.

"This is a prison some men would think a palace," she murmured to Gwenith, as they entered Edward the king's bright apartment and saw his comfortable surroundings.

Edward did not turn to look at her. He sat on a chest by a window, and pointedly stared out across the wide, scythed lawns across the moat. He was dressed exquisitely, in shades of blue. He still wore his favorite crown, a filet of gold, on his brow. But he had changed, she thought. He had lost weight and looked younger now. His hair was still buttercup; his eyes, so pointedly avoiding hers, gleamed azure. His travails hadn't left their mark on his face. He was, if anything, even more beautiful now.

"But then," she went on, pretending she hadn't noticed his sullen behavior, "Kenilworth is a palace, after all. Come, Edward, you would have done far worse to me had you been the one to win out."

This got his attention. His shoulders went up. "Aye," he said bitterly, "it would have been your lover carved up like—" He faltered. "I will not speak of it," he said, running a hand across his eyes.

"And I do not believe you would have put me in such pleasant confinement," she added calmly. "It was said you paid to have me poisoned. It was said you vowed to kill me yourself, with your knife or with your teeth. My own son told me that."

"And yet you don't fear me," he said savagely, turning to look at her. "You come to me alone? Are you not still in fear of your life?"

"I was never in fear of my life from you," she said softly. "Only for my son's life, and that too never from you. Your lover was ambitious, Edward. He would not have stopped at killing me, robbing the king or the country. His aim grew higher."

He grew still and looked away again.

"This is for the best, Edward," she said, drawing near to him so the knights poised in the hall outside the door could not hear her. "You have been repudiated. You betrayed your countrymen, and they now betray you. This is England. Even a king cannot rule without the consent of the people. For the sake of the line of kings you come from, for the sake of the kingdom they ruled, for the sake of England itself, you must step down. Sign the petition, cede the throne to Edward and be done with it."

"And my life!" he said angrily. "Don't think I don't know what you plot. Have me renounce my crown, and then have me slain with none to revenge me because I am no longer king. A pretty plan. But if you and Mortimer want the throne, you must kill me for it. Why wait? You are going to do it anyway. Will it be the ax? Or the noose? I only—" He stopped and turned his face to her again. She saw the crystalline tears on his cheeks. He cleared his throat. "I only beg you not to dispose of me as you did Hugh. I can face the executioner, but by the love of Christ, do not cut me into living pieces. I cannot face that."

She went to him and, on an impulse, sat at his side and embraced him. He unbent and leaned against her. His frame was lighter now. For all his height and strength, his bone structure had always been delicate. It was like holding a child. His heart beat so fast she could feel it against her own. She buried her face in his clean, soft, fair hair.

"Edward," she whispered, "for all the hurt we did each other, I never hated you. Indeed, I loved you from the first. I loved you very well. That was my mistake, and for that, I beg your pardon."

He drew back, and looked at her with suddenly grave eyes. "Nay, for that, I beg your pardon," he said. Then he threw up his hands. "Ah," he said, "it is folly for any king or queen to love. That is not our lot in life. A king is a tool. A queen is his helpmeet: They are made less than human so they can work for their people. And that is not bad. That is part of the bargain. It is only that we forget, because for all we are, we are yet human. And then we falter, and then we fail our people and ourselves. You should not have loved me. But you were so young, you didn't understand. I should have not loved Piers so well, but I had loved him since I was a boy. When he was murdered, I thought I had lost my heart. Others came to me, others left, but I felt nothing but idle pleasure, until Hugh. He ruled me. I know that now. But he never deceived me."

"And I did?" she asked.

"Did you not?" he asked with a twisted smile.

She looked away.

"I don't mean with Mortimer," he said. "That was to be expected. That I cannot blame you for, except in your choice of consort. I mean, before that. I'll speak plainly. Do you want me to give up my throne for a man who is not my son? Come, madam," he said with some of his old arrogance, "I speak to you as though from the grave now. The least I deserve is the truth. If it were so, it would make your victory even more delicious for you. And after all, what can I do about it? But I want to know."

She sat quietly a moment. Then she met his gaze. "There is no true answer to that," she said. "None that I can give you, and to that, I swear."

He took a long deep breath and let it out. "I see."

"And I will not have you slain—that, I vow," she said. "My solemn oath, I will swear to it. I will put it on paper, or in front of a priest, or God Himself. What need would there be for that anyway? You know I do not believe in spilling royal blood. It is a bad precedent. You will be given a good life, but not freedom. A long life, but not the one you were born to. But you threw that away when you took up with Hugh Despenser.

"It does not matter," she said, rising. "Edward is my son. The blood of kings runs in his veins. Now will you sign? You have nothing to lose, because you have nothing now. But the people are so angry with you, I wonder if you will escape death if you do not."

"I don't want to die," he said. "By God, when Hugh was with me, I laughed at death. And yet now, diminished as I am, I cling to life. My time with him was like a high fever I went through, leaving me weak and foolish now that it is over." He shook his head and rose. "Aye, madam," he said, "but if I sign your damned document, will you keep your vow to me? You cannot marry Mortimer while I live. Are you willing to accept that? Or will you have me killed to ease Mortimer's way to your wedding bed?"

"Mortimer has a wife and children," she said. "He is, for all that, a worthy knight and a good man, son of a baron and connected to noble houses." Her lips curled in a reminiscent smile as she added, "But though he claims kinship with the great Arthur of history, he is not of royal blood. Nay, it is my son I am thinking of."

She crossed herself and took another breath. There were no shouting, screaming or threats of violence, but this interview nevertheless hurt her to her bones. "I will do you no harm or cause any harm to come to you. I will write a document forbidding it when I return to London. On my oath, on my life, I do so vow."

He stood, lost in thought. And then looked at her again. He nodded. "On your oath? With all we have done to each other, I believe you. I will sign your cursed document." He reached up with trembling hands, removed the filet of gold that was his crown and handed it to her.

She took it, bowed her head and started to leave.

"But, Isabella?" he said, and she turned, because he had never called her that before. "Sometime, someday, when this is more a bad dream we had in the night than a memory, will you have the children come here, or to wherever you choose to put me? Will you ask them to come to see me?"

She saw him through her own tears: a misty outline glowing in blue and gold. She nodded. "Aye, that I will do. Good-bye, Edward."

He bowed. "Fare thee well, Isabella. You have won. But a last word, because of what we had, and might have had. Beware Mortimer. Aye. He is very like Hugh Despenser. Learn from my sorrow. Do not be like me."

Twenty-four

1327, SEPTEMBER
NINE MONTHS LATER
LONDON

Gwenith's life had changed. Her mission was fulfilled. She was no longer afraid, or guilty, or threatened. She loved, and she was loved. She still could scarcely believe it. Only one thing made her sad, and that was looking at her queen.

"I do not know how I can leave you," Gwenith told Isabella again, as they sat together in the queen's chambers.

"How? On a horse, or in a litter, or in a coach," Isabella told her. "But if you do not go soon, you can't go at all. Spring has turned to summer, and now it is September, and still you linger. Do you not want your babe born in your husband's castle?"

"Oh, aye, I do," Gwenith said. "But that will not be until Yuletide. There are some who can't even tell I carry a babe. Or so Owain says," she added, looking down at the swelling under her tunic.

"He is a very wise man," Isabella said, smiling.

Gwenith smiled back at her, but then looked sad again. "But leaving you will be like leaving a part of myself," she cried. "In truth, I was not whole when I came to you. I was half a heart, and that half steeped in anger and dark thoughts of revenge. You were kind to me beyond my deserts. You trusted me, spoke to me and brought me out of myself and into life again. I shall miss you so much, lady."

"Now listen to me," Isabella said sternly. "I was kind to you because I too was half a heart. My Therese left me forlorn and there was no one I trusted. You were young and alone—that is what called to me. But now you have a husband and are carrying his child. Good Mortimer has given him back his holdings, his land, his titles, his castle. He waits for you to return to Wales with him. Go with your Owain. Have the babe. Be happy in your new home, and when you think it time, then ask me to come to you and I shall. Now it grows late and I grow weary. I give you a good night."

Gwenith rose. "I cannot say that I miss sleeping near you, lady," she said, with a grin, "because now that I sleep with my husband, I am more than content. But, aye, in a way, I do miss it as well."

Isabella laughed. "I am your queen, and do enjoy your company, Gwenith, but even I do not think myself an adequate substitute for a loving husband."

They smiled at each other. It was as well, Gwenith thought, that she no longer shared the queen's chamber, because now Mortimer did. She didn't fear him. Indeed, she was grateful to him for keeping his word and restoring Owain. But now that the queen had a man in her life, she had no need to befriend homeless, friendless servants. Which is all she had been, Gwenith knew, and was again grateful for any crumb of her queen's regard. Mortimer would doubtless be here soon, but for the moment, he was still in the great hall for the gaming after the evening meal. But Isabella had sought her chamber, and Gwenith, of course, had come with her. She might not live under the queen's nose anymore, but she and Owain had the rare gift of a room in the Tower, and so she passed every waking moment the queen desired in her company.

She went to the door and opened it to find William, the squire, standing there, gray faced and wild eyed.

"William?" Gwenith said. "What's toward? You look like death."

"Worse," he said in a shaken voice. "Will you ask Her Majesty to receive me? I have news for her."

Isabella had heard. She stood. "Come in, William. Gwenith, you may stay."

William came in and bowed. "Majesty," he said. "Sad news. Edward is dead."

The color drained from Isabella's face so quickly that Gwenith was reminded of the ghastly sight of Thomas Lancaster's severed head. Isabella gripped the back of a chair until her knuckles were white.

"Edward?" she said. "But he was below stairs when I left. What? What happened? Surely not death in those few moments?"

"Majesty," William said. "I misspoke. Not your son our king. Edward, his father, who was king."

Isabella grew no less distressed. "But he is safe, at Berkeley now," she cried. "A goodly castle, a pleasant place. Indeed, I heard his chambers were sumptuous. He wrote to me and told me he approved the move from Kenilworth. He wrote of lawn games, visitors, great feasts. Edward visited him there and told me that he was very well treated. We sent an order specifically saying that he must not be harmed. I had not heard that he was ailing. What happened?"

William looked down.

"Nay, I will know!" Isabella cried.

"It is said," William began. "It is said that he was murdered, in a manner most foul."

Isabella sank to a chair. "Oh, sweet Jesus," she said, crossing herself. Then she looked up at William, her eyes wide. "How? Who did it and how?"

"It was done by men we have not yet discovered," Mortimer said as he strode into the room. "By means most vile, to be sure. They say that his murderers especially disliked his personal habits. And so they looked for a manner of death most apt. They are said to have held him down, taken a searing hot poker from the hearth and simulated that which was said he most enjoyed until he was dead."

Isabella put a hand to her mouth. She, who had stood dry eyed at the many violent executions of her enemies, could not speak.

Gwenith could not move.

"Oh, my dear God, oh, sweet Jesus," Isabella moaned, wrapping her arms around herself, because she ached so badly. "How could this happen? I promised him his life. To be sure of it, we wrote an order to that effect when I returned from seeing him, remember?" she asked Mortimer, her eyes searching his. "We forbade harm coming to him. You remember, do you not? We had the clerk write it up, in Latin, and then in our tongue, so there could be no mistaking it. I signed it. You signed it. It said no one was to kill or harm him."

Mortimer went to her and took one of her icy hands in his. "Murderers flout orders, even royal ones, and murder was done. Vile, indeed. Do not waste tears on him. He'd have killed you, and mayhap even your son, had Hugh Despenser lived and had I died."

She slid her hand from his. "He was King of England," she said. "Whatever else he was, or did, that is no fitting death for him."

"It cannot be undone," he said with a shrug.

"I can't speak to you now," Isabella said, her hand over her eyes. "My heart is shattered. I gave my word, and he believed me. I cannot bear this. Pray call my son Edward to me. We must talk."

Mortimer frowned. "But you should be easy in your mind now. Now there is no chance he will try to raise another army against us to regain the throne. I worried about that, and you should have done."

She waved her hands at him. "For the love of God, bring me

my son! We must make plans. His father may have been destroyed by depraved and contemptible means, but I will not have him buried alone, thrown into a charnel house like a homeless serf."

Mortimer nodded. "I can see that you would want to be at his interment, though surely his soul is no longer alone, but in heaven or hell now. But the king cannot leave now. There is too much for him to do. Now that I am his regent, until he reaches his majority, I try to keep him to his duties. He may not leave the Tower."

Isabella quieted, and looked at him so assessingly that he spoke again, in a more conciliatory manner.

"And too," Mortimer said, "having him at his father's funeral may enrage many of his subjects, not to mention the barons. They have not forgiven the last Edward as you seem to have done."

"Then I'll go alone," she said. "But I must to Gloucester, and I still must speak with my son. He is young, but not a child. He is named king, though he has but fifteen years, and he is sworn to marry next year."

"Aye, he is to marry a child of thirteen," Mortimer scoffed. "He will not master the ways of ruling for a while yet."

"You do not understand," she said coldly. "The death of kings is a matter of grave importance to a king. The means and manner no longer matter. But Edward was murdered, and his son must know, and seek the villains who did it."

"I'll summon him," Mortimer said. "But take a moment to collect your wits. You're striking out at those around you. No need to speak to me as if I were a servant. I am not king, but I am now an earl, and it is not as though I don't understand the thinking of kings."

"You do not," she said. "It is not a thing learned. It is a thing one is born to."

He looked at her and then, slowly, made an exaggerated bow. "Yes, Majesty," he said mockingly and left her.

Twenty-five

―――――

1327, OCTOBER
GLOUCESTER, ENGLAND

The funeral for the slain king was held at the cathedral at Gloucester. Several nobles and worthy knights who had once insisted on the king's removal were there, looking grim. The murder of a king was clearly a different matter from the ouster of one. The queen was supported on the arm of her faithful lady in waiting, Gwenith de Rhys. Isabella wept softly.

But her tears dried when she walked out into the sunlight again, and Henry, Earl of Lancaster, spoke to her.

"Majesty," Lancaster said as he came to her side. He bowed. "A word, if you would."

"Here?" she asked, looking around the churchyard.

"Aye," he said, "in the open air, where I can see all who might overhear."

She stopped weeping. "Then, speak. Gwenith," she said, "pray stay by me. Your husband will wait for you. She is dear to me," she told Lancaster. "I trust her, and beg you to as well."

"Of course," he said and bowed.

Isabella studied the earl. "So what is it that you must say that is so important it must be said in the presence of death?"

"Edward, our king, your son, is not here," he said. "Forgive me, but this looks very ill, almost as though he were party to the evil doings."

"You think that?" she asked angrily.

He put up his two hands. "Nay. Never. But I still say it looks ill. Majesty," he said quickly, "what I say is said for young Edward's benefit and yours. I know him and you. I know Roger Mortimer as well. It is not a good thing that Edward remains in the Tower. It almost appears as if he were prisoner there. It is not a good thing that Mortimer did not come here today. And it is not a good thing that the King of England is fostered by the man who . . ."

He paused and then spoke rapidly, as though he wished the words out before he could think better of saying them. "The man who escaped the Tower, became consort of his mother and helped her lead the war against the king, his father. I do not say what can be done. But I do say something must be done. A king does not rule only by God's command."

He looked around them and said, lower, "We see that here today. A king's people, his subjects both noble and common, must support him. They gave up their king once. The path has been cleared. They might do it again. I know how you feel about Mortimer, Majesty. But I also know how you feel about Edward, your son. And I tell you this is giving rise to ugly rumor, even though I know nothing uglier than what transpired in the dungeons of Berkeley Castle. I wanted Edward, God rest him, to leave the throne, but not in this way, not in this way. I am yet still your man, Majesty. And I am sworn to Edward, our new king. I only ask that you make that easier for me."

"Defeating rumor is like fencing with a shadow. You will never strike home. What would you wish me to do?" Isabella asked curiously.

"If the sun is let in, the shadow disappears," he said and, for the first time that day, saw her smile.

"You are a clever fellow," she said. "Go on."

"Let the sun in, Majesty. Let Edward leave the Tower, well protected, of course. I would go with him, if you wish, and I pledge my life for his, should the need arise. But let the people see he is a free man. Destroy the dark rumors about the taking of the crown. Because that is what they are saying, Majesty. That is exactly what they fear. You are queen, and Mortimer is a valiant knight. But one king has been murdered. What of the safety of another? The people will not take kindly to the thought of a new line of kings, especially a line of those who seek to be made kings."

"You have said enough," she said sharply. "It is also said that you are ambitious."

"For England," he said, his hand on his heart. "I so vow. Forgive me if I am overzealous in that ambition."

She made a small gesture, as though brushing something away. "Forgiven," she said. "But," she added in a softer voice, "you've given me much to think on. I shall. That, I promise you. Of all the treasures given to me to protect, there is none so valuable as my son. Know that. And know that I will consider what you said, and bear you no ill will for it."

"That is all I ask," he said, then hesitated.

"What more?" she asked.

"Finding you so forgiving, forgive me if I risk more," he said. "They say that a letter was come to Berkeley Castle, from you and Mortimer, telling Edward's captors, God rest him, that it would be wise if the king were killed."

"What?" she asked dumbfounded. "We sent a letter to his jailers, asking them to take particular care that no one slay him."

"The letter, it is said, read *'Edwardum oddicere nolite timere bonum este,'* which means, 'Fear not the killing of Edward. It is good.' It could not be clearer," he said sadly.

"No, no," she protested. "So it did read, but it was to say, 'No killing of Edward. It is good to fear.'"

"Then it was but a misplaced mark of punctuation, but still, the rumor is not then false," Lancaster said.

She stood, stricken. "A single misplaced mark of punctuation?" she whispered. "For a life? So small a thing to bring down a king?"

"The smallest things can bring down empires," he said. "Forgive me. I had to tell you, Majesty. For the good of England, and aye, for all my ambition for her great and bright future, and for her new king, Edward, by the grace of God."

He bowed and left her.

Isabella stood immobile, breathing quickly, until Gwenith took her hand and gently led her away.

Isabella walked into the great hall on Gwenith's arm and stopped, her legs suddenly weak, her heart beating like a hammer at what she saw. Her hand flew to her mouth. There, silhouetted by firelight, sat Hugh Despenser, thick bodied, dark, upon the king's throne, his head back, his legs stretched out before him. When he saw Isabella enter the hall, he stood and came toward her.

"You are back!" Mortimer said as he approached the queen. "Very good. I missed you. How went the proceedings?"

"Ill," she said shakily.

"You are ill?" he asked. "We shall call your physician."

"No," she said, blinking, still trying to see the real image that stood before her.

"I don't blame you," he said. "The royal physicians leave much to be desired."

"No, no," she said, "You mistake me. There is naught wrong with me but road sickness, and weariness."

A slow smile grew on his lips. "Can it be . . . ?" he asked. "It is not without the realm of possibility."

She looked at him.

"You are but two and thirty. Still able to produce a prince for me. It is what I had been hoping. This is great news!" he exulted. "To think that I should father a new prince for England."

She stared at him. "Nay," she said, "it is not that."

She saw his happiness fade.

"It was a long trip. The funeral was what made me sad," she said. "And my sadness makes me heartsick and weary." She looked past him. "Where is Edward, the king?"

"He is in the Red Tower."

Isabella started.

"Nay, don't distress yourself. He is well, and well taken care of. We've heard terrible rumors. He is kept there for his own good. He's but a boy. I only wish to keep him safe."

"I see," she said after a moment. Her eyes were clear and cool when she looked at him again. "Forgive me if I don't join you this night," she added. "I needs must rest after my journey."

"You are excused, of course," he said. "I give you good night, and I will see you later."

"Not this night, pray," she said. "I would sleep."

He smiled. "Rest and be well. We will meet in the morning. And make up for a lost night together tomorrow."

Isabella went slowly up the stair to her chamber, leaning on Gwenith's arm. The queen only turned once, to see Mortimer standing there, his back to her, legs apart, surveying the hall with the pride of possession.

When she arrived at her room, she closed the door behind her. She sat for a long while, then rose to summon a page and paced until he came. She whispered a message to him.

She waited for William, the squire, to come to her. When he arrived, she spoke to him briefly, handed him a purse, then saw him leave. When he had gone, the page returned with Owain de Rhys.

Owain took his wife's hand, and together they gazed at the queen with concern. Candlelight was supposed to be a flatterer, but Isabella suddenly looked much older to them than she had in the day.

"Gwenith," she said. "Owain. Now I can tell you why I asked you to return here instead of going to your new home. I didn't know, but I suspected . . . No matter. I would wish you and whatever company of knights you can muster, those you trust with your own life and your lady's," she told Owain, "to ride out from here, with Edward, the king."

"But we heard he's in the Tower," Owain said, "under lock and key."

"Aye, and so once was Mortimer. If you could help him then, you can help his king now. I have sent word. You will get the keys this night. There is no murder to be done this time. But it must be done in secret. As you and I kept our plans to ourselves when your man Mortimer escaped, so I ask you to pledge to keep this close. You may tell no one, not even Sir Mortimer. Do you so vow? If not, I will seek another to do my bidding."

"Highness," Owain said, sinking to one knee, "why mistrust me now? When I wed, I promised Gwenith I was your man as she wished. I would no more break that vow than one I made to her."

"Men's vows," Isabella sighed. "Still now I must trust my greatest love to my friends—or enemies. But who shall I trust if not you and my Gwenith? So then it will be done, and on your head and soul be it if you misspoke me. . . . Then, this night, you must ride out with your king and seek Lancaster and tell him he is to protect the new king and return with him to London only when I send word that it is safe to do so. And then go home and live in peace and joy, and never mention this night and what I have charged you with to anyone. Can you do this for me?"

Gwenith stood still, her eyes wide. Owain looked troubled, but nodded agreement and said, "To this I swear."

"And I," Gwenith said softly.

"As you once vowed to slay Edward the king," Isabella told Gwenith, "now I ask you to deliver him. Can you do this?"

"With a full heart, and all my soul," Gwenith said.

Isabella relaxed. "Tell Edward, your king, that I labor on his behalf. And ask him, as he loves me, not to speak of my part in this night."

Gwenith looked at her queen with worried eyes. "We will meet again?"

"Of a certainty," Isabella said. "Go now. And go with my blessing. I was right to choose you to be my confidante. You were sent here to destroy me, but see how God works? For all my sins, still He has smiled upon me. For now you will do me the greatest good. I am not sure of anything, but one thing, I know. I can trust you."

Gwenith impulsively clasped the queen's hand. "Trust me, lady. Now and forever."

"And me," Owain said.

Isabella grasped Gwenith's hand, then let it go. "Then Godspeed," she said.

When they had left, Isabella called in her body servants and prepared for bed as usual. But when they left, she never so much as sat down. She stood by her window and stared out into the blind night. She wished she could see in the dark, but only saw the sputtering torches that ringed the Tower grounds. Once, in the night, she heard the sound of horses clattering over the bridge that crossed the moat, and her hands unclenched. But still, she waited.

At dawn, she got word from William of the successful leave-taking of her lady in waiting, Sir Owain de Rhys and their company in the night. William lowered his voice when he stressed that it was a larger company than the one Gwenith and Owain had come with. Only then did Isabella smile again. But her smile was bitter.

Then William handed her a note. She scanned it quickly.

Madam, it said, in Gwenith's familiar handwriting, *We leave you with love, and with your love safe with us. Do not despair. All is well.*

Isabella let out her breath. "With my love safe with them. The girl is discreet. She has grown very wise."

"Yes, and I have seen what she says to be true," William said.

Isabella, the queen, nodded, even though she knew Gwenith was wrong. All was not well yet.

She had lost her devoted shadow. She would, Isabella realized, be agonizingly lonely from now on. But she had saved her son and her soul. The saddest thing was that she now also knew she must work ever harder to save her soul in future. Her husband was dead. Her lover awaited her. Neither had ever helped her, or loved her, for herself. But she had survived. She would continue to.

Twenty-six

1355, SEPTEMBER
TWENTY-EIGHT YEARS LATER
CASTLE RISING, NORFOLK

Her body seemed to grow more difficult every day, even as her soul grew lighter. The years weighed her down, making even walking difficult. But the lessening of guilt and sorrow made sleeping easier.

Isabella was old now, her beauty more legend than fact, or so at least she thought when she gazed into a looking glass. She hardly did anymore, so it did not distress her. Men still bowed to her, but she seldom saw many.

She was no longer queen. She lived under supervision. She could not leave the country or rule it, nor even sway her son, the king. She had little to say to the world, and few to hear her say it.

She couldn't remember when she'd been happier.

The years had ticked away, and as they had, they'd softened the blows she'd suffered as well as the joys she'd relished. Today, she sat in her chamber and waited to receive visitors. She used to travel to see her grandchildren; she hadn't been treated as a prisoner for years. She'd gone robed and hooded to visit them at the castle at first, and then, in time, went as freely as any other female. Age was a wonderful disguise. But now she grew weary more easily, and they were older, so they came to see her.

Beautiful Edward, already a warrior as brave and beautiful as his father, God rest his soul, and her own. Lionel, John, Edmund and now baby Thomas. But she seldom saw the baby. He was too young to travel, even as she was too old. She was also visited by her son's many by-blows. Edward loved them as well as his legitimate children. His poor wife, Philippa, Isabella thought. Was ever a queen happy?

Edward commanded a nation and an army, and did well for his people. He'd had a great monument built to his dead, deposed father. People visited it as a shrine. There was talk of sainthood for the murdered king. Isabella thought of how death had ennobled him as life had not.

So she thought about life, instead.

Gwenith and Owain visited with their mob of children and grandchildren. But Isabella's favorites were her own get. Her beloved grandson Edward was the image of his father. God willing, he'd never know that. God would forgive her for that, she knew. Her friend Elizabeth de Clare had founded an abbey and a holy order, the Poor Clares. Isabella was joining them, taking the veil in a few weeks to pray for her soul until the end of her life. Whether she'd be forgiven for Mortimer and his black deeds, she did not know. She prayed so.

For a year after Mortimer declared himself an earl, swanning around the Tower like a king, although the true king hid from him, she continued to suffer. She'd been brave, clever and manipulative, but when all was done, all she'd done was to replace her shame with humiliation. So when her son Edward burst into the royal chambers with his army one night, she was not surprised. She'd been waiting for them. Mortimer was surprised and shocked as he was dragged from her bed, and then to the City to be hanged in a public square like a common criminal. She'd been grateful. It had gone smoothly and quickly and it was over at last.

Then she'd been banished, by her own son. But not sent too far, and not to dwell in discomfort.

Now, in her old age, she tried to think about nothing but life. It wasn't easy. There was constant war with her native land; her own son had begun it. There were new diseases, and a great devastating plague swept throught the cities of Europe. Simply to live was now more difficult than it had ever been, for wellborn and peasant.

And yet men still slew each other. Did they not see the miracle of life? Isabella sighed. Because for all she'd done, not much had been done. Women still had little say about power and how it was to be used.

She heard hearty voices in the corridor outside her room, and smiled.

The children were coming. She rejoiced in that as she never had in anything in her life. Because they loved her, and after all these years, if she'd learned nothing else, it was that real love supplanted power, and was even rarer.

"Grandmama!" the boys shouted as they entered her chamber.

Most were men now, but she saw them as they had been. She smiled, and said a silent prayer.

"Children," she said and embraced them, filled with love, all her sins still upon her head, but none on her heart.

Afterword

In 1330, almost immediately after his marriage to Phillipa of Holland, King Edward Third arrested Roger Mortimer for treason, dragging him from the queen's own bed at Nottingham Castle. Mortimer, who had recently made himself Earl of March, was not taken to the Tower. He was hanged, by King Edward's decree, at Tyburn, in 1330, for the amusement of the common crowd. His estranged wife was pardoned and acquitted of all misdeeds.

In that same year, Queen Isabella was confined by her son Edward's decree, and then sent to Castle Rising, in Norfolk, to live in exile there. But contrary to popular rumors, she lived comfortably and well and at peace for the remaining twenty-nine years of her life, and was by all accounts content, and a doting grandmother. In her latter years, she became a nun of the order of the Poor Clares, and died on August 22, 1358.

Henry Plantagenet, Third Earl Lancaster, was appointed guardian to the new king Edward in 1329, before Roger Mortimer's capture and execution. He was also made captain general of the king's forces in the Scottish Marches. He went blind in 1330, and died of the plague in Leicester, in 1345.

King Edward Third ruled England for fifty years. He was handsome and athletic, and excelled at the joust. He was a stern man and a fierce warrior, waging war with both the Scots and the French in his time, with interruptions only for the scourge of the Black Death, which entered England for the first time during his reign. He also was a man of huge sexual appetites, and had many mistresses. Nevertheless he was said to be a kind husband and a good father. He had eleven children with his queen, Phillipa, and many illegitimate children as well.

On the death of his uncle, King Charles of France, Edward declared himself King of France, and declared war on King Charles' successor, Philip Sixth, in 1337. This precipitated what came to be called the Hundred Years War.

Edith Felber graduated from Hunter College in New York City with a degree in creative writing and theater. She worked for various media, including a radio station and a major motion picture company. The mother of three grown, brilliant children, Ms. Felber is fascinated by history. She has written more than thirty historical romances set in different eras, as well as two dozen novellas, all under the name Edith Layton.

She has received excellent reviews, awards and commendations from such publications as *Publishers Weekly, Library Journal, Booklist,* Romance Readers Anonymous, and *Romantic Times.*

Ms. Felber lives on Long Island with her rescued foundling pets, which include her dog, a parakeet and pond fish. They all can be reached at www.edithfelber.com.

Queen of Shadows

A Novel of Isabella,
Wife of King Edward II

Edith Felber

QUESTIONS
FOR DISCUSSION

1. *Queen of Shadows* is about Queen Isabella, but it has two heroines. One is royal, with all the power that involves. One has no power at all. But as time went on, which woman do you think had more influence over the other? Why?

2. How does Gwenith serve as a foil to Isabella? What qualities does she have that caused Isabella to make her a confidante? And why does Gwenith feel such sympathy and liking for Isabella? What is it that they have in common?

3. Edward Second was undeniably a weak man. Was he also cruel? Was he vicious? Given the time and place and his desires, could he have done better as a king and a husband? How?

4. How does the time period influence the characters? Gwenith was without birth, money or power. Yet she achieves a good life for herself. Would her position and progress be the same in the modern world? Could Isabella's situation be replicated in today's Western world?

5. Would a modern Western king who was gay have to conceal his sexuality? Would a world leader in today's world have to hide his homosexuality? Could he?

6. Why does royalty exert such a fascination for people—then and now?

7. Gwenith takes a solemn vow, yet then breaks it because of her growing feeling of kinship with Isabella. Is this a failure of courage on her part? Or does she feel so alone that she can't live without an ally? Could she have done anything else to bring down the house of Edward Longshanks?

8. Execution was performed as a spectator sport and carried out with great cruelty in the fourteenth century. This was thought to be just, and a deterrent to future treason and crime. Were people crueler then? Capital punishment, which is still carried out in many parts of the United States, is also said to be a deterrent to crime. Disembowelment and decapitation is still practiced in other countries. If it were legal to disembowel and behead as punishment in the Western world, would it still attract cheering crowds? If it were on television, would it get good ratings?

9. As a French princess and an English queen, Isabella had been taught pride, but also obedience. Yet she overthrew her husband, the King of England. Was she after power? Or was it revenge? After years of unhappiness and humiliation, what was it that finally moved her to such drastic action?